MATRYOSCHKA

CAUSALITY IS OPTIONAL

TERRY GENE

http://matryoschka.com

Those who cannot remember the past are condemned to repeat it.

— GEORGE SANTAYANA, REASON IN COMMON SENSE, THE LIFE
OF REASON, VOL.1

In a world seeming to run into chaos, it is easy to forget that this has happened before, and our ancestors overcame it. One theme of the *Matryoschka Heritage* Arc is the importance of not being a self-defined victim who hides behind *identity politics, role playing games, dystopias, or nihilisms*. Effective, lasting solutions are best self-generated without demanding that others take care of us.

A shout out to historical societies. They remind us that our ancestors failed and still persevered in conditions much worse than what we imagine ours to be.

http://ahsgr.org

One such society, the *American Historical Society of Germans From Russia*, follows ordinary German peasants and trades peoples devastated by the Seven Years War, who saw no hope of ever having a stable homeland. In the 17th and 18th centuries, they immigrated to the Russian eastern frontiers, where they restarted their families despite native uprisings, invasions, revolutions, and forced diasporas in railway cars in the middle of winter to Siberia and Kazakhstan. Those who escaped settled in the Great Plains of

Canada and the United States, and in South America, Brazil and Argentina.

The four-volume story arc of the Matryoschka Novels and the related Destenee short stories owes much to these ancestors for story, morality, and folkway. If any of these are misrepresented, it is the author's failing.

KIRKUS REVIEWS

... THIS SCI-FI TALE REMAINS THOUGHTFUL AND
EMOTIONAL

Alternative pasts and genders arise from a failed quantum energy experiment in this debut novel. Alexandria Jane Merk is a white Army veteran who, "at twenty-six, had left her soul on the streets of Tikrit, Iraq" when she couldn't save two young boys. She's now attending a university in Pullman, Washington, accompanied by friends Quentin Khan, a chubby, Arabic "man-child," and Katie Jo Parker, a very tall black woman and fellow vet.

Alex Jane becomes affected by a physics experiment that causes her to lose "contact with herself," creating alternative pasts for two separate identities into which she splits. One is college freshman Sarah Beth Merk, who generally feels that life is good, although she has almost-buried memories of a horrifying childhood event. The other is Alexander "Alex" James Monroe, an Army vet with disturbing child-hood memories of his own centering on his great-great-grandmother —"Babushka"— and the mental gymnastics she forced him to undergo with a set of matryoschka, Russian nesting dolls, covered with myste-rious writing.

And Sarah Beth/Alex are similar to these dolls, because she seemingly exists as a "flesh-hued thing" that slips on and off; in fact, she's "pure energy" and "the most dangerous thing on Earth." The dual entity, their friends, and government researchers must race to solve mounting puzzles before Sarah Beth loses control. ...

The gender what-if is central and has a remarkable twist, but Sarah Beth/Alex could be expected to explore their state with more curiosity. Gene's dialogue is naturalistic, although characterization sometimes falters. ... This sci-fi tale remains thoughtful and emotional.

PART I

SARAH

Too lonely to cry, Silli Sarai
Kissed shy boys, you Silli Sarai
When the boy was coy,
She chased the boy,
And ate him instead, silly, Silli Sarai

1

BIRDS FLEW OVER MY HEAD

ARCHIVES: WITNESS' STATEMENTS: THE SOUTH PACIFIC
INVASION CRISIS, FOLIO B.17.119, SARAH BETH MERK-
ADDAMS, PART 1, AGE 147.

Yes, this is Sarah Beth Addams, maiden name Merk, *the coward of the South Pacific Invasion*. Yes, I sat back and didn't lift even a quantum energy pinky to help the nine-nation Pacific Task Force fleet immobilized mid-ocean; sort of a house arrest or a timeout imposed by the invaders. I had my reasons, reasons few friends or enemies understood.

Get that damn pico-drone out of my face. I know I have no wrinkles. I've ducked photos for decades to hide that.

Martin Luther once said, "You can't keep flying birds from crapping on your head, but you can keep them from building a nest in your hair." Before anyone gets into a PC-motivated, "I'm offended" snit, that's the non-bowdlerized version. Your flat teeth show that you grind them down to the gums when you find "ass" correctly translated in your Bible as ass, instead of donkey.

But I'm stalling by picking a fight with you, my gentle interrogator. I've used that trick dozens of times with better interrogators than you...have you looked up Katie Jo Parker? She was legendary.

Anyway, to understand what happened, and why, I'll start with the first time I completely lost it, back when I called myself *Alexandria Jane,* Alex to my friends.

Don't get smug, this could be you. What you think of as Reality is tissue-thin.

DUST

ALEXANDRIA JANE MERK: PULLMAN, WASHINGTON

D ust.

There was always dust in Alex Jane's life. Back in Tikrit, it had dusted all morning, stopping only for the ambush. Dust all morning here, too. She traced patterns in the dust on the outdoor cast iron café table. Energy patterns like those her great-great-grandmother had obsessed about. Jenergija, she called them. Patterns claimed to break the bounds of the dimensions and time. Pure bullshit, but it kept Alex Jane from concentrating on why she was there.

The morning breeze kicked up dust from the plowed over failed soybean crop on the Palouse Hills. The morning *Pullman Daily News'* front page exuded optimism by harvest time the Chinese embargo of wheat would be over. Optimism was the currency of living.

Alex Jane was overdrawn at the bank.

In the outside courtyard, Quentin kept Alex Jane talking in the faux-retro café chairs at the Eye Scream Shoppe, in the Compton Student Union Building, aka the CUB, while Katie got their treat. Alex Jane was addicted to the Macadamia White Chocolate; Quentin liked to mash whatever fruit ice cream was on special into a second scoop of vanilla, and Katie went for the yellow style vanilla of her childhood in her Newark hood.

He'd purposefully placed his and Katie's chair to block her easy exit. He asked, "Any thoughts on if you'll declare your degree this fall?"

Alex grunted. She knew what they were here for and it wasn't about degree programs.

"Do you think it will rain tonight? Those look like lightning clouds." He continued.

She stared into the west to placate him but didn't say anything.

Before Quentin could try something else, Katie returned. As they smashed or spooned their ice cream, Quentin and Katie scooted their chairs closer and sat hip to sweating hip. They were an odd couple. Quentin, the man-child, ruddy-faced, obese with a double dough-white roll bursting out of the bottom of his T-shirt. Much taller, thin with little curves, Katie channeled her upbringing in the hood, never stopping her scan of her surroundings, the deliberate motions of a veteran who hadn't yet returned.

Quentin finished his double-sized dish first. He pulled back at Alex's stare and eyed the untouched ice cream in her bowl.

Katie nudged him. He and Alex had been best friends sharing everything, except sex, since first grade. The Alex in front of them had changed during her tours in Iraq. Where before, at eighteen when she enlisted, her eyes glistened with an intensity that at times scared him. Now, her eyes concentrated on nothing, reflected nothing, another veteran who at twenty-six, had left her soul on the streets of Tikrit, Iraq.

Katie nudged him again. As Alex's oldest friend, he had to man up and break their news. "I know I've only been here for a month, and I appreciate how you've found the double apartment for you and me. If you weren't here to push, I wouldn't be taking classes."

Alex dropped her spoon and swirled her hand in her family's "get on with it," disturbing the energy patterns in the dust.

"Since Katie came back from Newark, me and she, uh, have been spending a lot of time together at her apartment. We've decided to room together."

Alex avoided scratching her shoulder wound.

Alex and Katie had formed a mutual assistance friendship over the past year, based on their deep needs and anger at a Veteran's Administration which spent more on layers of staff and regulation than help for veterans. Katie finished the last half-spoonful of ice cream and ceased her scan of her surroundings. "Of course, we share classes, and we'll still hang between them."

Alex's dead-eye stare into the distance upset Quentin. He pulled on her hand, trying to peer into her eyes, but she found the antic of the fly stuck in her ice cream all-consuming. Alex's and his relationship was deep, so deep he doubted married couples had such a connection. She was pushing him out of her life; her silence said it all.

He tried another tack. "We're unpacking and arranging my stuff…" he paused when Alex slumped in her chair. "… but in a couple of days," —he glanced at Katie who gave him a nod— "we'll have you over for pizza and beer. We'll always have your favorite Hessian import in the 'fridge. Drop by any time."

"Especially when we have class assignments. I can't keep Quennie's attention on staying in college." Katie added, pushing her normal ability to connect, forcing a smile through her deep-set anger lines. She twigged her short Afro again, closed her eyes and attempted circle breathing, in through her wide nostrils, out through her tight but full lips. "Why aren't you eating your ice cream?"

"I just finished an apple," she lied. The apple sat in the bottom of her tan canvas satchel. Like an oversized purse, but with leather and substantial brass closures and laptop-sized compartments, also suitable for pistol magazines; it fit her. Alex avoided scratching her shoulder wound. Her neck felt as if rods ran the length of the muscles. She didn't dare massage it or the scar. She didn't want sympathy.

Typically, there was something about him that settled you. She'd counted on him to settle her for twenty years. Alex said, "I think you're right. There will be lightning tonight." *Lightning loud enough to cover the gunshot.*

Katie muscled her camouflage briefcase over her shoulder. "We have to go."

Quentin pulled on Alex's hand trying to peer into her eyes. She didn't reciprocate but instead found the antics of the fly stuck in her ice cream all-consuming.

Alex watched as they headed to Katie's car: she stiff-legged, toes pointed forward in military precision, he with his ambling gate, the left foot kicking outward.

The melting ice cream splatted onto the sides of the delft-blue dish. Her knife wound, still fresh on her mind. It itched like a possessed worm. Katie seemed to have forgotten.

She dropped the spoon again: *splat.*

They drove off into their future together. Their U-turn in the square pointed them toward their new apartment, their snuggery. Away from her.

But she needed them. *Splat.*

The sunbaked chair drew the sweat through her shirt. Desiccated clouds wisped overhead. Afternoon heat flowed from the Palouse Hills verdant with spring wheat. As the wind shifted, the scar on her face twitched. The air hinted of humidity and the tang of the dumpster contents behind the nearby Korean restaurant.

Splat.

Sweat dripped down her forehead. She let it sting her eyes but unconsciously wiped it from her facial scar. Time to go. She had a lot of prep work before the storm rolled in.

Splat.

She abandoned the puddle of untasted ice cream, grabbed her satchel, and headed downhill to her empty apartment.

One block away from the apartment, cutting through the alley, hunger provoked her to eat the apple. As she pulled it out, she lost contact with herself. Her senses collapsed into a miasma of undifferentiation. She tasted vermillion, touched squeals, smelled grit and saw salty. A fluorescent-green wind knocked her mind off its feet. Her last thought was, "Another panic attack?"

Day one, 02:01:13 PM

3

JOY

SARAH BETH MERK: DAY ONE, 1:47 PM, PULLMAN, WA

Juggling the two grocery bags on her lap while riding the bus that needed new shocks, Sarah snapped another selfie, making sure cherry juice dribbled down her chin. *Lemme see. This one goes to TD&H, cousins Tom, Dick, and Harry.* Another giggle of unadulterated joy slipped out. Just because his father named him "Sue," her uncle took revenge on the next generation, thus TD&H. It was still not as bad as the Marys: Mary Sue, Mary Me, Sallie Mae, and Fanny Mae, his daughters. They remained snots.

No doubt. Life is good, especially over a thousand miles away from home and starting college. She took four more photos and clipped them to her growing "brag board" on her *LuRRker* app. Only the best of the besties was allowed to be her LuRRkers, and Mom, of course. Which reminded her ... she thumbed the "okay to locate" icon to let her LuRRkers know where she was. She watched LuRRker track her progress on the bus and watched for landmarks for walking. A quick swipe confirmed most of her cousins were out in the prairie helping Uncle Helmut with the wheat harvest. She felt bad for them. She had promised to drive *Ol' Slomo*, the harvest truck, to help out.

Once she finished unpacking, she would ditch the giddiness and get serious on her matriculation and applying for local jobs. For now, she ignored her inner sense that this level of giddiness was unnatural.

Her overwhelming joy for life started four days earlier when she hugged her mom goodbye and drove with her cousins, Timmy and li'l snot Denise, for three days to the university in Pullman Washington. Timmy traded driving with her, Denise being too young. Even on vacation, Timmy spent most of his time coordinating his group back in Omaha. Denise sat in the back seat, created images of fictional beaus, and posted them on her lame-o Snap account. Every time they stopped, Sarah had to delete all she could find. Arriving at her pre-arranged apartment near campus, Timmy did most of the unloading, she and Denise contributing to the effort by opening and examining every closet, door, cabinet, and drawer.

They ended in the cozy kitchen, and Denise opened the oven. "Ain't you glad you don't cook? It would take a month of Sundays to clean that oven." She stuck her tongue out.

Pushing the final box onto the kitchen counter, Timmy said, "If you get your grades up, Denise, maybe you can score the scholarships to join her. Wouldn't that be precious? Sarah's never had a roommate. You could flip for who adds the boiling water to the ramen."

That night, as a celebration, the three of them hit up the Pullman nightlife—at least those places that would admit the underaged Sarah and Denise. Sarah reveled in being the independent one, the center of attention.

She felt guilty—not—when her joy peaked watching Timmy's car leave the next morning. Independence at last! She loved her cousins, all several dozens of them, but independence! After a few hours spent unpacking and organizing, her joy got old when hunger reared its head. Off to the grocery store, she went, regretting not keeping her cousins around for more of the settling in, if only for Timmy's car.

Even on the bumpy bus she stifled another giggle and tried to look like a serious academic. But something about proving herself, alone and over a thousand miles away from the safety net of her extended clan, burst her studied demeanor. Her giddiness brought a frown. She wasn't the giddy type. Then again, she'd been giddy when she placed in the State gymnastics finals. This was bound to surpass that.

Fall semester was only weeks away. She planned to settle in today, then find a job, preferably in retail. Mom would worry, that's what Mom's do. But Sarah was strong, and this was her opportunity to prove it.

She spat a cherry pit into one of the grocery bags, which caught the attention of another bus passenger. His smoldering glare ruined the moment and brought Sarah out of her bliss. The scent of street-living wafting from him further disrupted her joy. She was angry and upset with her attitude. She was raised better than that. Her stop was coming up, so she stood and handed the remaining cherries to the man. "You should try these. I've bought too many." She maintained her smile, her best feature, while the man pretended to reluctantly accept. This was best. She didn't want to be a stereotypical freshman who gained fifteen pounds. Besides, several of the Proverbs made it clear sharing with the less fortunate was its own reward.

Sarah pulled the stop-cord, pulled her purse's strap across her opposite shoulder with the clasp next to her hip and slipped her hands through the carry-holes in the two groceries bags. The weight pulled on her wrists, maybe she shouldn't have bought so many canned goods. Stumbling on the last step as she exited, she righted herself against the bus stop enclosure.

Dropping the bags on the bench, she reflexively rubbed her face scar and shoulder wound. Her shoulder didn't twinge, but what brought her out of her reverie was the lack of the ridge of her facial scar. Using the darkest side of the transparent bus stop, she examined her face. No scar. Turning on her heels, she confirmed no one was watching, and pulled her shirt off her shoulder. She couldn't see the still healing wound from Katie's last crazy spell.

A shiver started at her knees and ended with her teeth rattling. *Why am I checking for scars? I don't have any scars. Who is Katie?* Not sure about what had happened, she buttoned up her shirt.

She scanned the neighborhood—rambler and ranch-style houses giving way to apartments—and decided her best route was the way she had come; a full four blocks walk. Mid-day, she had the street to herself. Adjusting her load, she set out, when an alley she hadn't noticed before appeared. In fact, she was positive it hadn't been there earlier in the day. Gathering both bags into one hand, she lifted her other hand over her head to block the bright sunlight. She smiled. The alley would cut out a whole block.

In the bright summer morning, shadows deeply etched the alley. Shivering, she adjusted the bags to hold them again in both hands and checked her purse to ensure the clasp laid against her hip. She kept to the side without shadows. Something sensed but imperceptible disturbed her. *Silly.* It was mid-morning. It was no different than the alley behind her home.

When she was halfway down the alley, a dark green Caprice station wagon entered from the far end. Someone, short and skinny stepped out, keeping the sun behind him and her. Sarah sidled to one side, but the person mirrored her, staying between Sarah and the sun.

"I need to talk to you, Sarai. Your father didn't finish the experiment."

Who called me Sarai? Only li'l snot Denise dared. "I don't know you." The man shifted closer. His outline was familiar. Oh. *Please, not him.* It could only be the man who tortured her ten years ago. Thin, goat-like face, long ears, and a lipless mouth curled up on the left.

He grabbed her right wrist, breaking the bag handles, and tumbling the groceries onto the ground. The apple she bought as a treat rolled to one side. Forcing her down, he said, "Your father signed the contract."

"Daddy's been dead for ten years, and my name is not Sarai. It's Sarah." She rose to run.

Fluorescent green light infused her. Her skin moved as if it separated from her body, then formed crevasses deeper than her body. The last thing she saw was the apple collapsing, leaving only the skin. An electric-green wind knocked her mind off its feet.

Day one, 02:01:13 PM

4

A GIRL

ALEXANDER (ALEX) JAMES MONROE: NOVAE SPES
APARTMENTS, PULLMAN, WASHINGTON

I shake off the momentary belief I'm a woman. It grew into a shiver in my knees that rattled my teeth. I don't remember how I got back to my apartment after Katie and Quentin removed my last reason to live.

Where were the other rooms? Why did I think that this was a two-bedroom apartment? Along with the unpredictable trembles, it's another symptom and proof that seventeen months is too long. I should have died with the two street children in the Tikrit ambush.

The round glides into the chamber. I thumb the safety until I'm ready. I reach for the apple, but it isn't on the kitchenette counter. I don't remember returning, another sign of my disassociation.

Of course, my great-great-grandmother, "Babushka" is back, trying to get my attention—another sign I'm losing it. Dead for twenty years, she won't leave me alone. Her voice rasps like footfall on dried autumn leaves. Her last words to me, to anyone, were: *Alex, you die before you twenty-five.* Who tells a five-year-old great-great-grandson when he'll die?

I don't have time for Babushka. Besides, she's dead. "I know you trained me to save you," I say, "but I couldn't."

"She need you." This again? The last time she used this was a year ago.

"Go to hell, Babushka. Or kill me now." My rage exorcizes her voice. After what Katie and Quentin told me, I have no future. They abandoned me to live together. No one was left to care.

"She need you." Babushka was extra persistent today. Even though lightning flashes cast deep shadows across the orange and tan checked sofa, and thunder rattles the kitchenette window, she's as clear as the day she died, when she almost took me with her.

"She need you." Last time she used this line was to get me to talk to Katie.

"I said, go to hell." I don't need any more failures. In a few more minutes, I won't need anything.

For the last time, I run my hand over the hand-stamped copper plate on the olive-wood pistol case, made to fit my grandfather's service pistol, a Colt 1911A semi-automatic. *ThE StupidEst PErson to SurvivE an Ambush.* After we had survived the Tikrit ambush, my squad paid a local to make it. The artisan had lost the lowercase *e* stamp. They had slipped a long-neck beer into the case for the presentation.

I tossed the case at them. "Get it out of my sight." All I could see were the two street urchins laid out in the base mortuary and their sister— staring, staring into nothing.

No more failures after tonight.

My grandfather's service pistol cools my hand. Good to go. Returning the loaded Colt in the case, I set out my best clothes and shoes and draped the new vinyl shower curtain across the sofa-bed. If I stand at the front of the bed, then there should be no splatter on the wall four feet away. No one will say Alexander James Monroe left a mess when he offed himself.

A meadowlark sings outside the window.

"She need you." Babushka brings the scent of her favorite flower, lilacs. She's going all out this time.

"What part of 'go to hell' don't you understand?"

The handwriting could be better, but I'm in a rush. "If you find this note, please return the Colt, the service ribbons and the presentation case to my father. His address is in the case." My half-finished suicide letter is in the satchel. Screw everyone; I'll leave it undone. To keep it simple, I don't send a text to the manager at Lloyd and Donnelly's that I won't be coming in for my next work shift.

"Remember."

Babushka stopped visiting when Quentin moved in with me. It was a peaceful month. What little twist does she offer now?

And I *do* remember. Last year, outside of freshman orientation, standing at least six-foot-two, too tall for most men, taller than me. Melanin-rich, Katie could have loaned three-fourths out of her color and still be the darkest person on the campus quad. The fatigue pants she wore had screamed, "leave me alone." Eyes hard, she stared at one student after another until she found me and lingered.

But I won't let Babushka screw with me again, almost falling into her snare. After her death twenty years ago, it had taken months of therapy—and Quentin's family moving in next door—to return me to normal.

Babushka's voice leaves me shaken and holding my bathroom sink for support. I suck my knuckles and taste iron. Blood? How did I—Oh. I punched the mirror and the pain rescued me. How noir can you get? I don't remember stripping for a final shower, but I don't care. The broken mirror will come out of my security deposit. Which is hilarious. The clean-up of my blood in the room will probably eat up the deposit. Another scan of my face shows the scar is still there … maybe I should shave. Nah.

"She need you." Babushka's off her four-legged walker. Katie left me, not the other way around.

"Go away, Babushka. You've failed. I'm going through with this."

My debate with Babushka changed my mind about the letter. Rooting in my satchel for the notepad, I graze something cold, frictionless, and shifting like a snake. "What the—?"

I slip and land hard on my left hipbone. A flesh-hued thing attaches to my ring finger; the rest of it flows from my satchel. Flat, smooth like skin, it has no head, limbs, or body, just a featureless surface.

Where it attaches, it sets my muscles quivering up to my shoulder. It's not a snake. I wish it were. I killed plenty in Iraq. As I try to shake it off, the Flesh-Thing envelops my lower arm and moves upwards. All sense of pressure, warmth, anything, disappear where it touches.

"Stop!" I try to hold the other end down with my bare foot. The enveloping accelerates. I bite, pull, kick, squeeze, but nothing works. I grab the bathroom's doorjamb and stretch to reach my gun on the couch, just three feet away in this tiny efficiency. My arm goes dead as the Flesh-Thing surrounds it up to the shoulder. There, it gathers into a thick band, leaving behind a mitten which forms into a … a hand? A thin hand. I must be hallucinating; a reaction from stopping the VA meds a week ago.

A thinner, hairless arm has replaced mine. I can't move it. With a sound like sand falling down a dune. The Flesh-Thing thins out as it moves to cover my back and down my left arm encasing it, again leaving a different, thinner hand and arm. I'm numb but also ener-gized. I can't move my arms or do anything to stop it.

"Stop. Go to hell." Where's my rage? I'm defenseless without my rage. Down my back, past my hips, and down the back of both legs, numbing my skin as it moves. This—can't—be happening.

The Flesh-Thing wraps itself around my toes, up my legs, crotch, and starts on my belly. My toes and legs shrink—they're real but oddly shaped. My legs and hips stiffen, and I can't move them either. There's still no pain. No feeling.

Am I being eaten? Why did my arms and legs change, instead of disappearing? From both sides, the Flesh-Thing encloses my hips, my gut, and chest, leaving a gap from groin to neck.

Please, stop now.

The Flesh-Thing encloses the back of my neck. The sapping chill flashes into a headache. It slides into my ears, my mouth. In the fractured mirror, I watch the front gap close as it covers my eyes.

I lose the sense of my heart. My last sense, hearing, fills with that susurration sound.

THE NEXT THING I KNOW, I'm waking up on the sticky bathroom floor, and my hip still hurts. Strange, I've never blacked out before. Vision's blurry, but the digital clock on the vanity reveals that I was out for only thirty minutes. I palpate along the back of my hipbone. From the puffiness, the swelling has already started, but nothing seems broken. It would be ironic to break a hip and not be able to retrieve Ms. Colt.

Whatever it was, it's gone. Must have been a hallucination, nothing more. I weep in relief, then sniff it back. Weeping isn't me. Weeping before I off myself is silly. The thought makes my skin crawl. Goaded by my great-great-grandmother's voice, I had imagined that a Flesh-Thing ate me. How weird is that? I'm glad I stopped hallucinating before I was lost in it.

A meadowlark's song floats through my cracked bathroom window with a fresh sound. Color bursts with deeper hues. In the fading daylight, the tiny bathroom is somehow brighter. Now for my clothes.

Staggering to my feet, then falling back again, I hang onto the sink. It wobbles as I pull myself up. Too fast, the blood rushes out of my head, my feet slip backward, and I hit my chest on the edge.

"That hurt! You clumsy oaf." A female voice, expressive with ranges like a birdsong, stops my cursing before it starts.

"Who's there?" I say. "Is someone there?" Did I forget to lock the apartment door? The towel knotted around my waist, I look through the bathroom door, but there's no one there. My chest hurts, and I rub at the spot of the pain. It's soft … huh? I look down. Breasts?

I wobble, leaning on the sink. My right temple throbs like the blazes. I search for answers in the cracked, blood-stained mirror.

A girl stares back at me.

Her mouth opens, mimicking my scream.

5

ALIVE

SARAH: DAY 2, 7:31 AM

S arah woke to the sun glaring through the dirty window. She couldn't uncurl from her fetal position or remove her thumb from her mouth. A nightmare still held her hostage. She was being raped, being entered by a crew cut guy with a facial scar. Not on her first night of independence, she thought. How could she allow this?

Forcing herself, she uncurled and removed her thumb. The shaking didn't stop. She wiped her tears on the coarse bed sheets. Coarse sheets? She'd brought high thread-count sheets from home. What was she missing? This room was too small to be the apartment she rented.

She slipped her hand under her top to scratch her shoulder wound. Nothing. Puzzled, she withdrew her hand, unable to understand why she tried to scratch a wound she didn't have.

Sliding out from under the sheets that stank of a boy, she stepped onto the floor and stubbed her toes on a wooden box, sending sharp pain up her leg. Sitting back on the bed, she rubbed her toes. These weren't her jammies. This isn't her apartment. Where was she?

She stood again, to find water, and stepped on a gun. She nudged it under the bed. She might need it later, but for now, it was too much trouble to carry. She wished she had joined her many female cousins in target practice.

Gripping the kitchenette countertop to keep from swaying, she examined the tiny apartment. The walls, ceiling, and doors were painted in a semi-gloss, off-white beige, it combined in a ten by ten-foot combined bedroom and living room space with a tiny alcove for a kitchen separated by a counter. The door to the right of the kitchenette had to be the closet and bathroom. On the bed—a couch-bed combination—the bed sheets were tossed to one side as if she had been the only occupant. The ugly orange upholstery brought a shudder from her. A shower curtain lay, crumbled in one corner. She started to feel faint.

"Where am I?" A voice came from nowhere, but was comforting, filling a void she didn't know she had. The comfort vanished with her dizziness. It was if she had been someone else for a moment.

Where were her groceries? She saw no evidence of them anywhere. She tossed the piles of clothes spread around the floor, garbage bags with more beer cans than anything else, and the mattress. Where were her clothes, her phone, her purse? Why did the groceries seem so important?

Nothing seemed right. The counters and furniture were too short. Do built-in cabinets and furniture come in different heights? Stale beer and sour body odor threatened to gag her. The dirty-beige walls closed in, and her resolve wavered. Sarah's stomach flipped at the puke in the bathroom and her knees buckled at the thought of staying and rationally sorting out her situation. Her vision and breath closed in. She had to get out of there, back to her apartment. She'd brew coffee and chat with Mom, who'd be at work three time zones away in Omaha.

The apartment's metal door slammed with a solid ring on her exit. She took a couple steps down the corridor, the greasy carpet tickling her bare feet. At the sound of the elevator doors closing, she turned and shouted, "Wait." Too late, the doors closed before she could put her hand out to stop it. Even here the beige walls closed in. At the end of the corridor, a lit sign saying "stairs" beckoned, and she hit the door bar with a crash and sprinted down. She had difficulty in landing squarely on the steps, occasionally overreaching. After six flights of concrete steps and two landings, she bounced out the bottom door into a dirty, cramped lobby with desultory couches. Behind the fake ficus, a door swung shut, and Sarah followed it into the parking lot. Steam rose from the blacktop and gravel surfaces.

From the sun's position, it was morning.

She raced to the street, causing the singing meadowlarks to scurry aside. The parking lot's pavement gave way to sharp gravel that dug into the soles of her bare feet. This slowed her down, and she stopped to orient herself. *Am I still close to the Washington State University campus?* The letters spelling out "Pullman" on the white cylindrical water tower on the hill were lower and a different color than she remembered. The apartment complex shaded two sides of the parking lot. The other two sides were streets with parked cars and a field under construction. In the open grassy field across the street, the late model cars mingled with some held together with rust.

She was alone in the parking lot, except for the meadowlarks. With her hand shading her eyes, she read the one visible street sign, "Stadium Drive." That placed her on the north side of the campus, across town from her apartment. How had she gotten here?

Someone was waking up on the pickup parked to block four parking spots.

Three boys slid off the hood of their battered maroon over silver, rusted pickup, which had a keg mounted in its bed. Sweat poured off them as they removed their letter jackets to flex various muscles.

The shortest one said, "Heading to a slumber party? Or from one?" Even at this distance, this early in the day, their breath betrayed their inebriation.

They slipped around her, and the acne-pocked string bean grabbed her wrist. "You look confused. We can drive you to our place."

She pulled back, only to land in the arms of the third. He said, "She's made her choice. She's mine." He dragged her backwards towards the pick-up. Sarah squirmed and kicked to get out of his muscled embrace and the cloud of his alcoholic breath. *Asshole.* This was not a vague threat, like waking up in a strange room. Here was something she could see, smell, and … hurt. Rage took over.

6

RAGE

SARAH

Seventeen months earlier:

The Tikrit field mortuary reeked of embalming fluid, alcohol, and the ever-present dust. She watched the Army mortician prep the two boys laying on the stainless-steel table, side by side because the base had run out of tables. Two lives snuffed out, and their sister scarred for life. She hadn't saved them from the ambush set up for her squad. Their sister only greeted her with the stare of unfathomable loss. She never spoke again. They'd already lost their parents.
An Islamic cleric speaking through the interpreter advised the preparation.

Sarah's rage built, fueled by the memory of those two Muslim boys. *Gimme some leverage*, she thought, *and something's gonna hurt.* Gravel cut the soles of her feet as she tried to kick back into her captor. The added pain intensified her rage. He lifted her and dodged her backward headbutt. On the second try, her back-kick landed on something soft. He screamed and fell with her still in his arms. Releasing her, he grabbed his crotch.

The skinny one's steps crunched the gravel as he closed the distance to her, reminding her she was barefoot, and in pajamas that threatened to fall down. Not knowing what else to do, she sprinted back inside, up the stairs, stopping on the two landings to catch her breath. No sounds of pursuit followed. Having no other obvious choices, she slipped back into the apartment. She stopped and placed her ear to the door for several minutes.

How, she wondered, had she done that? She'd never had so much rage before. She'd never even seen the moves she'd made, much less performed them. And who were those Muslim boys on the table?

After the dry heaves and the weeping, she still saw no signs of the guy from last night. Washing her face at the bathroom sink, she sorted out her next steps.

In the mirror, a stranger stared back. Her left hand formed into a fist, and she swung it into an arc behind her. The expected head wasn't there, and she knocked the towel rack off the wall. No one was visible in the whole apartment, but she checked the chain and deadbolt on the door anyway.

Stalling. She was stalling. Never one for teen-slasher movies, this was too close for comfort. After she drank two glasses of water, she straightened up to confront the apparition in the mirror. Was it another victim of the scar-faced man?

Who was this? Eyes—an impossible green—instead of her light green with gray flecks—blinked at her. She edged closer and touched the mirror, then her face. This was her. Not a trick. No contacts. But how?

I'm Sarah Beth Merk, she thought, slowing her breathing to normal in and out, *I arrived early to settle in before the fall semester and to have a little fun.*

So, who was this? Her hair, almost an unnaturally shiny auburn was offset by electric green irises. She looked like a female action figure

from a role-playing game? The impossible person in the mirror—
narrower in the face than her but taller—could pass unseen in a crowd
if she covered her hair. In fact, with black-rimmed glasses, she'd be
almost invisible. Not bad looking, on the pretty side of plain, but definitely not Sarah.

I'm Sarah Beth, she rolled into a mantra cadence to emphasize her
determination, *I'm eighteen. I lost my daddy and brother and sister on my
eighth birthday. Mom and I have struggled for ten years. My hard-earned
scholarships got me here.*

But who was this? Her experience with drinking was limited, but she
was confident she wasn't drunk or hungover. Hallucinating? Less
experience there, as in none.

She continued, believing the apparition was not real. *I am Sarah Beth.
My Mom is Anne Marie Merk, family name Hergenreder. My closest cousins
are—are—Timmy! Timmy and Denise Hergenreder. Then who is this?* She
back-stepped to get away from the image, and the towel rack clattered
to the tile.

The affirmations didn't work. This was her. *I'm not me, so who am I?*

In her mind, a hollowness filled and a voice said, *"Please listen. We're
both in trouble."*

"I'm not listening." Her lower lip seized in response to her refusal to
cry. Crying didn't help. Denial hadn't helped. Affirmations about who
she was hadn't helped. Now her apparition wanted to talk? She
reached for the door.

"Don't do that. We need to talk. Please calm down. I'm alm ..."

Something she couldn't identify departed. How do you describe
missing something that couldn't be there? Or a hollowness that
expanded to larger than you?

After what happened, running off without a plan didn't appeal
anymore. She ransacked the postage stamp-sized kitchenette for the
sharpest knife with a blade short enough for her wrist to control. Prep-

ping steers for the family open-pit BBQ had taught Sarah how to handle a knife. Suitably armed, she searched again for her clothes, purse, wallet, shoes, anything. She found nothing of hers in that disgusting apartment. Where were the groceries? Why were groceries important?

Shaking out the bed linens hoping to find something, anything, a wallet stood out, bison leather, with its distinctive deep brown wrinkled texture. Dumping its contents on the bed, she sorted the IDs and other cards. The driver's license was for an Alexander James Monroe, Seattle, Washington. Crew Cut. The man from her nightmare. A nasty scar on his right cheek, but otherwise reasonable looking in a rough way. Six years older than Sarah. An old Army ID card included a picture without the scar. Two bucks were all he had to his name. Nothing else useful fell out of his wallet, no credit cards, just some charge cards for gasoline companies. She kept the driver's license. She had him, her rapist if she survived and got back to her apartment. Once safely there, she would call 911. And either he took his phone or didn't have one.

Going out in the pajamas had been a disaster, so she sorted through his clothes to find something suitable. Her nose wrinkled, from the odor or the color of each piece. Giving up, she pulled on the least objectionable shorts over her hips and wiggled into a polo shirt with only one stain. A thin belt looped into a square knot kept the shorts from falling when she moved. The knife hadn't left her hand except to secure the shorts. The wooden handle and iron edge comforted her.

Her lower lip quivered as she teased the tangles out of her hair with his comb. The mirror refused to budge in its reflection of her. This time, she was taking off, and no one and nothing would stop her. If she couldn't tell where she was, then she'd walk until she ran into a police officer or a campus po-po.

If the police couldn't help her, she may have to call in help from Omaha, a couple of her fave bone-crushing cousins, maybe even TD&H. They'd love missing a week or so of eating harvest dust. A grin tweaked her mouth, her first since waking up.

The void deep in her consciousness filled with something. *"Can you wait until I explain? I don't think I'll have another chance after this."* The inner voice remained calm, but a fringe of panic crept in towards the end.

This was her best chance to escape and find help, but something about that voice. She was raised better than this. The voice clearly needed help.

Sarah dropped her hand away from the doorknob, then returned it. She was haunted by a nightmare, a body that wasn't hers, and now a voice that could do things with her sense of wholeness. Was she hallucinating?

She dipped into her stubborn heritage and went with direct confrontation of the craziness. She'd better not be the clueless girl in a teen slasher movie who always ran upstairs to be trapped by the attacker. Cousin Denise would never let her forget it. Sarah could force the voice away from her new body if needed; that's what she'd been doing without understanding it.

She flipped the shower curtain off the least messy side of the bed, sat, and folded her arms, knife firmly in her grip. "Okay, say your peace. If I don't like it, I'm not listening to you again."

7

FOUCAULT'S PENDULUM

ALEX

I'm the thread holding Foucault's pendulum over the sand of her consciousness. A fraying thread.

Who is she? Why am I a girl? All I have is my mind, the rest is hers.

"Do you remember any of last night?" I ask her. Somehow, I'm able to speak aloud. My voice resonates higher in tone. My attempt to bring it into a more comfortable range causes a lisp, so I leave it alone.

She was the definition of crazy last night. Or am I the crazy one? Who thinks they changed sex in the middle of a suicide?

She frowns. "What about it?" Strange, she also speaks out loud, I can hear the echo off the walls.

"Please try."

She crosses her arms and blows between her lips. "Fine. When I finish, will you leave?"

I don't say anything.

She blows between her lips again, re-crosses her legs, and repositions her knife. "The last thing I remember was returning home with my groceries. I took a shortcut down an alley between the bus stop and the back of the apartment complex when … when…" She curls into a tight ball. "Oh no. I'm dead. Aren't I?"

I stall. Two, no, three choices here. The first is to force control over my delusion. I could hurt myself—wait a minute, that's silly, I *want* to kill myself. But, I want a clean death, not one with blood all over the place. Second is to give in and ride this, whatever it is, out. Don't like that. I didn't make squad leader by going with the flow. The third is to play along, wear out my delusion, then grab control.

Babushka, you've forgotten I can fight you off. Your illusion is pure evil genius. Much better than your cockroach illusion when I was fifteen. You've forgotten about how I wrested control from you when Quentin came over to play shoot-by-thumb games. Stupidly, I told him about being a cockroach. A month later, he presented me with a leather-bound set of Kafka's stories he found in an antiquarian shop below the Seattle Monorail. His excitement drew me in, and we laughed ourselves silly.

I go for the third choice, the one that conquered the cockroach. "I'm not certain living or dead applies. You're sentient and capable of independent thought, so you are living by my thinking."

"But … but … what about you?"

We have progress. We are communicating. Right now, I'm not confident I'm alive. I need to keep her off balance and not asking the real questions. She's in control. If she stumbles onto how thin the thread of my consciousness is, I'm toast. "Do you remember how we met?"

"Something about wrapping myself—oh my god—I'm a *thing*."

"No, you aren't a *thing*. Go on, tell me what happened."

"I sensed only warmth and pressure. I think I wrapped myself around you, then blacked out. I woke up on the bathroom tile and jabbered about lots of stuff. You must think I'm a total dim bulb."

Keep her engaged; this is working. She's rational, and the knife has slipped out of her hand. She's not going to stab herself to get at me.

"I don't think that. You were in trouble, and somehow you enveloped me. Except I don't think I'm in here anymore. I need to know. Could you disengage?"

She scrambles into the corner where I toss my dirty clothes and curls into a fetal position. "No."

It takes everything I know about PTSD to not lash out. I'm scared of my own PTSD-driven delusion? Yep. She scares me shitless.

I've got to get her to fade, or I'm due for pink room time at the VA. I need Katie. Katie can handle anything. Quentin would help soothe the situation like he did with every Babushka outrage over the past twenty years.

There's banging on the kitchenette window, probably the meadowlarks that have been dropping by.

Pain radiates from my cautious push to gain control of her left leg. She breaks her fetal curl of our(?) body. "What was that? It felt like a cramp, one of the bad ones I'd get from gymnastics."

"I was trying to straighten our leg. It was falling asleep."

"Thank you. You're kind, but you're not real. I can't be a thing."

I stifle my reaction to her hands running over my body.

She continues, "I can't be dead. I can't have an inner something injuring me. So, from now on, I move my body. Better yet, go away." Her last four words ascended in pitch. Now I've gotten her angry. At least she doesn't seem to the type to go hysterical or drop into catatonia. I must be careful though, her belief in her reality gains a deeper hold as the conversation continues

Arguing with myself isn't going to work. My knee stings, at least I can talk to her about that without a fight. *"Could you check the right knee? It burns. What happened to it?"*

"Where were you? Oh, that's right. You don't exist. Three goons with letter jackets tried to drag me into the back of their pickup. One will be walking hunched over for a few days." She uncurls out of the corner and pads to the pocket bathroom. Under the sink, she finds disinfectant. "You'd think I could create a better imaginary apartment. This place is a dump."

I can't keep silent. "*Hey!*"

"Hey, what? It's the truth. I won't say this wasn't fun, but I must get out of this delusional state and back to my own apartment. I probably never left it."

That's my opening. "Fine, I give up. See the gun under the bed? It's already loaded, safety off and round in the chamber. All you have to do is put the barrel under your chin pointing to the top of your head and squeeze the trigger."

"Okay."

8

WILL

SARAH

S he gripped the semi-automatic's handle between two fingers and a thumb and stepped with it to the kitchenette counter. She frowned at the suggestion. *Why would I tell myself to shoot myself? That couldn't be the only solution.*

Looking down, she sees that she's dropped the magazine she'd removed from the butt of the gun. Cartridges filled the magazine, but why would she want to check? Guns were not foreign to her mostly rural family. All of them, including most of the women, owned them. Of course, they made fun of the nut-wads who believed open-carry made them safer. Except when hunting, guns stayed in the trucks or locked up in the house.

But Sarah's family lived in the suburbs, and the only guns were the ones Daddy had had. Learning how to use them had never been important. Now that she looked closer, this was the same type of antique 45 caliber semi-automatic pistol that Daddy inherited from his Vietnam veteran father, who got it from his World War Two veteran father. Even the chips and pits on the barrel slide were the same. Flipping to the right, the newer black grip matched her memory. Spooky.

The faint banana-like odor from the gun oil reminded her of the times she had overnighted with cousins, and they chatted while one cleaned the hunting guns. The scent grew stronger. She'd done it again. This time she'd pulled the top slide, loading the chamber. Dropping everything, she scooted back on the counter stool.

Her arms reached out and reassembled the gun.

"Stop that!" There was no way she was allowing her dark side to kill her, even if it was to end her delusion. And when did she get a dark side? She needed to get away from the gun.

She scrambled to the bed and placed her back to the wall. Better. Unless she suffocated herself on the blankets. Something about shooting her hallucinated body to return to her real body seemed like a terrible idea.

She pushed against her dark delusion's attempts for control. She decided that talking to her inner psycho-voice could help. "Suicide seems extreme. There must be a non-violent way to regain my consciousness, surely."

No answer.

The feelings she picked up radiated an angry pout. "Seriously? You're upset? You're not even real. Now be part of the solution and help me get back to my real body."

"What makes you think this isn't real?"

Sarah lost it. "Are you friggin' blind? Look around. I would never put myself in a nasty apartment like this. Nothing's clean, it stinks of beer, and I stick to the bathroom tiles. And my clothes! I would never imagine dirty shorts and a grimy polo shirt."

She stopped, and breathed slowly, the way she had been taught after her daddy died. It would do no good if she slipped into a panic attack and hyperventilated.

"And you think you have better clothes?"

She stomped her foot, paused her open-handed slap when it occurred to her she would be slapping herself. "Do you think I run around nude? Of course, I have clothes. Boxes of them at my apartment. I can go get them." Her suicide ideation waned, and she no longer was drawn to the gun. Besides, Psycho-voice should disappear once she was in her apartment.

She hoped.

9

APPLE SKIN

ALEX

I've found the perfect opening to escape my delusion. *"I can drive there, but you have to let me go first."*

Our face opens into a smile. "That will happen. Not. Give it up. You're not real. How can you drive?"

"I have a car."

"Now that's convenient. My psycho-voice has a car. Let me guess, it's held together with rust, two of the tires are bald, and the engine bangs like it will blow up when you accelerate. Oh, and it's called Chitty-Chitty-Bang-Bang."

"So you let me go, and I drive us to your apartment?"

"Bogus. I can drive. Where are your keys?"

Too easy. She doesn't exist. Therefore, neither her apartment nor her stuff exists. The irresolvable conundrum will collapse my split personality, and I can continue my interrupted date with Ms. Colt. Yep, best idea yet. Except ... she knows the name of my car?

Within five minutes, we're off in Chitty-Chitty-Bang-Bang, my fourth-hand car bought before I enlisted. Like me, she enjoys rolling down all the windows to let the wind tickle our hair. Yes, this will turn out fine.

Sarah

Starting at the age of twelve, Sarah spent summers driving Uncle Helmut's two-ton, double-clutch diesel trucks chasing the grain combines. Bench seat pulled forward, her long legs had allowed her to double-shift with the best of her male cousins.

She kicked off his sandals, adjusted the seat and mirrors, and exited into busy traffic. She wiggled in the seat. She couldn't believe her hallucination included stiff, torn vinyl sticking to her butt.

A large, black van, dual axle, antennas sticking out like porcupine quills, careened from the outer lane to the median strip, knocking down two "wrong way" traffic signs, before returning to the center lane. It popped an illegal U-turn, on two wheels, and halted in a parking lot.

The rust-bucket she was driving might be a figment of her imagination, but in case she had just jacked a car, she at least would eat well. Frustrated by being lost in the new town, she stopped at a grocery store. Three bags of groceries filled the front passenger seat. At least she would be comfortably fed while she shucked her psycho-voice like a wormy ear of corn.

"When do I see your apartment?"

"Shut up."

Waves of unhappiness enveloped her. It wasn't her; it was Psycho-voice. He'd become a real pain in her newly skinnier posterior.

After a half hour of crisscrossing the neighborhood on the other side of Washington State University, she pulled into an alley. Her head on the steering wheel, she let tears flow. She didn't look like herself, a bitchy guy was hassling her, and now she was lost?

Since her Daddy's funeral, she'd never had any use for tears; tears didn't replace a plan. Hoping to get an idea, she parked in an alley and paced the broken macadam and gravel patches.

It looked familiar.

Dodging congregating meadowlarks, she slipped on a flat red object, apple shaped with yellow streaks.

10

ESCAPE

ALEX

What happened? I was so close to exorcizing her, then she slipped and collapsed. No concussion, otherwise I'd still be out. Standing, the jiggling and chafing of my breasts confirm my worst fear. I got rid of her, but I'm still a girl. I'm still the inner doll of this Matryoschka.

Pounding on the Bondo holding Chitty-Chitty-Bang-Bang together, I scream, "Son of a bitch!" In my other hand, the apple silhouette hangs onto the ends of my fingers. I shake to get rid of it, but it stays put.

A hand grabs my female shoulder. I wince, and my knees buckle.

"Ah," says a voice, "It's good of you to drop by for a social visit. We've been looking for you. Did you go to a beautician? You're not as tousled, and the hair is darker."

Unable to resist the sharp pain in the clavicle, I turn. At the other end of the iron grip is a runt, greasy face, oversized ears, and enough halitosis to fell a bison. He asks, "Where did you go? No matter, we've worn out our welcome here." A second person is positioned behind him, at least six feet, built like a fullback, but I think female. She's wearing fake military tactical gear, black, but her stance gives her away. She's seen too many Kung Fu movies and looks as if she needs to take a dump. The runty guy eases his grip, but only a little. "Come with us. We've moved the equipment to a safe house north of town."

The woman, who looks like she could crack my ribs with her fist, asks, "You mean that dirty cave in the state park?"

A fleer of anger from Greasy shuts his minion up. "Before I was interrupted, we need to stabilize your situation. You're taller. How'd you reform? I'm your only hope at being normal." He took a moment to glare again at his minion.

This is my chance to exploit my military training. Two opponents, one with a grip like a bench vice. The other one with knife sheaths and a suspicious lump under her right arm. She's a southpaw, and my assailant favors his right. I'm standing between them, inside their weak side.

I smile, I hope, encouragingly. "Sorry about the misunderstanding, but if you would let me get my purse?" These two think they know me so I can play that up. A light touch to his wrist and, startled, he lets go. "Watch in case I was followed." I can't believe this works, but the minion turns to look.

Under the front seat is the old-fashioned, solid iron tire iron. My delusion left my gun behind on the kitchenette counter. I think I'm five-eight and not an ounce over one-thirty, the iron will make a great equalizer. Greasy's eyes widen as I turn on the ball of my inner foot and swing with all the force of my turning abdomen. I clock him immediately above his left temple. Greasy crumples like an unstaked pup-tent in a Sirocco wind. He doesn't even twitch, but his eyes don't close.

His partner, at least one hundred pounds heavier than me, turns at the sound. Her pupils dilate, and a nasty grin exposes broken teeth. I'm off balance, and the iron is fully extended in the wrong direction. I kick out my off foot to regain balance.

I tumble, tuck, and roll out facing her back. I swing at her hand, and her knife drops to the ground. I regain my balance and move more like a gymnast than a street fighter. Smooth, balanced movements keep me in control and I knee-cap her. She falls overs as her scream fills me with dread that she'll get back up. She doesn't.

The tire iron is jarred out of my hand, and I'm too close to her to risk grabbing for. However, the knife lays within reach next to the passenger-side front tire of a dark green station wagon, parked between the two detached garages facing the alley. No markings or ID. Must be a rental. A knife plus tires is an opportunity too good to be true. I grab it and stab twice before I'm able to puncture the left front tire.

Through sheer grit, the guard is using my tire iron to brace herself as she tried to get up. The pure rage in her eyes burns a hole in my resolve, and I dive into my car.

Gunned and thrown into reverse, Chitty-Chitty-Bang-Bang does herself proud. A jerk on the steering wheel as I enter the street points me straight enough to shift into first gear. I see the minion struggling to unfasten the flap holding her gun. I don't wait to see how good a shot she's with her off hand. Tires smoke like a bad B-movie.

Two minutes later I spot the unexpected: the silhouette of my apartment building above the homes on this street. "I'm only two blocks from home?" My delusion had us traveling a circle around campus. The steering wheel slips from my hand when I turn into the parking lot; that damned apple peel had attached itself to the lower part of the wheel. It must have stayed in my hand during the fight. No matter how hard I try, it won't come off the wheel. Strange, but not as odd as dancing between my two attackers like a gymnast, instead of my practiced military hand-to-hand.

I stop the car but immediately change my mind. Parking here would paint a neon sign on the complex: Kidnap victim waiting inside. I circle the neighborhood three times and, spot the open grass lot where students park their junkers. Tall grass grows through the engine compartments of a couple in the middle. Perfect.

The diesel engine of the black porcupine van echoes between the walls of the office building, my apartment, and the one across the street. If I weren't worried about shaking my psychotic break, I'd be running them down. My Army Signal Corps background would help them. At least four of the antennas couldn't be properly grounded and working for whoever owned the test van would be more satisfying than my retail gig.

Reaching with my left hand to grab the three bags, I nudge those two lumps, reminding me I'm still a girl. One problem at a time. The big one is mean enough to come after me even with a flat tire and damaged kneecap.

Back in my efficiency with the door locked, chained, and my one bar stool propped against it, I wonder what just happened. Staring into the cracked mirror confirms I'm still a girl, about eighteen, with impossible green irises and auburn hair.

I recognize her. Please, not her. "She" would be my cousin, now almost thirty, married with three children. This is her at eighteen when she teased me into losing my virginity at fourteen. I didn't date for four years after that; couldn't handle the thoughts of what had happened.

But, on closer inspection, this isn't Helen. My delusional body's cheek bones and chin are more mannish, and there's a hardness to the eyes instead of Helen's twinkle.

Wearing what I have on, I wash everything else, including linens in the basement laundry room. Waiting on the dryers I do a minimalist cleaning of the bathroom and kitchenette. I make the bed with the clean linens and fold it into the couch and replace the cushions. This body comes with a cleaning gene? All this creeping around, checking for strangers burns me. If I was a guy, I'd call Katie, and we'd find my assailants, and leave enough for the cops, maybe. I still hate all this, but at least my little delusion isn't here to nag me. According to the clock over the range, it's 1:37 PM.

Why am I cleaning up this place? What's gotten into me? Why did I set aside three sets of clothes, white shirt, black or gray slacks, for my retail job at Lloyd and Donnelly? I'm barely holding down a panic attack to end all panic attacks. My best solution to my newfound gender dysphoria is to follow through on my plan. First the gun case …

I wake with a damp rag on my face. The gun case has been replaced. As an experiment, I place a fork in the grape jam jar I use as a tumbler and start my prep. First the gun case …

I wake with a damp rag on my face. The gun case has been replaced. The tumbler has two forks in it. I add a knife to the tumbler and start my prep. First the gun case …

I wake with a damp rag on my forehead. On the counter is the tumbler, with two forks, three spoons, and two knives. I've failed seven times. I only remember the preparation up to adding to the tumbler.

"I give up, Babushka. No more suicides."

The clock over the range shows 1:37 PM. The meadowlarks bang against the kitchenette window. What does that mean?

Something.

Something.

Got it.

Something is resetting time, only leaving the tumbler and its contents alone. I've read time doesn't have to travel only from the past to the future, and causality is not guaranteed.

This is too much.

"Go away. Find some other psychopath to harass." Slamming my hand on the kitchenette's window pane startles the meadowlarks and gives me the satisfaction of doing something physical. During one of my fugues, I must have stacked my textbooks and the laptop neatly on the kitchen counter near the wall outlet and pushed in my one stool.

As I cram my clothes into the highboy's drawers, a flicker that inverts the colors in the room teases me over my left shoulder. In the only empty corner of the efficiency stands four boxes, a purse and a back-pack that weren't there a couple of minutes ago. Now that's really weird.

"Oh, my clothes! Did you bring them? When?"

My delusion is back.

11

CLOTHES!

SARAH

"When did you get to my apartment?" Sarah bounced with joy, then looked around the apartment. "Hold that donkey. This is my imaginary apartment. How'd I get back here? Why are my clothes here?"

"I can't believe this. I'm back here!" She kicked the bottom box and the top box toppled onto her knee. "Am I expected to clean this pig pen?" She glanced around, stopped, and then did a full circle view. "Hey, this isn't too bad. It's tidy." Running her finger on the range top, she said, "But I could cook eggs here, without adding grease."

A beige bra hung out of the fallen box. "Clothes!"

She pulled open the box, found a set of undies, and then tore open the box labeled 'jeans-n-stuff.' "This will do. At least they're clean."

She headed to the shower, sniffed the bottles in it and said, "Hey Psycho-voice. Don't you have a better choice in shower gels?"

Alex gained enough control to say, "No shower gels. Guests use soap. Fresh washcloths are under the sink."

"Seriously? You expect me to use bar soap in my hair?" She lifted the ends to the mirror. "I'm already getting split ends." She ran her fingers through her hair. "Humph, the cut that came with this body works with the thinner face."

"Live with it."

"I have a better idea. I'll take a quick imaginary shower, put on fresh imaginary clothes, and drive nightmare car to either the grocery store again, or better yet, my real apartment."

"Can't."

"Can't what? In case you haven't noticed, I'm doing what I want, except ditching you, Psycho-voice."

"I hid the car."

"You did? How? Why?"

"Do you remember the alley you stopped in?"

"Vaguely." She shivered.

"Do you remember the apple skin?"

"I…" She dropped, and Alex grabbed control. He walked to the couch, the bed now folded inside it, and sat.

"You dropped out. I was attacked by two people who claimed to know you. One guy, short, greasy face, and a woman who could be a full-back. Friends?"

"No! I thought that was a nightmare."

"What?"

"I can't do this right now. G-go away. I'm taking a shower. Now I have my backpack…" she opened it and slipped out her laptop— "and laptop back, I need to check some things. Now go away." Her force of will stranded him in the background, unable to see, hear, feel, or react.

12

REALITY

ALEX

Oh, what a headache. Soft but rapid beeping wakes me, and a glow greets my opening eyes. I've fallen asleep on the keyboard of my laptop. Swell, I'm the stereotypical student who can't go to bed when tired.

The problem is, I don't remember working on the computer. The professors don't assign homework, you just read and parrot back their pontifications. God bless liberal arts teachers. Closing the lid, two things catch my attention: this isn't my computer, and my clothes bind, especially over the shoulder blades and crotch. Pulling off the shirt, chest hair bunches under and around the bra. I have chest hair? I have chest hair!

I tear the clothes in my haste to examine my regained masculinity. Alex is back. All of me. The chick clothes, including the bra and briefs that were killing me, and her sandals, miss the trash bin. No matter, I've plenty of time to clean up later.

Something is deeply wrong with me, and I need help. A fumble in my satchel brings out my cell phone. Thumbing my fave's list gives me a choice. Quentin or Katie? It's Saturday. By now Quentin and I would be on the quad, eyeballing coeds. Last year, Katie and I hit coffee houses and chilled at the outside tables.

I, I can't. Quentin would bring comfort and Katie strength, but they abandoned me. I have no one.

I shower. Afterward, still damp, I find an appropriately tattered T-shirt and shorts from my fresh laundry.

The laptop hasn't disappeared. And the boxes, purse, and backpack remain in the corner next to the door, leaning from the kick she planted in them. One box sits on the end of the couch with clothes scattered everywhere. On the countertop, next to the laptop, my spiral notebook is splayed open, full of notes in neat cursive handwriting. Arrows connect the notes. She, or I while unconscious, was attempting to mind-map ideas.

Flipping the pages back to the start of the left-handed cursive writing. "This is impossible to live with. I've shut down Psycho-voice, but nothing changed back to what I know as reality." I can't write in cursive, and I'm right-handed. My delusion gets more interesting.

Four pages of boxes follow, laying out a plan. In the first box, *Key Facts*, are lists of locations and things I don't know. The second box contains her memory of the details of the first list. The next pages are bubbles of thoughts, connected with lines and arrows. Some bubbles are crossed out in what I decide is an angry swipe, especially the ones with rips in the paper. My left-handed cursive-writing delusion was trying to reason her way out of the only conclusion, she's not real—I've got her.

The last page holds notes dotted with moisture. Tears?

"TD&H—gone, The Marys—gone. Uncle Sue—gone. Timmy and Denise—still here. Great Uncle Helmut—still here, but only has eight children. Mom—here, but now works for Daddy's old firm. She is up on social media, with pics of me, not as I remember, but the person I've become. My life has been erased and replaced by that thing I look like."

"I sense a deep fulfillment that conflicts with my losses. Something has…"

The notes stop there. So, my little psychotic delusion was searching for a life. I have to hand it to myself; my alter-ego had quite an imagination. Maybe I should become a writer.

Never mind that silliness. I'm going to be an engineer, contributing to society, like my father and my mother. I've had that goal since "take your child to work" day when I was six. It was intended to distract me from my depression of losing Babushka. It helped a little, but that visit to the design bullpens and the assembly plant fired my drive to become an engineer.

I wonder when my delusion's laptop, boxes and the writing in my notebook will disappear?

A susurration has been bothering me, and now my left ankle itches. I reach down to scratch it and find that same slippery surface from last night. The meadowlarks bounce off the window pane.

A thought forms in my mind. *"Help me."*

13

REALITY REVERSED

ALEX

I fall backward from the stool and crawl to the couch. Sitting on the couch, I shake the leg to displace the flesh-thing hanging on to my ankle.

"Help me."

Flesh-thing doesn't come off, but neither does it envelop me. My last experience is still too fresh in my mind; I don't tear at it with my hands. Even without movement, the susurration continues, forming a white noise that fills the apartment. Stalemate. My delusion has returned to finish me off. "Uh," I don't know its name, "is that you?"

"Yes. Where am I? I can't see or feel, Help me."

Fear surrounds me like a blanket, but it's not mine. Somehow, curiosity gets the better of my fear. I say, "I'll sit down, but don't climb higher." The thing remains wrapped around my left ankle, and my foot sticks out of the fleshy wrap. I wiggle my toes in my sandals and feel the movement.

I'm forming an idea, but it refuses to move forward so I can study it. I've been called an intuitive, which is a pain. Frequently, I just *know* the right answer but can't access the reasoning, or logical steps. It starts with an unexplained joy, and then ideas trickle into my head forming a solution.

I'm feeling that joy right now and can only wait out the developing idea. In the meantime, what am I to do with my delusional ankle-bracelet? "Hello. Are you still there?"

The thought forms in my mind. *"You told me to stay still."*

Not exactly what I told it, but close enough. "Can you unwrap yourself from my ankle?"

"Is that what I'm doing? So, this is what wrapping feels like. I wish I had the words for it." The words stop with a dead hollow filling an unknown part of my mind. *"About separating ... I don't want to."*

Wrong answer. Last time I touched it with my finger, it enveloped me in seconds.

The gun lies underneath the couch from when I couldn't kill myself. I wonder what would happen if I shot it. I'm afraid I already know the answer: nothing. With the right foot, I nudge the gun away from her—or it, I'm still not certain. Then I try a trick Quentin could do with a heavy bar: grip the barrel between my big toe and the next toe and lift. It slips and bounces on the carpet with a clunk.

"What was that?"

It can feel vibrations? "Oh, nothing. I shifted my other foot to relieve a Charlie-horse."

Bending, stretching muscles still somnolent from not being used for almost twenty-four hours, I reach again for the gun. Not thinking, I lift my wrapped leg and bring up almost a square meter of the throw rug with it. No rips, no weight, the fragment simply hangs flat in midair under my foot. This is too cool. I rotate my foot, and the fragment stays flat while matching the angle of the bottom of my foot. Way cool.

"Stop that. It makes me ill."

Huh? Then I see the rug intact below the "rug" attached to my foot. It's perfectly camouflaged, texture and all. Even the Concord wine stain is mimicked in perfect hue and reflection. If the government could get this into armor, no one could see them coming.

Without thinking, I reach to touch the faux-carpet fibers. The first impression is the needs-to-be-shampooed greasiness. The carpet flows up my arm, first covering it with carpet then converting to an exact copy of my skin. "Stop it!"

"What?"

"You're wrapping around me. Stop it."

"Say, I think I can see!"

It stops at my left shoulder. I touch my covered shoulder and can feel my shoulder through it, even the hair follicles tickle to a light touch. It's as if it isn't there. A filament hangs onto my finger. As I watch, it thickens and moves up my hand. "I said stop it." Any more, and I'll be unable to dive for my gun to finish myself off.

It releases the finger. *"Now I can hear your voice and smell what you smell. What did you clean the apartment with? No, don't tell me. We'll work that out later."*

14

KIVA

SARAH: DAY 2, SATURDAY AFTERNOON

Sarah realized Alex was having a male-kiva, complete with beer, in an attempt to center himself. He went to the 'fridge and pulled out a long neck beer, a brand she didn't know, and returned to the couch. He didn't say anything, and she did nothing to intrude more than she already had.

She appreciated her own privacy and did her best to not use his senses. As an only child, she cherished privacy. Even changing for the gym was a trial.

This wrapping-contact they were dealing with cut off her ability to manipulate the body, as it remained his, not their body. Miffed at not being able to check things out, she was also happy. This meant that as long as she kept silent, he wouldn't be interrupted.

This was the first real test of whether she was rational-thinking and not needs-driven. Unfortunately, this mode caused her to itch like falling into a nest of fire ants. The mismatch between her senses and the lack of a real body would be yet another trial.

Accidentally releasing Alex shook something loose. Her conviction that she was hallucinating the strange girl in the mirror vanished with her newfound and growing clarity. Even the notion of having a man within created more curiosity than revulsion. She couldn't ignore the possibility this was all real.

What am I missing? She wracked her mind. *How'd I get from the first day on campus buying groceries to this … this?*

Everything closed in on her, then opened to her. A non-glow glow emanated from all directions but didn't illuminate her. This state of existence would have terrified her if it didn't seem so normal. In fact, the more she didn't sense the physical world, the more comfortable she was. This was enticing! Her grip on her former existence faded.

To the North. She was being pulled to the north, and it was stronger when she wasn't as attached to the physical world.

Something broke through her sense of belonging in this strange place. Curiosity pulled her out, away from the comfortable. She couldn't place the new sensation, but it brought her back. She could again sense what he saw and heard. He was rubbing his arm, and thus her.

She'd forgotten about him. *"What are you doing?"*

"Did you know you have a tattoo?" He cocked his neck and pointed with his left hand. "Right here."

"I don't have any tattoos."

"I mean you're a chameleon. You perfectly mimic whatever you cover. I prefer it this way. I get to remain male."

"Let me see."

It took all her self-control to not be pushy; she waited for his eyes to settle on the spot. *"I'm sorry, it's blurry. Could you look to one side?"* This cleared the vision. *"Could you look at the other side of the tattoo?"* He did, and she could make it out now. *"Strange. I see better on the sides but can't make anything out in the middle. We must be neurally linked, but not completely. Interesting. You have a large blind or fuzzy spot in the middle. About the tattoo, I only see half."*

"No, you see it correctly. Senior year, Quentin and I got utterly blitzed and fell in with the wrong crowd. I woke up in a tattoo artist's chair. That half image is all I got before I gripped his hand. They thought..." He stopped and restarted drinking."

"Thought what?"

"I was going to say that '"I was a guy, thus the masculine tat. But I *am* a guy." He went silent and ignored her moving more fully around his shoulders.

"Who's Quentin?" She asked.

He rinsed out the beer bottle and dropped it into a recycling bin that had been empty when she explored the apartment before. The bottles and cans had cluttered most of the horizontal surfaces instead.

When he finished, he said, "What do you think of me?"

This was the moment she had tried to prep for. "You are real. Not a figment of my imagination. That means I'm some sort of thing, a parasite. I seem to need to be in contact with you."

He gripped his left shoulder with his right hand. "You're slipping. Do you want to be put somewhere?"

"*No!*"

"Did you know you were sliding off when you said parasite?"

"I felt sadness, but nothing else."

"Okay, you're back, maybe even higher. It's hard to tell, but I think you're across my shoulder. For what it's worth, I think you are real and in trouble. From your reactions, that girl we are when we fully merge is not you."

"No. There is a family resemblance. She looks like one of my homelier cousins.

"Oh, I never properly introduced myself. Hi! I am Sarah Beth Merk, from Omaha, this will ... would be my first year in college."

"I'm Alexander James Monroe, Ballard, sophomore going into engineering. Glad to meet you." He stared across the room.

"Is there a problem?"

"I think we're almost a dead ringer for my own cousin, Helen, when she was eighteen."

"I don't see—"

"She's four years older. Helen was … is everything I'm not, outgoing, friendly, the center of attention. She flirted with all the boys and receptive girls but told me she would never spread her legs or open her mouth until she did me first. I freaked and enlisted right after graduation."

"So, looking like her is…"

"Creepy. Our joint body even has the same dimples under the clavicles. She propositioned me after my last tour. There she was, three children, one on her lap, and she told me I would always be hers."

"I wish there was something I could do."

"That's the second reason I'm committed to finding a solution for you. You need an independent life. I read your notes. You are real. A real girl, but somehow translated into the thing you are. Oh, sorry about that."

"Don't be. We need to be honest, about everything."

"Thanks. With all the strangeness, dancing on eggshells is tough. My interest has a selfish element. I don't think I can handle being a girl, much less my cousin, for long."

He withdrew and stared into another corner. Sarah concluded he was either being kind or hadn't noticed she was like his cousin, except for the leg spreading. Her mother would kill her if she did.

Whatever Alex was thinking, that glowy thing suffusing him roiled. Sarah watched it in fascination. He always seemed to glow in a color she hadn't any name for.

Suddenly he said. "We can move your belongings in with some rear-ranging."

"You're much too kind." Lame, but he'd caught her by surprise. Her excitement caused her being to ripple. The next thing she knew, she was face down on the floor, in the strange girl's body. "Sorry. Sorry. I think excitement can shift me into full form. That and extreme energy loss." She rubbed her nose and flicked away the trace of blood.

He said, *"It's okay, I was going to suggest you take over for a while."* He was kind, again, trying to override the glower of pissed off emotions leaking to her. Sarah shucked and folded his clothes and slipped into something comfortable for nesting activities.

Alex kicked the dust ruffle of the couch. *"You're different this time."*

"Not really. When I attacked you, I think that was raw instinct. I barely remember the first night. Since then I've struggled with a weird sense of disassociation like I was some other person. I think this is more me. I'm definitely happier fully clothed."

Alex frowned. *"I had a couple of instances after we stabilized where I found myself completing something I don't remember starting."*

She added this to her mental "to-understand" list. Sarah wanted to capture what she remembered in case she lost her memory. She sat deep into the couch to prevent more accidents like tipping out onto the floor. "The greasy man was surprised I could move. He said where he sent my body should have paralyzed it. Do you understand that? My body still exists. It's somehow … decoupled. Maybe that's why or how I can think, remember, and make decisions. I'm both here and, also, wherever my body is."

Alex frowned. *"That's good news except for one thing, your shell is amorphous. In bright light, it looks like epidermis, like skin, but it does something to the available light. You don't have an "inside." Hmm, that's not clear. Your outer surface is visible, and tactile in a strange tingly way, but the underside can't be seen or felt."* He faded again as if he disconnected with their body.

She panicked. "Alex!"

Nothing.

"Alex!"

A resurfacing of inner warmth signaled the return of his presence. *"Did you need something?"*

She couldn't keep her eyes from tearing up. "I thought I lost you."

"Sorry about that. I wanted to study. I'd discovered a place where I can remember everything I've seen and can store mental notes for later. I knew I didn't need to worry about my—our—body, so I went there."

"Let me know next time!"

"Sure."

They needed a distraction. No sports games on TV. He had no one to call and chat with. Sarah didn't read Alex as someone who went in for "retail therapy," as her Mom called shopping. "Do you know of a movie we can watch?" Any movie, no matter how putrid, would beat her inner void when he wasn't present.

He said, "No. We need to review what we know."

15

MOTHER

SARAH

A lex's glow faded and was replaced by what she associated with his unhappiness about their blended state. *"I don't think your attackers are able to trace where you went. I'll keep watching. However, people may panic if you drop out of sight. Especially at home in Omaha. You can't become a nun. Staying in frequent touch is a way to protect yourself in case you are grabbed. You should make a list and a schedule to maintain contact with your friends.*

"For starters, I think you should call your parents."

How could she forget about Mommy? Her hand went to her mouth. "I —I've forgotten that I had had a life."

"Understandable. We'll need to work on getting you more connected. But you didn't lose your life. You have a life. Always keep that in your mind. We'll work this out somehow. The best place to start is to call your parents, then everyone you normally talk to, and expand that list to others to keep in touch."

"I only have a mother. Daddy died ten years ago." She couldn't continue with all the conflicting thoughts about her losses, turning her mind to mush. After a couple of moments, Alex nudged her back to their conversation. "What do I tell her?"

"You know her best, but I think telling her the truth, or even a partial truth such as you were mugged, may worry her."

Curled up on the couch, Sarah called her Mommy. "Sorry for the late call. I've been running full-out like when Uncle's bull chased me." She died a little inside over the lies she was telling her mother. They had always been open with each other. "I'm registered for the fall but haven't locked in the classes." More lies tore at her.

"Miss Independent," said her mother, "If you don't call me at least three times a week, I'll take up crocheting again, and make you take selfies wearing bunny ears in classes."

"Ma!" Alex's comforting presence was all that kept her from collapsing. Her voice went raw. "How's stuff at your end?"

"Oh, no. You don't get off easy. Why?"

"Why what?"

"Don't get coy with me. Why did you leave early?"

"Oh, that 'why.' Timmy's company had an IT changeout, and he offered to use his ten-day furlough to drive me."

"Ah-huh…"

"We had a great time. Saw a buffalo near Uncle Adam's ranch in Ogallala. Does he still run buffalo on his spread?

"And we stopped at both Little Americas in Wyoming."

Her mother kept up with non-committal "uh-huhs."

"The Great Divide was a disappointment. The interstate cuts through the low spot, and without the sign, you would never know you were dribbling downhill like the sink Mr. Kahn messed up."

"Uh, wait, who is Mr. Kahn?"

She dropped the phone. The Kahns had also disappeared? What was their son's name? Why couldn't she remember it? Alex reached with their arm and brought the phone back to her ear. She said, "Sorry, I was thinking about a different person. We decided to skip the Mormon temple and took the bypass to Idaho."

"Uh-huh…"

She knew what was twisting her mother's tail, and she wasn't about to go there. "So, what's new at your end?"

The banging pans at Mom's end announced she was about to lower the boom. Mom used either frenzied broom sweeping or banging pans in a drawer when a lecture was imminent. The swish of the broom wouldn't carry over the phone, so Sarah held the phone away from her ear, waiting for the end of the clanging-pans overture.

Her Mom said, "Why didn't you wait until after harvest? You always make great money and Uncle Helmut kept Ol' SloMo for you. He told me harvest was slower because your cousins and the hired hands didn't have you to compete with."

"I told you, Timmy had the days off."

"And" …"

"And what?"

"Don't get snippy with me. I'm not your cousin Denise. Why did you stand Douglas up?"

"Doofus wouldn't keep it to just-friends."

"What is wrong with Douglas? He'll finish his Associate's degree soon and has a bright future in his father's firm."

"And he would want a hausfrau to bed, pop out a half-dozen kids and have dinner on the table when he came home from the after-work bar gathering."

"Sarah!"

"It's true. He would be all over me, hinting and insisting I quit college and marry him. I want to get a full degree and take the time to decide what I want."

"You could do worse than Douglas, you know. His mother is not talking to me, the way you took off and didn't tell him. He showed up the next day for your date."

"I never agreed to any date. He declared it. I'd rather not talk about it. Can we change the topic?" She wracked her mind for something to distract her mom. "Please don't be mad about me not calling sooner. I was jogging, and I lost my phone and driver's license."

"Were you hurt?"

"No, Mom, I wasn't hurt. I only had the license for ID and the phone for emergencies. I think they fell out when I crossed a park. I went back but didn't find them."

"Well, be more careful. The state's online renewal is still buggy, that electro-putz—I think. I'll call Dolores at DMV to issue you a fresh license. She loves you and still expects you to call Douglas. If she's able to expedite without you coming back to Omaha, you'll need to call him a couple of times. It will make his month, well, his year."

"Yes, Mother." Pretending to be long-suffering was the game they played for each other's amusement. Sarah choked back a sniffle and caught the warmth of an Alex encouragement.

"This morning, on the way to work, I'll drop by the phone store at Fifth and Main and pick up a replacement. No telephone tag between you and Bangladesh."

"I can do it online."

"Where have you been? Ever since the Putz—or is it the Putsch? — electronic records have been scrambled. Especially here in the Midwest. I'm taking care of it. The governor has ordered the old paper forms be found, copied and used until everything comes online. You might get a paper printout with the county clerk's seal."

Sarah halted for a moment. *The electro-Putsch is that bad? I've so got to catch up.* Sensing Alex's imminent return from what she hoped was only a deep-thought moment snapped her out of her lapse of attention. "I'll transfer money to your account."

"Nonsense, Miss Independent, you will let me do this little favor. Now, where do I send the license and phone?"

Alex nudged her. "I forgot the good news. I got a wonderful room-mate. I broke my lease and moved in. Cut my living expenses in half. I told you coming months early would pay off."

"What's her name? May I talk to her?"

Oh, of course, a mother would assume her roommate was a girl. Alexi would work. "Alexi Monroe. She's out right now, grocery shopping."

At the Alexi fib, an amused tickle formed at the back of her mind, and a grin broke through. *"Quit smiling; I can't talk."*

Alex wrote their apartment number and address. He was getting quite good with their right hand.

After two rounds of repeats and writing it down, her mother said. "You're to put her on the phone next time. At least send me a photo made with your new-fangled phone." They chit-chatted for another fifteen or so. It was obvious their conversation was winding down, and Sarah was relieved she didn't get the lecture about waiting two days between calls. If that came up, she might burst out bawling.

Mom said, "I miss you."

"I miss you, too. You need to visit this fall. I understand the Palouse Hills are beautiful before the wheat harvest."

"I'll think about it. I used my vacation leave for my surgery last year. I must get dressed. If I'm lucky, I can mail all this and Doofus's phone number tonight. And don't forget, I do read texts. My independent daughter, I love the calls, and the sound of your voice, but you could also text me during your slow times. 'That would help this empty nester a lot."

"I promise. At least once a day. Love you."

"And I love you."

They hung up, and Sarah's eyes moistened.

"I'll remind you every day to call her."

"Figures. Always seeking reasons to nag me." She tagged with an affectionate emoting. He was a mother hen, but a sweet mother hen.

Sarah wondered if she'd ever see her mom again. She collapsed forward over her legs. Alex said nothing. Instead, he provided a sense of warmth and his wonderful hug. Alex was beyond wonderful, but she really did want to be independent.

She wanted to have a day when she wasn't scared.

16

NESTING

A lex's alarm pinged with the "Broomstick Song" from *Fantasia*, but Sarah was already awake. Another strange dream had woken her three hours earlier. Her night was dominated by the fear she was already dead, or her host would abandon her.

Setting this YAUP—yet another unfixable problem—to one side, she focused on how to keep Alex healthy and happy. This was his sophomore year and the first one where he would be taking serious engineering classes. He needed his study time. Last night, being the Helen-like-clone disturbed him so much he couldn't study. He begged Sarah to release him.

She tried several times and failed. "I don't know how." Tears rolled down their cheeks, and his anguish left her breathless.

Alex had to hold their body up. She let him. He said, *"Try again, we—you can do this."*

What if she couldn't? How Alex could trust her again? She wished to be the Sarah she remembered. A *Tsssk* sounded in the back of her mind, a sibilance like the top coming off a pressure cooker, and the Helena-clone disappeared, replaced by Alex.

Alex patted himself down. "This is great. How did you do it? Wait, where are you?"

"I don't know. I must be somewhere on you because I can hear you."

He patted himself, starting at his shoulders and working down. She said, "S*top. I sensed something."*

"Around my waist. And how about this?" They concluded she formed a disk from his chest down to his belly button. After an hour of experimenting with her movement, she wrapped around his shoulders leaving his neck free.

"Better. I can see and smell. Oh! I can hear birds. I can hear through your ears!"

Again, she was the perfect mimic, and he couldn't tell what was her and what was his uncovered skin.

After studying, he pulled out the sofa bed. "After you sense I'm asleep, you can try for the other body. We should find out if I can sleep through what you need to do." Unhappiness swirled out of his inner being, belying his chipper tone.

After twenty minutes of Alex's even breathing, Sarah made her move. He jerked as the blend into their composite form completed then settled back. She waited a couple of minutes to ensure he was still asleep then rose from the bed. Sarah went through her old gymnastics stretches. A smile, then a frown, then a smile formed as she discovered what parts of this strange new body followed her old body's flexibility. Not wanting to wake Alex, she refrained from pushing the stiffer joints and muscles. Maybe she could get him to join her in a workout. Maybe. But he broke out in a sweat whenever he saw the person he called Helen in the mirror.

A quick shower, and she slipped into cleaning clothes: drawstring pants and a loose T-shirt. Putting her long hair in a topknot held in place with a pen, she went to work on the apartment. The cleaning was surface-competent, but she wanted to do something about the odor of his—now their—apartment. Sniffing each corner, she cleaned as she crawled starting in the back corner and working toward the kitchenette. The water in the small bucket went from clear to beige to deep brown.

It looks like the nights are mine. I don't seem to get physically tired. Not done with the cleaning, she wrote a list of cleaning supplies and slipped it under the lid of his laptop. *Once we get better supplies, this place will be spotless and pleasant.*

Shucking the cleaning clothes into Alex's dirty clothes pile, she checked for Alex. He was still asleep, with the glow that she associated with, without knowing why, peace.

Another shower. She let the spray beat on her. A thought flickered that she should be worried about all the showers, but they were the only physical pleasure she had from her former life.

Afterward, she checked her bank account and credit cards. She closed the laptop with a smile. *I may be a parasite, but I have money to contribute.*

Instead of taking a break, she decided to investigate her condition. She tore around the Internet searching every word combination she could think of. She had to find out what was going on and how to get back her body. After fifteen minutes she was disgusted and almost slammed her laptop shut but slowed down to not damage it. Skin or coverings over live people was apparently a popular thing in porn. She wanted to puke.

Next, she decided to research everyone she could remember. She already knew Uncle Sue and Aunt Millicent no longer existed, along with their families. So, she listed everyone from school. Once finished, the list had over a third of the names crossed out, including half of her inner circle, and the Muslim boy she'd liked. All gone, as if they never existed, at least around Omaha, and as far as she could determine Nebraska.

She did the same with the over eight dozen cousins in and around Omaha. Well, the few dozens whose names she remembered. About a quarter gone, no record of them ever existing. The realization was a knife severing her connection to her old life. She couldn't continue looking, so she moved to the kitchenette, brewed some coffee and cried.

Alex stirred and mumbled something. She choked back her sniffles. *Life was easier when I thought he and this body were a delusion. At least I had a plan: get rid of them. What do I now?*

Via social media, old e-mail, old files on her computer, and in her cloud storage, she pieced together what was left of her Omaha life. All mentions of at least a quarter of her relatives had disappeared. *I wonder what my old yearbooks say?* That gave her a new idea, and she searched the archives of the Omaha *Daily Record*, the *Reader*, and the *World Herald*. The same results, with more relatives and their lives gone, including the new *Hergenreder Organics* dairy venture that employed twenty. This was big. Whatever had happened to her had also wiped out friends, about a quarter of her relatives and a couple hundred jobs?

A persistent news pop-up finally caught her attention. Variously called ElectroGeddon, DataGate, and electro-Putsch, something had crashed databases worldwide. No data appeared to be missing, but millions of links leading to nowhere. The greatest outages were in Kazakhstan, central Russia, the plains states of the USA and Canada, and Argentina. Something about those locations nudged her. Two, three(?) extended family steer roasts ago, her Aunt Millicent tried to get everyone interested in her photos of Argentina and Kazakhstan. Something about where their family came from and how spread out they were. She showed it to an empty living room. She'd been steamed.

Sarah shook off the feeling this was somehow connected to her crisis.

Taking a break from the insanity, she tore all her notes out of Alex's notebook and stuffed them into her backpack. *He has enough on his plate. I think he's the only thing that's keeping me alive.* He stirred, and her leg kicked out. Now that she'd confirmed her feelings of loss disturbed his sleep, she deep circle-breathed and calmed herself.

Washing her new face, she examined this new person they had become. For the first time, she did a detailed survey of her face. *She reminds me of someone. Helena?* Her distant cousin, maybe fourth, from

Ogallala, Nebraska. She searched her face, twisting to each side. *The ears seem familiar.* Dropping Alex's pajamas, she twisted to see her back. *Doesn't help. I don't think I ever saw Helena except in overalls on her father's farm.*

Her hand slammed forward into the mirror sending spikes of pain from her wrist to her elbow. "Helen, no! We can't." It wasn't her, but Alex, in a nightmare. There was more to his relationship with his cousin than he wanted to say. Why did they both have a cousin who looked like their composite body? Even the names were similar, Helen, Helena.

Back at her computer, she confirmed what she already suspected. Helena, her family, that entire side of the clan, was missing.

17

MATRYOSCHKA

SARAH

She stared at the screen, frozen in indecision. *Mom raised me better than this. I'm gonna live my life, screw whatever has happened.*

Not tired, and with the pre-dawn blooming like a sunflower raising its head in joy, Sarah made up the bed, folded up the couch, took a shower, and chose her wardrobe for the day. She settled on capris and a loose shirt to make Alex more comfortable. Now that she'd accepted her reality, she had moved to being protective of him, even if it meant that she'd wear clothes that didn't disturb him. Nothing looked good on this taller, thinner body.

She dropped onto the couch cushions and held herself. Deep breaths—in the nose, out through the mouth—repeated until her panic attack was over. Focusing on Alex's needs wasn't enough to patch over her fear, but she didn't have any solution other than staying with the relationship until they could be separated. His fear couldn't handle hers added to it. She sensed his panic slithering in the dark recesses of his mind. She needed a way to keep Alex stable.

The obvious choice and the easiest was to cook breakfast. Some midwestern soul food would be a balm on both their souls. *This morning Alex is getting Granna Hergenreder's special recipe flapjacks.*

She'd bought all the ingredients during her attempt to find her apartment—which she was now convinced had disappeared into the hole in her former life. The cheap aluminum pan didn't cooperate, and she got grease splatters on her sleeve, and overcooked spots on her flapjacks but they got made.

Alex woke and asked, "What do I smell?"

"Flapjacks."

"You cooked?"

"Of course, I cooked. What do you want on them? Next time I choose the topping."

Finished, overstuffed, and uncomfortable, Alex said, "I gotta learn to eat like a girl." And ran to the bathroom.

Returning, and sitting on the couch, Alex flipped their right hand over, palm up. "*We need to explore more than the skin and core aspects of our Matryoschka existence.*"

"Marty? Who's Marty?"

"*Mah-tree-oosh-ka. Ever see those nesting dolls with an outer shell which comes off, to reveal the next doll? The Russian name is Matryoschka. You're the outer shell; I'm the inner. Together, we are 'Matryoschka Sarah.'*"

"I don't like that. It's creepy. But it does describe us. Hopefully, there aren't five of us in here. Where'd you come up with Matryoschka?"

He stopped and shuffled his feet. They stared above the oven's clock for several moments. She noted that she'd need to do some serious degreasing of the old-fashioned tile there. "Oma Anna Maria, my maternal great-great-grandmother, had a set she brought when she emigrated from the German colonies along the Volga River in Russia. We all called her "Babushka." One day, she caught me playing with them. She made me play with them, every weekend, but with 'rules' about how to think while playing. This stopped when I started first grade. She declared I was the only child or grandchild to inherit the family Matryoschka. I thought she meant I got the creepy nesting dolls. She died the next week.

"My Aunt Millie locked the dolls in a safe."

His pain took over and swept her with it. This was the first time Sarah's emotions had been overridden. Matryoschka Sarah wasn't only hard for her—it was tearing her host apart. She sat on the couch; it was still an ugly orange. She experimented with the best way to comfort her body partner. His glowy thing felt like this wasn't about them, Matryoschka Sarah. This was something deep; scary. Alex was scared. He hurt in many ways. He was needy, as much as she was, and had been for a long time.

She tried hugging herself. He looked up. "I'm supposed to be the strong one. We have something else to talk about."

18

TRIAL SEPARATION

ALEX: 8:13 AM

I can't stall any longer. Time to clean up and leave before I'm late for classes.

Our first extended separation. I'm conflicted. The past four days, almost full time, I was a woman. As a man, I've learned to control my emotional swings. As a woman, the hormones, even our skin sensitivity defeats me. I don't see women breaking down, controlled by their hormones. How do they do it?

Now with my "independence" in sight, I'm scared. What will I be like? Will I be a woman inside, and a scarred veteran outside?

"Sarah, we need to separate. I have my classes. "

"*No.*"

I was afraid of this. "Why?"

"*You're all I have, and you will leave me.*"

"You've got to trust me like I trust you. This is only to go to classes, work, and errands."

"*If I let you go, you'll leave me.*"

"No. Yes. But—you know what I mean. I'll come back. I have issues I need to work on, without distractions." Sarah holds back her emotions and separates into her *thing* form. I cry as I fold her into a bundle and place her in the bottom drawer of the highboy. I wonder how she survived before we met.

No time to walk to class, so I take my car. More expense for parking which I can't afford. Mistakes like that I won't be able to support Sarah until we find a solution for her. This can't be as simple as her hanging on me. Her food choices are not for me. Her clothes will wear out. Every available space in my micro-bathroom contains her personal care products.

Classes are my zone-out time. Last year, my major, electrical engineering, was my refuge from the world. It was the one place where I could ignore everything that had happened to me. As it's the summer inter-semester, I have a light course load, two liberal arts with Katie and Quentin.

The first class is in an amphitheater classroom. It's been three days since our *Eye Scream Shoppe* disaster. That was enough to send me over the edge. My breath halts raggedly like before I cry. Perspiration hangs on me, and my face twitches around the scar. Three days isn't enough. Especially when you spent almost every hour of it obsessing over a girl with an existential crisis.

I stop at the classroom door and bolt.

19

COSTS OF INDEPENDENCE

ALEX

S afe in a study carrel nestled in the basement old-and-never-browsed section, at the in the Terrill Library, I touch the side walls and the shelf above the desk. Safe. Whom am I kidding? Slipping in the earbuds, I bring up the streaming vid of the lecture.

Too soon. Katie is at the front, before class starts, challenging the professor again. Quentin stands to one side, patently not paying any attention. Quentin is his own person. I hope Katie catches on and doesn't ruin their relationship by hounding him into studying. He'd only fake compliance, then slide back to his slacker persona. He won't discuss it, but something happened between his mother and him after I enlisted. He worked on her research project, then quit. He quit college, socialized at all the after-hours clubs, and took a series of dead-end jobs until I returned.

The prof has a well-honed drone, with perfect intonation. "To be moral is not to follow one's nature, but quite the opposite; it's to go against nature. We don't desire something, as Spinoza writes, because we say it's good, rather we say something is good because we desire it." I remember a sci-fi novella built on this premise of Spinoza's Ethics. Too bad I've forgotten both title and author.

Next is French Medieval Romance Literature. The prof's nasal, slightly lisping delivery rolls most sentences from low to high tenor and back, like a mid-ocean SonoBuoy, except where he finds the breath to end a sentence with an upward lilt like an airhead Valley girl. This stuff is as exciting as the flatulent Voltaire. I so have to convert this to pass/fail before time runs out and it affects my GPA.

The next thing I know, I'm watching a cleaning crew work on a spill in front of the lecturer's table. That's the third time during the past two weeks I've lost track of time during a lecture. Something gets me obsessing about my combat issues. But this time, it was about Sarah's situation. Normally, someone knowing my situation has had to nudge me to get up and to the next lecture.

According to the clock in the lower, right-hand corner of the laptop, I've been sitting here for almost eight hours. My back screams as I stand and straighten. The next class day, I'll face my fears of rejection and sit again with my friends.

20

TSSSKT

SARAH: 4:55 PM

It wasn't fair. *Tssskt*. She had had everything. She was the Chess Club champion. She placed in the inter-state gymnastics competition. *Tssskt*. She had the third highest GPA of a class of over 500 students. She was even awarded an academic scholarship.

How could this happen to her? Instead of a full life, she spent another day in the second drawer of the highboy dresser. She cleaned, cooked, and made his demons go away. All she asked for was to walk a little inside the building. *Tssskt*. No, he even did the laundry. He said it was because he worried about me. For eighteen years—ten of which were after Daddy died with her brother and sister—she'd taken care of herself with minimum effort by Mom.

She had a plan to fix this. She sensed his approach in stages, far away, then outside their door. About time. A little closer …

Ow. Ow. Ow! Her entire body throbbed. She made another note to herself, don't do that again. Oh, he fainted. That's why she had forced a painful blend, to keep him from interfering. Time to clean up and go out for—something. She'd had a plan, but it hadn't survived the blending. Well, he had cash in his wallet, and she had some in her purse. She could take his car and with their money … and do … what?

Alex came around as she remembered the plan. He asked, "Are you okay? Are you ill?" Nauseous and dizzy, he ran their body to the toilet and knelt in front of it. Nothing came out.

"Never better. Instead of staying here, I'm going out."

"We've been through that. You could be in danger."

"Not the way I see it. Where's your gun? I know you must have one. You're ex-military. Some souvenir you smuggled home."

Regaining control, she stepped to the couch and reached underneath. That must be it. She pulled it out. There was just a wire on the latch; she twisted off. Inside the case, a slim handmade presentation box had a plate inscribed with *The StupidEst PErson EvEr to SurvivE a FirEfight.* Inside was her goal, a pistol like the John Wayne war movie Daddy made her watch. He wanted her to understand that even an old pistol could mean duty, honor, and sacrifice.

She stalled by running her hand over the cold blue steel. The pistol was the same as her father's, including the same mismatched brown and black grip plates.

Then she remembered. She remembered the man, Greasy, torturing her with her father watching. That day her father, brother, and sister all died in a mysterious accident. She always believed that Greasy had had something to do with the accident. The plan, in all its illogic, came back to her.

"Ah'm goin' huntin'. You understand huntin', don't you? I'll drive around until I find the greasy man. He'll turn me back. I'll get my body back. I bet he'll cooperate with this in his mouth. After Greasy, I'll go home and take care of another ten-year-overdue problem." The day she left for college, she'd read the man who T-boned her family's car was released from jail.

Alex attempted to gain control of their body and failed. "You can't go out with a gun. Too many things can go wrong. You don't have training. You could kill him. You could be mistaken and kill the wrong person. Once you kill, you will never be whole."

"Then *you* shoot him." Alex missed the most obvious solutions.

She had a gun and bullets, though her memories of how to use it failed her. It was strange, but a mere memory lapse wouldn't stop her. How would she put bullets into the gun? She peered down the hole at the end of the gun. Looked right. The bullet went part way in but stopped at the brassy end. Did she have to open it somehow to put the bullets in?

"Alex, how do you—Eek."

Alex seized the counter-top. Both hands. She fought him. Couldn't-break-his-grip. Harder. Twisted.

"*Snap*" echoed in the room. Their wrists broke.

Snap. Their lower arms cracked.

Snap. Pain. Intense. Alex's will was staggering. He was in as much pain as she. She couldn't compete. She had to give up.

Alex grabbed full control. He manipulated the bones of both wrists and lower arms. "Like I expected. No breaks. Nothing was torn. Now, ... can we talk?"

She stifled a sigh, as she couldn't blame him. She remained quiescent, waiting out the consequences.

Alex

I'm the worst possible person for Sarah.

A write-off for the mental stability award. I fail her.

I suspect she's suffering as much as I am. The attack by a man left her without a body, and now only with the help of a different man does she have a body. How does she cope with the stress? Her irrational reactions line up with some of what that stress disorder quack yammered about. Most, but not all. Was she schizophrenic before she came here and was attacked? What about all the showers?

After downing one of the beers I brought home, I ask "Well?"

Amazing, I'm catching emotions of extreme contrition. *"Well, what?"*

"Speak out loud; we need the practice anyway. Well—what was that all about?"

Sarah says, "I'm sorry, but I felt. No, not felt, but sensed a deep need. If I remember our meeting, it was like that."

"You have a kitchen timer?"

"What?"

"Poor metaphor. You have a limit on how long you can stay separate before you start leaking rationality?"

Swell, now the tears come. I'll never be a counselor. I'm no better than the VA shrinks. I say, "Here, use my handkerchief." She accepts it, hesitantly, but I let our arms and head go limp, and she blows our nose.

"I didn't think about it, but I can't spend too much time away from you. It's deeper than emotional. I lose my sense of self. As if I'll slip into someplace else."

I nudge my arms, and she lets go. After retrieving and slugging a gulp of beer, I ask, "I was gone ten hours. How was it have before this happened?"

"I don't have much sense of time passing, but I think my deep need started just before you came home."

"To be safe, I'll never leave you more than eight hours. Will that work?" The tears start again. I can't blame her. I want to cry, too, but for the loss of my individuality. I must save her.

I'm exhausted. I could have sworn I just saw those color overlays Sarah talks about.

21

LOST

SARAH: 6:42 PM

Alex maintained a tight grip on her leash. She satisfied herself with the closeness she felt when she conformed over his shoulders. If he had been totally pissed, he may have demanded they separate. Draped on him, she could read what he read. *"Alex, I wonder if..."*

"No, I have to study. I've already lost too much time."

She faded back to give him space.

Waiting for Alex to take a break, she worked on sorting out that Spinoza fellow. His Ethics promoted personal accountability and sacrifices even during a loss. Not because society demands it, but because it's core to the human condition. She understood why Alex latched on to it as his personal philosophy. The next section covered loss, which reminded her ...

Ten years ago

"Sarai, you're quite the brave little girl."

She wished this green blob would quit calling her by her baby name.

Her name was Sarah. Better yet, she wished the blob would hush. Her new black dress scratched her neck, arms, and legs. Its stiffness kept her from leaning or bending her arms. Mommy knew she hated dresses.

Colored blobs surrounded her. They appeared when she cried at the graveyard as Daddy, Brother, and Little Sis were lowered into the ground. They wouldn't go away unless she pressed hard on her eyes until she saw stars. Auntie Gertie made her stop pressing on her eyes, and the blobs came back. Green blob finally shut up and went away.

The peace was short lived when an ugly black and orange blob dropped to her eye level. Not saying a word, it stayed there. She pressed her eyes hard with her palms until the blobs disappeared. Ugh, the goat-faced man, who put needles in her. He stared into her eyes. Rudely turning away, she saw her fave cousin Timmy, her age, and his little snot sister, Denise.

Timmy smirked. "Sarah Beth, don't you know braids are for little snots?"

"Ah'll go to my room and take them out. Ah'll do a ponytail. Wanna come?" Little Snot joined them, and they spent the rest of the day pretending nothin' was happening downstairs. The blobs faded and never came back.

WHAT AN ODD THING TO REMEMBER. That had been ten years ago. She'd forgotten why she never wore braids. Next time they were blended, she should call Timmy, and ask him if he could show her how to braid her hair. It would bring an overdue laugh with her favorite cousin. Alex would enjoy it.

But there's more. Her memories convicted her that at the age of ten, she'd handled the loss of her daddy, brother, and sister wrong. She should have told someone about what he, Mr. Y'Arty, did to her. Instead, she ran away to play with dolls. Now he was back. Whom else would he kill? She was positive he had something to do with daddy's death.

She'd failed. What if she failed Alex?

The only way she could tell time was to roll forward and look through his eyes. He said they tingle when I do that, but it doesn't disturb him.

Rats. No phone or another clock in his field of vision. She decided to study his homework like she had the other four or so times when she checked up on him.

She confronted the reality that the classwork made no sense, that she was lost. Alex's homework all looked the same.

Wait. She thought back. Oh no. Her memory of each instance brought up the information on all the pages. She'd somehow gained a photographic memory, and it confirmed Alex had stopped at the first page. "*Alex. .... Alex.*" She waited. "*Alex. ... Alex.*" Her concern overwhelmed her promises to not violate his me-time. Finally, she rippled into body sharing.

Fully reconstituted as Sarah, she found herself staring at the page. She carefully took control of each muscle group. No resistance. He had propped up his head on his hands. She said, "ALEX!" both verbally and mentally. Nothing. She didn't sense him in the background, no sleeping, no dark, or other Alex-static. This was all wrong, all of it. Where was Alex?

She worried if supporting all her strangeness may have killed Alex. She forced back her urge to run to the toilet and be ill. Alex first. She had an idea. Well, it was more of a desperation play, a "Hail Mary" tossed into the whatever that sustained her sheet form. He couldn't be hard to find. It was a deep instinct she couldn't explain, like not having to think about breathing. The problem was that the only time she'd slipped into that form of existence, she almost stayed. It was only Alex's curiosity and rubbing her surface that had distracted her back to physical reality.

Her heart seized then banged against her rib cage. Perspiration flowed over her brows into her eyes. Except here in no-space, she had no body. Her mind was attempting to translate her terror into familiar sensations. No Alex. They'd lost her owner's manual, and her limbic survival reflexes rebelled against going further.

All in for Alex. This level of dedication and concentration came as a long-lost friend. A friend that had been sitting above her in the bleachers, waiting for her to turn around and say hi. She had faced her terrors of the day of her family's funeral, of the colored blobs, and the goat-faced man—Greasy's—unnatural attention to her at the post-funeral reception. Ten years ago, she ran away from it all, pushing it out of her memory to play with her cousins. This was all tied to her state of being. This was the reason Alex was lost.

A moment's hesitation and she went in—whatever this was. There he was. She was drawn to him like a moth to a candle. There was nothing here but non-glow and the green thing she sensed he was in.

She admonished herself to quit stalling, suck it up and shock Alex back. All she needed to do was "touch" him.

Pain shot through her right shoulder, and she was staring at the ceiling and the bottom of the coffee table. She must have fallen on its corner. The stool rested over her left leg. Her limbic survival instincts had tossed her out of her sensing Alex, and off the stool.

She'd failed to shock Alex out of there from the outside. She grabbed a water glass, held it tight to her mouth and breathed. Her hyperventilation spell passed.

A lesson she remembered from before her first grade came to her: she could disconnect from the physical. This would add to her ability to sense and manipulate whatever the rest of her was. How'd she know that? Who taught her? Did it have anything to do with her later ability to see people as colors? Alex was gone, and her attempt to reach him failed. She'd save Alex.

Even if she was lost in the attempt.

To conserve energy, she shimmied out of Alex's clothes, pulled on her warmest jammie, wrapped herself in her fuzzy housecoat, and buttoned Alex's winter coat over it. As a final precaution, she filled an adult sippy cup with a hydrating sports drink and placed a paper bag within reach. She unfolded the bed, added extra blankets, climbed in and tucked all the covers around herself. That was the best she could do for safety. She wished she had someone to watch their body.

Remembering her mysterious lessons, she dropped away from her body. A quick mental push before she was tossed out got her inside the green glow that somehow contained the essence of Alex she sensed. Her skin burned like she had rolled in a field of nettles ... and she thought, "My God, it's full of stars."

Not stars, color blobs. So many, like a moonless, cloud-free, dust-free night on the prairie. It was overwhelming. She knew she needed to hang around and study this.

Abruptly, Sarah realized she was falling into the trap of this place. A voice from her past nudges her. *"Focus and get out quickly."* This was more complicated than she had thought.

It wouldn't hurt to take a little time to understand how these colors congregated.

"Focus." That voice again. A voice that was and was not familiar. Breaking like walking through dried autumn leaves.

Focus on Alex. Ah. There he was. Thinking about Alex moved her toward him, slowly. Thinking harder about Alex and the non-distance between them vanished faster. Harder. Harder. ... Finally. She touched him with her no-hands.

Both screamed as if they were burning into ash.

Sarah: Day 4, 4 PM

A tinny rendition of Beethoven's Ninth assaulted her ears. She slipped in and out of consciousness. The mystery voice had left, and the scent of sweaty sheets brought a smile to her face. She rolled over to luxuriate at all the senses of being alive. The music repeated. Alex's phone and she couldn't answer it as no one local knew about her. Why wasn't Alex waking? *"Alex … Alex … Alex."*

Dropping into her strongest emoting mode, she pushed her alert. *"Alex, wake up, you have a call. You need to answer it."* She separated and draped over his chest. *"Answer-the-phone."*

"Okay, I'll pick up the phone before you have a cat." The phone stopped ringing, but a pleasant-looking man's grin beamed from the display. Alex touched speed-dial. "Hi, Quentin, did you call?"

"Where have you been?" This Quentin's voice inflected upward in a worried tone.

"What do you mean?"

"Katie and I were concerned when you didn't show up for classes. Are you okay?"

"Something like the flu. Joints ache, been having a love affair with the porcelain appliance. I'm fine and will cook up some soup."

"Certain? We can come over."

"And contaminate you? Don't be silly. I'm getting better. I'll see you tomorrow. I'll call if I relapse. Bye."

Palm down on his chest, he gave the three-tap signal they had agreed on, and Sarah was whole. Alex held their head. "Damn, what a headache. What happened?"

"You were studying math before lunch. You disappeared. I don't know when. It took me a while to realize it. I was desperate. I detached from our physical body."

"And you went in after me? Are you crazy?"

"Like I had a choice?"

Alex's inner colors rippled in disbelief. "Damn headache. I remember studying, getting tired. Decided to take a break. I thought of one of those Matryoschka doll games Babushka made me do over and over. No dolls, so I visualized them. I saw people, or some form of color I assumed were people. It was fun, so I scanned further and further. I don't remember anything until you woke me."

He squinted at the bedside alarm clock. "This can't be right. Cell phone says four in the afternoon. More than nineteen hours. And I'm still tired." Sarah staggered and held the countertop. He asked, "What's the stench?"

"It's us. We smell like sewer sludge. We exuded something disgusting through our skin. I'll put us and the clothes through the shower, then we eat. Then to bed."

Alex scratched their chin. "Why do I have a nagging feeling I'm missing something?"

Sarah shrugged their shoulders. *"Can't help you there. However, I've got news. I can help find Greasy. Our crisis released memories. I can find, sense, detect, not certain what to call it, people. Greasy's distinct and I sense him. Tomorrow, we can work on how to find him. After we recover."*

22

GAGGLE OF GEEKS

SARAH: DAY 5, AM

Their left eye socket pulsed with pain. She'd fallen out of bed, and the chair had probably jumped up at the right moment to hit their eye. She checked on Alex; still sound asleep. How did he sleep through her nightmares?

She also checked in on Greasy. He was. ... somewhere ... near. Now that she had a handle on that strange knowledge about sensing people, she realized that her jumpiness and flights of fear had been her reaction to perceiving him. He had been somewhere to the north. Now he had returned to the immediate Pullman area. She'd find him. Even if he couldn't help their situation, he had had a lot to account for back in Omaha.

Alex asked, "Are you awake?" Duh. She'd been cooking breakfast after two hours of tidying and reading his textbooks. "I fell asleep last night before I could work on how we report your attack. What do you have? Did you say you sense him?"

"Yes, but vaguely. He's here somewhere but too far away to get a direction or distance. Give me a moment… He's still there. If this sense has any reliability, he doesn't around move much." She headed to the bathroom for her third shower of the morning. They still stank.

"I have an idea. You're going to work with me. On the way there, you tell me if you sense anything more. If we can't get distance and direction directly, then we'll triangulate based on what you sense from different locations. After work, there's a group that may be able to help."

She stumbled on the shower sill. "*Ah'm goin' out?*"

"Don't you want to? I can leave you here. Seriously though, only as the transparent shawl around my neck. We can't take the risk of being recognized in our new body, and I need to work the hours for the money." A wide, face-splitting grin pulled on their cheek muscles. Alex was incorrigible. She loved it.

She separated onto his shoulders and positioned herself to where he was happy. Alex still was not convinced their blending took care of all his hygiene needs, showered, checked in the mirror, decided not to shave, but used his cologne and antiperspirant. He kept the tie loose, and they left. They were out the door, and she was not hysterical. She hadn't been under a real shirt as his shawl before. It was nice and warm. This was gonna be a nice day.

As they passed through the small lobby, she asked, "*Wait, did I see a mirror?*"

"No." "*Oh, I shouldn't be talking to myself. What mirror?*"

"*The one to the right before we went through the door.*"

Alex returned to the lobby. "*Probably has been here all year and I never noticed it. Say, you're good at watching through my eyes. It takes a girl to spot a mirror.*"

"*Funny. Stand in front of it. I want to be proud of my host. Can you do something about that cowlick? You need a haircut. Now stand sidewise, I need to ensure I don't look like a bra line under your shirt.*"

She practiced her personal commitment not to ask to see more than what he normally did and to not distract him with questions. They entered a side door in a downtown Pullman building without her knowing where they were. Before he clocked in, she needed to tell him about her problem. *"This sensing is exasperating. As you drove here, the distance to Greasy fluctuated wildly, and I never got a direction. If it means anything, I think he is at the same distance here as at the apartment."*

"Don't despair." Seeing a couple of women wearing the same white shirt and dark slacks he wore, he switched to internal. *"This is great. The Intel helps us triangulate his position. I'll pull up a map on the laptop tonight, but I think that puts him on the other side of the main campus from the apartment. We're zeroing in on him. We'll get him."*

A heavy-built but not fat man, with a receding blond hairline, greeted Alex. He glanced with a frown at the time clock.

"A bit close, but I'm dressed, and here's the name badge. Where do I start?" Alex's tremor returned. She didn't need to use any preternatural senses to tell he was faking happy. However, this was an excellent opportunity for some people surfing, but almost all the staff were students. This would be so boring, she'd probably fall off his shoulders into his pants. The guy who had greeted them, though, he had a copper glow with lots of roiling, nothing dark. She thought she was looking at worry. *"Who was the guy by the time clock?"*

"Dave, the store's general manager. He's lost most of his managers, and we students don't have the heart for the job."

"What is this place?" She'd never asked.

"It's a department store. Lloyd and Donnelly, LDO."

Alex grabbed her as she reacted with a joyful writhing. She said, *"Sorry, I've been an associate with LDO for the past two years. Before that, I did three years in Ma and Pa stores paid under the table."*

They spent the day in merchandise accepting deliveries organizing the backroom, and replenishing store stock. She gave him tips on how to arrange, fold, and handle the merchandise. Dave even smiled as he walked by. There was no direct customer interaction. She'd work on his people skills, and they'd be the top salesperson.

As he finished the restocking, Alex surprised her. *"Tonight you're going out again. I wrangled an invitation to a weekly bull session by physics grad students. I'll be the only undergrad. I've proposed a problem—you—for them to study. It's at Ferdinand's Ice Creamery. After work, we'll drop by and listen in."*

Sarah: PM, Ferdinand's Ice Creamery

Iconic large black and white linoleum squares, glistening with paste wax, set the stage for the group of eleven crowded around two white Formica tables pushed together. The bent metal red chairs pulled around the table were filled, and one chair had two sharing it. The sun had set, and the picture windows reflected the group.

"I see the *Creamery* manager giving us the evil eye," said the facilitator, an obvious momma's boy who was all spiffed up in perfect eighties yuppie-wear, complete with thick round-framed glasses. But he radiated confidence and had kept this gaggle of geeks on track for two hours. "Also, I want to thank Alex for bringing us our 'moot Conundrum' for this week, and for springing for coffee and milkshakes."

She tried to project an image of a smirk to Alex and failed. *"Told you it was a good idea to bring my debit card."* She wished she had understood more of what they are saying. She didn't have the background. She hadn't taken physics in high school.

"We'll talk later. I don't want to lose the thread here."

Alex was right, but she had been bored with not understanding. Besides, that girl, Clarice, in the corner aggravated her like she did everyone else in the room. She didn't have the decency to keep her snotty and superior attitude to herself. When she wasn't a pain, her face rolled in worry, and her fingers flew over her phone, likely exchanging messages. Sarah felt sorry for her older sib who was stuck babysitting her this evening. She couldn't be old enough to be here, much less in college. She flashed a wide smile at someone who showed up wheezing and took a chair near the service counter. His reflection showed he was an old professor type, short and in a vested suit. Sarah wondered who wore suits in the summer but quickly lost interest.

The moderator waited for the group to finish thanking Alex. "To summarize our week's moot conundrum. Can an organic artifact exist that if worn would transform someone into the facsimile of another? A 'skin-suit' like the movie *Men in Black*, if you need a visualization.

"The consensus is that it's not possible. An alternate approach would be to have an n-dimensional manifold, which could create the effect. In our physical three dimensions, it could appear as an enclosure of epidermis. As it would occupy several of the theoretical dimensions, it would be pliable and have significant stretch to our physical senses. As to which of the theoretical dimensions it would occupy, we are not agreed. The minimum is seven of the eleven dimensions."

Clarice's ponytail bobbed side to side as she objected. "Ten. Eleven dimensions are not needed to make the equations work." She reminded Sarah of Little Snot, Denise, her younger cousin.

The facilitator replied with a short laugh. "Or ten. Clarice, you'll not give up, will you? Where was I? Oh, yes. The artifact could resemble skin but would not be truly organic. Again, thanks to Alex for the question. You're invited back, and you don't have to buy coffee and ice cream. Clarice, next week the moot conundrum is yours to state and could you not turn it into another ten versus eleven fight?"

Back in the car, Sarah was glad they were skin-to-skin talking; she could block out the noises. Chitty-baby whistled through the gaps in the door gaskets, and the engine banged when Alex accelerated. *"Could you explain what happened in the last two hours? I got lost. What eleven dimensions? There are three, four if you call time a dimension, right?"*

Alex laughed with the vibrations she loved. She wished she could hear his laugh as a real person. "I had a tiny taste of it in a math concepts survey class. I hope to keep up with the math so I can take more classes. The basic theory is all phenomena can be explained with equations using only eleven theoretical dimensions. Mathematical dimensions, not sci-fi dimensions. Ten if you follow a different set of theories."

"That doesn't help. Three, seven, or all eleven, where does that leave me?"

Alex tugged at her. When 'talking,' she tended to grip tighter to his neck. She loosened up. Alex shrugged his shoulders. "Actually, it does help. Up to now, we had me enveloped by you, and automagically I became your near-twin. This group of geeks seems to be on track to explaining us, without magic."

"Gaggle."

"Gaggle? There are no geese here. Oh. A gaggle of geeks. Very funny. Back on topic, we have a theory but no path to a solution. Did you spot anyone who may have more insight?"

"Just the little snot with the ponytail. She kept fading out as if she was thinking deeply. She also was messaging half the time."

"Shit." With a short curse, he slowed, popped a U-turn, and returned to their missed turn. "I'll approach her at next week's bull session. I can't rush this, or we will lose the goodwill we've made."

"You mean you want to ask her out. I saw how you kept checking her. Forget it. I know the type. She'll only want you for your brains."

He circled his apartment's neighborhood. *"I've seen several parking spots. Why are you circling the neighborhood?"* asked Sarah.

"OpSec. Operational Security. I'm circling to see if anyone is watching or changes position."

He parked in a lot away from the apartment and got out of his car. He rubbed his shoulder as if it was stiff. He was really getting better contact with her. If she could, she would have purred from the contentment his rubbing gave her. He said, "You're cranky."

"Huh?"

"You're cranky. I felt the non-verbal sniping at the girl. You're short on energy again. Right?"

This devastated Sarah. *"I was trying to hold out longer to give you more time as you."*

"Not a good idea." He closed the apartment door. "Blend and do whatever makes you happy. I'll study in the background."

In case he came back early, she wore loose, comfortable clothes and a bra. He still had issues with jiggling. With her panic and anxiety controlled, mostly, she planned on surprising her Alex. Logging in on her computer; she researched the local police procedures. Her attacker chose in-town, so it was the Pullman Police Department. She downloaded and filled in the details, turning it into an assault that conventional police could handle. The more she thought, the more she remembered about the attack, right down to the license number on the station wagon, and the odd scratch in the grill. In the morning she would report to Alex that her photographic memory was expanding even to minute details before they met.

She worried if this was a good idea? Could she handle it? What if Alex was harmed? She reached for the paper bag kept handy to quell hyperventilation.

Alex

She senses my return and closes her laptop. To one side is the paper bag. She's been hyperventilating again. She frowns and asks, "Wazzup?"

I feel the burn on our cheeks. I'll give her the benefit of the doubt. Besides, I do have an issue. Sucking in an extra breath, I say, "How we fix Matryoschka Sarah?" Shuddering breath, eyes welling up. Now I'm sniffling. Damn emotions. Ever since she arrived, I cry so easily.

"We'll work this out together."

I bring out my spiral-bound notebook, the journal where I've documented my ideas since Sarah convinced me she was real. She dubbed it the "Cat Journal" after the cartoon cat printed on the cover. "I can't even come up with questions to adequately cover our situation. The physics grads have ideas, but they would take years to even set up the theory and a test."

"I tried your trick of extended range sensing."

I said, "Why, are you crazy? I slipped away from reality trying that."

"Maybe I'm crazy, but in-shell I have much more control. I hunted for another natural Matryoschka, another you. With any luck, we would gain synergy and traction on my problem." She drops into non-verbal to hide the emotional inflection. *"But there was no one."*

I drop our head, unfocus, and scuff our left foot against the railing. I had one ace. The one lead to tell us all. "One last thing. I called Mom about the Matryoschka dolls. She set up the call for when Aunt Mil, the one who locked them away, was visiting. They confirmed out of ten children and over fifty grandchildren and great-great-grandchildren, Babushka allowed me and only me to play with the dolls more than once. She trained me in something, but all I got out of it was a deep psychosis that lasted about a year.

"Anyway, it's been almost twenty years, and Aunt Mil still seethes. I asked them several different ways what they remember about what I did with Babushka. Their grandmother adamantly only talked with me. No help for us."

She says, "I've written down everything I can remember about the attack. We can approach the Pullman police after your morning classes. If I start panicking, you may have to do the real talking."

The clock that came with the apartment clicks with each swing of the fake pendulum. People move outside the door. Someone honks and shouts in the parking lot. Water drips somewhere. The fridge compressor cycles several times. We are quiet in our thoughts. I feel despair. Our despair.

Sarah speaks first. "We need help, don't we?"

The diesel engine of the porcupine van rumbles the two times it drives by. The couple across the hall returns, laughing about something before going into their apartment.

"Yes … We do."

The meadowlarks haven't sung in days.

23

HI, I'M SARAH

ALEX

Depression hangs over my class preparation. We emote mutual encouragement even though it's hollow. After she's safely in her comfy drawer, I leave for classes.

A half-mile side excursion around campus hill, avoiding the hill climb, confronts me with a crowd consuming my worst addiction. Bagels, made the right way, boiled, and baked, no oil. The crisp outer crust, soft, chewy interior, simultaneously melting anxiety and frustration.

The shop door leaks high humidity from the boiling vats, visible in the morning sun. Some wit has written "intolerant people, please stay outside" on the window's condensation. Another scrawl beside it announces, "First Amendment trumps PC." Once inside, the yeast and gluten aroma draws me by the nose through the moisture to the counter.

The round café tables are already occupied. The first by the bitch-trio who mock my facial scar. The second by two guys hunched over their phones as if someone will steal them or break their thumbs while they compete against each other. The third table sports a coed who smiles my way. Rumpled shirt, cut-off cargo-pocket dungarees, and a face that would not be noticed; she's my type. I don't know her, but sharing a table with someone who doesn't cringe when I smile would help turn my attitude. At the counter, the pock-marked baker's assistant recognizes me. "Alex, I'm sorry, we've run out of honey-walnut schmear." Fists gripped, I prepare to …

Crack!

The underside of the café table sports generations of bubble gum. Cordite permeates the moisture, and I draw my worn canvas and leather satchel to me as a comfort blanket while staring at the coed's legs. Rubbing the canvas satchel always helps. Not this time. The shakes start again while I rummage in the satchel for my gun. Not there. Instead, there are the child-proofed meds the VA demands I take. They interfere with even the liberal arts courses and create a disaster with engineering. I stopped taking them months ago.

Ignoring the helping hands, my satchel and I crouch and dive out the side door as someone says, "It was a pallet breaking." I still smell the cordite.

Leaning against a rusted and tagged dumpster, the fluorescent green tag "God Saves" consumes my attention. My eyes follow the flowing tail of the final S to the bottom of the dumpster, resting on a piece of rustling trash. I bang on the metal side to get the rat to move. A touch on my shoulder receives a tightened fist backhand, barely stopped when I see the baker's assistant. "I'm sorry Bro. I've had bad days also. Bossman's tied up scooping broken hundred-pound bags of bagel flour, otherwise, he'd be here." He hands over a bag that has to hold at least two bagels. "On the house."

Munching the first bagel, straight cream cheese spread, I hoof it over campus hill to classes. With plenty of time, I slow and enjoy the meadowlarks singing in the nature conservancy plot.

A block from the physics buildings, I spot the "porcupine" van. In the last few days, they've added more unusual lengths and configurations of antennas. They still aren't properly grounding some of the antennas. This time, a skinny, nerdy student directs the two burly weightlifter specimens who are bolting more racks into the already stuffed interior.

You've got to be kidding; he's even wearing horn-rim glasses with tape at the bridge.

This tweaks my intuition, so I peek inside. An annoyed side of beef glares. "Get lost."

There are always engineering study projects roaming campus and Pullman, and this is one of the most interesting, with electronics filling racks and suspended from the ceiling. I'll check with the electrical engineering department. Maybe it's a project I can join. Any project as mixed up as that van must be interesting. With my veteran status and my two tours overseas with the Signal Corps, I should have an easy in.

Might even be able to wrangle a work-study and drop my detested job at the department store. Even when I pull my desired stockroom and receiving gig, there can be too many people. Morons cutting up, using current sitcom references, pretending to be trendy.

First period. Spinoza. I need this distraction from our plan to involve the cops.

But I seize again, bolt and end up in the same study carrel following the vid feed from its safety.

Spinoza's ethics of self-awareness and responsibility convicts me, reminding me of my duties. The conclusion of Spinoza is inescapable —we are individually responsible for our actions, and for the consequences. There is no out to make us feel better.

I needed this distraction from my depressing reality. I'm going to fail Sarah like I failed those children in Tikrit. I failed my great-great-grandmother when I was five. Failure is what I am.

No, I was never that way. Failure is not what I am. I'm rejoining the world, starting with sitting with Katie and Quentin in the next class like I've always done. If they follow habit, I can catch them for coffee before the next class.

I'm stalling, but a quick stop in the men's room should help my flagging courage. To keep calm, I avoid the two unisex lavatories. This may be the modern world but running into a woman in the restroom is a bit much for me. At last, the far end of Johnson Tower, a Men's logo appears. The cool tiles echo the slap, slap of my sandals, and the walls and ceiling are painted the same gloss white as the floor tiles. Calm, conventional, non-threatening. Cool water on the face and the back of the neck revives me. A splash of cologne and I'll be good to go. I reach into my satchel and touch something warm, motile—familiar. Oh no!

At least blending with Sarah no longer is a major physical shock. As she pulls us up and straightens our knees, Sarah's biggest, most dazzling smile replaces my mug in the mirror. Bad idea. Can we dodge Katie and Quentin? If she suspects what's happened, Katie may decide to pull her Ka-Bar knife and skin Sarah off me. Quentin is more likely to dose up with an enhancement drug in a marathon effort to screw her off me.

She says, "Surprise. Did you miss me? Please say yes."

"This is the men's room."

"I know, Honey. I would worry about you if this were the Ladies' room." She's in a happy mood, and I'm reluctant to puncture it.

My pants and briefs had fallen to the floor. Pulling them up, she calmly shuffle-walks in my sandals to the door. She pops us into the unisex lavatory room and into a stall.

"Someone may see us!"

"Humph. You know better than that. I sense anyone near. Before you recover enough to say anything you'll regret, I just had to get out. Trust me. This will work, really. Greasy didn't come to us. Hanging with you, I cover more territory. If he isn't hiding in a bush between here and the police department, we make the report. If he is, we can take him. This will work. I can jump onto his head, but not blend, and you beat him until he spills how to restore me. Now hold still, I must dress. I bought something in Omaha special for my first day of classes here."

She pulls out new baby-blue heeled sandals, ivory bra, and panties— lacy, of course—a flouncy ivory blouse and a short pencil skirt in baby blue. After checking both sides and the front in the mirror, she frowns and buttons the blouse to the top. "This may not be the best look after all."

I can't help blushing. The heat on our cheeks could cook an egg. My clothes and sandals go into the now overstuffed satchel, laptop balanced on top. In the mirror, she adjusts our makeup.

I say, "This has gone too far. You're not registered. You don't even know where the class is."

"Bogus. Where do you suggest that I go? Seriously, not back into the bag, I'm too lonely and useless. Besides, do you really believe they will even notice we aren't a student? Trust me. Afterward, we report to the police. Think of the time you'll save."

We argue with her winning. Except I know where the class is. *"Don't do anything to embarrass us. I'm doing the walking. Watch. Don't do anything."* I control the body, at least for now. A pyrrhic victory; I try to calm the jiggle factor, but the baby-blue heeled sandals render it a lost cause. Practicing on high heels never crossed my mind. Watching my foot placement to not twist an ankle, I spot baby-blue toenail polish. She'd been planning this for a while.

Sarah's delight is palpable. *"My first University Class!"*

Entering the lecture hall, I head us to my regular seat in front of Kate-Quen. I freeze. I can't go anywhere near them like this. The next student stumbles into us, and almost face-plants himself into the seats. Flustered, he picks up his cell phone and my laptop. Another freckled redhead with a blush reaction that can be used for railroad crossing lights. *"Sarah, we need to sit next to this flustered kid. Put on the charm."* Away from KateQuen. I glance over. Katie stares at us. Damn.

Sarah emotes puzzlement but complies. "My, you're so nice, really you are. Do you mind if I sit next to you? Over here? Looks comfy."

Seated, she demonstrates aggravation. *"What was that all about? Seriously, if you expect me to flirt, I would appreciate a little notice so I can work up to it."*

I pull the reins in on my anger. *"You could have just conformed and mimicked my body. Why did you have to blend?"*

"I, I don't know. Something about lying around, unable to sense the physical, just the emotions of people walking by, got to me. You're right, but that solution didn't occur to me. I had to go out full-body, even if it meant this body." She grips her arms to calm herself.

I don't know where to take our argument, so I punt. *"Enjoy the lecture; it's Romance."*

Focus on the lecture. Pretend nothing's amiss. Medieval Romance Literature. Why'd Katie have thought this would broaden me? I attempt to take notes though it's a crashing bore. A guy, knight or noble, is frustrated in his virtuous (no sex here, uh huh) pursuit of the maiden, a lower-level noble lady with skin like alabaster because she hasn't seen the light of day since birth because her father or guardian or master wants her pure to sell—excuse me—marry off to the highest bidder—excuse me—the man best for her.

However, I'll wax enthusiastic the next time I meet KateQuen. Which reminds me, I glance in their direction. Katie still stares at us. Double damn. Quentin's sleeping, why can't Katie?

Sarah

She devoured the lecture. She loved it. She didn't have the background to understand everything the prof was saying, but he spoke well, clearly and with significant passion.

The whole culture of romance was so much richer than the contemporary romance novellas she read in middle school. The concepts of love, honor, even dying if necessary, for an ideal, filled her with a passion for more. Centuries of this literature for her to unearth; she had found her major.

Lost in the lecture, she forgot she was the parasite.

She couldn't miss Alex turning their attention to the left, past the geek to a couple. The black girl in the aisle seat stared at us. Tall, must be over six feet, her legs are longer than the auditorium seating tier, so she extended them down to the next level. Sarah was fascinated, she had small tits, and ass, or T&A as they said in her almost-banned school production of *A Chorus Line*. The male was short, pudgy, cute, and was too distracted by the girl to notice anyone else. She wondered if this was the infamous KateQuen. She thought, talk about an odd couple! Sarah had to meet them.

Her sensing extended in all directions, and the position of their head was immaterial. The Amazon was complex, with an undertone of angry pink. A rare non-boring person; she definitely wanted to meet her. Cutie was a pleasant mix of amber and puce, almost no undertones.

Alex broke her reverie. "*Sarah, give me control. I'll pack and walk us out of here at the bell.*"

"*Huh? I know you don't have anything to get to other than the police. Can't I hang a little and meet people?*"

"*I'll explain later. We need to leave. Now.*"

The bell rung, startling the Prof. He reeled off a rapid-fire string of reading assignments Sarah doubted anyone caught. Alex packed and hustled them to the exit. The Amazon moved faster. She stepped in front of them, bent at the waist, and with intense mahogany eyes flashing fire and brimstone asked. "Who the hell are you? And what are you doing with Alex's satchel and laptop?" A trace of musk-like scent hovered in the air between them.

She cracked open her camo-ballistic cloth briefcase enough to show Sarah—a gun.

PART II

ALEX

"In the mind, there is no absolute or free will; but the mind is determined to wish this or that by a cause, which has also been determined by another cause, and this last by another cause, and so on to infinity."

— BARUCH SPINOZA

24

KATIE
ALEX

T his isn't how I planned to approach Katie and Quentin.

I had envisioned a private discussion in the coffee shop. Then we would go in Katie's car to my apartment and introduce Sarah. We would strategize, using Katie's military police background on how to proceed.

Struggling with hyperventilation and perspiration in the over-cooled lecture hall, I gather up my most winsome smile, "Hi Katie. I'm on my way to meet you and Quentin for coffee." The new chill I'm fighting isn't only because of Sarah's clothes.

I need somewhere more private to work this. Those few minutes should help me gather my wits and give Sarah time to centering.

I walk, wiggle, there. Damn high heels. Stunned, KateQuen follows but too close for me to make a break for it. Damn high heels. The tight pencil skirt doesn't help.

At the ReUnion coffee shop, Katie moves ahead. Long legs in flats beat short in heels any day. Despite the situation, I admire her self-assur-ance. Three tours in Iraq and Afghanistan as a military police officer will do that. She commandeers a corner table, pulls out a chair for us in the deepest corner, positions Quentin on one side, and takes the other. They usually share the same side, cozy. Today isn't going to be that day. Quentin arrives with our coffees.

Katie stands, leans over the table, glares down at us, and repeats her question. "Who are you? What are you doing with Alex's stuff?" I never thought I would be on the receiving end of Katie's interviewing skills.

I flash on a story told over beers with her MP friend. A contractor suspected of creative five-finger discounting of US military rations. She'd leaned over him and "pleasantly talked." After ten minutes, the thief soiled his clothes. She left. The interrogation team did the clean-up of the crime and him.

"I am Alex." Lame, but I'm rattled.

"Stop shittin' me, I know better." She drops her briefcase on the table with a clunk. She's packing again.

Quentin opens my satchel and pulls out my clothes. His face pales, and his hands freeze over the satchel. He's too nice for his own good. He doesn't see others in a bad way, except for his mother.

I squirm in the tight chick gear.

Inspiration. I exchange a two-year-old verbal sign/countersign with her.

"Silly ... silly ... silly ... silly ..."

Katie catches on. "Goose?"

"Goes to...."

"the market...."

"to see...."

"The Butcher. And what the fuck is this about?"

I exhale. We're past the crisis point but not safe. My breasts follow my breathing in sympathy. This isn't a good time to be distracted. I thought I was past self-voyeurism. I give her the short version, ending with, "Sarah needs me to be her core to survive."

Katie's face ripples with disbelief, concern, and finally anger. Her hand moves into the briefcase, but Quentin stops her. "Hold," he says. "This sounds insane, but those are Alex's cadences beneath the accent."

Quentin re-stuffs and snaps the satchel shut, and fidgets in his seat. "I have some questions for uh … her."

Katie waves him off and goes in for the kill. "Who picked the little number you're wearing today? Who wears skirts and blouses to class?" Katie's shifted gears and is targeting Sarah. If we don't convince her there are two of us, all credibility is gone.

No answer that I, a male, can give will work with her. Given her training, several unpleasant scenarios torture me. Another inspiration pops up.

"Sarah. Help!"

Sarah

"Got it, Honey. Just sit back."

Lady Amazon was unapproachable, so she decided to reach cutie pie with a reprise of the first day's giggling airhead. Sarah stood and started a twirl, but the tight corner prevented finishing it.

She tried a giggle. "I did. I wanted something sexy but restrained for my impromptu coming out party. Please say you like it."

Alex said, *"Don't do that. Katie'll be pissed."*

"Hush, your rational approach fizzled. I'm trying for cute to distract her long enough to for you to try again."

Katie's chair bounced twice as she fell into it. "Wait, your voice changed,"

Quentin interjected. "Not changed. Same sexy voice but the cadences are like a birdsong." He got the evil-eye from Katie, and he returned a sorry-honey shrug. At least her furrowed brow loosened. "The dialect shifted from the Ballard hood in Seattle, to something Midwest."

She forced a giggle. "Poor Alex struggles with speaking in our voice. I think he's still trying to sound like himself."

"Wait? Is this 'Sarah?'" The anger drained from Katie's face, and Sarah sensed fear and uncertainty. The musk scent reasserted itself. Katie produced a big knife and slid it into a notebook where only they could see it. Her deep umber skin shifted from an undertone of ruddy to white, which combined with the renewed perspiration, gave her an ashen sheen.

Sarah wanted to sense how they were reacting, but this was too dangerous to split her attention. "Yes, I'm Sarah."

"And you're aware and can talk without Alex's control?"

"And dress, walk, put on make-up, all while chewing bubble gum."

Alex spoke to the back of her mind. *"Back off the bimbo stuff. It caught her by surprise, but any more will set off alarms. Her training and experiences makes her deeply suspicious of the unexpected."*

Quentin burst out with an avalanche of questions. How much male, how much female, the length of time combined, side effects, and did they need Alex's conscious effort to move? He was smitten with the whole concept of "Matryoschka Sarah." Sarah did the answering except when it was too technical or male-specific when Alex took over.

Sarah reached into Alex's satchel, and Katie's hand moved to her knife. Sarah said, "Just the laptop." She opened the file she had shared with Alex, containing the details of the attack, descriptions, "Greasy," the car, the alley, and the strange tube thing with electronics on it. Sarah started to gulp air.

Alex moved forward. *"No need for you to stay forward and risk a panic attack like before. Take a break. I can handle this now."*

Katie leaned against the back of her chair, assessing. She glowered at

Quentin's interest in the sexual side but let it pass. When he wound down, she asked, flashing a megawatt smile, "Girlfriend, how often do you leave the apartment?"

With a broad smile, Sarah hid her unhappiness at being apartment-bound. "Well, only twice to retrieve my boxes at my old apartment and to check where I..." She admonished herself. Suck it up; these were Alex's friends. He needed them. "... was attacked. I do call and talk to my mother in Omaha."

Katie stood, leaned over the table, and smiled down at them. Her eyes regained their flashing hell and brimstone. "Alexander James Monroe, you're a stone-cold sexist pig. Take off that pretty face and put on something more comfortable like a pig's snout and ears."

The barest musk-like scent wafted across their nose.

"Sorry, I'm late. We went extra innings."

The ancient woman lay on the polished red oak floor. Eyes an impossible glowing fluorescent green pierced me as I came through the door. Her skin folded in creases appearing deeper than her body. Creepy nesting dolls were scattered in a semi-circle. The smallest, the one she would never show me, was crushed in her hand like a lover's Dear John letter. Her last words to me were, "Never come late on Wednesdays."

WHAT WAS THAT?

Who was that woman on the floor? Sarah couldn't remember any such incident in her life.

Sarah regained consciousness while Alex righted them in the chair, but still captured by Katie's glare. He said, "Who are you to act like my mother?"

"I-am-NOT-your-mother.   I-am-the-bee-itch-who-will-skin-you-and-eat-your-balls."

They were attracting attention from the others in the café. Katie will sit down soon. He asked, "What do you mean by 'sexist'?"

"You find a totally dependent doxie; keep her a virtual slave in your apartment waiting for the return of her man."

Conflicted and angered by whatever she "saw" when she passed out, Sarah took over their body, stood and leaned with her knuckles on the table top. "Who the heck are you? Don't you dare say that about my Alex. He's been nothing but kind. If you can't be civil, we're leaving."

Both Katie and Quentin said, "Heck?"

Alex said, *"Don't do that. She's on edge, I'll explain later."*

"Shut up Alex. No one treats you that way." Katie and Quentin jerk back at the one-sided argument.

"You don't understand; she's dropped into interrogation mode. She might even be flashing back to something dangerous. I must handle this."

Alex

"Okay. So, what's it you want?" A tactical retreat. This might not be so bad. Katie keeps us locked in her glare and slowly sits, this time not scraping the chair legs.

"Stay there." Katie touches Quentin and stuffs the knife into her brief-case. They stand with an admonition from Katie. "If you're really part Alex, you'll understand why. If not, then you'll not have to worry about your future problems if you attempt to leave."

The two whisper while not taking their eyes from us.

I catch snippets. From Katie's rumble, "We'll hold them until…" and "Some sort of sick game." Quentin argues in softer tones, and I only catch, "Somehow, it's Alex. We must save Alex."

I needed to work this out before Sarah showed herself. Katie's swooping in for the kill. She devastated her opponents in frosh mock-debates, not from her brilliant arguments but her intensity. Her body loosens in a deceptive drop of the shoulders.

Gazing at Quentin with an affectionate smile she's never had for me, she says, "Quennie, be a doll and bring the car around. We'll meet you in the front circle." Quentin leaves at a fast walk.

"Sarah, we're going in a moment. Is there anything you needed to say without Quentin here?"

Sarah says, "Nothing."

"No? Alex?"

"No, Katie. Quentin is my oldest friend. We've never had secrets."

"Until a couple of days ago. Time to move to the embarkation point."

She slings her camouflaged military briefcase and my satchel over her shoulder. I reach for it and catch the Katie-glare. She's in serious bitch-mode. Keeping our hand unstabbed motivates my decision to not insist.

At the curb, Quentin waits at the wheel with his grin, sweaty from the run, the front passenger side door open. Katie steps in front of us and closes the door. She opens and pushes us into the back seat. She follows, locks the door on the other side, and buckles herself and us up.

As we pull out, the porcupine van rolls up. If we sort out Sarah's problem, I want in on that project.

"To Alex's apartment—we need his car." Turning to the two of us, Katie says, "First, we'll verify your unbelievable and insane story. Quennie, when you pass the practice field, do I remember a large tree? Yes? Park in the deepest shade." This isn't going well. Sarah's interested and worried, but she should be scared.

We pull up and park. Katie places her left hand over the middle pocket of her briefcase and with her right pulls out her tactical five-inch blade, edge glistening in the dappled sun coming through the leaves. "I want to see Alex. Separate, whatever you do and Quennie, eyes front, and I don't mean in the mirror."

I squirm. "Sorry can't. I'll either cut off a limb or tear Sarah's clothes to shreds when I expand to my normal size."

Katie's unimpressed. "Then strip. Quen-tin get your eyes out of the mirror."

A last-minute thought comes to me. *"Don't conform to my body. I'll fold your sheet-form and hold it against my chest. I don't want to explain how you disappeared."*

Thankfully, Sarah slips her own clothes off, sparing embarrassment. She separates into my arms. *"Keep our eyes on that Amazon. I want to see if she makes a move. Her overlay glaringly roils. You have scary friends."*

Katie takes my chin and turns my head side to side. A meadowlark sits on the hood, singing.

I'm angry. "Do you need to check the teeth before bidding?" The slave auction jibe doesn't faze her.

"Shut up. Quennie, outside, we need to talk. Lock the doors." She glares at me. "Last time home in the hood, I installed high-security locks. You won't be able to get out."

"What's going on?" Sarah asks.

"Not certain. Katie didn't like something but doesn't want to do anything without talking it over with Quentin."

They argue again standing at the car's hood, this time unheard because of the closed windows. Katie draws up rigid, emphasizing her full six-foot-two frame. Quentin looks up into her eyes, gestures with both hands and his head.

"Watch Quentin. The argument's heated. He rarely drops into Arabic gestures. The head and eye up-roll probably is 'No.' Likewise wagging the right index finger. Oh, something's changed. That open hand dipping down means "patience."

"Your black Amazon doesn't like any of this."

"I agree." What I won't say is that her body movements subtly shift into the attack stance I last saw when she stabbed me.

Katie shouts something. The car reverberates with the thrum of her fist hitting the fender. Quentin resumes his grin and uses the unusually shaped remote to open the doors. From the sound, only two doors—the ones they use—open.

Once inside, Katie says, "Okay, turn around. Is this Alex?" She backs away, hand deeper in the briefcase.

Quentin turns around while I scoot to the middle of the seat. "Yep, it's Alex."

"Could you ask a question only you and the real Alex could answer?"

Big grin on Quentin's face. Not a good sign. He has a wicked sense of humor for an inveterate nice-guy. "When did I last see you totally naked? And I want all the details."

25

NOBODY EXPECTS THE INQUISITION

ALEX

I'll never forgive him for having to relive this.

"Summer between junior and senior years. We took a week off from summer jobs and hiked the Cascade trail. Late afternoon, dripping hot, we found a deep, glacier-fed pool. We'd seen no one all day, so we stripped on a pink granite boulder and jumped in Commando. Ice cold, my balls started to solidify. As I scrambled out, three blond girls ran down the path, stripped, and jumped over me into the pool. I tried to cover up in the crystal-clear water. I was mortified, frozen in place. They laughed and splashed you. After five minutes, they climbed out, laughing, and disappeared. The way clear, we climbed out. They'd taken our clothes, packs, and water, leaving only our wallets and boots. Naked, we found the trail across the ridge to Concrete. The County Mountie stopped us. He'd driven out to check a report about two nude boys trying to slip into town. After amusing him with our tale, he covered us with a stinky, scratchy horse blanket. We called Quentin's father, who was working back shift at Boeing. He rescued us. We scratched for days until my mother asked if I had fleas."

It was the most humiliating moment of my life, and now Katie knows. And, as she's draped over my arms, Sarah.

"Satisfied, Quentin?" asked Katie.

"Yep, it's Alex. Sh-he would never tell anyone. I never did. Dad chuckled all the way home, but never asked us about it, and never hinted to Mother."

Katie swirls her knife towards Sarah's form. "Hand her over. I've got your back; now we can decide what to do about your pet monster."

"No."

Sarah writhes on the side nearest to my skin. She's about to do something.

"I don't recall giving you an option." Her knife edges closer.

"She isn't a Pokémon. She's a real person and in deep trouble. I won't abandon her." Maybe I can disarm Katie with less damage to me this time. She outclasses me in hand to hand.

Katie points her knife away from us. "Good enough. That's the Alex I know. I'm not convinced, but we can work with this."

She pulls her left hand out of the briefcase and whacks Quentin on the back of the head. "Whatcha waiting for? We need Alex's car." He grins into the rearview.

"Alex put yourself back together, yous nekked like a jaybird." A moment of relief. Katie has dropped into the Newark First Ward dialect of her youth.

Katie Jo Parker: Lutheran Church three blocks from Alex's apartment.

She'd spotted the location last year while taking a shortcut to a party. Quiet suburban street, a church with little daytime traffic, lots of trees and berms creating difficult lines of sight for watchers. Picnic tables, grassy spaces, spacious shaded areas created the perfect location for privacy without any concern for pre-set vid or audio monitoring. Subconsciously filed away, Katie'd never thought about it, until today.

The perfect safe location for whatever might happen next. Just her, this Alex and Alex's whatever-it-was, mano-a-mano, like in the original definition, each fighting for survival in the bullring. Except this was an arena of bulls of the unknown. Katie had never had to deal with strangeness. Stupidity, yes. Violence, yes. Lazy privates, yes. Not understanding why a mob attacked armed military troops, yes.

Strangeness like this, never.

Katie Jo Parker had fought and escaped the "safety net" of the Welfare State. In reality, it merely enforced the power of political parties which created interlocked layers of lowered expectations. Those who fought for better found themselves suffocated by the poverty industry wielding regulations and money to keep generations in line. The Welfare State expected her to have one child, and again pregnant by age seventeen, by an abusive but mostly absent man. All dreams killed by an entrenched single-party system that paid more to pop out babies than to keep her in school.

Nothing more than the plantation system, updated to include lip gloss.

The only way out for her was to go military. After sailing through boot camp, joining the Military Police was a short and easy step to show she wasn't to be underestimated. What she hadn't counted on was how she was a natural, with her innate bullshit detector and preternatural sense of impending danger honed in the First Ward.

Cissy! Where are you? The mystery of what happened to her six-year-old daughter tore at her. Like she did nearly every day, she rose above her gut crunching grief and guilt and focused on the immediate.

Never, ever had she faced strangeness. Quentin consumed this shit, by the book and vidful. She shook her head in disbelief as she followed his lead. If it weren't for Quentin's quiet influence, she couldn't have survived the past hour without being tied down and heading to the Spokane VA's psych unit. Likely after she shot this strange creature that called itself Alex. It couldn't be Alex. But it did seem to have Alex's memories.

Quentin was out prepping the next step. For the next three hours, she was on her own but in her most comfortable role as an interrogator. Just her and her two guests, seated at this picnic table. Anyone driving by would only see a couple quietly enjoying the late summer day.

The hair of her close-cropped Afro stood out so much that it tingled. Her muscles cramped with the effort to avoid the shakes. Even in the shade under this gnarly, pathetic Washington State excuse for an oak tree, she dripped sweat. A dusky skipper butterfly landed in her hair and got tangled in the kinks. She brushed it off. Wings crushed, it fluttered into a glob of pitch oozing out of the planks of the new picnic table and stuck there. Watching, she was consumed in its final struggles.

That could have been me. Dreams crushed, stuck in the gooey comfort of the Welfare State set up to give me no options except to pop out more babies. Babies to grow up into voters to perpetuate the Party that survived by exploiting their despair, ignorance, and fears. And grow more babies.

A rustle brought her back to the problem she'd been trying to avoid while fighting an anxiety attack. Across from her, in jeans and a spotted T-shirt grabbed from his apartment, Alex sat with his hand in his canvas satchel. She waited for him, knowing the first to speak always ultimately loses.

Katie and the real Alex had supported each other for the past year. They'd stumbled into each other at Freshman Orientation, confused, angry, and blown off by the Veterans Administration for needed psych help. Their mutual assistance bond now went deep and was the other reason she was tolerating this false-Alex. *What if this was the real Alex, who didn't know how deep the changes were?*

A largish bird with a yellow chest landed in front of Katie, cocked its head to look at her and stared with one eye. "Damn bird." She backhanded it off the table.

Alex blanched. "That's a meadowlark. They're friendly."

"I don't care if it's a gold encrusted royal peacock, I'm not letting a bird shit in front of me. In First Ward, they left no place to sit."

Alex twitched as he eyed the ground, in the oak tree branches and the table. "What about the others?"

"Other what?" Despite herself, she broke her stare with this Alex to scan the area. Nothing interesting, other than a car, windows rolled up, passing the park at well over the speed limit.

"Nothing." He kept his hand in the satchel as if he was holding back a flow of molasses.

Katie pointed to the far side of the large round picnic table. "You can stop fondling, scratching, or stroking it. Put it here, and you sit on my right side." Within reach of her dominant left hand. "Get your hand out of there."

Alex said, "I must let her know. I tell her everything."

Katie slipped out her combat knife and flipped it, hiding it by her long arm. "Make it quick, but afterward, she stays more than an arm's length from you."

Alex said, "We're in the park near the apartment." His eyes flickered. "She wants to drape over my shoulders. That way she can see and hear."

Katie shook her head and exposed the knife edge. Her nostrils flared and shoulders bunched into the ready position, just like three weeks ago in front of Alex's apartment.

Alex

The full sun momentarily blinded me as I emerged from the front door of my apartment building, but the shouts caught my attention.

"Hey bitch, put the pig sticker away. We want to show you a good time." The voice was familiar but from where?

Another voice, "Three of us, one of you. Put it away, and we'll make it easy on you." It was the three parking-lot-Einsteins who offered beer to any coed who walked by.

My eyes cleared enough for me to spot Katie, on the balls of her feet, semi-crouched, elbows in, her favorite pig-sticker blade-up in her large hand and backed into a blind corner created by the apartment's back door and dumpster.

The idiots sauntered forward, arms out to grab her. This wasn't football pass interception practice. The three Einsteins were going to get killed.

I sprinted towards Katie as the largest jumped for her arm. She rolled out of his grasp, grabbed his wrist and twisted to one side. There was a resounding pop, and he screamed. The other two moved, but not in coordination, giving her enough space to slip between them. The one on the right received her elbow to the bridge of his nose, and the one to the left stumbled and missed getting sliced by an inch. She turned to the one she elbowed, who was cursing and wiping blood flowing from his nose.

"Get up you pussies," he said, "She needs to be taught some manners." They stood as Katie slipped to their right, keeping their backs against the dumpster and limiting their maneuvering room.

"Katie, no!" Her nose flared, her eyes glazed. She was in one of her flash violence episodes. She slowed down enough to pull her second knife from her calf sheath, reversed the grip, and stepped forward. I didn't have the speed or strength to counter her, especially when she slipped into one of her dissociative states. These three would end up sliced into small pieces.

I ended this with my only move. As she swept forward, I stepped into her parry, hoping her weak side wouldn't cause me too much damage. Searing pain, like when I was shot in Iraq, ripped into my shoulder.

Her eyes focused, and she stumbled. I leaned against her,

holding her arms to her side to stop any more violence. We fell to our knees.

"Alex! What the hell?"

"Sorry to interrupt … your fun. We have lunch plans … we would be late."

She wept and wrapped her long arms around me but kept her grip on the knives. Her long neck stretched upwards, and she said to the three, "I hurt my friend. Leave, now, or I'll finish you off, yous mudderfukrs." They stumbled past her. Two assisting the one with the bad arm.

A siren blared in the distance. She holstered one knife and searched for something to wipe the blood, my blood, off the other. "Give it to me." I rubbed the handle and blade and left only my fingerprints. "You came up to pick me up and found me with this knife. You saw nothing else."

Then I fainted.

Katie

Katie's eyes glazed.

Alex said, "Sarah, stay where you are. You'll be in the satchel but within easy reach." His eyes flickered. "It'll be okay. Don't move unless you feel my signal." He rubbed his right shoulder. Katie's eyes cleared.

Katie sat between the satchel and Alex and positioned herself to watch both. She asked, "She can hear you?"

"Only when we're touching. The more surface we share, the better we can communicate. We don't need to say it out loud; that was for you." He hesitated. "If we're touching, with enough surface contact, she can see and hear through me; some sort of neural binding."

Katie slid her knife into its sheath but kept the retaining clip unfastened. "I wanted some time with you without Quennie and your little monster around. I'll settle for this, but only if she stays out of sight. I don't understand your situation, but I do understand things are better off dead." She waved off his objection and slid into her thrust, counter-thrust interrogation mode.

Physically separating this-Alex and the Sarah-thing gave her the control. The next step would be to offer an olive branch of goodwill. If this was really Alex, it would also clear her guilt. "First, I want to apologize for how Quennie and I treated you. We got caught up in each other and forgot about you. Sticking you with an apartment you couldn't afford was terrible. Me and Quennie are sorry. I haven't forgotten about 'Shadow and the Ghost'; S-and-G." They both smiled at the nickname their fellow students had given them.

"I understood but was angry. Then I got preoccupied…" Alex said, pointing to the satchel.

"How are your parents?" Katie asked. This was the make or break. If he was evasive or couldn't answer, then her Alex was still missing. Katie had guided them into their old-Alex familiar conversation style, questions, and answers, sliding into laughter about in-jokes. Alex's body posture eased. Only once did he stall, staring into the distance. She asked, "Something wrong?"

"No. I guess not. For a moment, I thought there was something else I remembered, but apparently not."

Their conversation had gone for over two hours without a single glitch between her memories and his interactions, now this. Was it significant? Nothing he said about his family that conflicted with her memory. She had about a half hour to wrap this up, her only conclusion was that this fake-Alex had the moves, gestures, and openness Alex always had. She couldn't believe that somehow her Alex could physically change this much.

While she checked the time on her phone, he asked, "How were your Newark folks?"

She flashed a rare smile. "They were surprised to see me. My cousin Rashaad spotted my craziness and insisted I take my VA meds which keep me mellow, and zombie-polite. That and about a key of weed. I had to relearn weediquette. It was a good visit. Can I look?" She pointed the shoulder he'd been rubbing.

He unbuttoned enough to show the wound in his right shoulder. "No infection, and once the Steri-Strips fell off, no itching."

"Did you always heal this quickly?"

"Maybe it wasn't as deep as it looked."

"You saved my ass. Those three roid-junkies could've ended up dead. I'll never forget you jumping in front of my knife. Have they come back?"

"Last week, but the campus po-po caught them at the end of another attempt and made them feel unwelcome again."

"White-gr-boy, I guess you won't stop looking at the time, so let's go." She forced her widest smile. The blatant racist slur was her signal she was copacetic with Alex, no matter what dumb thing had happened. For the next step, this Alex needed to feel safe.

He reached for the satchel, only to be grabbed by Katie. She scanned the park for anyone who could observe. "She won't do that thing, will she? Turn you into a girl?"

"No. We've worked it out. I'll have to give her some time soon, though." He reached in and touched Sarah. "We're fine and going back to the apartment." Withdrawing contact, he asked Katie, "Are we good?"

"We're always good. My question was if you were good. I'm fairly convinced you're my best friend ever. With that thing, and when you're that girl, I'm still working on it." She chided herself for her slip. She had spoken her subconscious desire that this was the real Alex, disguised somehow.

"What's the plan?"

"Simple. You and your monster are being feted to the welcome we should have given you instead of walking out last week. Quennie has set it up, and his texts are frantic about food getting cold."

Katie did not divulge their real plan. They were working this unholy symbiotic creature with only one goal in mind, getting the real, not the present, Alex back.

What happened to the monster was not a consideration.

26

QADIR NADIM

QUENTIN (QADIR NADIM, ROUGH TRANSLATION, CAPABLE
FRIEND) KAHN

K atie texted, >>Sticking to pln. some issues. ltr.<<

That meant she'd had some success. Otherwise, she'd be killing the thing and the false-Alex by now. Whatever the issues were, she planned on working them here. Now it was his turn. Katie, growing up in the survival zone of the hood, didn't have his suburban luxury of dwelling on the strange.

Alex's apartment was as ready as it could be. Quentin had drawn on all his skills gained in restaurant gigs to create a comfortable setting in the efficiency. Moving around the supplies and dinner courses without bumping into something would test his agility. Right now, he was rotating the warm food through the tiny oven to keep it all at the proper temperature.

Never would he have imagined that moving in with the rough-edged and hair-trigger Katie would put him in a position of responsibility. Their attraction was raw sex, or that's what they told themselves. Over the past few days, something else had happened. Each generated something in the other, something lost. Quentin had a rush of responsibility, and in their private moments, Katie smiled, truly smiled.

Now Katie was counting on his wastrel talents to fill in where her kick-ass practicality failed. He ticked off the possibilities from his youth and adult reading pulps as well as more respectable fantasy and science fiction, bolstered with hundreds of hours playing in illogical virtual reality—VR—worlds. Though, to be honest none of the gaming betrayed innovations in thinking, philosophy, or themes. For that, one had to read.

He also brought something else to the strange. No one, except bitch-Mom, knew about his "added-extra." He knew his presence soothed people. At the age of five, this ability, more than his goofy sense of humor, had kept the five-year-old Alex from the next suicide attempt. Today, he learned that his recent mental distresses, like a migraine, were associated with false-Alex and the sheet-thing. It clanged like a Navy klaxon whenever the false-Alex and the sheet-thing were separate.

He used his fussing over the food temperatures to inventory the possibilities, and hopefully give him an idea of how to get the real Alex back.

Was this Alex a golem? That was silly, his forehead had nothing written on it. Besides, that doesn't account for sheet-thing.

Was this Alex an artificial intelligence construct? No, Katie would have gutted any Lisa or Turing programming in her interrogation, then disposed of Alex-the-thing.

Was Alex a doppelganger? Interesting. Hold that one on the possibilities stack. It might be able to pass Katie's interrogation. Which would mean the other twin, the real Alex, would be out there, somewhere.

A changeling? A replacement, indistinguishable not only in body but in everything else. This was the first theory that explained the sheet-thing, Sarah. She could be the prime mover, manipulating this Alex.

Sarah, the thing. What was it? The folding and shape manipulation was beyond physical. Twice while Alex sat in the back seat of the car, he could have sworn it flipped into a doubled Mobius strip. Which left three possibilities.

Sarah is an illusion, projected by the false Alex. Tough to do when you're nude, he hoped.

An outside illusion caster? There was Stanislaw Lem's *Solaris* planet-thing. It did that to an orbiting space lab. What could have set this Gaian creation loose? Too bad the TV series and the two movies sucked.

He decided that the third possibility—Sarah as an energy entity—answered the most questions. That would mean she would have no true physical shape. The shape they saw was their minds adjusting, creating a shape to "see" what they couldn't perceive. It could even be mostly in one of those extra-dimensions he loved to read about. It confused his added-extra with wildly varying and vivid impressions. A standing energy wave could do that.

What worked for both of them? None of the above completely covered what he sensed. There was the added-extra his bitch-mom poured into him with no more concern than if she was topping off a beer stein with the right amount of head. The reaction of his added-extra didn't line up with most of the explanations. That left the two scariest and dangerous possibilities.

Both were energy creatures, holding the real Alex in stasis. He doubted anyone could detect their energy-matter boundaries. Without knowing that boundary, they had no chance of bringing them down and saving the real Alex.

He settled on a working hypothesis: They were one entity, most likely on a quest they didn't know they were on. The problem was that a quest's goal is usually unachievable without the death of something within the seeker.

Quentin's instincts told him he was on the right trail, even if his analysis thus far was deficient. The rising claxon-jangle signaling their presence prevented further thought.

He pondered on the thought no one wrote books about readers of books, or about the passive victims of experiments. After—if he survived—he resolved to no longer be passive and finally confront his bitch-Mom.

He readied his trap to lull the composite entity with physical sense overload, cause it to slip up and reveal something they could use to recover the real Alex.

I'm sticking to plan A. I'm going to get them drunk.

27

WHAT WINE GOES WITH SQUEAL?

ALEX

My apartment! "What did you do to my apartment?"

Quentin gives a nonplussed half-smile. "Nothing. I shoved your service box into the closet and pushed the hideaway out of the center of the room. I rented a card table, three chairs, china, silverware, tablecloths—three to tie back cover the chairs—candle holders, and a few other party goods."

Katie grins. "Lover, you're a keeper."

I stand there, anger building over the violation of my space. My face distorts, and my feet shuffle into an attack stance. Katie turns to me and knows I've lost it. Instead of cuffing me across the tiny room, she wraps her long arms around me, locks them behind my back, bends me backward, and gives me a passionate kiss that would shame the VE-Day kiss. Eyes open, but I can't see. Scalp on fire, I go limp.

Once I recover, I ask, "What's that about? You've never kissed me before."

"Why? You needed some sense of worth before you tore the plaster off the walls. The kiss was because you've been awesome. You took in a total stranger with the most freaked out tale I hope never to hear again. Anyone less brave, self-assured, and compassionate would have either run or attempted to destroy her.

"Okay, you two, can you both be visibly present at the same time?"

Sarah and I repartner, and Sarah says, "Sorry, we tried, but it's an all or nothing thing."

I'm exhausted and need rest. Mentally. For some reason, I'm never physically tired. *"Katie is rough around the edges, but she's all right. And, you need some people time. This whole day has been too much for. I need some selfish me-time to center and not feel angry. With Katie here, I can. She can protect you better than I ever could. Enjoy yourself. You deserve it."*

Katie flashes her megawatt smile. "Girlfriend, you need to find your best and be ready in less than twenty minutes."

As Sarah takes our body back, she does her mental squeal of delight. I hope I never get over how I love her squeal.

Sarah

"Katie's inner color no longer sparks but is still an angry pink."

"Possibly her normal state. She's had a bad history," Alex said.

"Could you fill me in?"

"Don't you have a party to get ready for?"

There was apparently much more to her Alex and Katie than either would tell her.

The card table glistened with silver edged china and crystal, starched napkins, and starched tablecloth. The rental chairs were also draped with starched white tablecloths, the extra fabric was used to create a tie-back bow. Incense and candles lined the kitchenette countertop as there was no room on the card table. His friend Quentin placed heavy emphasis on the niceties. No beer in sight. From her angle, at least three types of wine would be in play. Never much of a wine person, she committed that for tonight, for Alex's sake, she was.

Her party outfit for tonight had arrived with the rest of her moving boxes. Alex was still reluctant to discuss how he found them. An unbidden blush filled her face. She'd let herself get talked into it by li'l snot, Denise. It was a risqué powder pink number and exposed her midriff, lower thigh, and cleavage. A year ago, she would have never worn, much less bought, such. At least the pink showed off the nails and make-up. While she was adjusting makeup in the little table mirror, Katie used the bathroom.

Despite Alex's warming emoting, she needed to clarify something. *"Should I worry about being normal with your friends?"*

Alex chuckled. *"Good point, you've done great so far. Watch Quentin, he's a hopeless lust machine. If he made a move, Katie would slit your throat on the spot."*

She said, *"I need to concentrate. Could you please fade back?"* Another white lie. She needed Alex out of action so she could adjust her party dress. It had fit perfectly in Omaha. It was bra-less, but she needed some tissue paper … She twisted to examine her waist and sighed when she saw more skin than she remembered. At least it was muscle, not fat. Again, she admonished herself: *Just remember, life is good.*

Alex slid forward long enough to say, *"Have fun."* He retreated.

Quentin seated Katie and Sarah facing each other. He opened the doors on the hot and cold Cambros, food from the fanciest restaurant within fifty miles. He expertly dished it up as if he trained at a high-end restaurant. She resolved to ask Alex more about Quentin—but not now. The incense and hunger made her giddy with anticipation. He retrieved the first-course wine, a Chablis, from the ice in the sink, opened it, checked a sample, and poured it into the taller, narrower stemware. So, this was real wine; better than the stuff that comes with plastic stoppers. They drank through three courses with different wine and stemware for each course. She was mellow, but not drunk.

Quentin

Katie couldn't loosen but continued to stare at the new girl. He understood, at least partly. The male Alex looked like their missing Alex Jane, like a near cousin. The new girl Sarah was spookily like Alex, like a sibling. When the two were collaborating, one could forget this female amalgam was not Alex. The main difference was that the was fleshier, rounder, and not as hard as the missing Alex.

Katie's body language reflected her inability to connect with this impossibility. Sarah said that she was from Omaha and had that mid-country accent. Quentin was drawn to it as if he should be using the same accent.

Sarah fidgeted when they sat, knocking the tie-back off her chair. After they stood, Quentin rearranged the tablecloth to cover her chair and tied it back in a more secure, but less, decorative knot.

Their body went stiff, no movement until their face drained of emotion then refilled with the open smile he associated with Sarah. Alex Jane's smile was always controlled, reserved. She poked at her salad, and asked, "What is the…" and her eyes went blank.

She knocked the chair over as she launched into a flying leap over its back followed by a right pirouette, and a pirouette on the other foot. Skipping behind his chair, she bent backward, while spiraling her hands. To keep her balance, she placed one leg, glorious leg, over his shoulder. She asked, "Well, Quennie? Tell me. Does that look like a fine piece to you?"

Quentin flushed with embarrassment and his natural reaction to close female flesh. He kept his hands in his lap and asked Katie, "Could you?"

Lightning and worse formed in Katie's eyes as she unwrapped Sarah from his shoulders.

Seated back at the table, Sarah picked up the dropped fork and her glazed look faded. Looking back and forth between Katie and him, she asked, "What?" She looked like she nearly was in tears. "All I did was ask what the vinaigrette was made of."

Interceding before Katie could blow, Quentin said, "I'm not supposed to say, but I invented it myself. I use ten-year-old aged Balsamic vinegar and crush dried cranberries in a mortar and pestle to infuse it." Katie's breathing evened out, and he served the next course.

Over the next courses, Sarah didn't return to her previous happy mode. Between her being scared spitless and Katie's hidden anger, Quentin was exhausted. Quentin gave up on Katie and carried the conversation.

Sarah's eyes dimmed but didn't glaze again. Even Quentin had caught on to the fact that such moments were when Sarah and Alex talked internally. Good enough. Quentin relaxed in his chair, enjoying the respite. She said, "I'll be right back. The alcohol isn't sitting well with me."

Alex

Feeling guilty, and my ego partly mollified, I drop back into cognizance of what's going on. Quentin is faking bonhomie. Katie, well Katie alternated between hacking at her food and shoving it around her plate. Sarah's emotions remain positive but have a tinge that I've come to associate with her about to break into a panic attack. I ask Sarah for some time with my friends, and she jumps at the chance.

I'm going nuts in all this chick gear. Before I slip into the bathroom, I grab a tie, a freshly pressed dress shirt and slacks, and belt. I had set them out for my interrupted—now canceled—suicide.

In the bathroom, I'm eager and start on the unfamiliar snaps and hooks. Sarah nudges me aside, unclothes, and separates into my arms. I carefully fold her into her plush towel. I sense her contentment in the back of my mind. Fascinating how I'm tuned to her feelings.

After Sarah separates, I'm always pristinely clean, but psychologically I need to wash. Probably some emotional intertwining with Sarah's need for showers immediately after blending.

I do a stand-up, washcloth bath … can't start the shower without getting their attention, though I certainly would appreciate the needle spray. The belt fits two holes tighter than last week, and the shirt and slacks hang loose. Regardless, my clothes, not hers, feel good, feels *normal*. Another quick glance in the mirror and I slide out the door. Shoeless, but hey, it's my apartment.

KateQuen are whispering head to head. I ask, "Is it too much to ask when dessert will be served?"

Quentin knocks over two wine glasses and a half bottle of cabernet. I recognize the label and groan inwardly at the cost. Katie, as expected, does a seamless shift to her "Hi buddy" smile.

Quentin's mouth opens to start a question, but I say, "Dessert first."

Waiting only for my first bite, Quentin bursts with questions. "I couldn't ask some things in front of a girl." Quentin's hiding nervousness. I ignore it as I'm too happy with my reunion with my two best friends.

He didn't realize he implied Katie isn't a girl. He's sweet. Where did THAT come from?

She accepts it with a caricature of an airhead eye roll and reaches out to hold his hands. "Before you ask about Alex and Sarah's body sharing, we need to clarify something else." Turning to Quentin, she says, "We need to talk. First, did you see anyone unusual hanging around here?"

"Not really. Just the students who were here when Alex and I had the downstairs apartment."

"I watched on the drive back. We weren't followed." She turns to me. "Do you know where her attacker is?"

This is what I wanted to talk to Katie about. "We think, actually Sarah's the one who thinks, that he's somewhere on the other side of the main campus."

Quentin drops a dish in the kitchenette. I'm now down to three. "Wait a minute. You've been attacked and never called me?"

"Not me, Sarah. How'd you think she got into her condition?"

"Uh, well, you know. I didn't get that far. I was still putting my mind around …"

Katie taps her pursed lips. That's a rare eye flare of fear. "Can she reach us?"

"Yes, but slowly. Her movement is slow. However, once she touches, she can be lightning fast in the blend. Why are you asking?"

"One more question: Can she tell what your mood is?"

I shrug. "I don't think much about it, but yes. When she drapes on me, or when we blend, I can't withhold emotions without effort. Not touching, she senses my emotions, but vaguely. What's your issue? I'm not going to be interrogated. I deserve better from you. What is it you want to know?"

Katie closes her eyes and squeezes them more. Quentin reaches and holds her hand. "It's okay. We'll be all right."

She waves her other hand but doesn't withdraw the one he's holding. Her eyes open, and stare into mine. "The two of you have the weirdest co-dependency thing going. Even earlier, your reaction was too mellow, for you. My stunt of kissing you was my only option to hitting the two of you. It worked. We have to work on how you remain stable emotionally and spiritually."

"I won't abandon Sarah." I'm still having issues with pulling up my rage, so I cross my arms.

Quentin fidgets, his sanguine complexion paling. Katie removes her hand from his and turns to me. "That's what I meant. Even Quennie caught it. Your relative calmness isn't you adjusting, it's you giving up. We're not leaving you again."

"What about Sarah? She didn't deserve what happened to her."

"What about needing to be joined for about eighteen hours each day?"

I say, "We tried less, but something inside her snaps. I'm afraid she'll kill someone if she goes back to feral. We don't know how she didn't kill me when we first met." Which reminds me of my memory involving Babushka's training. Is that the real answer? Was I conditioned twenty years ago?

Katie's eyes harden and flash. "So we have a dangerous monster. Why not kill it?"

A sound like dry sand falling down a dune, a susurration, catches my attention. I jump the two steps to where Sarah's slipping from within her favorite towel. I flat palm her to speak. "Sorry about that. Let me tuck you back in. Katie and I bring out the worst and best in each other."

Sarah emotes concern but allows me to refold her.

Back at the table, I drop my head onto the surface. "That was close. She does that when she senses I'm unhappy. She has no notion of how dangerous she is. I think she's all energy. I can't easily explain it, but what we think we see of her is only how we process the energy she has in the three physical dimensions."

She isn't solid, or even a physical being. After the physics grad-student bull session, I must accept she's the most dangerous thing on Earth. She's pure energy, and their quick guesses placed a phenomenon such as her at twice the energy released by the largest Soviet thermonuclear weapon. She forms in our physical and time dimensions as apparently physical but is continually reforming. Her self-image of what she should look like is all that holds her from losing control.

"Sarah's been struggling through terrors about being attacked again. You know how that affects you." Katie winces. "Yesterday was the first day I felt she was stable enough to set up a meet with you to get your perspective as a former MP."

Katie loosens her shoulders. "Fair enough. I don't think she's stable yet. When you aren't … what do you call it … forward? She has brief moments of strangeness like she's a different person."

"I didn't know."

Katie pulls her briefcase closer. I sadden at the realization that she's packing that hand-cannon again. Quentin will get a lecture on how to handle Katie. She doesn't need to be armed on a rural campus.

Quentin catches my glare and fidgets. He knows my moods. Katie sees but ignores our moment. "From now on, one of us is with you two all the time. We need to scope out a place more defensible with fewer access points where we can be together. We'll move you two to our apartment, but that will only be temporary until we find better. What about the police?"

Love having Katie in charge.

"We planned on going in today as Sarah to file an assault-and-battery. She has an amazing memory…"

"… and we interrupted your plans. Tomorrow morning, we'll go together. I can do the cop-to-cop thing and increase interest in investigating. Brotherhood of Blue and all that. We're sleeping here tonight. You two have free-wheeled too long."

KateQuen exchange glances. Something unsaid passes between them. I'm jealous. Three weeks ago, Katie and I had had the same intimacy of communication.

Quentin says, "Okay. Where do we start? I couldn't handle you killing her. She's real, just beyond strange."

This is what I've wanted since Sarah arrived. But we had to stabilize. Quentin's acceptance of responsibility surprises me. "I always planned on getting Katie, and you, involved, but Sarah and I have had a bad adjustment time."

Katie stands up, drains her champagne from the tall, thin flute. She refills, drains it again. She refills and takes it with her to the bathroom. She hand-motions for Quentin and me to follow her. Positioning me in front of the vanity, she points the flute at my image in the mirror.

"Where's your facial scar?"

28

CAVALRY

SARAH: DAY 8, FRIDAY

For once, Alex was in a happy place. He needed his friends. His happiness was Sarah's happiness. She recompacted herself, and Alex finished folding her into her fave plush towel.

KateQuen must have been too drunk to drive. They pulled out the hideaway, and they all slept together. She was in her favorite position when not blended or conforming to his shoulders, wrapped like a cat near Alex's head. As she didn't sleep in this form, she studied his friends. Katie was just plain dangerous; wound too tight for words. However, her commitment to Alex was unquestionable. Quennie, she decided that he looked more like a Quennie than a Quentin, remained the nice guy, though puzzling. But he's Alex's best friend.

She pushed awareness outward to check the neighborhood.

A deep disquiet jerked her out of her snooping. Something dark and evil drew near. Where? How could it get this close?

It was ... Quennie?

The darkness flickered then disappeared. It was as if it hadn't liked being watched. It hurt Sarah to study it.

It was back, and it hurt her. Then it was gone. She'd had enough psychic trauma with the two of them, but she had to think of Alex. His stability depended on his friends, but it seemed they were as much a danger as salvation.

To calm down, she shifted outwards to study people at a party three blocks over.

SOMETHING WAS WRONG.

She'd been uneasy for some time, but nothing appeared unusual. Some people were milling around, but this apartment building was dominated by students, and that was expected regardless of the hour.

Now, people with unusual hues congregated and moved together toward the apartment.

Sarah blended with Alex and screamed into his metaphorical ear. *"Visitors. And they're not friendly."*

"Huh, what?"

Katie woke and reached for her knife sheath.

Sarah repeated, "Visitors and they're not friendly. Wake up!"

The door vibrated with the pounding. "Open up. We need to speak with you."

Katie drove a sharp elbow into Quennie's ribs shocking him out of his rumbling snore. "Quennie, move behind the kitchenette counter and stay down. Don't look for clothes. Go!"

She watched as he ducked behind the counter, and Alex said to Katie, "Thanks for that. Quentin has no experience or training." He frowned. "And you, separate right now, this is not for civilians, and I have height and reach over us."

"No."

"Yes."

She stomped her foot. "No, I will not lay around helpless and let you get harmed. Those people are worse than the three jocks. Besides, you move much faster as us. Quit arguing before they bust the door down. I'm not going to separate, and you can't make me." She ignored Katie's raised eyebrow.

Katie strapped her knife sheath between her shoulder blades and slipped a shirt over her lanky body. She slipped the other knife sheath into the back of the shorts she'd worn yesterday, then sat on the edge of the bed, her camo briefcase near her lap, her left hand casually draped over the opening.

Alex squared their shoulders and faced the door. "Are you sure you don't want to disappear until this is over?"

Sarah ignored Alex and said loudly. "Don't break it down; it comes out my security deposit." She did her best to sound hung over.

As ready as they would ever be, Sarah opened the door to a barrel of a man who was less than five feet in height, wearing a three-piece wool suit. He stood in the doorway and pointed a gadget with loose wires and spinning lights at them, then Katie, then the kitchenette.

A puzzled expression flowed over the intruder's face before he said over his shoulder, "Objective confirmed," gesturing to Sarah, then, "two bystanders" gesturing to Katie and the kitchenette. Two mountainous guys in black uniforms move forward. The short man waved them off. "Stand down. One in this door, the other down by the elevator. No interruptions. And, can you act casual and not scare someone into calling the local police?" He stepped into the room and handed the gadget over his shoulder to the closest man. Their intruder's sad, haunted eyes concerned Sarah.

Sarah nudged Alex. "He's not hostile, but there's something about him I can't figure out."

The intruder wheezed before speaking. "You can't escape; we've sealed all windows and vents." He sadly gazes up into our eyes. "Do you have any idea what you've done?"

Alex says, "Take this. They see a girl. They need to hear a girl's cadences."

Sarah agrees. "Who the heck are you, and what's with the four AM wake-up call with two gorillas? A ten-buck alarm clock would've been as effective." She was serious. She didn't even think about giggling or using her bubblehead approach with this man. Only Alex's emoting calm kept her from screeching.

Shorty wasn't flustered. "Why'd you kill her?"

"Who?"

"The woman whose body provides you structure and nutrition."

"What woman?" A sharp snap of pain rippled along their jaw muscles. A second sharp snap and they slumped, stars erupting behind their eyes. Their talking simultaneously caused pain in their jaw.

Shorty stepped back, his eyes widening. The nearest guy moved up, his face hard. The bedsprings complained as Katie stood. He froze.

Shorty stared over Sarah's shoulder without changing his expression. "Drop the knife, and we can keep this civil."

There was a muted clunk on the throw rug behind her. Katie's large hand rested on Sarah's right shoulder, keeping her strong left arm free. She had complied but used the moment to move into a better defensive stance.

Sarah faded back. "*Alex, take it.*"

Alex

Grateful that I wouldn't have to fight with Sarah in front of whoever these people were, I exhale and say, "I'm not dead."

Halfway through the door, our uninvited guest's pupils dilate, return to normal, and he gestures for his device. This time, the light patterns change, and he mumbles to himself. "Odd, that shouldn't happen." He peers into our eyes. "Does this mean the host lives?"

"Of course, why wouldn't I?" This line of questioning puzzles me. I shrug our shoulders.

"Can you get out when you want?"

"When Sarah lets go. Why?"

"Can you separate now?"

I check what I'm wearing. I realize Sarah kept my T-shirt and boxer; no clothes changing needed, I'll fit as me. I say, *"Separate slowly. Don't show off. We may need the edge where we can change faster than they think we can."*

Sarah objects. *"No! Let's kick runt-man in the balls and run."*

"We should go with this. Katie's already disarmed herself. She has better instincts than I do. She must believe that's the better choice."

Sarah separates, taking a leisurely twelve seconds, exaggerating the separation at the limbs. I fold and hold her against to my chest.

Sarah says, *"I'm good. I can see and hear."*

It looks like our uninvited guest is having a seizure as his eyes pop. "You're a ... man," he says.

"That's what Dad always beat into me." I show my fiercest toothy smile.

"Impossible." He recomposes himself. His eyes grow distant for a moment, then he's back. Returning the device to the man behind him, he says. "Wait outside this door. No hostiles, unless I don't leave the room first." The guy starts to object, but Shorty stops him. "No, maintain station unless I don't come through this door first."

He turns to me and says, "I'm unarmed. We need to talk. You all are in deep danger."

Katie steps back and with her foot nudges her combat knife closer to the intruder. "Return it, but right now, it's a sign of our good will."

Quentin jumps into the conversation. "I'll make tea." He surprises me with his quick thinking. He's contributing by moving into his host mode.

I glance at Katie. She responds in our facial shorthand, "VIP." I concur. This little man is not the normal government nose picker with an attitude.

I fill in Sarah. *"Don't let the size fool you. Think Napoleon. He's used to being in charge and being obeyed. He sees civilians, so he's giving us slack. My problem is that toward the end of my last deployment I built up resentment towards authority. You may need to carry the ball."* Another problem occurs to me. *"Are there more people outside?"*

"I've been watching a tight cluster of four who either stay in one spot or move at traffic speed. If that is what you mean, then yes."

I wish I could let Katie know about the back-up. She already picked up this guy is military. Those outside the door are black-ops contractors, likely ex-military. As our intruder didn't bother with identifying himself or show a search warrant, this may not be a legal ops. Bad news.

Sarah emotes deep fear. I block my own to not add to hers.

She says, *"I've never seen people like this outside of TV or a movie. What are they doing at a rural university? The nearest terrorist is probably at a Starbucks on Yesler in Seattle. Ah'm gettin' outta here."*

A couple of moments pass before she starts again. *"Bogus. Both ends of the hallway blocked by a yellow aura. Fire escapes, both up and down, are covered. The small staircase only the coeds use for the basement is also covered. I wonder what they covered the windows with and how hard it is to break."*

"Cousin Timmy taught me how to hot-wire a car. I'm goin' back to Omaha. I have cousins on the police force. Why don't we kick this runt out and call

the cops? If you don't want to, I will. I always beat my cousins in wrestling."

She's hyper. I need to squash her good intentions and bad instincts. *"Did you see their badges?"*

That got her attention. Her rattling stopped. *"What badges?"*

Before she jumps me and makes a run for it, I explain. *"That's the problem. Anyone confident enough to roust a citizen and not flash a badge has serious juice or is dangerously stupid. Just play along. Katie's thinking, playing for time. Quentin's overdoing the tea prep making unnecessary noises to cover for Katie."*

Sarah asks, *"What about the men in black outside?"*

"I believe they're stone cold mercenary types. Probably ex-military, not a problem if we keep our uninvited guest happy. We'll hold you against my chest. Don't want to give away any Intel including the mimic trick of yours."

What I'm not telling her is they're carrying heavier than standard-issue pistols. In Iraq, we stayed away from them. The causalities were too high, theirs and others, when they engaged. Good news is this is a rural university and not Fallujah. The bad news is they're here at a rural university.

My arms are full of Sarah, so Katie grabs a chair from the counter and pulls up the rental chairs. She clears the remains of dessert and champagne into a corner of the room but leaves the rented tablecloth. She seats us with our back to the kitchenette counter. Across from us, Katie offers the counter chair to our uninvited guest. On the raised seat, he's almost at eye height with me. Katie sits to my right, where she can reach Shorty with her right hand, while still leaving her left hand loosely over the open briefcase.

Sarah interrupts. *"I knew it. We know him."*

Impossible. *"He'd stand out in any crowd."*

"Think back. At the Geekfest at the cow-dairy. Remember the obnoxious Clarice? When she wasn't interrupting, she was in deep thought. Otherwise,

she was frantically texting. In the last fifteen minutes of the meeting, this guy came in and sat behind us. I saw his reflection in the window partition when you were watching the moderator. Also, he may have been with the van with the antennas that almost hit us."

They missed us at the Geekfest. I'd seen that van several times when we were out, and of course, on campus yesterday. It never occurred to me that it wasn't some research project. That would explain the constant cruising and changes in gear. They've been looking for us. Or at least Sarah. I don't have time to think this through. I have to stay in the moment.

I held Sarah tighter in my arms. Standoff. A chin-lift by Shorty confirms he knows I've drawn the line.

Our uninvited guest starts, "As a show of good faith, I'll first tell you a story. After a physics experiment, a researcher found a pliable cat skin in a test chamber. The unanticipated result of a practical joke of putting a dead cat in the chamber. Only the skin remained. A series of unauthorized experiments created the pliable shell of a recently deceased twenty-year-old girl. The experiments stopped when an audit showed misapplication of resources. The research, now properly authorized, and under tight security and review, repeated the results. The most interesting result was that "wearing" the shell would result in a "blended-person" completely indistinguishable by any medical test or even close family examination from the original pre-death person."

He stops staring at me and glances for reaction from KateQuen. Katie's back in her chair, arms folded, forehead creased. Quentin's wide-eyed and leaning forward. Situation normal for both. For me, I pass on judging the converted-cadaver story. I don't know if I believe him, but Sarah was living and breathing when she was attacked. Right now, the important question is how deep is the crap we're in. *"Sarah, how many are out there?"*

"Knew you'd need to know. They've added some. Those two are still outside in the hall. I count the same four yellows who've been milled around the past few days across the street. They're with someone with a unique color, and four more I don't recognize in the staircase above and below this floor."

A full-sized squad. What's so dangerous about us? *"Interrupt if they move. He may be wired so he can communicate with those outside."*

Given the scale of this intrusion, with no real options, and an eyebrow ripple "go-ahead" from Katie, I decide to bluff. "Interesting, but why are you here?"

Shorty grimaces. "I'm getting to that. You're all in danger. Your friend was attacked by a mole who decided to freelance. He stole a compact prototype, but by then all our experimental cadavers were protected. In his desperation to get away, he used it on a living girl. That's what he told us when we picked him up last week. Since then, we've been attempting to locate the victim. We used the faint shell emanations and obtained a triangulation fix on this block. Yesterday, we got readings in the center of campus."

He wiped his forehead. The window A/C unit had never kept up with the summer heat, and he was in a three-piece wool suit. His face started to flush. I wonder if I should offer him a glass of water.

"Also, yesterday, we got another break. We found the third car the mole had stolen, a station wagon, before the local police. We retrieved Ms. Merk's clothes, groceries, purse, hairbrush, cell phone, and driver's license. We reported the car to the Pullman Police. I talked with her mother—a delightful woman—who enthusiastically thanked us, believing we were the local police, for finding her daughter's belongings. She gave us this address to return them." He flashes a carnivore's smile he must think is friendly. "And, here we are."

The twitching of his eyes betrays his studied urbanity. "Two items of info before we finish.

"One, over 90% of the blends fail, disintegrating the shell and killing the volunteer host. The remaining 'successful' 10% must separate within eight hours. Otherwise, the host is trapped and dies a terrible death within twenty-hours."

Quentin reaches out and touches my shoulder. He's lost his grin. Katie leans back in her chair.

Shorty waits as we process this. "Two, immense moral outrage aside, no one ever believed a living human would work as a shell. It was never proposed, let alone tried."

A chill rolls up my back. We, Matryoschka Sarah, are the only success, ever. Our guest has a lot of firepower outside the apartment. My guess is the porcupine van contains over a quarter million dollars in tricked-up electronics. We'll lose either our freedom or our lives if we fight. I decide to not tell Sarah. I need her as calm as possible.

How do I warn Katie? She doesn't know about the outside forces.

Very kindly, our guest reaches across the table to open my arms. "Now, I'll remove Miss Sarah, take her where she'll be treated with respect and honor, and we'll find why and how she's the only exception."

Sarah panics and jumps me. Blended as us, she backflips over the counter into the kitchenette. As I clear my head from vertigo, I see Katie, but still can't speak. She has Shorty by the throat with her right hand, and BMFG, *big mudda fk'n gun*, her 10mm Smith and Wesson, safety off, in her left, the barrel touching his temple.

29

BMFG

KATIE

The intruder had accepted her knife and assumed it was Katie's only weapon. In his eagerness to play good cop, he didn't notice the briefcase next to her chair; that was her backup card. Once he was separated from the overly eager guard detail he came with, she could regain the advantage. None of what he had said made sense, to her, but Quennie was nodding like an idiot. She'd followed his lead so far, and if this continued to pass his weird-filter, then she would act accordingly.

Her opportunity came when the VIP leaned across the table, placing his throat within her reach while leaving her within reach of BMFG. She leveled it at his head, clicking the safety off so he could hear it. With her right hand wrapped around his throat, she hadn't cycled a round into the chamber. She hoped that he didn't notice.

She dropped her voice into her best command-MP register. "I'm starting the renegotiations. Let me tell you what will happen. We'll leave here unmolested. We'll make ourselves presentable. At thirteen hundred we'll meet you at the teahouse on the Pullman Square at the most publicly visible outside table. Over tea, we'll work something out. You're buying. You can have the run of the apartment, to convince yourself nothing is here. You can copy the entire guts of any computer here, but leave the computers, we're students, and it's nearly time for finals. As a cover story, your goon squad will install a new window in the bathroom. The super is too cheap to fix it. You will also remove the damn seal; it's stuffy in here, and you will remember to lock up when you leave."

The uninvited guest asked, "Anything else?" Other than the steel in his gaze, he showed no emotion. However, he hadn't sounded an alarm either. No sounds or people had come through the door.

Satisfied he wasn't going to make any sudden moves, Katie laid BMFG down, retrieved her tactical notepad, and wrote down her name and military service number. Quennie recovered from his faint, wrote his name and as an afterthought, his social security number. The blended Sarah, still frozen and eyes glazed, stood behind the kitchenette counter. They remained locked in some form of argument. Good enough. Neither was stable and wouldn't be an asset in what happened next.

Spotting Alex's boxers draped on the back of his chair, Katie said. "Quennie, hand them some clothes. I think her stuff is in the lower drawers of the highboy." Turning to the guest, she handed the information sheet to him. He turned his head up to indicate the still frozen Sarah. She said, "They'll be a while. I think they're arguing."

Quennie did her proud. He rejected frilly things for a complete set of cottons. He handed them over the counter with his back turned toward them.

Katie's attention was still on the guest. She raised her voice, "Could the two of you table the discussion until we work this out?" A shuffle and a grunt signaled clothes being pulled on. Blended Sarah moved back to the table and glanced at Katie. Now it was Alex, assuming eye color followed, who is in control. She passed the notepad to them, "Name and military service number. Sarah, your name and social security number should be enough for ID."

Their right hand wrote his name. The left hand wrote Sarah's name, social security number, and home address. It stopped, then placed a heart over every "I."

Alex asked, "With a heart?" His eyes glazed over, and they dropped into another argument.

She handed the second sheet to the VIP. He handed her a business card with a cell phone number on the back. He stared at the blended Sarah. Katie said, "You'll get used to that. We don't think they're in any trouble, just arguing."

He asked again, "Anything else?"

Katie said, "Yes. Get something decent to wear on the Square; it's midsummer for Christ's sake."

30

BETTY BTFSPLIK

QUENTIN

K atie took her eyes off the road and peered into Quentin's face. "Are you going to be okay, lover?"

He held a plastic shopping bag to his mouth and breathed into it. Back in the apartment had been the first time he'd seen the whites of her eyes, veined with faint red capillary webs. Her deep-brown (never say chocolate!) eyes flicked back and forth as she tried to watch the road, him and their following escort.

Unlike Alex's Chitty-Chitty-Bang-Bang, her full-sized Toyota was quiet and sedate. His questioning raised eyebrows when she'd first picked him up—was it really only a little over a week ago? —received her response: "I need the leg room. Besides, Southern boys and girls know how to build cars."

The bag helped his hyperventilation and anxiety. Finally, he was able to turn in his seat to ask, "How are you doing?" He realized he didn't know if he meant him, her, or them. The Sarah-thing in the back seat gave a stone-faced nod and her eyes glazed over again. That would have been the male-Alex. The Sarah part would have never shown that face.

He'd never had this much responsibility. The Sarah-thing in the back with its fake Alex was *their* only link to the real Alex. The people following in at least two cars believed in their crazy shit, which meant he believed it. Even if Katie didn't believe it, she trusted Quentin and was improvising as fast as possible. He'd counted six people watching as they left Alex's apartment. Katie had counted eight, and the Sarah-thing reported three unseen. The thought of knowing about unseen people almost sent Quentin back to his breathing bag.

Screw up, lazy, slacker, wastrel. All these words and more had been tossed at him by his mother. Though there had been those three months where he was respected. Three months working for his mother in the lab until he discovered what she did there. He had cut and run from bitch-Mom and all her machinations. He breathed again into the bag.

Alex Jane, where ever she was, needed him. Katie needed him to control her flash violence. His running away had stopped.

People needed him.

Alex: 7:32 AM

My first time in KateQuen's apartment. Double the size of mine, separate bedroom, full-sized bathroom, great picture window, dove-gray walls, a new red couch and dining table set in red. Nice touches, including contrasting throw pillows, Quentin's touch. Katie never expressed any interest.

We break down for another cry. I understand Sarah's emotions. She's never experienced a life-threatening crisis. Before this craziness started, I always stuffed everything into the neck of a tall cool beer or got angry, very angry. But together? We cry. Something's wrong with us.

Sarah says, *"I've never been a crier. At least not since Daddy died."*

Katie's the true rock, the true professional. She insisted on a garbage bag with a change of clothes, shoes, makeup, etc. She drove us to their apartment. She rotates us through the bathroom, including me while separated, to clean up.

I shower first, but as usual, I don't have to shave. I may be pale skinned, but normally I have morning bristles like a boar. That changes, like many other parts of my life when Sarah found me.

Coming out, I find Quentin prostrate on the floor, Katie's ministering damp rags and ice packs on his forehead. He turns and groans in response to my footfall. "Do Sarah first. The migraine will pass soon."

Odd. Quentin was always the hale and hearty one.

I grab the towel I folded Sarah into and signal I'm ready. We reform, and she skips us into the shower. There is no mistaking her wide-toothy smile of joy.

This time I stay forward. First because of Katie's warning last night, and second, if Sarah disappears leaving me stuck in this body, I should know the basics. After folding our hair into Katie's shower cap, she answers my puzzled feeling. "We don't have time to dry our hair. I'll do my best to comb it out." Wetting down, she examines the shower toiletries, pads out, and cracks the bathroom door open. "Could someone be a dear and…" A black hand with Sarah's fave bath gel appears. "Thank you, Katie!"

After ten minutes with our face in the shower stream, and a knock on the door, I ask, "Why are we standing here?"

She says, "I can't explain it, but the shower beating on my face centers me. All my anxieties become bearable." That would explain the sensation of the past few minutes that reminded me of a cat purring. "I've been grateful you're a sound sleeper. I shower two or three times a night. That bad night when we fought, I showered four times."

"We have to…"

"I heard the knock." She raises her voice. "I'll be right out."

Quentin rushes in as we exit, wrapped in a towel. "Migraine disappeared." He grabs the shower cap. His hair is longer than ours. Normally, he keeps it in a half-assed pony-tail.

Seated on the bed, opposite the mirror, she runs our fingers through our hair. Time to deliver the good news to her. *"At least one problem is behind us."*

Sarah stops pulling Katie's Afro-comb through the tangled mess of our hair. *"What?"*

"Katie's shifted from protecting me to protecting us. To her, you're real, and we're both independent, at least in identity."

"I'm missing something."

"Sorry, you don't know Katie. If she was only protecting me, she would've held me down and let our intruder take you. She pulled the gun to protect you."

"What about Quentin?"

"I'm going to have to spend some bro-time with him. He's supporting us, but something's wrong." Why did he get these frequent migraines, and how did they disappear quickly?

Katie's on the phone constantly, sometimes demanding, sometimes promising, sometimes screaming. She showers, and over Quentin's breakfast at the dining table, she convenes a meeting. "Here's the situation. None of my MP or contractor friends could tell me who's out there." She waves at the parking lot. "You saw his name on the card. Mr. Samuel Johnson. A probable pseudonym. You understand we have to work with them?"

Sarah ignores my calming. "No, I don't. How dare they? I'm calling the cops."

I can't stop her reaching for Quentin's phone. She's right about the shabby treatment, but if she doesn't calm down... *"Either they will do a quick snatch and run or have the juice to legally pry us from the local police. Katie's right, we need to bolster our negotiating position to score freedom while keeping whomever they represent happy."* Sarah lays the phone down.

Katie grips our clavicle with her iron-like grip. "You do that again; I backhand you across the room. Alex, get her under control. A very thin thread keeps us from incarceration or being shot. The wrong move will break it."

I need a diversion to defuse the tension. Katie may know why they're not acting like military. I ask, "Why do I get the feeling this group is a little odd?"

She releases our clavicle. "I noticed that too. We're still in their net, but we shouldn't have been able to waltz out of your apartment that easily. This isn't strictly a black-ops, either. They may be a split command. One black ops, and another … something else. They want you, Sarah, badly, but something is holding them back from detaining us and snatching you. Are you willing to go along until we know more?"

Sarah crosses our arms and scowls. "Okay."

Katie sits at the dining table. "Quennie, Sarah, please sit across from me." She takes Quentin's hands in hers, lifts them and kisses them. "Leave. Now. It's the only sane choice for you."

Quentin jerks his hands back. "No."

"You're the only one who can still walk off. Hear me out. I pulled a gun on someone with power. Sarah's the prize. Alex is the way to hold the prize. You're the innocent bystander. Walk out, get into your car and don't stop until you're home in Seattle. Find better friends next time. I'll make sure your stuff gets shipped to you."

"No, I don't abandon my friends or my love."

Katie's eyes well up. She sniffs. "Listen to what I'm saying. When you hear it all, I expect you to stand up and walk out."

Turning to us, she asks, "I think I understand your situation Sarah, but we need to be clear. How long can you go without a core?"

Sarah pushes against the tabletop and starts to stand. I force her back into the chair. "Sarah, you need to face this."

Sarah says, "This isn't fair." I let her process her emotions. She regains control after a couple of seconds. "We accidentally experimented before you discovered us. We didn't know how unstable I am unblended. Without sixteen hours a day together, I lose rationality. Soon after that, I'm as feral as a raccoon with rabies. I don't know how long it was after I was created when I took over Alex's body. Nothing can stop me once I go feral."

Katie shakes her head. "A rogue element of a rogue government group created you. They've been killing people trying to create a viable Sarah. They haven't stopped, but they have one success. Leave, Quentin. Now."

"I don't care." Quentin's grin disappears, replaced by hard eyes, thinning lips, and tightly folded arms.

Katie kisses him. "Idiot. I may club you and send you home to be safe." She holds onto his hand and reaches for ours. "Which brings me to Alex. Are you certain? Sarah will be a handful—sorry girlfriend—and deadly without you. You could refuse to help them."

In my rush to respond, I shove Sarah out of the front.

She humphs. *"Hey, You could just nudge. I release quickly."*

I emote contrition. She's right, but Katie needs to know. "Don't go there. I don't leave comrades on the battlefield. End of discussion."

Katie purses her lips. "As for me, well, I'm the Amazon bitch with the trigger finger itch. They won't let that go."

"I'm not leaving." Quentin reaches out to hold both ours and Katie's hands. "I haven't done anything useful in six years. It's time I did."

Katie sniffs back welling tears. "I need to go to church again if we survive this. I stopped after Afghanistan. My first prayer will be to save me from insane lovers."

Releasing our hands, she gathers herself and turns to us. "The next few hours will be critical to Sarah. We must position ourselves as aggressively cooperating. Something they can deal with without learning new tricks." She stops to see if we have questions. "Speaking for myself, I don't want to live in some undisclosed location, watching the guards change shifts. The trick is to not force them to go underground with you." She stops again.

"Sarah and Quennie, listen up. This is the SitRep. Whatever it is we ran into is covert and they believe in their rightness and authority. A bad combination to fight."

Quentin's pursing his lips. I hadn't seen him do that since middle school when he last was serious about classwork. He asks, "Alex seems to be copacetic with your contractor plan, but I don't have a clue. I doubt that Sarah understands either. How does working for the man keep us safe?"

I signal with a lifted finger. "Think of it this way. We've fallen into something dangerous enough to kill people to make it happen. Up to now, they've used volunteers, accidentally killed them and with no payoff. The only success, Sarah, isn't a volunteer and they have no reason to trust that she'll cooperate. If they force her by threatening us, they have an unstable situation that could be exposed at any time.

"Katie's idea is brilliant. She's trying to shift them back to their volunteer approach, except this time the volunteers get paid. The government has more contractors than civil servants. We aren't asking them to do anything they don't do all the time."

I signal for a halt. Sarah says, "I caught it also. The six who followed us switched positions … and … two are at the door."

At the knock, Katie motions for us to remain seated at the table kicks her briefcase behind the door before she opens it and asks, "Hi. Is there something we can do for you." It's the two who were with Mr. Samuel Johnson when he inserted himself into our lives.

The beefiest looks up at her, runs his hand through his hair, and says,

"Ma'am, sorry to be a bother, but this is an unsecured area. We'd like to assess it."

"Go ahead. I'm an ex-MP, so I understand. We'll sit to stay out of your way." She returns to the table.

A couple of hand signals to someone in the hallway precede their entry. "We know your service record, ma'am."

"What's up. They seem to be polite but…"

She's right, but I don't see a legitimate goal here. *"I agree this is fishy. Follow Katie's lead. These are her type of people."*

The two don't even pull out drawers or look under the furniture, though they open one of the two closets. "Clear." The other one replies, "Clear. Thank you, ma'am. Please carry on." And they leave.

Quentin and I keep our grip on Katie's arms under the table. It's like gripping a python, strong, motile, and about to break out. Once she opens her fists, four deep half-moon impressions remain on her palms. She says, "You can let go. That bastard."

Quentin asks, "Why didn't they search anything?"

"It was a warning. They already knew about the 10mm I pack. They didn't try to find it. I've used similar tactics on a real hard case to shake him up."

Sarah's voice warbles, "What do we do? Couldn't we have said no?"

"It wouldn't have made any difference. We now know they're extra-legal. They left their guns outside which means they have the classified part of my personnel record. I would have blown if I had seen a gun.

"Let go of my arms and listen up. The good news is except Mr. Johnson, everyone we've seen are contractors. Black-ops, but contractors. This works to our advantage."

"No. No one takes me anywhere. Ah'm outta here." Sarah's still processing this and coming to the wrong conclusions. Conclusions that can get us killed. She alternates between flight, flight, and freeze. Understandable for her age and lack of experience with violence.

Katie's approach may work, and it will prevent casualties. Only someone who has never seen blood thinks violence is a solution. Sarah fights for control and I momentarily freeze. Katie refrains from her glare, but a raised eyebrow communicates to me to put a damper on my guest.

Sarah struggles against my control as I say, "*Listen to Katie. She was a Lieutenant in the Military Police. She's dealt with contractors like those outside. I was in the service for six years. Trust me. This is the best plan. Running is more likely to involve others who may get hurt.*"

Katie continues. "Like I said, we can't walk out of this. Sarah and Alex are stuck because they represent the only payoff for an expensive and dangerous government program. Me, well, they can't trust me not to come looking for you and bust you out." She looks directly in our eyes. "They're right."

"Since we can't fight them, we join them. We offer to comply but as paid contractors. This also works for the mystery agency. Paid contractors are much simpler and easier to explain than secret detainees. And cheaper. The people I contacted offered to be our *Prime Contractor*, with us signing on as independent consultants. Our prime will handle all the legal stuff and keep it legitimate. Whatever agency we're facing will understand our attempt to cooperate."

"The prime must never know, ever, about Sarah's special circumstances. The temptation to exploit her would be overwhelming."

Katie yawns. "I need a nap. Did any of Mr. Johnson's physics bafflegab help the two of you?"

Sarah returns the yawn. "Huh?"

"The part about how they shove cadavers into a chamber and presto, they have a Sarah-shell for someone to blend with."

Sarah fights tears.

I say, "I'm not certain I'm at all happy with the *blend* terminology, but it beats inventing some Sci-fi jargon such as *Betty Btfsplk*. *Blending* lines up with how we look, namely mostly Sarah with some Alex, and matches theories proposed by the physics geeks we talked with. So, yeah, it will fly."

"I've always wanted to be a Betty..." I can't tell if Sarah's serious.

"Forget it. It's probably copyrighted anyway." In a couple of hours, we will be reluctant collaborators with a covert agency or hauled off to a secret location. I can only hope Katie's contacts have the juice to make this stick.

31

TEA

ALEX: 1 PM

K atie glides like a runway model to the designated table and flashes her most electric smile. We're in full makeup, with hair-style sprayed-stiff. Even Quentin broke with his stubbly aspect and shaved. Sarah launched into de-tangling his mop and combing it into a neat ponytail, which gave me needed downtime to decompress.

The recent renovations of the Pullman Square had replaced the dying trees with ones more adapted to Pullman's low rainfall and hot summers. Unfortunately, this meant that any outside seating was in the full summer sun, and businesses raced to add café umbrellas to keep their clients cool. Someone had already positioned the umbrella to keep our table in the shade. Only one building loomed more than two stories, the one over the tea house. It sported a full brick façade with no windows. An odd architectural choice, as only the Edward Morrow communications studies building similarly had no windows. The rest of the square had an eclectic mix of cafes, boutiques, one shoe store, and the Merrill Lynch offices, which was located opposite to where we were seated.

We smile, even Katie. We're depending on her in-theater experience in negotiating with people who would rather shoot her. In Afghanistan, she tumbled on the civilizing veneer of sipping tea before starting anything confrontational. And nothing could be as confrontational as refusing to be detained. Especially when you are harboring a known monster.

Katie told us we have to put up with whatever happens with our host. She may have misread him.

Sarah overdoes the cuteness. My fault, I should have briefed her on how to handle this. *"Tone it down. Treat Mr. Johnson as if he's your grand-father and show respect."* She emotes flustered-followed-by-consent. She keeps her open toothy smile, which is her best feature. Mr. Johnson pulls out our chair for us.

As Quentin moves to pull out Katie's chair, she leans over Mr. Johnson, fakes an air kiss, and says in his ear, "We won't die because you hire idiots who attract attention. Send the kid driving the second follow-car back to training. He's too obvious. "

This gets a frown from Mr. Johnson.

Katie continues, "And if I ever spot someone within rifle distance whose haircut screams Fed or military as much as the guy in the third-floor corner office in the Merrill Lynch building, I'll shoot him myself." Quentin finishes seating her, and she flashes a wide smile. "Now, what does a lady need to do to get a menu?" Katie's pulling out all the stops to establish equal standing with our mystery agency.

Mr. Johnson seems distracted, then moves his hands in a series of quick motions. I recognize a couple of the hand signals. He's wired and has ordered someone to stand down. I don't tell Sarah; she needs to be calm. Katie? Yes, she read the hand signals, and a lifted eyebrow confirms she's okay with it.

I catch a sniffle, Quentin's signal from our grade school days. He's seen our little drama. Katie and I are a well-greased team. Together we'll make this work for Sarah. As long as she stays calm. I doubt bullets would bother her in-shell, but I'm sure blended we'd bleed.

I glance across the square to the Merrill Lynch building as a shadow drops below the window casing. As if by magic, a waiter lumbers forward, and distributes menus, upside down. I groan.

Sarah asks, *"What? Didn't I do right?"*

"No, you're doing fine. It's our ersatz waiter. If he isn't part of the security, I'll eat the menu." Sarah holds our menu high to hide her unvoiced giggle.

Mr. Johnson's shoulders loosen, and he straightens. I assume we passed the first test of many by not being aggressive. We harbor a known monster with an unassessed threat profile.

Johnson starts with, "I apologize, but my tea knowledge remains plebian. Could someone suggest something for this old codger?" He's accepted the civilized veneer of the afternoon tea to keep tempers in place. The test will come with the last of the mini-pots of tea.

Quentin speaks up. "I may be able to help. The Oolong is a strong tea. Fujian is like putting hair back on your chest, while the Darjeeling is smoother but somewhat sweet."

"Thank you. Ladies first."

Katie hands the menu to the waiter and says, "I'm familiar with the Darjeeling. I'll have the de Triomphe." After a smile to the waiter, she continues, "And a round of tea cakes and sandwiches for all of us."

A flush and frown roll over Mr. Johnson's face. She's usurped his host role. He recovers with a small half-smile. Score one for Katie. He likes her.

She's playing a close game, and so far, she's been pitch perfect. However, the stiffness of her movements betrays how close she is to losing it.

Our eye tingles, signaling Sarah's intense interest. I say, *"Time to participate. What would you like for tea? Your taste buds, so I'm deferring to you. For the Pashtun three-cups-of-tea etiquette to work, everyone participates and waits for the last cup to conduct business."*

"Oh, I don't know. I was checking out the neighborhood. The people here are more diverse than student housing. Our collection of yellows is scattered around the square. Now that I know about them, I'm certain they've been in our neighborhood for the past week. The odd one moves back and forth in the office Katie wants to shoot up."

She's distracted. I gently nudge her back to business. *"If you deign to join us, it might get tight, and we need to be following Katie's lead."*

Handing the menu to the waiter, I say, "We, ah, I would love the Nepalese White."

Mr. Johnson frowns, purses his lips, and hands the menu to the waiter. "The Oolong Fujian for me."

Quentin's left lip lifts in a semi-smile. Oh no, he purposely 'possumed, getting himself passed over. He's up to something.

"Waiter, could you bring a couple of bags of Lipton?"

I'm so startled at his breach of protocol, I release control, and Sarah takes us on a giggle fit for all to enjoy. Through our tears of mirth, I catch Mr. Johnson and Katie exchanging smiles.

From the burning of our cheeks; we're obviously red-faced. Sarah says, "I'm sorry, but it was funny." To me. *"Sorry for overwhelming you."*

"Actually, it's a good thing. We needed it, even the nervous waiter. This gives me an idea. Stay forward and enjoy the party. I'm interested in how this crew deploys." I can feel our lips open with our beaming smile.

"On second thought, make my order the same Darjeeling." Quentin, you saved this meeting, but someday someone's gonna pop you one.

I'm happy with my decision to hand-off to Sarah. She's the life of the party, engaging and laughing. Mr. Johnson's a brilliant host, keeping the conversation as fresh as his linen suit bought today from my hated employer. It had been tagged to be returned to central distribution.

This gives me plenty of time to do recon. This sensing thingy's handy. Two line-of-sight positioned on rooftops, likely snipers. I'd like to visually confirm, but that would give away our tactical advantage. This places Katie and Quentin at risk of being killed. Sarah, if she panics and separated, will be unstoppable. I wish I could tell Katie.

I wait for a break in the conversation. *"If I ask, release immediately. I may need to jump Katie if she gets excited."* Sarah emotes understanding. Quentin touches our hand, and our quivering stops. Katie's eyebrows lift, and I go for an encouraging smile. This may be too much for Katie. She's carrying the entire load, putting her trust in the same government that left her in a filthy Afghani hut while it bungled days of attempts to find her.

With the potential Katie problem covered, I resume my surveillance. Three in the Merrill Lynch corner office. Probably a listening and command post. Sarah's right, one is unique. Another five to nine possibles scattered in the café and around the square. They're backup and to prevent escape. And of course, our sorry excuse for a waiter. We picked the worst location thinking it gave us an advantage. We are isolated from any crowd cover.

We walked into their trap.

32

THE DEAL

ALEX

As we wind down, Katie picks up the lead. "We've considered the offer you passed through our contracting officer, and we accept. I assume you and our Prime Contractor's lead, Ms. Ernő Rubik, completed negotiations. Any problems?" Katie, as usual, pushes the envelope. She's forcing him to accept our offer to be paid consultants.

If he doesn't bite, we run until we're captured.

Mr. Johnson pulls a thin portfolio from under the table and hands out folders with our names. Katie's folder is the thickest, double mine. Quentin's and Sarah's are the thinnest. "This is a formality, but could you confirm the information here is correct?"

Katie opens her folder, confirms her name, service number, dates of service, and closes it without reading further. An emotion flickers on her face, and she goes stoic. I wish she didn't have to re-live her personal hell like this.

Quentin riffles his and grunts assent.

My service record is thicker than I thought, including some "unreported" incidents. About thirty pages including my post-deployment issues.

"Sarah."

"Yes."

"Read this. It's my record., Some unpleasant stuff, but it's accurate."

"Why?"

I'm out of my league here. No one should know about my failures, the deaths I couldn't stop. For Sarah, I'm doing it for Sarah. *"We don't know how long our condition will last. We need to be totally honest about our less pleasant sides to make our relationship work. Read every page. I'll answer any questions."*

The incident at Tikrit is included. Sarah rereads that page. Her eyes slow down on how many civilians died in the crossfire intended for me. She has no questions. I catch a churn of conflicting emotions, but she doesn't explicitly emote a specific one. With her concerns and her perfect memory, I expect discussions later.

We finish and close my military and VA record. Then she opens her folder.

I tell her, *"Slowly, flip the pages as we read."*

I'm active-reserve, my life is available with a simple computer query. Sarah's a civilian. It's been seven hours since the first contact with Johnson. This can't be right. These people have collected comprehensive school, doctor, and state DMV info, and a pile of reports from Nebraska and Fed agencies. Everything is online but allegedly protected behind encrypted firewalls controlled by different commercial and government agencies. They have the juice to ignore laws and obtain Sarah's school and doctor records, and force agencies to respond in hours instead of weeks.

"Sarah, let me control for a moment, I need to get Katie's attention."

Katie examines the flow of people in the square, and her posture stiffens. She's spotted the people out of place in the civilian flow. I signal that I know about them and indicate that she should examine Sarah's folder. Katie reads upside down without being obvious. Her pupils dilate and reduce. She agrees with my assessment.

Even if I'd had any doubts, I'm now ecstatic about our collaborative negotiating stance. These would be dangerous opponents.

Sarah's records reveal interesting details. Academically, solid math and science curriculum, with advanced placement in the liberal arts. President of the Chess Club? Lettered two years in gymnastics and last year competed at the Nebraska State finals. Her backflip in my efficiency was no fluke. GPA 3.995, and the Class Salutatorian. This girl's well above me. I'm ashamed I treated her as a dimwit. If we survive this meeting, that stops. Broken clavicle and metatarsal two years ago. Pointing to the page, I ask, "*Sarah, gymnastics?*" Sarah emotes agreement. Emoting is faster than talking. I'll have to remember that.

Katie, Quentin and I hand gesture confirmation. Sarah speaks up, "That's me and my Omaha records are good."

Mr. Johnson slides out a tablet and flicks open a street map of Pullman. "I'd like to stabilize the location where Ms. Merk had her unfortunate incident. You'll get your belongings, which the mole left in his car, once we confirm there are no contaminants." He stops, listening to someone. I can't spot the receiver he's wearing. "Everything is cleared, but to be safe, we'll dry clean the soft goods and return them to you Monday afternoon." Apparently, no one wants to break into local dry cleaners for expedited service.

Sarah slides the tablet to face her, frowns, then finger-spreads to focus the map on one set of streets. "I know exactly. I walked from the bus stop to the apartment through this alley. Here. He came from between two identical garages on the left. He grabbed and pushed me down. He stayed between me and the garages." Her speech comes in spurts, so I take over our body to help her anxiety. As she retreats, she emotes thanks.

Mr. Johnson talks into the air. "Alley northeast of the complex, two garages." He smiles at Sarah. "Young lady, thank you. We'll return anything of yours. As for the houses on the alley—in a few minutes, a construction crew will remove the pavement and resurface the alley. We'll haul everything to a lab elsewhere to examine for traces of the attack."

Sarah flashes her smile. *"Honey. We found our help. They have the resources to work Matryoschka Sarah."*

I move in to control her shaking. I let the tears go. She sniffs them back quickly. I'm nonplussed. Yes, the cavalry has arrived. We cooperated because we saw no alternative. This is unexpected. They are interested in more than exploiting Sarah and show a willingness to expend serious cash to investigate even the blacktop and dirt in the alley. At least I know what to do with the flattened apple in my freezer. "We picked up something there. We'll get it to you." This isn't the place to talk about a seamless apple skin. I'm not going to assume that our mystery agency is the only one with ears on our table.

While everyone is copacetic, I need to bring up one concern: how to protect our families from 'accidents.' I work up my best Sarah-talk. "Mr. Johnson, we absolutely believe your organization is what we need to fix our problem."

He waits for the "but." Smart man. I like him. "I'd appreciate not raising questions back home. Katie and Alex are Active Reserve. No one will question yet another request for their records. However, for Quentin and myself, people may ask questions." I leave out the obvious extra-legal activity of the past few hours. "If you'll provide release forms, including medical, for what you've already acquired and might need, we'll sign them. We don't need any accidents back home."

His frown disappears, and the crinkles around his eyes lessen. "We'll get right on it. Great team, you got here, Ms. Parker." Yep, he likes Katie. Mr. Johnson moves to pull out our chair, and Quentin follows suit with Katie.

Katie, her smile flirtatious, hands Mr. Johnson a slip of paper. "You need an inconspicuous safe house; hide-in-plain-sight. Here's the address. Ground floor, easily controlled access, clear lines of sight.

We'll handle the decorating. Feel free to supplement with what you need for security but remember to let us know. I'd be devastated if something valuable accidentally fell into the garbage disposal." Katie did it again, forcing a solution. She's right. We should be together for security reasons, but even more for mutual support.

KateQuen and I are back together, joined by Sarah. Sarah picks the decorating.

We're all quiet on the ride back. I'm emotionally exhausted. You could have cut the tension at the teahouse meeting with a knife and sold it on eBay. Mr. Johnson and Katie had kept it below the surface, and Sarah and I handled it with tactical body-control swaps when one was having difficulties. Quentin, well, he loves drama.

Katie finessed a miracle. She'd shifted us from potential detainees under the byzantine Homeland Security Act to paid contractors. We've retained the freedom to continue our college studies. Although, depending on how demanding our mystery agency is, we may have to cut back on classes.

I emote exhaustion. Sarah takes the body, and I scan what's following us.

Katie watches the rear-view mirror "We're still being followed. Their role has changed. They're our archangels watching over us."

I say, "I confirm. Five following in two cars."

Katie's face droops. "Alex, or Sarah, whoever that is, you must tell me how you do that. But not today."

Back at KateQuen's apartment, everyone kicks off their shoes, and Quentin rummages for cold beer. Katie's face bunches up, and she leans forward as if she's sick. Instead, she lets out a loud sob and cries uncontrollably. It's continuous, no breaks except to catch her breath.

Before I can ask, Sarah stands up, turns our back to Quentin, and takes off our clothes. She separates onto my shoulders back. *"Thanks for understanding. Keep track of our new friends outside. Shout if they start moving."*

Quentin mouths "Thank you." He and I hold Katie for over an hour until she cries herself out. The tension we rode throughout the tea party almost got the better of me. Without Sarah's naturally positive influence, I would have gone physical over the stress. With Katie's unresolved issues, the last thing she needed was the challenge of keeping us out of the hands of the government she had served. The government that had failed her.

Through her final sniffles, Katie says, "Thank you, Alex, Quennie, and you too Sarah." Looking again at me, she grins. "Yous nekked as a Jaybird. Is that how you were raised?"

"Quentin's clothes won't fit, so Sarah?" She jumps me, turns around, and hums as she redresses.

As we drink the now-warm beer, Sarah runs her finger over the condensation on the label. "Something from Hesse, Germany. Tastes like pig spit." I emote deep satisfaction with the brew. She emotes disgust. Another item for the Cat Journal. The puzzle of what we are only grows deeper.

Katie picks up her ringing phone. "Yes, it looked good at our end. What about yours? Any contract or other glitches ... Really, civilian? This had all the earmarks of military ops. Oh ... Thanks. You'll earn your fifteen percent on this one. Call me anytime, especially at night if something comes up."

Watching the condensation drip on her second beer, Katie exhales. "As you guessed, that was Ms. Rubik, our prime's contracting officer. She confirms the paperwork is approved and we'll sign within a week after the standard contractor processes are met. The surprise is that our men-in-black are civilians. They're an FFRDC, a Congressionally authorized federally funded research and development center. The research remains with the civilians. Due to a recent breach, the military controls the security; I think your Greasy's the reason. Ms. Rubik believes this isn't a happy marriage. The original research project had no security implications. Happily, our contract is with the civilians."

"Katie, that doesn't add up. Mr. Johnson is military. How'd he get in charge if this is civilian?"

Katie shrugs. "You'll need to practice your Sarah-talk. They'll want Sarah, and I've spotted when you two change out to relieve each other. You need to be less noticeable."

She has a point, but right now I don't care. I want to go home to my familiar lumpy hide-a-bed. "Katie, can we borrow your phone? I want to program a speed dial for Mr. Johnson's number in both of our phones. We'll call him to let him know we're heading home."

As I program my phone with our right hand, Sarah calls Mr. Johnson with our left on Katie's phone. Being ambidextrous is cool. "Hi. Mr. Johnson? Say that was a nice time. Why thank you. You're sweet. I'd like to go home, tidy up and crash early tonight."

I hear discussions in the background. They've already agreed, they're just organizing the details.

We collect our street clothes and the cell phone into the garbage bag. Sarah surprises Quentin with a cheek kiss. He'll grin for at least an hour. Katie extends her hand. Sarah locks eyes with her. "Either you smile, or I'll climb up there and lay a juicy one on you, too." Katie smiles. I think I'll faint. Katie rarely smiles.

A couple of blocks later, I interrupt Sarah's chatter with the two hunks —they've lost their goon status. Good news, all the people except one follows us. With any luck, the one left behind will stay out of Katie's sight. She needs serious decompression. *"When we get out at the apartment, walk slowly through the lobby, I want to do recon. They're friendlies, but I like to know who and how many are at my back."*

We're all exhausted, but I can't forget we're in their control. The next few days will show if we'll be free will participants or forced subjects.

33

RATTUS RATTUS

QUENTIN AND KATIE'S APARTMENT, TWO HOURS LATER

A firm knock at the door broke up their argument. Katie sat in the loveseat. The rose undertone in her complexion came from her and Quentin's first argument. Quentin, in a chair instead of his usual spot on the love seat, stood to answer it.

At the door, he turned and said, "Have it your way. We'll rat her out. You have the experience as an MP but remember Alex Jane's been my best friend for twenty years more than you've known her. I'll fight for Alex's independence and happiness." Quentin's key rattled in the double-sided deadbolt as he opened it.

Katie rubbed her hands on her shorts to not have a clammy hand-shake. She'd changed into the shorts to effect a more casual, "Trust me. I don't shoot" image. This is where the 'gutteh-chile' from Newark's First Ward proved she was more than a collection of failures, hers and others.

Despite her training, her eyes flickered to her briefcase holding BMFG.

"That's the whole point. We have to get Alex back whole first, then work on the happiness part. We'll hold the Sarah-thing discussion for later." They were all in for Alex Jane. If needed, they'd kick Sarah-thing to the government. After all, it was what the government cared about.

The deadbolt receded with a snick.

After examining Katie with her forced smile and informal clothes, Mr. Johnson waved to someone in the hallway and entered.

Katie handed Mr. Johnson her BMFG wrapped in her shoulder holster. "A sign of good faith. Besides, you'll want to verify the ballistics. It's pattern-registered, but you can check."

His eyebrow went up as he double gripped the too-large semi-automatic. "Earlier you almost blew my brains into the next apartment. What's changed?"

"We're still desperate, but now we think you're part of the solution."

He handed the semi-automatic to the person in the hallway. "Standard checks, then return it." He swept the room with a calculated gaze. "Thanks, we do need to verify its ballistics. Why did you threaten me earlier with an unloaded gun?"

"You knew?"

"Of course. That's the main reason I accepted your invitation. You have a pair of brass ones. You didn't intend to kill me, but you wanted me and anyone listening to believe it. That makes you worth listening to."

Quentin's near perpetual grin was gone as his hand swept the room. "Would you like the seat facing the window or the door?"

He took Quentin's usual spot on the love seat with his back to the door. Smart, that meant he had full coverage outside the door. Katie straddled the other chair, arms draped over the chair back in front of her. Quentin pulled up another chair from the dining table.

Mr. Johnson asked, "Why such a big gun?"

"It fits my hand."

Quentin handed out beers. "You run a tight ship. Is it military?"

Their guest's eyes shifted left and right.

Katie interrupted, "We'll know soon enough. Isn't that right, General?"

"Who told you?"

"Give me some credit. Three combat tours plus MP training and you can sense the energy levels a general gives off. Enjoy your beer; this will be a dry conversation."

Quentin wiggled in his seat but obeyed Katie's quiet gesture to remain silent.

After a long swig, Mr. Johnson placed his bottle down. "You understand why I'm not advertising that I'm a general?" Katie nodded. "Lieutenant, why did you want to meet?"

"We have a situation. And it's Katie, I'm decommissioned." *A situation*, the universal military polite-talk for the more honest SNAFU. "We'll assume whoever is monitoring has high clearances."

Johnson held his right index finger up and touched behind his ear with the other hand. "Come in. Remove all the listening equipment and bring in a recorder." A stocky woman, hair in a graying pageboy, slipped into the apartment. Katie admired her smooth movements, deliberate steps, and quiet as a cat stalking a bird. The tech removed the microphone and transmitters from under Johnson's shirt, and he handed her the earbud.

Buttoning up, he said, "Let's just call what remains is health verification." He placed the recorder where the flashing LED could be seen. "Your MP record is exemplary, but the paperwork for commendations and a grade increase seem to have been lost. I'll take care of that."

Katie looked away. "There was an incident. I requested there be no commendations for anything I did."

"I disagree. Your restraint is something we could include in combat schools, but the outcries would never stop. Did you know all similar incidents stopped for over a year after what you did?"

Katie's eyes glistened, as she turned them to Quentin. "Quentin doesn't agree with us confiding our issues about Alex and Sarah, but he does agree on the issues. He'll fill in or disagree as he sees fit." She took a couple of deep breaths, then stopped. "I can't start. Quentin, why don't you start?"

With a blush and tremble starting at his knees and ending at his shoulders, Quentin said. "Alex and I have been best friends since first grade, over twenty years ago. We were always in trouble. Every vice-principal knew us on sight. We spent summers together, including summer jobs. We even skinny dipped, more than once, together." A frown creases his face.

"Tell them about the sex." It was that non-verbalized voice prodding Quentin. He hadn't heard it in weeks.

He said, "I've never thought about it, but something tells me I should say we never screwed."

Katie cleared her throat, and he glanced at her before continuing, "Katie, this is my story. I'll tell it my way. The only time we separated was when Alex enlisted in the Army, and I stayed home to pursue my college degree. When Alex came back, everything changed. No sense of humor, jumping at most noises, nightmares. Our parents sent me here to finish my degree and to stay with Alex. I was to help Alex along with Katie. About a..." He broke down, gulping deep breaths. Grabbing a pillow, he breathed into it. "I can't. Katie?"

Katie stooped over Quentin, held him then turned to Mr. Johnson. "Are the military and civvy records you have on Alex complete?"

"Certainly. Every inductee has their records digitized and included in their package."

"Were there any anomalies?"

"We did a cursory check, but we were more interested in Sarah. Nothing stood out. Why?"

"That's the problem. The Alex in your records? The Alex you and we see now didn't exist a week ago."

"That's impossible. How could that all be modified in secure computers right down to eye scans and fingerprints?"

"I don't know, and I don't think anyone committed a fraud. At least that is what my instincts and MP training tell me. This is bigger. It may be tied to the same phenomena that created the Sarah-thing."

Quentin paled some more. "Tell him about the dependency thing."

This was the crux. Either the group Mr. Johnson represented could help or couldn't, and they'd be in the way. If the latter, she would grab Alex and run. "According to *this* Alex, the thing needs at least sixteen hours a day in full-body, any less, and it becomes feral. This means Alex only has a max of eight hours a day of independent existence." She waited for Johnson to process this. "It gets worse. He thinks she's pure energy and could do immense damage if excited. He stays in the combined mode as much as he can stand. He's trying to keep her from striking out in confusion."

Johnson said, "I'm reactivating the project. Most of the original researchers are still around. I have a friend who can do a med assessment without major equipment."

"There's more."

"Yes?"

"We believe their relationship is dangerously co-dependent and potentially symbiotic. We need to permanently separate them before this Alex is no more. We both believe the male Alex we see is key to recovering the Alex that disappeared. Your records, everything has changed in the past week."

They stop to lay Quentin down with a plastic bag to breath into. He said, barely audible, "How am I going to tell her parents?"

Mr. Johnson asked, "Who?"

"The real Alex—Alex Jane Monroe—was female. The male Alex we now have looks somewhat like her, except for hair and eyes, but is a man, all the way."

Quentin turned his head away, into the loveseat's back. "I was supposed to keep her safe."

34

NO PLAN SURVIVES THE FIRST CONTACT

GENERAL SAMUEL JOHNSON

The dust had settled everywhere, creating a tan tableau. Swept by the movement of his green sedan, the dust formed into streaks. The streaks reminded General Samuel Johnson of the olive drab uniforms of the previous generations of the US Army. He was heading back the project's HQ. The plan had been to give orders to quickly and decisively finish this excursion.

The driver asked, "General?" Stocky, with muscles showing through even his dungarees, he was one of the two who had accompanied the General in his initial raid on the unknown phenomena. Out of sight from those in the room, he and his partner had had backup armament: an assault shotgun loaded with depleted uranium double-aught buck-shot, a flamethrower, and a nitric acid projector. Ready in the elevator was a stored-charge EMP device. He'd been stunned when they found three perfectly healthy students surviving with the creature.

"General?" he repeated and waited for the general's answer.

The sight of an Army MP Lieutenant crying with her partner was more than the general had expected. He had exited while they were wrapped together, forgetting he was still in the room.

He'd left a note. "I'll be in contact. We can handle this." Hollow, cheap words. It wasn't a matter of budget. In his line of work, that was rarely a problem. He had a few Congressionally mandated black-works projects he could tap. No one knew who he really was. A few calls and he would delegate all the other black projects to subordinates. This one affected him in a way he'd never been affected before.

He'd never heard of a sentient energy being. And that was the problem.

The driver slowed down to confirm his next orders. "Do we go back to HQ?" Still no answer. "Sir?"

General Johnson asked, "How many people on the project know I'm a general?"

"Only those loaned by the intelligence agencies and a couple of the staff from the original project."

"Put out orders I'm only to be addressed as Mr. Johnson from now on. We can't scare off these people. That includes all paperwork, briefings, and discussions. Let's go back to HQ. I need a secured line. Everything has changed. We need heavy support, including better security."

He'd pulled the plug on the previous project due to its danger. Clearly not soon enough. The danger was out and roaming. Like worms crawling out of the bait can all over the dock.

The project also needed a great and facile mind as its physics lead. The tall, black-haired model-type, Carla? from the original project would be ideal.

He closed his eyes until the driver said, "We're here sir. Surveillance reports no observers, and our tail reports no one followed."

They pulled behind the tea house where he'd met with the friends that afternoon. The car parked behind a partition painted and textured to appear like the brick wall of the building, he climbed out and headed to a rusty door with no identification. He checked the time. It was still early enough to get the new funding out of his classified location in Crystal City, Virginia. He turned to his driver and aide-de-camp and said, "New project orders. Cancel all plans to sweep up Ms. Parker and Mr. Kahn."

He had intended to sign anything, then sequester all involved people until his team controlled the situation. Of course, the myth of independence would have required the deposits of consultancy fees to their accounts. But until he had everything under control, the four wouldn't have had access to the money.

That plan had died before the first shot in this new war. The sincerity of the two friends about the danger convinced him a more nuanced approach was needed.

Upstairs, past anonymous offices with no markings on the doors, he arrived at his office. A 24-hour camera blinked in the upper left front corner. The occupancy sensor turned on the lights and the monitoring equipment. The bare beige walls provided the calm he needed. Before he opaqued the outside window, he checked the square below. A couple sat at the table he met the four friends earlier today. There were no obvious watchers. Not that he expected any. They had hidden cameras surrounding the HQ and the contiguous streets.

He opened the secured safe using the eye scanner, and he pulled the personnel files from the last project. Most were bright, and he liked them, but they had no sense of confidentiality, and worse, no sense of security. Lab space would be difficult to procure as the corporate sponsors had already vultured the old equipment.

Most important —were the sensors. Their sensors had left them vulnerable. If the lieutenant and her partner were correct, without this Alex, whoever or whatever he was, forming the bottle for the Sarah-thing they'd have a combined Godzilla-Mothra-like rampage.

With a shudder, he initiated his personnel requisitions, starting with the Addams twins. The problem with the Addams sibs was they came as a set. Jimmy Addams' designs formed the core of many military and most intel sensors. His sister Clarice was the problem. She was the one who had texted him when the grad students' bull session slipped into classified territory. She was probably the smartest person he'd ever known, but he couldn't let her loose on the project. He'd have to find a safe, unclassified task for her.

She'd still find a way to get into trouble.

35

DADDY

Daddy stood between the skinny, yellowish man and me. "Are you certain?" he asked. The skinny man looked like a goat, and he talked funny. Daddy said to not make fun of him; he came from Russia.

I hated this stinky room. It was in the basement of Daddy's company, and the only entrance was down an outside, slippery staircase. When I came here, I knew that I would not meet any other fun people.

He pulled Daddy to one side and said, "Absolutely. This can't harm her. It only activates the bio-energy perception we all have. She's got the highest reading of all the test subjects. You know she complains about how she tingles when she's around certain people?"

"Like you, Mort." Daddy shuffled some papers with lines on them. "I'm still not certain making her more sensitive is a good idea."

"You know from the animal trials it flushes out of the body. Even in the worst-case scenario, she won't have physical problems. It's State Testing day at her school. I'll be around. I signed up to proctor the test. After this, you can take her there, and then she'll have the weekend to rest before school Monday."

Daddy pulled a sheet of paper out of the piles, sat down, and read. "If this was as harmless as you say, why does this release for a one-time experiment require seventeen pages and four signatures?"

"Lawyers. What can I say?" I swear the man's eyes glowed.

I said, "I wanna up. I want to see the hamsters." Maybe if I left, they'd forget about me until Daddy took me to school. I didn't want to be in this stinky basement on my birthday. I turned eight today. Yep, I was a big girl. I didn't like needles, and I shouldn't be stuck on my birthday, but the straps on the chair didn't let me wiggle. "Ah wanna go."

Daddy ruffled my hair. I hated it when he did that. "I know, dearest. We've discussed this. I've worked very hard on things that will make boys and girls better. You're special. My tests show that your brain is ready for more neural-plasticity development."

"I don't want a plastic brain!"

"I know this can be scary, but what if we get waffles on the way to school?"

I stopped squirming. "With sprinkles and three types of syrup?"

Daddy grimaced. "Yes, if we can put a large napkin on you. We don't want Mother upset over the stains."

I wanted to pout, but thoughts of forbidden waffles won. "Okay." The strange colors glowed when I closed my eyes, and now I smelled each color.

Daddy signed the paper while the goat-faced, greasy man—Mort was his name; I kept forgetting it—said, "You may want to look the other way while I give you this shot. It may pinch."

It didn't pinch, it hurt. I did my best to not squirm—waffles—but I stuck my tongue out at him and watched everything he did. Waffles.

Daddy watched a large TV with lots of squirming lines, and said, "Theta waves jumped, and the waveform is like nothing I've seen before. The ocular nerve also…" He turned around and asked, "Sarah, what do you see?"

I looked around as much as I could in the thing they strapped on my head. "This stinky basement room, but now the walls aren't as gray. They have some other color."

Mort nudged Daddy. "She's shifted into energy sensing. The steam lines pass through that wall."

I closed my eyes and thought about the waffles. It was a long time, but Daddy finally unstrapped me. He said, "We have just enough time for the waffles and then get you to the school test. Uh, don't tell your mother about the waffles. Okay?"

I grinned all the way up the stairs, out into the sunlight and to the car where I was strapped in for the ride. Waffles. It must have been the waffles that made everything brighter. Even the people glowed like big candles. I couldn't stop thinking about all the fun things I learned in school, even those from last year, and even way back to when Mommy first smiled at me in my crib.

36

GANG'S TOY

SARAH: THEIR APARTMENT, EARLY MORNING

Sarah's snore woke her,

Or was it Alex's snore in their body? She didn't think she'd snored before she was attacked.

The alarm clock read 02:37 AM, but she couldn't sleep. Was that a nightmare or was it a memory? How could she have dreamed Daddy would ever violate his eldest daughter in that way?

Mom was her only friend, and she couldn't help now. Sarah couldn't even get to her. *They* watched. Without understanding her new-found ability, she instinctively knew where each watcher lurked.

She tossed until she was tangled in the sheets. The AC didn't keep the heat off, so they slept with only the top sheet as a cover. Who knew what perverted things Alex has done to their body while she was asleep. She was a pleasure thing, the Greasy man said as much, and she was convinced Alex thought this all the time. He only faked being weirded out.

Alex's friends were worse. That Quennie, what a horn-dog. Katie? She was violent with no notice, and she creeped Sarah out with the way she gazed at her when she thought Sarah wasn't watching.

She couldn't handle this. Everyone around her treated her nicely, but they were only sizing her up, buttering her up like a turkey heading into the oven. She wasn't brave, and she couldn't fight everyone off. And now that strange man with his bully boys wanted a piece of the action.

She was no gang's toy. She couldn't control what she was, the greasy man took that away from her.

However, she could control how her life went from here.

She tossed a double handful of lilac-scented bath salts into the tub and ran the water as hot as she could tolerate. In the kitchen, she found the sharpest knife and tested it against her palm. She winced. "Bogus, that hurts. But not for long."

The bath had filled. She gripped the knife and climbed in.

37

IT BEGINS

SARAH: THEIR APARTMENT, EARLY MORNING

Sarah wakes me when she unexpectedly separates. I'm startled. Feels strange to stretch awake as Alex. Laying my palm flat on her, to initiate skin-contact communications, I emote confusion.

She compacts herself tighter. "Ah don't like always watching my back. In-shell, Ah've got no back."

This probably isn't the time to point out that she has no front either. *"That makes no sense. Are you the shell-equivalent of drunk?"*

"Also, in-shell, Greasy can't get me."

"What?"

"I get nightmares when we're blended. In-shell, I don't. Go away."

I don't need to understand. Give her slack, she's six years younger with no combat experience. If I have anything to say about it, she won't see trauma like the kind Katie and I have.

To give her space and demand less from her, I drop into the sensing mode and recon the area. Only two days ago, this was a fun and relaxing game we played. We made up stories of the different colors and their interactions. It loosened us up after a bad day.

Without her strength, it's fuzzier and limited to a couple of blocks. I'm probably riding on her abilities, with a small talent of my own to activate it. Still good enough to spot the likely four security on shadow detail, two in close, two further away. The kitchenette window faces the right direction, and the dark green sedan down the block correlates with the two further off. At least they have the sense not to use black cars.

Still fuzzy, but I locate a tight cluster of four. From the kitchenette window, I see the entire block, so they must be around the corner.

In the mirror, I spot a red streak dried on my right arm. Rubbing it removes what could only be blood. As I fold the bed into the couch, the sheet slips showing a red butterfly-like splotch. Did she, we, start our period? Maybe that's why she separated. I'll have to get used to it, but I'm not looking forward to everything that goes with it. Katie, having no female friends on campus, spared me none of the details about cramps and other monthly visitors. Anyway, a quick shower will take care of all this, and I'll take the linens to the laundry room afterward.

There was nothing for us to do but wait. We were told by our new boss, Mr. Johnson, that they had to set up the appropriate lab space. We were free until Monday, except to ensure we didn't accidentally ditch our security. No problem, both Katie and I are security aware.

Which leaves my LDO gig. My shift starts at ten. Hopefully, Sarah's up to going to work. With Sarah conformed over my shoulders and chest under the dress shirt, time passes pleasantly. She's funny and keeps me sane while working the mundane. To be honest, with her retail experience, she's a major help.

I may as well take a page from Sarah's *Life is Good* manual and shower. Sometimes I think Sarah lives in the shower. My bar soap refreshes me as does the needle spray. Finished, I check in the mirror. Can't get used to this mug without the four-inch scar. The scar's gone, but something … yes … no. Using both hands, I run my fingernails lightly over both sides of my face. I don't believe it. Feeling has returned to my right cheek. The nerve reconnected itself. I'll eat steaks for physical therapy.

The scratching sensation, no whiskers, pushes me to examine closely in the mirror. No facial hair, no shaving needed. If this continues, I should find a doctor to check what's going on. For now, another item for the Cat Journal. I found it in a dusty corner in the off-campus bookstore. Ugly as sin, with a ridiculous cat on it, it met my whimsy.

Now to implement Sarah's entire Life is Good and apply make-up. Applying makeup centers her when she's agitated. I reach for the brush she starts with ...

No, drop the thought. Why'd I even think that? It was as if I momentarily dropped out and was someone else.

Instead of pacing, I fidget in my chair while eating breakfast. I sense a change with our watchers. I wonder how long between shifts. I'm handling my downtime poorly. Our abrupt change from care-free students to government contractors has left me rattled. Come to think of it, our duties weren't defined. I wonder what type of boss Mr. Johnson is. At least he likes Katie.

Ring.

Thank God, I was going bonkers. "Good Morning."

It's Katie. "Hi, Alex. Mr. Johnson, some of his friends, and I'll be over in about an hour for preliminaries. Is that okay?"

"Ye-Yes," I stutter. "Certainly. I'll call work and beg off. Sarah's strung out and recuperating in-shell, but she'll be fine. Wait, we don't have refreshments. Could you delay a half hour so I can run down to the corner store?" Our new job starts today, not Monday? I have first day nerves?

"No need, Quennie's already on it."

Sarah refuses my signal to blend. Another first in our relationship. I talk through surface contact. *"Guests arriving in about an hour. Our new employment starts today."*

"Go away, all today is me-time."

"No can do. Whatever they want, we don't know who knows about our relationship. We need to maintain the illusion it's you and not us. We only know two—our new boss, and the body-builder who stays close—who know about our partnership." 'She doesn't respond, and I assume she needs time to process. I continue, "However, looking around at this mess, I can do the cleanup easier as Alex."

No emoting from her; she always emotes. She's usually a babbling brook of emoting. She's really out of it. It must be those nightmares she doesn't want to talk about. When we find some downtime, I'll make her tell me. If her disconnect with us-as-Sarah continues, I might have to be full-time Sarah while somehow maintaining my life as Alex. I don't think I can keep the two identities without her active partnering. Not spending the sixteen to eighteen hours blended with Sarah is not an option. She'd either die or accidentally kill someone.

After folding the dirty linens into the hide-a-bed, I carry the first load of Quentin's party rentals and food containers into the elevator. A casual loiterer sits in the lobby reading yesterday's paper. A quick sensing recon; one of ours. I hold up my first load and smile to ensure he knows I'm a friendly. "Big party last night. Little Miss will cut my tenders if she sees the mess. I'm hiding everything in the storage locker." The guard gestures at someone around the corner.

The first guy precedes me downstairs, checks the corners and winks, "I know how it is."

Two trips later—one to the dumpster—I can see the floor. I vacuum and wipe a damp rag over the more objectionable surfaces, the card table, and chairs. I straighten the bed and fold it into the couch. After moving it back to its spot, I signal, and we blend. *"About forty minutes left, sorry I took so long."*

Sarah

Not certain what to expect, she pulled out loose slacks, a shirt, and her penny loafers, in I-wish-I-hadn't-bought lime-green. That would have to do. Pulling the shower cap on, she spotted *it*.

Oh, hell, no. That was a nightmare. She didn't commit suicide with a steak knife in the tub. Did she?

She needed some privacy, so she hinted to Alex that girly stuff followed. He dropped out. It worked every time.

Her first stop was a close examination in the bathroom mirror. No wrist scars from the cuts in her nightmare. Likewise, no scar from right to left cut her jugular. Picking up the knife, the edge remained moist enough to smear. A taste confirmed it: blood.

No scars, but the knife was bloody. She had done it! She healed faster than she could exsanguinate. *Alex! What type of monster have you been helping?* She pushed off the issues created by her monster side to when they'd be alone. More deep breaths. Almost showtime with their mystery employer.

As she pulled on thigh high socks and her lime-green penny loafers, Alex slipped back, but in increments. She had to laugh. "All clear of the girly zone." He joined her laughter. Everything was better with Alex to lean on.

She said, "Now I'm getting practice; emotions are easier to identify. I sense Katie and Quennie, and that Johnson guy. An entire herd is walking up the stairs. Four coming out of the elevator. Something's different about them. They may be carrying stuff. The same group is milling around across the street, and not happy. They're not mad, just not happy. Say, what day is this?"

"Saturday," Alex said. "Until we know who Mr. Johnson has briefed about us, there's only Sarah. We'll split duties. You need to be undistracted and responding corporally. I'll handle the sensing. Your oddly glowing person is about to knock. Wait for the knock."

A man slipped in, looking in both directions, with his right hand under his shirt. He wore newly torn jeans, a country-style sleeveless shirt, a spiked hair wig, and an attempt at metrosexual makeup.

She started then smothered a giggle. *"I'm sorry, he caught me by surprise. What's that all about?"*

"Protecting us, at least indirectly. He adjusted his clothes and hair to blend in."

After he checked the nooks in the efficiency, he waved everyone in. She gave him thumbs up and an encouraging smile.

He left, and five strangers walked in with Mr. Johnson and Katie. Last in was Quentin with a skinny kid. They carried an ice chest and bags of munchies. Nine in the room. The window AC would be overloaded if the day got hot.

Alex relaxed, giving her a warm go-ahead in the back of their mind. *"Flash our million-dollar smile and be the gracious hostess. Don't mention me. If I come up, Mr. Johnson should provide an adequate explanation for my absence. Or he's a total fool. This is the time to find out."*

"Good morning, I'm Sarah! Please, don't be strangers, spread out as you need. Be comfortable."

Mr. Johnson signaled. The four unpacked various lab and medical equipment onto the card table, the counter and floor. The room filled with screens, boops, and beeps, and wires. Lots of wires with no other function than to be attached to Sarah. One person left for extension cords.

She shot an emoting to Alex. He responded. *"I agree. Why didn't they escort us to a lab?"* Once again, she was filled with warmth that they worked on the same level.

The fifth, who came in with Quennie, returned with a hard case metal portfolio, diffidently sat on the couch and laid out various electronic gadgetry on their foldaway make-up vanity.

He held Alex's interest. *"The 'grad student' I saw at the porcupine van."*

"And the one who stands out in this herd as the nicest."

"Down girl. We aren't in the clear yet."

"Spoilsport. You're right. We need these people. I promise to be good, but you must promise to stay with me in case I'm inappropriate. No zoning out today."

"Never happen with Katie here." They both smiled, sharing muscles without pain.

Sarah was pleased with herself. She hadn't had a silliness spell since Shorty, oops, Mr. Johnson, and his crew banged on their door yesterday morning. Before Alex could catch the emotion, she pushed down thoughts of her suicide attempt.

She glanced at Katie. It bothered her she refused two offers for a chair. Alex detected her nervousness. *"Katie isn't relaxed, but she's also not on her guard. She's okay with what's happening."*

Mr. Johnson said, "We know this is abrupt, and we appreciate your flexibility. We don't have proper lab set-ups, but we want to take some baseline readings." He motioned to the grim shaggy-haired female lab tech. Sarah couldn't avoid comparing her to a collie needing a brush-out.

She relaxed. "How do we start?" The female lab tech, or maybe doctor, sat her on the far side of the table.

No—no—no. All those needles. She pushed the chair back. Katie moved forward as Sarah searched for the path, bathroom, or hall, with the fewest obstacles.

Catching her building panic, Alex said, *"Move over and as you say, chillax. I don't like needles either, but in the service, you get used to them."* He pulled them back to the card table and waved an okay.

Her retreat left her feeling guilty. Finally, she came forward, but not enough to see or feel the needles. She didn't want to, but they needed some partner-only time. Something had happened last night, the nightmare did mean something, and she was certain it had to do with her reaction to needles and her attempted suicide. He emoted an okay and stretched their arm while the tech patted it to find a juicy vein. Sarah decided that she'd had enough. Before the needle was inserted she bailed. To be fair to Alex, she remained aware of what was happening in case she was needed.

The four took turns swabbing, sticking, pumping, reading, and drawing more samples than Dracula. A dozen sensors were stuck to their body with wires running back to the bank of beepers and boopers on the kitchenette counter.

Questions, intrusive, nosy, detailed questions that never stopped, forcing her to be forward and active. The techs relieved each other, which got her—more questions. *"I need a break; can you talk to these people?"*

Alex emoted confidence to her. *"Sorry, I can handle the needles, but you're the only one who can answer personal questions. Also, if I slip in one of my grunts you hate, they might form the wrong opinion of you."*

Bogus. What she wanted was an excuse to tell them where to shove their ugly armored laptop.

The shaggy-haired woman tugged on long, blue nitrile gloves and grabbed a try of shiny instruments. "Into the bathroom, Missy, we need to take more samples." Orders! No bedside manner from her. She visually appealed to Katie, who opened the bathroom door. Alex chuckled. As she passed, she flashed Katie her "not happy with you" dagger look.

Alex disappeared at the first sample. *"Coward."*

Three hours of this later, all the readings, tests, and health history complete, Mr. Johnson had the techs pack and leave the equipment in the corridor where it was guarded. They came back in and checked for anything, including stains that might give away what had happened.

The four techs huddled with Mr. Johnson. After twenty minutes of hushed but intense discussion, he kept the tablet. As she exited, shaggy-hair woman glared at him.

After the rest leave, he radiated worried, as he sat at the table with Katie and them. They were the only ones in the room.

Sarah said, "*Alex.*"

He comes forward. "*I'm here.*"

"*Our new boss isn't doing happy.*"

Finally, Mr. Johnson said, "We still have dozens of tests left and will courier samples to the appropriate labs. With what we can field analyze, you're completely normal." Definitely not a happy face.

Katie, always with the killer question, asked. "Why is this such a disaster?"

With a start, Mr. Johnson said, "Oh, I'm sorry, please excuse my distraction. This is good news for you. I-we-had hoped for an early 'ah-ha' moment to point the way on how to understand you. As I stated the first time we met, you're a total mystery." He stared directly at us, ignoring Katie. "I'm assuming you're curious about how you exist?"

"Damn straight." Oops, that was Alex verbalizing. He blushed, and Sarah attempted to cover. Mr. Johnson's right eye twitched. He may have caught the switch in who was speaking. They needed to be more careful until they knew who was to be trusted.

"I can assure you have my complete attention on anything which may help us. You know what my personal agenda is." Sarah glanced at the skinny guy, who had returned to the apartment with Quentin, then back to Mr. Johnson, who shook his head. With Skinny potentially listening and not cleared by their boss, Sarah was stymied. She had many questions.

"And of course, Alex would be interested in the same results, so he can get on with his studies." Lame, and less than 10% of what she wanted to say. She wouldn't accept a salary for cooperation without some serious progress on releasing Alex from his stupid, loving sacrifice.

Another item she would negotiate—well demand—she wanted some quality time with Greasy. She'd call a couple of her Omaha cousins. They'd help Greasy see the light. She mentally shuddered. Where did *that* come from? She'd never been either violent or into retribution.

During the probing and poking, Skinny Guy with the yummy energy-color overlay had alternated between conferring with Mr. Johnson and Katie. With Katie, arguing would have been the better term. Katie clearly overpowered Skinny in both size and power of projection. Their argument extended to hallway conversations Sarah heard through the door. He didn't back down. Good for him. She wondered how many men or women could claim the same.

Skinny covered the card table with a large array of gadgets and explained what each did and didn't do. All monitored something. Some were audio, meaning she couldn't argue with Alex out loud anymore. Others sounded like a high school science fair booth, measuring things like static. Like from her hair?

She was about to cry-out for back-up when Alex assisted. *"I'm impressed. This overlaps with my training. I had no idea these sensors could be this small. Again, we're seeing a serious investment in us."*

Skinny finished with, "Our proposal is that we install everything here in the apartment. Your friend objects to these." He waved his hand over a third of the table. "I believe they're necessary for your safety. However, she's right. You'll have no privacy. She's agreed since it's your privacy, you should decide."

His eyes were a light tan with green flecks set in a longish face with a birthmark under the corner of the left eye. His mousy brown hair was carelessly combed to one side over the ear. He could use a haircut. The hair was long enough for a style to bring out his eyes. Full lips for a man, waiting for …

Alex interrupted. *"The man asked you a question. Quit staring at him as if you're contemplating kissing him."*

To Skinny she said, "Give me a moment." She was in over her head. Time to call in her soldier. "I've had another emotion-regression. We'll need to discuss why I regress and what to do about it. Right now, what do you think?"

"Katie is right, and your Skinny is right. They need a tiebreaker, you. Don't worry about me. Not having privacy is like active service. You're the one most battered and abused. Whatever you decide, we'll back you."

Her soldier thumbed-up the cute tech. The lab techs had as much personality as a sea slug. Even with her full intelligence back, a little flirt would loosen the tension that had been building all morning. "Well." With right index finger to lower lip, and a small half-smile on the left, she said sweetly, but shyly, "Well, I guess my answer depends on if you're a pervert."

Skinny Guy stammered and turned beet red. Definitely the shy type, he was now her "Shy Guy." Mr. Johnson gasped. Katie finally cracked a smile. Quennie dropped the plate he was washing, and Alex metaphysically rolled on the ground laughing.

"I guess that means you're not." That got a dark scowl from Katie, Sarah shrugged her shoulders to say, "in for a penny, in for a pound."

"One thing?" She caught Shy Guys" attention. Those eyes gaze directly into her eyes …

Alex mentally thwapped the back of their head.

"As you aren't a pervert, nothing in the bathroom. I don't need protection there. Agreed?" She emphasized the last word.

He looked to Mr. Johnson, who said, "Of course, sorry for any confusion. Bathroom sensors would add no security."

Alex said, *"We'll go over the sensors later. Did you capture them in your memory?"*

"Sure, but I may need to be separated for full retrieval."

"Good, we can wait. Most aren't security, but sensors across the entire electromagnetic range, radiation, electrostatic, and, I think, gravity. They're trying to discover what you and thus we are. Worse than a canary on display,

but it's for our benefit. Lots of people are puzzling over us, or at least our sensor readings."

She'd already guessed most of that. Alex was a mother hen. She picked up one sensor that would make a pretty ear dangler. Shy Guy blanched, so she placed it in his palm. "How long do you need us to be gone?"

"About an hour, two max, and you will never know they're here."

She had a lot to say to Alex and Katie. From his emoting and her glowering, they had a lot to say to Sarah, too.

Life is Good.

She was playing the compliant girl for only one reason: to get Greasy. If Alex was right about they're being a military group, they would schedule meetings. That's when she'd make her demands.

She could wait. Greasy was contained and hers.

38

IMPOSSIBLE

SARAH

On the way to lunch, to Sarah's delight, Katie insisted on using her car with all the bells, whistles, and lux upholstery. She luxuriated on the soft leather seats, no tears, and drew in that new-car-smell. Sarah loved the quirks of Chitty-Chitty-Bang-Bang, but she admitted that what it needed was a date with a car crusher.

The initial happiness with her ride over, she decided she'd had enough. Alex and Katie had issues. They could wait. She was the one getting prodded, poked, and stabbed with needles. "I've been the good girl, but I want answers. First, what do they really want?"

From the back seat, Quennie said, "I doubt the security people know. I chatted them up during the tour." Sweet Quennie, of course, he would. He'd be the only one non-threatening enough to get away with talking to guards.

Katie glanced over from the steering wheel. "It should be safe to talk here, but in the future, they'll probably wire the car. I would. Alex, with your training, you'd probably spot them. Don't touch them. We need the credibility of cooperating.

"We did get a few hints. While you swooned over the needles, the cheerless med tech exchanged glares with Mr. Johnson, and I caught a terse exchange of words. Mr. Johnson dropped a couple of hints as well. Best I can figure; you can't exist. The whole blending phenomenon was abandoned as impossible. They're mystified. A sentient shell freaks them out. A viable long-term host destroys their theories."

"So, what? I'm a freak. I don't need a ring of goons and walls full of geekware to remind me."

"That's the point. You're the ultimate impossibility. They need to understand you." Each of us took a moment to absorb this. She hesitated, and muscles moved on her face. A slight tremble threatened to affect the steering.

Alex said, "*Get ready, she's almost at a breakdown. We'll need to get her to pull over and hold her.*"

Her facial tics ceased, and her shoulder tremors calmed. She focused again on driving.

"*She's never come back without help before. That's amazing. Something's changed.*"

Katie finally exhaled a breath too long held. "In case you or others like you are a danger to National Security."

39

SLICING ALEX

ALEX: SUNDAY

She touches the blade of my paring knife, and says, "This'll do," and slices across our arm above the wrist. The warmth of the blood rolls down onto our wrist and fingers.

I pull back, "What the hell?"

She holds control and says, "Just watch."

Not able to slip past her control, I watch in horror. I can't even get in a gasp. Blood drips into the sink, and the burn from the cut nerves almost flash me back to Tikrit. Sweat forms on our forehead.

She says, "It's almost over, calm down." Utterly past the sanity threshold, she starts to grin. "Watch—what do you see?"

"What the hell? We're calling our emergency number and get some psych help."

"Pay attention. What do you see?"

The blood has slowed. No, it's *stopped*. We clot quickly. She washes the cut, revealing severed flesh and muscle. No blood. Curious, this is a deep cut. At my nudge, she brings it closer to our eyes. All along the surface of the cut, fleshy fibers flash and disappear, then stay in place. As we watch, the wound closes, becomes a white scar.

Then the scar vanishes.

She lets out a breath. "I had a clean dish towel ready if I was wrong. I'm positive I cut myself last night and climbed into a tub of warm water. When I woke up, the cuts weren't there. Look at the blood on our arm."

Bad memories surface from the insurgents' bullets shredding my face, shoulder and the kids' bodies, fighting my attempts to avoid hyper-ventilating. "Where'd it go?" If she wasn't controlling our body, things might start flying. Only my commitment to keep her under control prevents my outburst.

"Not certain. I tried this again this morning, using your razor blade, smaller cut while getting ready for our guests. It closed like this, and the blood disappeared except what had dripped on the bathroom vanity."

"Don't do that again!"

I've got to process this utter violation of our growing trust in each other. For now, we need to make plans. "You're exhausted, and I'm bummed out. We'll bring this up, high priority, at our first meeting tomorrow morning. I'll text Katie to give her a head's up we have something to report, and I'll pull her aside to tell her before the meet-ing." I compose the text and show it to Sarah. She's unhappy but quiescent. I want to call Katie, but that would violate standard Opsec.

We have a lot to sort out. Tomorrow.

The meadowlarks sing outside our window.

40

ON THE JOB

SARAH: DAY 10, 0511 AM

A large building, made from metal panels, appeared to Sarah, and it was inside another building. Inside the innermost room, he sat, alone. In front of a three-screen terminal, he typed something and watched the results. Lines connected on the middle screen. He designed a tube, octagon shaped. Curves moved, and numbers rolled off the left screen. The screens stopped, freezing the lines and numbers in place. He studied the results on the right monitor. His smile reflected in the left monitor.

He turned around and smiled at Sarah.

Alex: 0512 AM

"Sarah. Sarah. Do you need me?" Either a twitch or her saying something woke me.

"I think I had a nightmare. Strange. I haven't had a nightmare since this all started." She yawned and punched the pillow. "We're getting a decent bed."

She was asleep before I could ask another question.

Sarah: University Physics Annex 0930 AM

"Screw you. Ah held this in for over a week." The blended Sarah-Alex's forehead throbbed with each heartbeat. As she leaned over Mr. Johnson, her clenched fists prop them on the tabletop brought in with chairs for this, our first debriefing. "Now Ah'm with'n reach, and he's pay'n. Where is he? I want him now." Sarah screeched and didn't care. Besides, the closet where Mr. Johnson had brought them stunk of something she didn't want to hang around to identify.

"Sarah, calm down." Alex calmed.

Instead of her expected reaction, Katie exuded calm, and support. Alex was right, Katie had passed some emotional threshold. This wasn't the same person who had scared the blank out of her.

Mr. Johnson wiped his forehead. "He's not available." His energy overlay had a tinge she suspected was fear. His eyes pleaded with Katie. She scooted closer to place a comforting hand on Sarah's shoulder. She was her friend. Sarah sat down.

She knew they were contractors. Sticking it to the man wasn't good behavior, but she didn't care. The security people, never less than four around her 24/7, pressed in on her. Even those out of sight distracted her. Hours of humiliating med tests; they had even taken her earwax. Her earwax! Why would they need her earwax?

It was time Sarah got hers. First up, Greasy needed some bare-knuckle justice for what he'd done to her, and even more for what was happening to Alex. He didn't deserve to be stuck sixteen hours a day as a female. "Wrong answer. Either bring him here or take me to him. Roll me up and toss me into whatever room he's in. In five minutes, he'll confess to everything his sliminess has ever done, including stealing candy in preschool."

Alex failed again to gain the upper hand. She ignored Katie's non-verbal signals. Unless she missed her guess, it was a demand for Alex to control her.

"As much as that would be justice, I can't." Mr. Johnson rotated his hand, palm up. "Friday, while we located you, another agency swept him up before I stop them. I've attempted to contact them. I'm sorry, but my hands are beyond tied." Mr. Johnson's manner cleared during his confession of inadequacy. "He was part of the hijacking of the project to create a means to change people's identity. Totally unauthorized and it caused half of the deaths. We want him badly. He disappeared with lab records and destroyed the backup drives."

Sarah slid back into her seat. "I need a moment." As much as screaming might bring satisfaction, with the new information, she believed her soldier had a better grip on what was happening here.

She'd thought the excitement of the past two days interfered with her sensing Greasy. It never occurred to her he had disappeared. *Someday Greasy, we'll meet.*

She consulted Alex. *"I'm struggling with my overreactions, but shouldn't we be offered more details, like who has Greasy, what is being done to get us to him, that stuff?"*

"I agree but remember we're only on day three of our contract. They've gone to a lot of effort and expense to make this work for us. Their security is impressive in how inconspicuous it is. Once we've built credibility, we can ask. I won't let this go."

"Okay, I believe you. Now, I have a development to report." Katie twitched. She and Alex had argued about this. She wanted to withhold it until she was more comfortable with their mystery agency. Sarah agreed, but Alex's ethics won out. It would be trial for Sarah to be tied to a perpetual Boy Scout. At least he didn't know that her first cutting hadn't been an accident but a real suicide attempt.

Following Alex's instructions on proper decorum, she straightened in the chair and squared her shoulders. "We have blazingly fast healing. I accidentally cut myself Saturday night and healed before I could stop the blood flow. Yesterday, with Alex watching, I tried it again." She held up her arm with the wrist facing Mr. Johnson. "Here is where I did it less than twelve hours ago. There isn't even a scar."

"I would appreciate it if you don't intentionally wound yourself again." His eyes harden. "If your healing becomes important, we'll come up with a safe test protocol."

After a quiet moment, he asked, "Mr. Monroe. What did you have to do with this?"

"Nothing sir. She caught me by surprise. Whoever is forward can block the partner from interfering."

"I'm sorry to push on this, but are you certain this doesn't have anything to do with your medical history?"

Alex said, "Positive sir. You don't have to hint around. Katie and Sarah know about my dicey mental issues. I'd rather you don't spread it around to others though."

"There will be one other. We've gained a medical researcher. We'll introduce you. Anything else you want to mention?"

"May I ask for a favor?" She concentrated on sweetness, but she was still worked up over Greasy, and her freakiness.

Mr. Johnson leaned back in his chair. "Okay."

"When you're addressing us, say 'Sarah Beth.' That's who we are most of the time. I can't do anything when I'm separated other than lie around looking disgusting. Please tell everyone we insist on being called Sarah Beth. When you want just me, the girl still in here some-where, say Sarah." She needed this team, so it was time for some fence mending. "Of course, Alex doesn't have identity issues." Alex groaned in the background, and Katie's eyebrows jumped. So much for her attempted levity.

"*That's not completely true.*" Alex was right. He was also forgetting he couldn't come out of the closet without putting himself and all descendants of his Babushka under the control of this two-headed covert operation. Someone could tumble on to the notion of others of the clan having been trained or the possibility of a gene-linked talent.

"*Hush. Quit being a Boy Scout. First, we needed some way to tell if they were addressing us or me. Second, this protects you and your family. We'll always maintain you're only the core strengthening me. If this party boat springs a leak, you walk away."*

"Excellent suggestion. Everyone will comply," Mr. Johnson said.

He then launched into a mind-withering string of administrivia. After a minute, she gave up. *"Alex, do you follow this?"*

"Sure, standard OpSec, and C and C. Sorry, Operational Security, and Command and Control. Why?"

"It's boring, you follow. Tell me what I need to know when it's over. I'm searching for Greasy."

Alex said, *"Promise me you'll stay within your safe limit. Since it's only Mr. Johnson and Katie, I'll let him know it's mostly me."*

She emoted compliance. Freed up, she surfed with her senses. First a quick scan out to her known safe limit. Rats. No Greasy. *Why couldn't secret-agency-number-two lease an annex within city limits?* She'd work with Alex to expand the combined safe limit. They couldn't risk slipping into their other state again. It was too difficult to gather the forcefulness to leave.

With nothing to report, she soon became bored with watching students. She came forward in their consciousness. Good timing, Mr. Johnson appeared to be finishing.

She'd decided to disclose her nightmares. She was putting Alex under too much pressure with her issues. They now had an extended team, and this was a good way to show that she was ready to trust them.

To a point.

"I don't know how to say this, and Alex, I'm sorry I haven't mentioned this before." Katie pulled up her chair and Mr. Johnson's expression bunched. "I haven't discussed this with Alex. He's been on my case to discuss my nightmares, but they didn't seem important. Now, I'm not as certain." She hoped that covered Alex's credibility.

Mr. Johnson brought out a tablet; touched a screen open. "Nightmares? I would like to record this."

She said, "No issue with me." Alex emoted concurrence and curiosity. This would be the first time he'd heard the details. "I've had the nightmares since the beginning, but they haven't been clear enough for me to understand and remember. They all involve my attacker doing things in a lab. Sometimes in front of some type of design software; other times it's not as clear. In the end, every time, he turns and smiles directly at me. "

She paused.

"I think he's trying to contact me."

41

UNTESTABLE

Reading people from inside a sealed box in the Psych Lab was a crushing bore. She'd thought sensing people walking by would be fun. Instead, it was like counting sheep. Worse than counting sheep. She'd counted her Uncle Hergenreder's flocks without falling asleep.

At least Katie refused to stay away and was their constant companion in the hothouse of a room. Actually, it was a used twenty-foot steel shipping container, complete with dents and large swaths of rust. The interior was not much better. Only an exhaust fan concealed in the ceiling provided circulation. The doors sealed from the outside. Unable to predict what she'd have to do, she brought along a change of clothes in Alex's ever-present satchel. Even then, in this box, she wanted to pull her shirt off and her shorts stuck to her thighs. Katie never complained, never varied from her long-sleeved shirt and long slacks. If this was boring to Sarah, Katie had to be leaking patience by the bucket. Sarah would check with Quentin on what she could do to thank her.

Alex emoted encouragement. *"I can do this. I've gotten the same scores as you for over an hour."* He couldn't hide his excitement at this new ability.

"Oh, thank you. But remember, stick to a monotone. Not even Katie can know about your Matryoschka curse." Katie remained the uptight straight-shooter. No point in telling her and then asking her to not report it. To her, that would be lying. She'd taken on everything she could for them that didn't require their direct participation. Like this test gone soporific.

"Gift, it's a gift. Give the restart and fade back, I can handle this."

The promise to let them attend classes had turned out to be easier to fulfill than anyone had thought. The project invested multiple hours, evident from the wires dangling in this box, designing and assembling each test. Sarah Beth finished each test in less than half the allocated time.

Tedious, yes, but this dreary experiment could work. Mr. Johnson had spread some ad hoc grants to the Psych department. Volunteers filled out a seventy-page online psych questionnaire. When finished, the volunteers printed a voucher for payment.

The real test was when the volunteers walked to where they were paid. Each passed the soundproofed shipping container, and Sarah Beth recorded subjective suitability rating as a host from zero to ten. Ten was her dearest Alex. Their rating and their psych factors were real-time correlated. The study should break the lock on the puzzle box of how her senses differentiated people. Life was good.

The volunteers finished for the day and security opened the container. They needed better ventilation. Katie took them by the arm for the next test.

Katie followed orders. Alex followed orders. Sarah only followed orders that made sense to her.

"No, I'm going to the briefing. There." She pointed with their free arm. "Along with everyone else." Coop her up in a box for hours, and she wanted to know what happened. Alex didn't interfere.

Judging by her puckered expression, and the way she tapped her man-sized military wristwatch, Katie was exasperated. She gestured to the guards, and they followed the crowded. They got Katie's stare and raised eyebrow that signaled, *I'll talk to you later, Alex.* Alex always caught it from Katie when Sarah didn't toe whatever line she chose to ignore. He remained loyal and supportive.

The meeting had already started.

"This is puzzling. The survey form correlates more than eighty factors." The team leader's eyebrows furrowed like a crawling caterpillar. She was average sized, wearing an off-white fitted shirt and narrow navy-blue tie in the current fashion under her lab coat. Sarah had thought only scientists in old movies wore ties and dress shirts.

Pursing her lips, she continued. "Excluding the five percent who faked their answers, the psych factor correlations are better than most studies. However, we find no correlation between any of the factors and Sarah Beth's compatibility readings."

She wasn't positive what the chief researcher had said, but she worried she had sunk four hours into nothing.

Only three techs were cleared to know the data from the box was merely Sarah Beth touching numbers from 1 to 10 on a pad. This was the reading they had failed to correlate to their most detailed psyche questionnaire. No psyche factors correlated with the "suitability to blend." No one managing the test knew what the numbers meant.

The frowns and disgruntled demeanor emanating from the three cleared techs confirmed it. They doubted the sensing phenomena. Sarah was afraid this one item would ruin their credibility. She'd lose the research muscle to fix her and release Alex from his idiotic promise to her.

She was late to the next test. They hadn't scheduled for Sarah's recalcitrance and demand to sit in on debriefings. They'd have to learn she wasn't a pigeon waiting for food to drop in response to ringing a bell. She clung to being a human and demanded all the respect of being a human.

42

DOCTOR STRINGY HAIR

SARAH, UNIVERSITY HOSPITAL, RADIOLOGY DEPARTMENT

O h, no. It was an MRI. She couldn't stand confinement. Stringy Hair, the lead med tech from Saturday, barked orders. "Follow the tech and change into a gown." She still looks like a collie that needs a brush out.

"Please tell me I'm not the plugin for that orifice." She was answered with a don't-sass-me stare. "Well, for how long?"

"About three hours. The orders are to scan for everything and anything. Taking enough image slices takes time."

Her gut in knots, Sarah sweated like she'd just finished a major work-out. She thought, "I can't. I can't. I can't." Little-snot Denise had locked her in a root cellar, and no one had found her for a day. To hide her weakened knees, she pulled on an open drawer of a medical cart. The cart tipped towards her.

Alex nudged the back of her mind and stiffened their knees. *"Chillax. I can take this. I did this many times during recovery. I'll sleep through the banging and buzzing. They'll hear snoring. Drop out and do the surfing you do when you should be paying attention."*

"Stinky."

"*Snot.*" Alex projected a rolling-eyes image.

They were acting like siblings? She happily started a new surfing trick. She divided the area into quadrants and did a systematic evaluation. She pushed each result to her newfound perfect memory. The failed psych test had given her ideas. She'd look up how correlations work, and do her own analysis, but on groupings of people. Something from her youth nudged a memory, just beyond her grasp ... she should be examining groupings, not individuals.

She felt a buzzing. It had to be Alex. "*Yes?*"

"*Glad that worked. I never tried to reach you when you weren't forward. I'm uncomfortable.*"

Bogus. He was gloomy again. A tease was in order. She interrupted him, "*I stopped wearing sexy undies. I'm wearing cotton.*"

She felt mirth, followed by annoyance. "*Stop deflecting the topic. I'm uncomfortable about staying in the closet about my Matryoschka abilities to sense people up to a half-block away.*"

"*What did I tell you about your Boy Scout attitude? Let's go over this again. You probably inherited your talent from your Babushka. She trained you to take her place up to the day she died. Your abilities didn't manifest until I swallowed you whole and tormented you for a week.*"

"*Which is why we should tell Mr. Johnson and his team.*"

"*Why'd I pick a stupid host? No, don't say it. My way, we gain heavy research muscle to rescue us from this mess. If this doesn't work out, I'm stuck in the gilded cage no matter who holds the key. You walk away as the innocent bystander who saw the accident but was never involved. Remember, this is a two-headed dog we're riding. The visible doggy head smiles. Ever wonder what the other head looks like?*"

"*Girl, your dark side is showing.*"

"*Thank you. Now, remember it.*"

He projected an image of folding his arms. "*I signed up for the duration.*"

"You're a bra size, double-D. Dense, and in denial. You helped a damsel in distress. You had no concept what was involved. Also, why are you so callous about your family? The other descendants of your Babushka, what about them? What if our two-headed dog, or a bigger dog that eats our friendly one, listens to you and decides to get into the undetectable new-person business? I think some form of shock or torture is needed to force latent abilities. What about your Babushka's descendants? All seventy-five? Why expose all your family to our bosses?"

Only the need to remain still in the MRI kept him from his "unhappy dance," where he rolled from side to side on the balls of his feet. *"What about you? I'm afraid to fall asleep before you for fear what your father did to you will activate another suicide attempt. Why aren't you disclosing that?"*

That hurt. One suicide attempt and he wouldn't stop yammering. Bogus, she was getting another silliness attack. She pushed back and forced her mind into serious-mode. Satisfied, she responded, *"I promised you if that happens, I'll wake you. Plus, I'm not certain the experiments in my Daddy's company's basement aren't a false memory. I'm not siccing anyone on my family until I know for sure."*

Then, before he could recover, she asks, *"Anything else? Otherwise, we have time to discuss my instability."* He confirms interest. *"I know you have drop-outs, but they are momentary and don't affect what you do. Mine can last for minutes, and I act as if I'm some giggly High School airhead. I'm at my wit's end. Will I ever get over the effects of the attack? How do I handle this?"*

Alex didn't answer. That was a good sign. It meant—he was thinking. She waited him out but withdrew from hearing as the MRI's sledge-hammer chorus gave her a headache. He smiled at her move. *"So far, it's only been embarrassing. Let's give it to the end of the week. If we can't keep you stable, I'd like to talk to Katie first then approach the project lead on getting help. If your flirting and other obsessions grow, then we hit the panic button."*

She emoted assent and withdrew to check out the neighborhood. There were fascinating clusters, and she took her time studying them. How people clustered fascinated her, and she looked for the cause. After she finished, she dropped back to check on Alex.

Something was happening. They were being manhandled.

"I'm not an invalid." She stood up and fell into Katie's hands.

Alex chortled in the background. *"If you left me in control, we wouldn't be embarrassed. You lose coordination lying too long in one position."*

"Stinky."

"Snot."

The scent of burnt beef grease overlaid the antiseptics used here. Hamburgers? That couldn't be right. They were in a sanitized lab.

Quennie stuck his head in from the hall. "If you're finished stumbling around, you can eat." Quennie. Sweet Quennie. He had brought burgers with all the fix'ns, fries, and salads. "Mr. Johnson called and suggested as you'd be working late, a break would help everyone. I cooked everything myself."

Sarah learned something new. When she surfed farther out, she missed local stuff. She had missed the arrival of Mr. Johnson and the change of the security team. Someone new, a woman, was with them. The new woman was interesting. Sarah wondered if 'they'd meet.

Stringy Hair, a new tech, male, and Mr. Johnson frowned their way past the movable feast. Quennie stepped in front of them. "Now what would Mom think if people walked away from my cooking?" Sarah's mouth dropped. He could charm a rattler in mid-strike. His shallowness was only show. They stopped and collected plates of food.

Over burgers, Stringy Hair, the med tech, and Mr. Johnson watch the thousands of MRI views. From this angle, the four friends saw the clashing colors of a confusing movie.

Alex bit into the burger and wiped their chin. *"Catch the argument in the viewing room?"*

"Good or bad for us?"

"They aren't looking at us. It's not us but something esoteric. The tech's losing."

Stringy Hair dismissed the tech. He slammed both the observation room and the hall doors as he left.

She pulled four chairs to the table and motioned Sarah Beth and Katie to sit. Alex attempted a Sarah mimic. "One more chair. Quentin's my friend. I don't keep anything from him."

Mr. Johnson looked at Katie, then Stringy Hair. He got no assistance. Turning face to face with Quennie, he asked, "If you join this, do you agree to the same security monitoring and movement limitations."

Quennie bounced on his toes and wetted his lips. "Will the discussion be weird?"

Johnson stiffened, and his jaw dropped, "Yes, you could say that."

Quennie pulled up a stool. "I'm in. For the sake of security, the cute guard outside can sleep with me." He caught Katie's glare. "Okay, even the ugly gorilla, I'm not going to miss anything weird." He winked at Sarah. Alex winked back for them. Sarah let it pass that she never learned how to wink.

Once everyone was seated, Johnson prompted, "I should introduce you to our medical lead. This is Doctor Timsen. The man with the great hamburgers is Quentin Kahn, next to me is Katie Jo Parker, and across from you is Sarah Beth. Well, Doctor Timsen, what are your findings?"

Doctor Timsen said, "Preliminary findings; we'll be reviewing the scans in detail for weeks. Sarah Beth is a textbook example of an athletic eighteen-year-old. No breaks, no fractures, perfect dentition."

Sarah interrupted. "Dentition?"

"Your teeth." Doctor Timsen slipped in a half-smile and continued. "All internal organs are normal. Absolutely no evidence of a subcutaneous interface. All organs are female. There is no Alex."

"What?" Alex jumped us out of the chair and backed us to the door.

"Timsen isn't on the "need the know" list. We need to get out of here." Katie joined them, slipping her hand into her briefcase. Quennie froze on his stool, too stunned to move.

"Wait! I can explain." Mr. Johnson pleaded.

Sarah tried to grin and sat down. Trusting their preternatural senses, Katie also sat, though her left-hand remained in her briefcase.

"I need an XO to help me on this. I'm out of experience working in non-adversarial situations." He looked straight at Katie, and his face smoothed. He'd made a decision. "Ms. Parker, I've contacted your previous military superiors. If you accept it, I would like you to re-enlist and be my second in command, my XO." He flashed a rare grin. "That way I don't have to demand you turn in your gun."

Katie's forehead furrowed, and she turned to us, "How does that work for you?"

Alex answered for us, "I think it is a great idea. You have the background, and it's obvious the staff respects you. A bonus is Sarah will listen to you more than me."

"Hey!" Sarah's outburst set off laughter in the room.

Johnson said, "Now I've filled the hole in my project, I'd like to answer your concern. Doctor Timsen is an old friend. Post doc in physics, and a diplomat of the Gynecology Board of the AMA. I know, an odd combination. She'll explain over a beer. She works at NASA. This year she escaped to the university on a rotation fellowship."

Sarah felt dumb, she didn't understand. What did a Physics Ph.D./Gynecologist do during office hours? And what was an XO? *"Alex?"*

"An Executive Officer, the second in command who handles the scut work. Did I anticipate your question?" Again, she was warmed by their ability to know each other's unstated needs.

Doctor Timsen interrupted and held Johnson's hand. "Over the past year, Sammy here tantalized my grad assistant with a succession of grisly pieces of blood-soaked human flesh. The blood DNA never matched the skin. We were stumped."

Johnson winced visibly at the use of his nickname.

Doctor Timsen's love came through clearly. It was rare when Sarah sensed people's emotions without first dropping away from her physical senses. Love. Deeper, stronger than any she'd ever sensed. She was in love with Johnson, had been for decades. Sarah filed that away for later.

"I was about to turn his ass over to—can't tell you whom—when he called me last Friday night, requesting I fetch my best med techs to an apartment first thing in the morning. He wanted me to cancel the first outing of a golf foursome that took months to arrange. But I could never turn down cloak-and-dagger Sammy."

Alex was impatient. "And how does that get us here?" Sarah was fascinated with their relationship, but this was Alex's existential issue. Where was his body?

"Last Saturday, the tests we performed on you pointed to something dangerous. Sorry, but that was my conclusion. I cornered Sammy, with a threat to go up the chain. He cleared me into your project." She stood. With a wide grin, she hugged Sarah Beth. "I can't tell you how much the two of you mean to me. Yes, I saw the video of your separations. In NASA, the most excitement I'd had was treating measles on a shuttle payload specialist." She hugged them harder.

"You're grinning like Quennie does, like a loon." Alex emoted both relief and liking for Doctor Timsen.

"Oh, hush. You know I love hugs." She emanated joy onto Alex. She felt his annoyance for the violation of his emotional control. *"Oh, sorry. It got away from me. Forgive me."*

Johnson asked, "Satisfied?" to Katie. She closed her briefcase and dropped it to the floor in response. Johnson continued, "This is the confirmation of what we suspected. Alex, you keep your consciousness, memory, emotions, intellect, and the full ability to control the

Sarah Beth body. You don't lose your body because it's always there when you separate. We're clueless why it doesn't show up in tests. The sensors in your apartment and during your blend/deblend exercises should help our analysis. We're also setting up time on brain scan equipment."

It was Sarah's turn. She'd avoided the question out of respect for Alex, but she had to know. "What about me? Do I still have all my female parts?"

Linda said, "Why yes, and you're fertile. The blending apparently interrupts the hormone cycle, which is why we found no menses indications."

Johnson prompted, "Linda, tell her about healing."

Doc Timsen stopped, studying our changing facial expressions. "Sarah, we suspected, but the MRIs prove it. Sarah, the injuries in your school and medical records aren't just healed—they disappeared. No scars, no weak points. It's as though they never existed."

AS THEY WALKED out to Katie's car, Sarah asked, "Where do I buy a six-pack of the Hessian pig spit you and Alex like?"

"There's a specialty store in Idaho. Why?"

"I think this is a six-pack night. Idaho is too far away. Alex needs to start soon."

"Girlfriend, I can handle this." She fast dialed. "Quennie, do you still have Alex's apartment keys? Great. Take the two six-packs of Alex's and my brew to his apartment. Let's see, they're warm so take the ice from our fridge, and set up the beer in his sink. I'll meet you there."

"You and Quennie aren't invited."

She scrunched her face and tapped the steering wheel. "I'm preprogrammed as "2" on Alex's phone. Anytime, no excuses. Got me?" Flashes flared behind her irises.

"Thank you. This has to be a private discussion." Sarah couldn't tell Katie that her best bud had curled in a fetal position in the back of their mind. This was what she'd been afraid of, Alex giving up.

He'd signed the check and was heading for the door.

43

FOUR PIG SPITS

SARAH, AT THEIR APARTMENT

S arah kissed Katie on the cheek before she could pull back and hopped out. She spotted Quennie exit the stairwell, but didn't attempt to get his attention as she pushed the elevator call button.

"*Alex, we're home.*" No response. It was her third try since the lab. She did some slow breathing in the elevator to keep her panic from adding to his issues.

Inside the apartment, she slipped the frozen pizza out of its box and into the oven.

"*Is pizza okay? It's kinda late for real cooking.*" Still no response. She dumped her clothes on the way to the bathroom for a quick shower. After drying off, and she patted on the lilac-scented powder he liked. For the first time since the start of their partnership, the shower didn't center her.

"Should we discuss your concerns about your family?" No response.

She slipped on Alex's PJs, in case they needed Alex to be in his body. She sighed, pulled the long neck out of the ice, popped the top and took a long swig. Uhng, pig spit.

"Quennie brought over your fave Hessian brew. At this rate, I'll finish the six pack in an hour." Nothing. She'd hoped going verbal would help.

The oven timer's *ding* announced the pizza was ready. Beer and pizza, his idea of a balanced meal. This had to work.

She tried again, "I'd pour out this Hessian pig spit out the window, but I might be fined for killing the bushes. Also, it's the only thing that will kill the taste of the Rex Max pizza." She wolfed down a slice, Alex style.

"Hey. Treat it with respect. You know how much it costs? Move over. I'll show you how to enjoy beer and pizza."

She held back her tears. She thought she'd lost him. She was the one with the existential crisis, but he was the one who could disappear.

After consuming half the pizza and four pig spits, Alex whimpered into the bottle. "I don't exist. I'm a figment of your imagination."

She reached back as far as she could and swung. Damn, that hurt.

Rubbing their cheek, and picking up the spilled bottle, he asked, "What's the slap about?"

"Well, asshole, the slap is because I can't shock you to your senses with a kiss."

"Would've preferred the kiss."

"That's more like it. Before you get too drunk to talk, would you prefer to separate?"

Alex thought for a moment. "No, I had enough phenomenology philosophy to know I either exist or I don't. Blended or in the flesh. How do I know I exist?"

Sarah reached back again, this time with her right, and formed a fist.

"No, hear me out. I could be a fevered image you got from some bad food you bought the first day you arrived. You never were attacked.

You're in bed in your nice apartment wrestling with your senses. I may be 'an undigested bit of beef, a blot of mustard, a crumb of cheese, a fragment of an underdone potato. There's more of gravy than of grave' about me, and that is what's been disrupting your dreams."

"Yeah, and I'm the butterfly, dreaming I'm a geisha, dreaming I'm a butterfly. This gets us nowhere. Where's your phone?"

"End pocket of the satchel, why?"

"Because we're getting guests."

I touch 2 on his phone. "Katie, code whatever, come over."

44

NORMAL PEOPLE

SARAH: DAY 12, WEDNESDAY, 6 AM

Sleeping Beauty awakened, an hour early. Sigh. At least she got in her daily call with her mother before he could listen and interject with his 'helpful' suggestions. He should be calling his own parents. She was away from home, her friends, her cousins, and her mother. At least half of her extended family had disappeared as if they'd never existed. She pulled up her courage to fight Alex, if need be, to interact with the world. People, lots of people, centered her. Why did he act like a monk in lock-down?

Alex started his normal yawn. "Why are we doing makeup?"

"Are we a butterfly or a geisha this morning?"

"Judging by the makeup…" He wiped the steam off the bedroom mirror. With all the windows sealed, the A/C couldn't keep up with the shower's steam. A small price to pay; showers also centered her, though they also reminded her of how she wasn't the old her. She'd never luxuriated in showers before.

"Get serious. The make-up jokes are getting old. Okay, the first few days were over the top, but I had issues with being real. More importantly, are you okay with Sarah Beth again?"

Alex scratched their nonexistent beard. "Guess so. When did Katie and Quentin leave?"

His morning rituals slowed her down because she had to drop control to let him do them. She didn't object to his rituals, she needed Alex balanced. But it seemed each day he was less stable, and the bad periods extended longer each day. If she didn't keep him engaged as Sarah Beth, he riffed into Alex-gloom.

"About an hour after you asked to blend for quality rest. You fell asleep before we finished blending. You were rude. I brewed coffee and talked until I convinced them you were copasetic."

"Fine. Do I have to ask again about the make-up?"

"I'm late getting ready for work, honey. So please stay back and let me finish. This requires a light touch; I don't want to look like you applied it." She hoped the tease would wake him. When she had time to shop, she needed a different foundation. Her complexion was darker than when she left home, another affect of her dual existence.

"You don't have a job."

"Wrong. *You* don't have a job."

"Sure, I do. There's the drudge drag at LDOs."

"No, you don't, you quit your job four days ago."

"I'm certain I'd remember quitting a job I hated."

"Sorry, sweetie, the day after our contract negotiations with our two-headed agency, your LDO boss called to ask about your absences. I passed your apologies and said you quit."

"Huh? It's too early to be funny."

"Okay, I'll be serious. You hate the job. I love this type of work. It's finally some way I can contribute without being merely the parasite cleaning the apartment. I applied right then for the job, said I was your cuter, younger cousin, eighteen years old, with four years of retail experience. Corporate personnel still lists me as an employee, and today's my first day."

More morning rituals. He ran our tongue over their teeth and examined their eyes. "Uh, ah, wait a minute. You had a retail job at fourteen? Isn't that illegal? What about…"

"If you suggest that I earned my money babysitting little snots I'll slap both of us. Boys get away with lots of under the table employment."

"I guess you aren't kidding. I hated that job's soul-sucking tedium. With our new contracts, I would've quit anyway. Next time don't do that. I'm a responsible adult. I'll handle my own exits." Next, he rounded, then straightened their shoulders three times, and twisted their back to pop a couple of vertebrae. It never worked.

She sensed a quick shift in emotion. He concentrated on their image. "This isn't you. Did Katie put you up to this?"

"Seriously, you never knew who I was. You're my macho Army guy, and I love you for it. You keep me alive. During our dinner the first night, I told Katie about my retail jobs. She pointed out how you hated your job, besides retail is a safe way to meet people."

"I thought…"

"What? That I'm a wilted daisy? Except for Quennie, the rest of you are too wound up for me to talk to. Even the two nice guards from the first day were always distracted. I love being with people. I need normal people."

"What about classes?"

"I worked it out Mr. Moore, your LDO boss. We've scheduled around classes. I love French Medieval Romance Literature."

"This may work. I could use the time for the abstractions on the math tensors. I'm way behind the others in the class. Wait a minute, how are you going to get there? This will drive security nuts."

She practiced her wink. Quennie winked best. She'd asked him to tutor her. "I'm not taking your car. Too expensive and takes too long to find a decent parking spot. Plus, you waste time and money feeding the meter. Did you know the bus stops on this block?"

"No, never checked. What about strangers? This will drive security nuts." He progressed to checking their teeth.

"A public bus is safer than driving. When was the last time you heard about a jacked bus half-full of passengers? Okay, outside of idiotic, illogical movies. Who would dare with veterans all over campus? Anyway, Monday, I called 'Mr. Johnson's magic number.' A delightful guy answered and wrote down the bus schedule. I'm willing to bet I'll hook a cute hunk on the bus."

"Fine, whatever." She let his glower through, even though it, like, totally screwed with her makeup prep. He wasn't taking the tease well.

White noise. Alex dropped out like a light switched off. This was another Alex-slump day. She feared not forcing him to keep the retail job was a dumb idea. She had to get him off that depressing Spinoza.

Oops. They'd had the entire discussion verbally, with the bathroom door open. Hopefully, the mics hadn't picked them up.

On the plus side, she seized this opportunity to get back to normal. Even without her, uh, singular existence, she was at college, away from everything familiar. A part-time job gave her a smidgen of something familiar to hang on to, even if it was only folding clothes dropped in and around the dressing room by an entitled brat continually affirmed they were special.

Alex remained aware but not responding to her prods to get him to talk. She hesitated at their door but went through when she didn't sense any objection. Outside, their apartment building sported a recently steam-cleaned white brick exterior. The steps were safety striped, and the handrails leaned inward with pipes painted easy-grip yellow for the perpetually inattentive. The parking lot striping included blue for handicapped, and red for electric cars. Even the gravel lot had been raked smooth. The rose bush competed with the Rose of Sharon and the Butterfly Bush for the most butterflies. It was like her great-great-grandmother's garden. Her house had the shotgun room-style layout. She pushed back the giggle. You could shoot a shotgun through the front door, and the slug would pass through all the rooms and before it exited the back door. She hadn't thought about her for, like forever. What was her name? Great-Great-Grandmother had been was more than a little 'off,' always playing with wooden Russian nesting dolls and muttering to herself. Other than the image of the garden, why couldn't she remember the house or where it had been?

For that matter, why hadn't she noticed before how pretty this neighborhood was?

Captain Obvious calls. Because every other time she had been out, she was scared down to the ends of her painted toenails.

Even the grass between the sidewalk and the street curb was mowed and cleanly edged. Fall-blooming flowers, she wasn't certain which ones, pushed toward the sun, ready to pop their blooms.

With each step from the apartment, Alex's tension grew. She wished Alex could take a step back and just enjoy.

Being miffed about not being chauffeured couldn't damper her raw joy. Katie explained to Sarah that using security to drive her around would draw attention. She hadn't considered taxis, or the new call-a-ride services as they were too expensive, but apparently, they created even bigger security issues. She now saw why Alex deferred to Katie. Her MP background may stifle, but it was also like a warm blanket against the chill of their situation.

45

GRAVITON

KATIE: SECURED PROJECT HQ. 1300 PM

N ano-autoreflectors opaqued the windows; the only illumination were the light cones recessed into the ceiling, one per seated position. With the rest of the room darkened, the only indication others were present was the occasional *thnnng* sound made by the chair's torsion bar when its occupant moved.

Carla, emaciated as a supermodel, exuded both competence and seductiveness, used her interpersonal skills to the max. She finished her detailed briefing on the project code-name "Graviton" including time-sequenced topological maps and the "blinking magnetic monopole." Graviton remained the only known source of magnetic monopoles. The blinking was shorthand for the monopoles switching polarity between north and south.

When motionless, Graviton was undetectable. In motion, it created a gravitational distortion more than twice that of the moon. A couple of water fountains sloshed over during one extended separation where Alex was moved from lab to lab. Occasionally, with no known correlation, a directed plume of magnetic monopoles appeared orthogonal to the direction of travel.

"Thank you." Mr. Johnson said and waited. Carla held for a few moments then acquiesced to the dismissal. The tap, tap, tap of her four-inch heels receded through the door which opened on her approach, then closed behind her. Only Katie caught the micro-expression of Carla's anger at being dismissed. Katie, as the only other woman in the briefing, was not even a consideration for Carla, thus the slip. Being discounted by potential adversaries had saved Katie more than once. She had schooled her body posture to emulate boredom.

Doctor Timsen had given her report, depressing as always, about how the male-Alex showed no illness or organic distress but was clearly dying.

Left in the room was the head of the Physics Department, Stan, Mr. Johnson, Katie, and their resident spook in the corner. Apart from the Johnson, no one knew his name, or even how he managed to get into the darkest corner without being seen first. He said, "Fire her."

Steve said, "But she's the best in the university. No one outside even knows enough about this type of phenomena or the predecessor's lab work to step in."

"She's trouble. Right now, she's bedding five on the project, three males, and two females. This isn't libido, but a campaign to get something." Something the men missed, at least on the conscious level, was who wears heels in a lab? Katie at times wondered if the woman slept in heels. Carla even curled her eyelashes for work.

Johnson said, "Keep watching her movements. I can't afford to lose more researchers. The Graviton phenomena has already cost us four resignations." He glanced over at Katie.

Katie stepped to the projection of the ceiling to floor display. "This confirms what we already suspected. Whenever the Subject Two," She understood but giving everyone a code name rankled her first-name-only upbringing in the hood: Alex was Subject Two. Sarah was Subject One. "Moved from intimate association with Subject One, at exactly twenty-one minutes, thirty-seven seconds, nineteen milliseconds, Subject One becomes Graviton. It followed Subject Two, changing trajectory to match the subject's position every eleven seconds."

Placing a map in the middle panel, she continued. "This is the most problematic, at least to me as a layman. It slid through all obstructions, without slowing or affecting the material. In this plot, you see how it traversed the radiation sensor calibration pile. That's two walls of three feet of lead shielding bricks, a cobalt test sample, and of course, the radiation shielding to protect the personnel. There no was affect on it or what it passed through, even people.

She brought up the second set of plots. "This is the one that has security most concerned." A hush and a lack of chair noise punctuated her presentation. "In this, and the next three events, Graviton passed through Biology test areas, through liquid nitrogen containment bottles, Dewar's. No effect, not even a momentary slowdown. In short, we have no known method, including freezing, of containing it.

"The only good news is that none of this is intentional. Graviton definitely doesn't know about moving outside the shielded test box or the safe house."

Johnson asked, "What is your recommendation for when we need Subject Two for more than twenty minutes."

Katie, though she had been on the project for only a few days, had had enough of the code words and impossible threats. She was already contemplating reactivating her lieutenant's grade to go where threats didn't tingle the back of her Afro. She continued, "We have two solutions, but we should trade them out. One is to ease the ban on Graviton's conformal attachment to Subject Three." Despite all her attempts, Quennie had accidentally inserted himself into the project as a needed option. "Neither had had an issue with it before the ban. They share their impression about tests and briefings anyway." She drummed the conference table top with two fingers. "Subject One and Three have been "apartment sitting" together. It conforms like with the Subject Two but has limited access to his physical senses. When they are together, Subject One does not move outside the immediate area."

She didn't want to discuss how she would come home and find Quennie, wrapped in "that woman," invisibly, of course, engaging in exchanges of witticisms and giggling.

"So, you buy the "boredom" hypothesis?"

"I do. It doesn't sense any of the tests we perform on it and gets bored. I absolutely recommend Subjects One or Two not be separated at any time. Neither feels 'right' unless near the other. All we have to do is either keep it in the apartment with Subject Three or return Subject Two for her to believe she never left."

Johnson tapped his secure tablet. "I'm still not comfortable with the extreme freedom of movement you talked me into."

Katie replied, "The preliminary psyche profile states that she needs human contact. Lots of it." Before they ask, Katie fills in, "The male subject has severe depression issues, so we can't assume he'll remain stable. Also, unlike the male, who is a veteran, she has no experience in being closely controlled. By letting her maintain an illusion of having a real life, she is less likely to exhibit instability." Katie touched a blinking icon on her tablet. "Everyone is in place. She's arrived at LDO and should be under our constant supervision, without her knowing, of course."

Steve pointed to the projected charts. "We should keep the van following Graviton. The GPS shows its position in real time."

The shadowy person twisted in his chair. His chair's torsion bar thnnnged in complaint. "We know our job. Just keep your monster under control."

46

LEALA

SARAH: DAY 13, LDO DEPARTMENT STORE, PULLMAN
WASHINGTON

In the housewares department, she found Mr. "call me Dave" Moore with a solid coppery sense about him. Waving his covered mug of coffee, he rushed through introductions, including another young woman, older than Sarah, hired late the day before.

She introduced herself with a half-smile and a firm handshake. "I'm Leala, but please call me Le-ah." Another good energy color, claret, but closed in a way Sarah couldn't describe. Now she thought of it, claret was Shy Guy's color, too. Angular instead of curvy, Lea exuded a sense of purpose that Sarah was drawn to. Even without makeup, her strong features, squarish jawline, protruding cheekbones, and heavy eyebrows made you want to trust her. There was something familiar … hmm, Sarah could almost put her finger on it.

Dave took them to their new supervisor. Retail was old hat to her, and her experience got noticed. She was moved to more involved work before the first break. Lea remained quiet but paid close attention to instruction and was a real trooper. Several times, Sarah caught her checking where she was.

During her first break, Sarah skipped through the men's departments to check the fashions for the fall. Once she replenished her bank account, Alex needed a wardrobe rescue.

She checked out several other departments during the break. As the break ends, Lea appeared. This wasn't a large L&D but following her was the only explanation for her timely approach. Katie hadn't said anything, but Sarah couldn't believe that this level of freedom came without restriction. It was just a little creepy.

As she refolded a pile of children's clothes from the morning rush, a handsome, if somewhat fleshy and prematurely balding guy touched a onesie, toddler sized, pink and blue with spaceships, and asked, "Is this on sale?"

Sarah flashed her biggest smile. Yes! Her first sale! She leaned in and half-whispered, "No, but it will be next week. I can use my code, and you can get the sale price early."

He said, "Could you? I ruined my daughter's in the laundry. I want to replace it before the spousal-unit finds out."

She loved personal interactions. Helping, talking, she loved the connections. By the time he checked out, he'd bought a second onesie, some sandals, and a set of hair ribbons. She almost hugged herself. "Direct sales, here I come!"

Poor Alex had tuned out from the moment the building came into view. He was aware but paid no attention to external things. Their eyes tingled when they both looked. She occasionally caught him checking up on her. She hoped this would help his mood swings.

Katie waited for them at the bus stop, guided them to the lecture auditorium, and a seat between her and Quennie. Another compromise and a small freedom clipped. She'd have sat in the cluster of boys three rows down. She hoped it wasn't her silliness-regression kicking in, but rather her urge to be normal. However, now that she was not hiding, she could concentrate on the lecture on Spinoza's *Ethics*. She loved it. Her mind leaped to new philosophies, centuries old.

Alex returned and followed the lecture. She was warmed to her innermost being when he was forward.

Huh? A disturbance washed over her from the left. *"Quennie? What was his problem?"*

Alex jumped in with an explanation. *"Quentin's used to spending more time attending to Katie than the lecture. I'll fill you in later."*

Quennie was sad, and his emotions threatened to affect Sarah. She'd found a skill she didn't know she had and struggled to dampen his emoting onto her. Her presence and needs had become the cause of her friend's unhappiness. Like the Btfsplk character in the comics, her mere presence rained disaster on her friends.

Toward the middle of the lecture, she followed Alex's view to the back of the lecture hall. She didn't know her co-hire at the department was taking classes. Funny that Lea hadn't mentioned it. Katie also stared in her direction. She and Alex exchanged something in hand motions.

In a lull in the lecture, Sarah said, *"Lea from work is taking the class."*

"From work? Where is she?"

"Top row, furthest from the top entry."

"The one in the ponytail? Katie and I think she's security."

"What?"

Alex kept her from turning around and emoted satisfaction. He even did one of his rare Sarah Beth smiles. *"This is good. We now know one of the security team. When we stand to leave, wave and smile. If you can act natural, walk up and say something about how you're enjoying the course. Don't invite her over yet. Katie will check on their preferred OpSec. It's best if she becomes a fellow student doing drop-ins."*

She emoted disgruntlement.

Alex asked, *"What this time?"*

"I don't like not knowing what you and Katie decide. All those hand motions and eyebrow stuff makes me feel stupid because I can't follow."

"Sorry for leaving you out. Last year, we developed a mod on military hand signals combined with American Sign Language. We used it to 'pass notes.' I'll translate from now on."

As they left the lecture hall, they waved at Lea and smiled. Lea waved back but rushed out ahead of them.

Sarah: Day 14

Today she dressed for comfort and warmth, but still a touch flirty. Clothing that tortured Alex's prudishness also chilled her in the heavy A/C of the department store and the French Lit lecture hall. Slacks were for the farm. *No. Stop that. Alex will detect you're crying again. I don't want to admit I'm homesick for the earthy odor of pigsties. He has enough issues without me crying on our shoulders.*

News of her prior retail knowledge had spread quickly. A new department supervisor claimed her at her first break. Lea was moved to the same department. Sarah was miffed that Katie wouldn't fill in what she knew about Lea.

After she clocked out to go to classes, Lea saw her. "Sorry about running off yesterday, I needed to call my boyfriend. I'm new on campus, and I'd die for a stiff caffeine fix after Philosophy. Is there somewhere you go between lectures?"

Sarah flashed her best "friend" smile. "Certainly. In fact, want to join my friends and me? The coffee's strong."

Alex, your attitude adjustment will start between classes. Keeping him engaged as Sarah Beth exhausted Sarah. Lea watched, so she kept a straight face. No breakdown over her failures to nurture Alex.

Alex

I can't describe how happy I am with Sarah's sudden wardrobe reformation. I'm no longer cold all the time. When did she change? I don't recognize this outfit. We must spend thirty minutes each day pondering what to wear. As a bonus, I can stop wanting to pop guys who stare at my chest instead of my eyes. They stare at Sarah Beth, not Alex, but I'm still offended. Her new skirt outfit doesn't encourage voyeurism.

Yesterday, I asked her how she put up with the eye-to-breast contact. She shrugged and said, "It's a boy thing. Either you get used to talking to boys who look down, or you stay angry all the time."

Katie had conferred with Johnson and his security exec. The damage done by using Lea for lecture coverage wasn't reversible short of making her disappear.

Sarah breaks out of Katie's marching order, between Katie and Quentin, and runs over to Lea, sitting by herself on the top row in the lecture hall. "Lea! Unless your beau's coming, you sit with us." She plops next to Lea. Lea reseats herself between us and the door.

Katie's eyebrow tells me that I'm not handling Sarah well. No kidding. Quentin smirks, he gets to sit next to Katie again. Exchanging shrugs with Lea, Katie sits him next to Lea, and she takes the seat closest to the door. Sarah and Quentin exchange smirks. I don't miss that Lea and Katie had maneuvered us to the most protected position.

This happened too fast for me to intercede. She gave me no warning. A dressing-down is in order. *"It's not appropriate; messing with the security folks. You'll jeopardize our safety."*

"Katie and Lea are packing, and the two yellows who pace at opposite ends the outside corridor are also packing. Besides, my sense kicks in when someone non-boring comes within a half kilometer. Chillax. You're too jumpy."

Can't fault her logic and arguing about her attitude is fruitless. She's amenable to changing her actions, but not her attitude. I'm glad

Sarah's not here for the credits. Otherwise, we'd be taking left and right-handed notes.

At the ReUnion coffee shop between classes, Leala's wonderful, displaying old-style vivaciousness. Leala, I love that name. Leala rolls off the tongue like honey. I'm right, she's a southpaw, and the slight bulge on the right is a holster. Not big like Katie's hand cannon, it's a nine-millimeter or a .380. The way she swings her legs around chairs, she wears a backup piece on her thigh. Smart, and confident, my type. How do I meet her as Alex?

Over coffee, she and Sarah become inseparable, cutting KateQuen out completely. Leala deftly turns the conversation to include them. Nothing to do, I drop into observer mode, doing Sarah's chillax. Something about Leala ... why do I want to say "yummy?" I don't say yummy. Leala engages Quentin in a discussion of teas and tea parties. Hired in after all the fun, she wants to catch up on the more exciting events.

"Stop it." Sarah's disgust-emanation drives through me like a bolt from a crossbow. It leaves a slight headache in the right temporal. Something new to add to my overly long list of things I doubt I'll understand.

"Stop what? Since the class, all I've done is chill."

Sarah shoots another bolt of disgust. *"And?"* She's got her panties in a twist. I'm helpless to respond. *"And?"* Not knowing what she's expecting, I try emoting puzzlement.

Another bolt of disgust, but she relents and fills me in. *"Are you clueless? Every chance you get you ogle Lea. You slip in when I'm distracted. Quennie spotted it. That's why he asked her if she heard about when Katie threatened to decorate the apartment across the hall with Mr. Johnson's brains when she shot him."*

"Sorry, I thought I was merely hanging out." Leala is a phenomenon. Latina, not a beauty or even cute, just self-assured, and outgoing. How does she keep the men off her? I need to patch this, somehow. Sorry, won't cover this. *"What do I do?"*

"Katie and Quennie realize it's you. They're covering for us while we sort this out."

I listen to Quentin's overly dramatic description of Katie's choking Mr. Johnson. He sees us return from our internal discussion, then continues before Lea's attention shifts to Sarah Beth. Sneaking a glance at Katie, I can tell she's not happy with Quentin's blow-by-blow. She catches my eye. She wants to wrap this up.

"What do you suggest?" I'm beyond mortified. My parents raised me better than this. My best friends are scrambling to cover.

Sarah smiles to cover our conversation. *"Our shadows are behind us, so they didn't spot it. My reputation as hetero is safe. Sorry about the angry, but when people see Sarah Beth, they think 'Sarah' not 'Alex" and I don't swing that way. No! What's happening to me?"*

47

BLOW UP

ALEX

A chasm opens in my consciousness. Sarah has closed off, retreating backward. She's never done that. She loves being forward. She doesn't respond. I check for *Tssskt*, that strange feeling we get when we're missing blending time, energy levels, everything, and get nothing. I sense for her 'static,' and it's low. I touch Quentin to get his attention. "Sorry to interrupt, but I need to go to the little girl's room. Keep filling Leala in." Katie's eyebrows go up.

Leala stands. I forgot she's on duty. I knit my eyebrows to signal to Katie I'm in trouble. "Sorry, Lea, I need some space. Katie, anyone nearby who's new?" Katie signals and a thirty-something woman stands. "Lea, this has nothing to do with you. Sometimes, my condition needs distance from the familiar."

Lea's pissed. I want her with me, holding my hand, but any friend too close to us would complicate what I need to do. Whatever has happened needs intense privacy without us sensing familiar people. That would confuse our senses. This could lock our body into an apparent coma and scare everyone.

In the lavatory, I turn to my escort. "Thanks. This may take a while. I'll be in the end stall."

Seated, I search for Sarah. If I can't retrieve her sitting down, I'll have to get to a bed and create panic in the project.

Still no response to any of my signals.

Another inconvenience of being Sarah Beth. As Alex, I could wedge myself into a sitting position. In this smaller body, the best I can do is tie our belt around our wrist and the assist bar on the wall and lean on it. That will keep us from falling. "*Sarah?*"

I can't go in too far. They might find us comatose. No answer. I plunge deeper and find her curled in a fetal position. What could have caused this? I nudge her. "*Sarah, please talk to me.*" No response, so I nudge again. This deep in, neither of us have a sense of the passage of time. We could already be in an ambulance.

"*I'm not that type of person. I'm not that type of person …*" She's muttering to herself.

"*Sarah. We need to talk, then regain consciousness before we scare people.*"

She responds. "*I'm not a homophobe. I've never had any issues before. I never cared if someone called me a lesbian.*"

"*Then you aren't homophobic. You're suffering from gender dysphoria.*"

"*Huh?*"

Got her attention. I've been terrified all my Sarah Beth time would spill over into my Alex-body time. That people would get the wrong idea about who I am. It never occurred to me my body-partner could have the same struggles. "*The blending with the mixed emotions and hormones does a number on us. In my case, your female hormones. In your case…*" I avoid pointing out that her extreme emotional swings may be tied to this. Doctor Timsen's reports give no conclusions.

"*I get it. All your male reactions even while working as Sarah Beth, and the wild emotional swings. They affect me. I still need time. Go out. I'll stay forward in case you need me, but I need to process this.*"

I catch her deliberately calming, as though she's taking deep, slow breaths. Okay, she's ready to work us out of this. She comes fully forward and looks, puzzled, at the belt around our wrist. *"This is also my fault. You're all man. I forget with you being girly all night and most of the day; you need outlets. For now, before Katie throttles us, our best way out is for you to engage Lea as Sarah Beth. You're not a letch, so talking to her will stop the slips."*

Why didn't I think of that? Nothing keeps me from being Sarah Beth in most circumstances. *"Thanks, I appreciate it."* I catch some weariness in Sarah. She's drawing out her vowels.

I wash our face, check our make-up, and thank our patient shadow. "How long was it?"

"Twenty minutes. Ms. Parker came in to check but left."

"Sorry about that. I wish you were cleared. Just chalk it up to a weird assignment."

"Trust me, Ms. Merk. This job is a cakewalk compared to what I normally do. We're all pulling for you. We don't know what the issue is, but we all care."

As we walk back to the table, Quentin smoothly wraps up his tale of the tea party. Quentin could talk a wart off a toad. I do my best Sarah smile, and ask, "Lea, this may sound stupid, but after listening to a recounting of our tea party on the square last week, well, could you drop in after your shift? I promise more than just tea."

If I can happen to be Alex when she's off shift …

Something dazzles multiple colors in its tumble from the ceiling.

48

DODECAHEDRON

ALEX

I ndigo.

Blue. NO!

My training screams "grenade," and I twist and jump to intercept it. Not used to our body, I can't keep my wrist from slamming into the bottom of the table as I turn.

Green. I launch our body out of the café chair, catching one leg on it. The chair flies to one side as I scramble backward. I see three of everything.

Yellow. Each pentagonal facet flashes a distinct color as it spins, and my vision stabilizes. I smell the yellow.

Orange. The chair skitters to my left and more facets appear as it reverses its spin. The orange itches like a bad case of hives.

Red, then nothing.

Overhead, I get the impression of a thin hand receding and pulling the false ceiling panel back into place.

Indigo. The sequence starts again, and it bounces off the tiled floor, to the left.

Blue. It's something like a grenade, shit. I lurch to my left.

Green. I see the smell of burning rubber. It hits the tile on edge between the facets and spins to the right. I lose coherence in my vision again.

Yellow. GOT IT! I pull it into my chest as I land face down.

Someone bigger lands on me. "Fuck'n idiot." It's Katie, trying to take the blow. "Get off."

"No." Do I hear meadowlarks?

49

THE NEW GIRL

SARAH

Those sounds. The beeps, boops, and swooshes filled her with terror. They are the same sounds. Daddy made when they had him in that dim room with her brother and sister.

Aunt Gertie found Sarah in the mortuary's reposing room. The floor lamps gave enough light to show that the bottom of the walls were a rich earthy brown and the tops tan. The chair rail was painted the same tan but glossy. Someone, somewhere, played the piano. The sound surrounded her with calm.

She didn't want to be calm, and she kicked the tables to feel something, anything.

Aunt Gertie said, "You shouldn't be in here. I've brought Timmy and Denise. We'll go to the playroom, and the three of you will play while I watch."

She didn't want to move. Surrounded by three boxes, one long, two shorter, she was comforted. These were the prettiest boxes she'd ever seen. The dark swirls of grain in the red and tan wood combined into the imagined faces of her family. The slippery surface defeated her attempt to touch their faces. Her Daddy, big brother and little Munchie reached out from their closed caskets to say, "We're okay."

She heard them talk to each other about what was next. Her tears flowed. She may have been eight, but even she knew that being dead was not okay.

Her birthday cake, never eaten, forgotten when they found out about the accident, sat in the freezer—its own coffin. Candles displaced by the rush to clear the birthday decorations tilted like tombstones in a neglected cemetery. Forgotten by everyone but her.

They passed the sallow-faced man. The one who hurt her with the needles three days ago on the morning of her birthday. He seemed to have a private joke. She kicked him in the shins.

Aunt Gertie pulled her back. "Sorry. Her father and brother and sister are in the viewing room. Normally, she's a sweet kid."

A SQUEEZING HAND WOKE SARAH. The sounds refused to go away, so she refused to open her eyes. If her eyes are closed, none of this was real.

"The brain monitor shows you're awake. We need to talk." It was Katie. Her best friend ever. They had spent the past year together. They'd had some wild times.

She opened her eyes and tried to sit up. The pain in her chest caught her breath. Her hands gripped both sides of some sort of brace over her chest, and her breasts felt as if someone had tried to rip them off. She had to see. "Bring me a mirror."

A doctor she didn't recognize swam in her vision. "Not yet. Could you answer some questions?"

"No. First I see why I hurt. Then, maybe."

Another doctor slid up to her side. "Get her the mirror. Everyone but Ms. Parker clears the room." They left. Sarah smiled as best as she could. As short as he was, she doubted many women smiled at him.

He opened a metal briefcase on the table tray and used both hands to raise a Plexiglas tube, sealed at the ends. "I won't let you lift it. The dodecahedron inside weighs over two kilograms."

After checking that contraption on her chest, then all her smiles in the mirror—only a couple of bruises to the left of her mouth—she paid attention to what the strange doctor held. Inside the tube laid an almost-sphere, with twelve facets. Each facet was a pentagram. Dark as pencil lead, light seemed to disappear into it, leaving a dead feeling. This is the "dodecahedron" he wanted her to see?

Sarah asked, "That's over four pounds? It couldn't be more than an inch in diameter."

"That's the problem. It was the size of a grapefruit when it dropped from the ceiling. After you grabbed and covered it, it pulverized over a meter of the concrete floor down to a half meter, exposing the retaining rods. However, you only got a cracked sternum and bruising. When we pulled you off, it was this size. Do you have any idea where the energy went?"

She turned to Katie. "Who's this idiot and what's he doing in my room?"

50

HOLLOWNESS

SARAH: DAY 16

Sarah woke at exactly 6 AM in her new and messy bedroom. Because of the silliness at the hospital, she'd only had time to retrieve her toiletries and a change of clothes to bring to the new apartment, before falling asleep on the floor. A quick check confirmed the bruising faded to a small patch of yellow on her sternum. Something deep, hollowed her core, but what the hell, she was fine.

She reached for her phone to LuRRk. But her LuRRker wasn't on her laptop or her backup phone. What was going on? How would she let everyone know how she was? She didn't know their e-mail addresses. So, she called Mom, like she did every morning, just as she finished breakfast before work.

"Hi, Mom!"

"Oh, I love to hear your voice. Something wrong? You normally vid-message me on that app-wazit."

"LuRRk. It's missing off my phone and laptop. I'm hoping I didn't lose my LuRRkers."

"What is wrong? There's something different."

"I guess I fell and bumped my head. I don't remember it, but the docs decided to let me go rather than try to keep me in the hospital."

"That's my Sarah. Did you hear about what your younger cousin did?"

"What this time?"

They finished in five minutes. She liked to arrive before her boss. Unfortunately, their call, which normally started her day on a high note, reminded her of the dead-zone in the back of her mind.

Mother hadn't raised a wilting daisy. The idiots at the hospital had been beyond exasperating. They had claimed she had a broken sternum that threatened to puncture her heart. What a pile of crap. There was nothing wrong with her, except some short-term memory gaps. She took Katie's word for it that she had been in an accident. She promised to tell her more after we both had a good night's sleep. The doctors had fretted about a concussion, so she let them place a head harness with patches against her skin, so she didn't have to put up with people waking her every hour.

Rushing out of her bedroom into the living room, dressed for work, she saw a strange man, ruddy complexion, in sleep shorts with a crescent moon and Arabic letter pendant around his neck, puttering in the kitchen. Katie was at the dining room table still wearing yesterday's clothes, her Afro crushed on one side. She looked like hell.

Sarah asked, "Who's the guy?"

Katie went stone-faced, then said, "Quennie, come out here and introduce yourself. Sarah this is Quentin Kahn, my current squeeze. Quennie, this is Sarah. She's the one I told you about."

Quentin left ashen-faced and slammed the door to Katie's room. She could have told Sarah that she'd invited a man to live with them. She was surprised at this side of Katie, the ultimate personification of feminism, without the baggage, taking up with a Muslim. At least she thought he was a Muslim. If they could establish a friendly relationship, she could ask about Muslim beliefs about women.

A light knock at the apartment's door announced my ride, Leala. Sarah told Katie. "I'll get off early to move the rest of my stuff down from my apartment."

Quentin had returned and was whispering with Katie. She stopped her whispering. "No need, Quentin has the day off."

"I'll move my own clothes and toiletries, don't touch them. My new mattress will be delivered from L&D today. I've got to decide what to do about the old sofa-sleeper." She blew her hair out of her face. Why'd she let it get so long? Long hair was for floozies.

Further whispering grabbed her attention. It was Quentin. "What about...."

Katie said, "Put them in our room."

Shrugging her shoulders, she joined Leala in the hall. "Glad you found my new digs. Thanks again for saving me from the local buses."

They slipped through the front door. Leala asked, "No problem. Any word on Alex?"

She shrugged her shoulders to answer. Who is this Alex everyone asks about? Every time she heard the name, a hollow opened in her.

51

ALEX JANE IS BACK?

QUENTIN

His retreat to the bedroom hadn't been a panic attack but to deal with whatever had torn within him. Similar, but not as deep as what nearly collapsed him each time "Sarah Beth" separated into male-Alex and the Sarah-thing. Even as far away as across the hilltop between the Physics labs and the apartment, he felt—not really felt, but something deeper—every time they separated. His experiences varied, but most frequently, he smelled green, felt odors, heard salty, and a miasma of other senses he had no name for.

She—the self-named Sarah—brought with her a lower, tolerable disruption of his being, but he still smelled colors, felt odors, and heard spices. The latter was handy in that he didn't have to read the labels as he cooked. That last thought solidified the sense of losing his grip on sanity.

This new Sarah didn't know it, but she needed him. From Katie's description of Sarah's fit at the hospital, the old Alex Jane had returned. The 'tude was there. Alex Jane had never suffered fools. A few minutes ago, she had even blown the hair out of her face with an Alex Jane scowl that could curdle sour milk.

His Alex Jane was back, but she didn't remember him? Twenty plus years of rowdy companionship and Alex Jane had completely forgotten he existed. It was a cut, deep in his psyche, like when bitch-Mom had experimented on him. This Sarah Beth resembled his Alex Jane except for something he couldn't put his finger on. Sarah Beth was rounder and even smiled more easily, just like the prepubescent girl he'd known before it all changed.

That was it. This is how Alex Jane would have turned out if she hadn't obtained illegal testosterone at the age of eleven. She'd made it a condition of their bro-ship that he inject her in the buttocks. Even at eleven, she wanted to follow in her dead father's footsteps into the military.

That was when she started to call herself Alex, after her father and older brother. Jane had been her younger sister, whom he had only known as "li'l Muncie." But her father was alive. Wasn't he? Another tear gutted his sense of reality. What was Alex Jane's real name before she got the court order to change it? A burn like a railway spike heated cherry-red burst between his eyeballs. Why would he think she had had another name?

The swirl of inconsistencies in his memories left him face down on his bed.

Quentin returned to the main room after composing himself in his and Katie's bedroom. The apartment had started to fill with more people. Katie asked the skinny guy whose electronics gear drove male-Alex green with envy. "Is this location secure?"

"No intrusions detected. InfoSec reports the entire project is still black in the chatter," he responded.

Johnson slipped in with the head of security. As always, the energy levels changed. Quentin prepped to host what promised to be a full meeting. He knew nothing about security but suspected they purpose-fully drifted to the apartment in ones and twos to confuse any watchers. Meeting in the apartment and not in their secured location would be a bold, unexpected move.

Screw project security. He would slip away, get a burner phone and call his adopted sister, Aliyah. He always felt better after talking to her. Besides he was overdue in checking to ensure bitch-Mom hadn't started to work on the little girl Alex Jane had saved in Iraq.

With all the craziness, he hadn't been calling Aliyah every day. The few times he called, no one answered the phone. She might be in after-school activities. He didn't want to think she could've already been swept up in bitch-Mom's machinations.

He gathered his laptop and a couple of books to legitimize his cover of going to the library for some peace. His peck on Katie's neck and the explanation got her "what are you up to" raised eyebrow, but she returned to the group of people who were filling all the chairs, stools and the couch. At least now she wouldn't have to explain how he, an uncleared civvy, traipsed back and forth while a classified meeting was being conducted.

In his car, he pulled the battery out of his phone. Safe, and untraceable. He powered down his laptop. He'd learned about how phones could be located, even when turned off. Even tablets and computers had this capability. Which reminded him; he removed the laptop's battery. Not spyware but a needed element of network stability. Based on where phones and other connected equipment were, resources were adjusted, tables rebuilt, and timing algorithms fine-tuned. Except, the government watchers were overly fond of using it. He had Alex, the Signal Corps Sergeant, to thank for that tidbit. Alex Jane, not the fake male-Alex. This reminder stiffened his commitment to the true Alex.

In the parking lot of the bodega he'd spotted during a beer run to Moscow, Idaho, to replenish Katie's Hessian beer stock, he used the burner phone he bought there with cash. It was four PM. Aliyah should be home waiting for Mom to come home.

His father answered. "Hello, who is this? I don't recognize the number. Answer before I hang up." Ever vigilant and protective, his father had bought a caller-ID coupled with a cloud-based reverse number search.

"Hold, hold. This is Quentin. I was calling Aliyah."

"What are you doing with a strange phone and who is Aliyah?" His father totally doted on the six-year-old girl, buying her things to make up for her life as a street-orphan in a war zone. Her bedroom closet overflowed: ten shelves installed for all the toys and a second clothes rack bolted to the closet door for school uniforms. The redecorated room had been an explosion of Pepto-Bismol pink, canopy bed, ruffles and all.

Quentin had had to explain Aliyah was having nightmares about how close the color was to blood. She'd picked a new color, tan, like the uniform Alex Jane had worn when she saved Aliyah. Quentin had taken a day off during one of Aliyah's school holidays, and they had repainted the walls, and most of the pinkalicious furniture, and each other. That night his parents took them out for dinner. They thought it was to avoid the paint fumes. Instead, his parents brought out the application to adopt Aliyah. All the federal red tape had been expedited, and now they wanted Aliyah's input. Like the six-year-old she was, she screamed and danced. Quentin hugged her.

"Aliyah."

"Who is this really? I don't like jokes." His father hung up the phone.

Anger wiped out Quentin's habitual panic attack. If bitch-Mom was already experimenting on her …

He needed someplace where he could activate his virtual private network, VPN, on his laptop, another gift from Alex Jane.

The study carrels of the Holland/Terrell Library were the logical choice, especially if Katie had someone check on his whereabouts. There he found a carrel that couldn't be watched and linked to the cameras in his home. His father, a total security nut, had installed cameras in all the rooms, outside the house and even surreptitiously mounted several on nearby utility poles, painted and textured to resemble the poles. The fifteen-character password still worked on the server, and he thumbed through the rooms to get to …

Aliyah's bedroom was all wrong. The pale blue off-the-shelf paint was from fourteen months ago, as were the computers and old electronics stacked in two corners, and the closet door still hung off its hinges, left unrepaired by the previous owners twenty years ago. His father wasn't handy, and as the storage/dump room, it hadn't been important. Quentin had repaired the door before Aliyah arrived. The breeze riffled the curtains proving it was a live feed. The oversized analog clock he'd bought for her wasn't visible. She preferred analog over digital, and he'd had to visit antiquarian shops in a three-county area before she was happy. No sign that Aliyah ever was in the room or that it had been redecorated.

I could use a beer. Following a hunch, he flipped to the kitchen to read the elementary school calendar and see Aliyah's artwork lovingly preserved on the refrigerator door. Gone, as was the new refrigerator they had bought using Aliyah's arrival as an excuse.

Next, he searched online archives of the *Seattle Times, Seattle P-I, UW Campus Daily,* and as an afterthought, the *Ballard News-Tribune,* his hometown newspaper. All had had features on the story of Alex Jane, hard-bitten two-tour veteran, fighting the bureaucracy and mass indifference to bring street child Aliyah to a suburban family.

He couldn't find anything about the story. Alex's return was a small paragraph and photo in the Ballard N-T. Except this was the male Alex James, not Alex Jane.

Somehow, history had been rewritten.

Back at his apartment, he ignored the war council. They returned the favor. Something about gravity was the day's tail-twister. There was a moment's hesitation before he decided not to weigh in. Gravity was the mutual effect of two masses. Which added to the mystery of why it was being discussed in hushed tones. What did gravity have to do with an energy entity?

He let the shower beat on him for a half hour but gained no idea of what he could do. Only he remembered people who no longer existed.

Gravity didn't need him.

52

BLOUSES

SARAH AT LDO DEPARTMENT STORE

I t was creepy how Leala followed her around work. Sarah refolded blouses; Leala was there. Sarah prepped for the holiday sale, Leala was there. Sarah decided a quick break to the lady's room is in order, and Leala, well, was there.

Leala asked, "Are you okay?"

"Sure. Why?"

"You haven't called me "Lea" all morning."

The hollowness in her chest blossomed, but Sarah forced it back.

The general manager found them in the back correcting the inventory on the computer. "I know you need to be home to accept delivery of the mattress you bought. Make up the time next week. Have a great rest of the weekend."

Leala deposited her at the door of Sarah's apartment and chatted with some people coming and going. They were carrying in stuff. Sarah said, "Hey, that's from my old apartment."

She remembered these two but from where? The smaller one—Harry—

with muscles showing even through his jeans, said, "Katie asked us to help. The super was in a hurry to clear your old apartment upstairs."

"Fine." She wanted to tear someone a new one, but she was caught off-guard by some obvious guy clothes they were carrying in. Katie pointed to her room, and they took everything there.

Sitting at the dining table, the strange little doctor from the hospital—she thought he was a doctor—sipped tea and chatted with Quentin. Katie waved off the two helpers and said, "Quennie, Lea, could you give us some time?"

They left, and Katie pulled out a chair for Sarah.

She'd gone stone-faced, again. In the year Sarah had known her, well, it wasn't good. She sat rigidly in her chair. "Sarah, how long have we known each other?"

"A little over a year, why?"

"How did we meet?"

"Huh? Frosh orientation confused more than explained for both of us. We stumbled into each other and went to the ReUnion to commiserate over coffee."

Mr. Johnson fidgeted, hands opened stiffly, and his face whitened. Katie said to him, "See what I mean?"

Katie flipped through her tablet, showing pictures of a pleasant looking guy, nasty cheek scar, some in uniform, some with her next to him. "Does he look familiar?"

"No." Sarah touched the photos. "An old boyfriend of yours?"

"Not exactly." She dismissed the photos, hovering first over the ones with her in them. "His name was—is—Alex."

"I should introduce myself. I'm sorry that I didn't last night. I'm Samuel Johnson."

Mr. Johnson laid two folders on the table. "There was an accident.

You've had a concussion and memory loss. Do you still not remember me, or Alex?"

Sarah folded her arms. "Of course, you got me the mirror." He was nice enough, but his voic activated that weird internal hollowness she couldn't lose.

"How many people are outside in the hall?"

This was getting weird. "I'm sorry, but I don't have a clue." How would she know that?

"You don't remember the attack a couple of weeks ago?" Sarah shook her head. "After that, you were found by Alex Monroe." Another head shake. Not even a tickle, except that hollowness. "Okay, we can re-brief you, but the short story is you, and Alex joined a government project. Here is your contract."

Her signature. It even had that silly heart she only used when she was trying to loosen up a situation. She scanned for details. She was a contractor on some study project. Wow, she made a lot of money. More than what Mother made with her two jobs.

She was shaken. "Wh-what do I do?"

Mr. Johnson said, "We'll do full debrief in a secured location. For now, avoid the man who attacked you. He was part of our project before he went rogue. His name is Tod Engle. He uses the pseudonym Mort Y'Arty. This is the ID photo."

Her sallow-faced man…Greasy? Sarah remembered, but what? She pulled the tablet closer. The photo was like an anchor to something valuable. "Could you send it to my phone? I don't remember him, but I feel like I should."

Mr. Johnson swiped the photo to the send icon. "If you sense him, hit the panic button. You'd probably die trying to take him on."

Why would she do anything other than run?

She remembered—his face leering at her laying on the ground. Noting else. "Agreed." A chill ran up her spine, and perspiration broke out on her neck. "Wait. What panic button?"

Katie reached out to touch, to comfort Sarah. She rarely comforted anyone. Katie said, "The one on your phone. It takes a special finger swipe to activate. I'll give you all the ops briefings."

Mr. Johnson said, "Every place he left, research records have disappeared. We've backtracked him, eleven years so far. Coincidently, the company he worked for is headquartered in Omaha, your hometown."

A memory pushed into her inner hollowness, and she fell out of her chair.

———

Her eighth birthday! Finally, after all those nasty needles, she knew Mommy and Daddy were cooking something up. Daddy dropped her off at school for the state test. Mommy had other plans. They weren't fooling me. She kept her joy. The creepy guy with the sallow, goat face watched her the entire time. She finished and dropped the test on the teacher's desk.
He stopped her at the door. "Sarai. My, you finished fast. That was a new state record. You can call me Uncle Mort."
"You're not my uncle." She skipped out to the car, eager to be whisked to her surprise birthday party.

53

GIANT'S TEETH

ALEX

The giant's teeth, row upon row, erupted from the field, threatened to consume the unwary. Some gleamed. Some stained tobacco-tan with the passing of the ages or green verdigris leached from pennies left on them. Two, over there, exuded the scent of the whiskey poured out by old buddies. Occasionally, a cross or an angel capped and protected a tooth. More rarely, a voice only the five-year-old Alex heard stood guard over the most neglected gravestones. Blessed were the deaf.

No one came to the cemetery except for those who remembered their grandparents' Sunday homages. Generations ago, the one-way lanes jammed with people rushing to visit great-uncle-whozzit after the Sunday sermon and before the Sunday pot roast could overcook.

Yesterday's late evening Chinook had melted the powder snow, but only the surface, before a Blue Norther refroze everything. Glare from the cloudy ice over the snow combined with bands of winter fog to create a dappled world of half-light and half-terror blindness. Blessed were the blind.

Someplace back there, hidden by the low rise and the flat-bed truck that had skidded off the lane was Aunt Mil's car. Pulled along in her iron grip, Alex dug the toes of his Sunday-only dress shoes into the milky ice covering the powder snow. Behind him, a trail alternated between his left then his right, then his left toe trying to get traction. He couldn't easily stand on the ice, but his mom and Aunt Mil broke through the crust. Each snap of the breaking ice reminded him of dogs cracking pot roast bones for the marrow.

His silent beseeching eyes were met only once by his mother's. She exchanged looks with her sister, but he only scored a regrip, harsher than before.

Their silence, punctuated only by glares at each other, didn't make any difference anymore. They would have been drowned out by the sentinel voices anyway. He even heard the meadowlarks that kept vigil during the summer.

The guardian of the destination row of giant's teeth, a gnarled Bios d'Arc tree, reached out to stop him and tore his suit jacket. His aunt expelled an angry huff and jerked him free. The motion left a vertical bleeding scratch on his right cheek.

Twenty years later a bullet would open his cheek along the same line.

A CONSCIOUSNESS FILLED HIS BEING. A dry, raspy voice like a footfall on dried leaves asked, "What are you doing here, and what's this about giant's teeth?" Of course, it had to be Babushka, interfering with whatever *this* was.

Twenty-six-year-old Alex said, "Go away."

"Can't. You came here, and I can't leave. Why are you here?"

"Where else is there?"

"If you knew, then you'd belong here. That explains why you seem strange. Something is off about you."

"Go away."

"At least you retained your stubbornness. Turn that stubbornness into something useful. You need to fight. You're not whole. If you're not whole, you haven't finished something important. Fight your way back."

54

RETURN OF THE SOLDIER

SARAH

S he hated water in her face. Sputtering and turning, she asked, "What's that stench, and why are we in the shower?"

Alex said, "You passed out and were writhing on the deck. That and some movement of energy pushed me back. Your spasm kept you incommunicative, so I took control. The stench is what we excreted through our skin. It's awful."

She glowed from every pore. *Alex!* She remembered! "I'm so sorry."

"About what?"

"I had some form of amnesia."

"Understandable…"

"Please don't interrupt. If I don't get this out … Okay, I forgot who I was, and completely about you. I appropriated your memories of the last year and thought I had been here for a year and that Katie was my best friend."

"I didn't think about you when I jumped on the grenade. I'm sorry."

"You're missing the point. I took over your life and didn't even know it."

"We've never been able to share our memories or thoughts. We'll need to watch out. Are you certain you're okay? Can you tell which memories are mine?"

Putting their hand over the showerhead, she said, "Positive. I came here about two weeks ago. Anything about the campus, or Katie, or anything before that is your memory. It's confusing, and I have to stop to sort them out. The creepiest memories are those of you talking to me while looking in the mirror. Luckily they seem to be fading."

Drying their hair in front of the mirror, she asked, "How long was I out this time?"

He touched his phone and displayed the old-fashioned analog clock app. "Don't know about the total time, but I've been in control for about twenty minutes."

Wrapped in her long robe and her hair in a towel, they exited to see Doc Timsen and Katie whispering in their new bedroom. The new mattress set was against the wall, and her—their—furniture laid about the room. Doc Timsen grinned and winked at them as she crammed their stench-laden clothes in a garbage bag. Some people had the strangest hobbies. Sarah never want to see those clothes again. The first set they had stenched never lost the odor. They'd double bagged the laundered clothes, and Alex had tossed it into the outside dumpster.

Alex closed the door. *"We have a lot to talk about. I'm so sorry for getting us into this by jumping the grenade."*

"What about me taking over as if you never existed?"

"Like I said, we need to work this out, without an audience. I think I was busy, but the memory's vague." He was too bland. Sarah would have been hysterical by now.

Katie tapped on the door, peeked in, confirmed they're decently clothed, and strode into their bedroom with Johnson. He said, "We now know the sensors work. The common room isn't wired, but whatever happened to you set off several sensors in your bedroom. Mr. Addams will provide a full briefing." A new name, she wondered who Mr. Addams was. Stepping to peer directly into their eyes, he asked, "What happened?"

Alex glanced up from Sarah making final adjustment to their clothes. *"Let's discuss this later. They're watching."*

Fib time. Sarah decided to lead as she didn't trust Alex to keep quiet about their issues until they decided what the answers were. "I've discussed this with Alex. He's back, and solid. The thought of Greasy in my hometown was too much for me. But I think you really want to talk to Alex. He'll be right out."

She rummaged through his drawers and laid out clothes for him. "I'm sick about how easily I took over. I'm going to separate, and you can talk to Alex, as himself." She separated with instructions to him. *"Take all the time you need. Do it in the main room but leave me here. Both of us need some separation to think this through."*

"Agreed, but I never liked this T-shirt. I'll wear the blue one."

Alex was taking this too well. Had she damaged him during the takeover? Yes, there was some weird-ass grenade, she vaguely remembered that, but still ...

More importantly, anger and fear were competing to overwhelm her. Her false memories weren't false. Daddy let the sallow-faced man, Mort, experiment on her. She remembered the basement and the equipment. Most of all, she remembered the experiment, the morning of her birthday. On the same day, she and Mom got the word Daddy, big brother, and little sis had died in a suspicious auto accident.

In her grief at the funeral, she saw colored blobs where people should have been. Her first manifestation, which thankfully faded the same day, taking with it all memories of the experiments.

Until now. Damn you "call me Uncle Mort." Why'd he have to find her, then attack her? Anger took over. He'd stolen her innocence, twice. If it took the rest of her life, she'd find him.

Hold it. Alex signaled her to reblend. How much time had passed? He adjusted his T-shirt to not show their nipples. "We've got to do this blended. Once we separated, I lost memory of what I experienced after jumping on the grenade. Together, I'll remember more." He opened the door and waved through to the other room. "We'll be out once we get decent clothes on."

She couldn't stand the residual stench. "*Let go. You missed some of it because of your sensitivity about our body. I can scrub what needs to be scrubbed.*" He released with a blush. "*I've remembered that two weeks ago wasn't my first sensing experience. I've suppressed the memory for years. I think Daddy allowed someone to experiment on me.*"

Alex emoted concern, panic, and determination. "*That would explain your weeklong psychotic episode when we met. It parallelled my experience when my great-great-grandmother died. My memory is fuzzy, but I think I had Quentin as a friend for two months before I finally shook my psychotic Babushka's influence.*" He went silent, thinking. "*Something in all this explains us. I think we're linked, beyond our accidental union.*"

Anything to get Alex back. She didn't realize it at the time, but she had been slowly unraveling. She opened the door to face the inevitable interrogation. "*Greasy's attack on me my first day here in Pullman can't be a coincidence.*"

55

GRENADE

ALEX

The project head, Mr. Johnson, stands as we come in. "I took the liberty of ordering your favorite food. I hadn't anticipated I would offend Quentin." A diverse spread of traditional Korean food steams on the table.

That's the unhappiness I picked up as we left the bedroom. I never knew Quentin, my oldest friend, was such a strong emoter. Grabbing chopsticks, I join them. "Now I'm reblended, I can tell you what little I remember. I had no sense of time or body. I did sense something suffusing me. Then it was as if I was being tossed out. Sorry. I'll write up anything else comes to me and send it to you." Quentin's a great cook, but something about kimchi swirled with spicy-sweet bulgogi soothes my raw nerves. The gluten of the scallion pancakes doesn't hurt either.

"Sarah didn't talk to you about our results?" Johnson asks.

All I'm getting from Sarah is embarrassment, so I jump in. "No, we've only had time to exchange personal info."

"That's okay. Sarah, please listen up, it may be important for you to know. Someone dropped or tossed a device. We don't know where it came from."

"I saw a thin hand drop it from a ceiling panel."

"Glad you saw that. We checked but discounted the over-ceiling space. We'll recheck, but with forensic equipment. We didn't catch the attacker. All project personnel have been accounted for. Did either of you pick up on anything before the attack?"

Sarah emotes "not going there," so I answer. "We were preoccupied."

Johnson lets it go. He's getting used to what he calls our lovers' spats. "You were attacked with a dodecahedron device twice the size of a grapefruit."

I interrupt. "I don't know why, but it's important it be called a grenade. I guess I'm having difficulties with the notion of jumping on a device. I'm sorry, my ego gets the better of my judgment."

"Grenade it is. Grenade probably is the best term anyway. It's new to everyone in the government we've been able to securely query, and we didn't have a name. Anyway, the electronics van picked up an energy surge in the electromagnetic bands where we've hypothesized your blending works. We haven't invented a way to simulate that, and to be honest, we don't how to test without hurting you. We think the device was meant to overload Sarah's binding with what they assumed was a host she killed."

"Ewww." Sarah puts our hand over our mouth. The grisly fates of the earlier volunteers are never far from her mind

Moving to break the awkward moment, I ask, "Any idea if they knew about me?"

"The fact that Sarah Beth is a partnership of two living people is our closest guarded secret. Your symbiotic relationship probably saved both of you."

I have to think this through. Those physics grad students could help if I'm careful with the question set-up. "Are you checking for gravity and magnetic fluxes? And also, what about the weak and strong force?" This brings a twitch from the Johnson. I change topics. The grenade is also interesting. "Sarah did mention something about a tiny but heavy spheroid."

Katie says, "That part I understand. Afterward, it was about three centimeters in diameter and heavy. It packed enough energy to pulverize about a meter of reinforced concrete, but only cracked your joint body's sternum. Anyone but you two blended would have been splattered over the cafeteria."

"We do heal quickly."

Johnson touches his tablet, and a sequence of photos and graphs appear. The video-selfies by a clutch of coeds also show us jumping on what I'd thought was a grenade, multi-colored flashes, and us rising in the air a few inches. "What is important is no self-healing can explain how your body didn't disintegrate. Something moved the energy before it could complete its purpose. The same phenomena sucked most of the energy out of the device, collapsing it. The elements are there, but the electrons are at the lowest quantum state."

Sarah interjects internally. *"Don't you dare tell them how. I was nursing my ego when it happened. It had to be you. Don't put them on the trail of your background."*

I need time to think this through. Besides, fighting with Sarah hasn't been a winning proposition. I'm rescued by Mr. Johnson. He says, "We can take this up with Steve in Physics, but you're missing the important question. Not where the energy of the device went; it's where it came from in the first place. Only two energy storage methods could fit in that space: a battery or a super-capacitor. Neither could hold enough energy to pulverize cured concrete."

Or lift us off the floor.

56

PUERILISM

ALEX: NEXT AFTERNOON

The post-attack series of rushed physics lab tests gained us nothing, but exhaustion. We collapsed into bed without unblending or even removing our clothes.

After three days of no Alex-time, we returned to the standard test rotation. I'm feeling great, despite this being the longest non-Alex-body time since the start of our partnership. For the first time since this started, the strange fatigue that follows me dissipated.

As we walk up for Dr. Timsen's weekly baseline physical, the doctor and Katie exchange a flicker of a smile. The flair of mutual respect and happiness pushes out to where I sense it. Dr. Timsen grins even as she orders everyone around. For the first time in her professional life, she's wrestling a true conundrum: us.

I read the measurements over the shoulder of the lab techs. Fifteen pounds gained in less than two weeks?

Sarah loses it. "Hand me a hammer. Ah'll beat the truth into that machine. Ah'm not 125 pounds and five-foot-seven and a half. Ah'm 110 and five-foot-six." The last baseline had disturbed Sarah, but not this much. Last week's gain was ten pounds, which set her privately weeping. But fifteen is too much.

Dr. Timsen glances at a senior technician. "We'll recheck the calibration."

He checks the certification sticker on the scale. "The calibration service is in Spokane. We can get them here within a couple of days."

"Good, and I want a report on what my weight really is. And by the way, no way did I grow an inch and a half. The State Gymnastics League measured me." She's sniffling. I cautiously emote comfort.

Back in the car, this time Leala drives, with our new omnipresent armed passenger in the back. I tell Leala in Sarah-cadences, "The fitness baseline test exhausted me. I'm laying back."

Sarah and I've been dancing around the Sarah Beth body issue since the first day of our partnership. I purposefully push a rude jangle to force her out of the back, and we move to our internal voices for privacy.

"Spill. It's been weeks, and you still meltdown over our joint body. I should be the one with the issues. After all, I'm a man in a young woman's body."

"You don't understand." She goes silent. We have a silent-contest.

She opens our eyes and looks around. *"Fine. We have time for this. Ever hear the phrase "Plain since 1867?" It's a joke about how flat Nebraska is, and how plain the people are. Until I turned seventeen, I had as many curves as Katie, namely none. I was beside myself when I blossomed and could buy cuter clothes for college. Don't say it, it was shallow of me, but no one looked at me all through school."*

"So, you came here to pull a metamorphosis, with new clothes and, make-up and plans to take the college by storm. I'd say I get it, but I guess I don't."

"When we blended, I lost most of my curves. My face became plainer, and I've also lost much of my hard-earned gymnastics flexibility. Bottom line: I'm taller, heavier, clumsier, my joints are stiffer, and my clothes don't fit. But the

more important part is we are growing, in height and muscles, with no sign of stopping."

I don't bring up my loss of height and weight. As long as I don't have a meltdown, I can keep it from Sarah. *"Are you going to be okay?"*

"I needed someone to talk to about it. Sorry, it had to be on your shoulders. You have enough Sarah Beth trauma in your life."

"I guess that's why we're so close."

"Funny. Lea's holding the door for us. We have to stop doing drop-outs when others are waiting. Any chance we can get her cleared? She seems to be a good listener."

Sarah, the next day. University Hospital Medical Arts annex

Doc Timsen stiff-armed Katie. "You can stay outside. This is doctor-patient talk and thus confidential. You have no need to sit in. If it makes you feel better, stand outside and scowl at people."

Sarah shrugged and smiled at Katie to show she was fine with it. After being escorted into the doctor's office, she asked, "What was that all about?"

"Just what I said. The results of your tests, both the initial and the follow-up have been analyzed to death. We need to discuss them, and you need to decide how much to tell Alex."

Sarah jangled Alex. Luckily, he was only resting and not in study mode. "Alex is present. I don't keep secrets. It would be silly."

Alex yawned. "Wazzup?"

She was thrilled they could both talk without damage. "Doc Timsen has the med reports."

"Oh, you have my reports?"

Doc Timsen shook her head. "This is for Sarah Beth. We have a little more work for you when you are independent." She handed them a data chip. "For you, if you wish to read on your computer or reader."

"Is any of this classified?" Sarah asked.

"No. We scrubbed it. But it is protected as patient private data."

Sarah stood and opened the door. "Katie, if you can, could you come in?"

Katie entered, frowning in confusion. Sarah said, "Katie should know everything about me. She's stuck with me in the apartment and ensuring I'm protected elsewhere."

"Okay. Then I'll jump to the only new item. You already know about your rapid healing, and we still have no notion of how to explain it. We think your sporadic puerilism is explained by major fluctuations during the day in your biogenic amines."

A quick glance at Katie confirms she's as lost as them. He asks, "What, what, and whoozit?"

"Sorry, I should explain the jargon. Puerilism refers to childish behavior in an adult." Alex perked up. "Your irrational moments could be explained by, and sorry about this, the post-traumatic stress from your attack. However, you don't consistently respond to stressors. The flux in your amines is another explanation."

Sarah was about to cry, and it wasn't her being childish. "Alex, Katie, take the lead. I need to chill. Don't hold back on describing what you've seen me do. I'll stay aware."

Alex asked, "Is the flux every day?"

"No. We can't discern a pattern. For example, sometimes the deblend/blend cycle helps, sometimes it creates a major attack."

Running their right hand through their hair, Alex pursed their lips and asked, "Are there other symptoms we should be aware of?"

"According to the medical literature, lethargy is also a symptom."

"I don't remember lethargy, just normal tiredness. Katie, do you remember anything?"

"No. Together, you are age appropriate as a freshman, when you're not bouncing off the walls."

Sarah confirmed. "I don't remember any lethargy."

Doc Timsen said, "The treatment is a cocktail of anti-psychotics tailored to the individual. We already know your joint body requires extremely high dosages of any pharmaceutical to be effective. That's why we don't treat you anymore. I believe the best course is to let a limited number of staff personnel know about the symptoms and Alex's hug therapy." How many times had Alex put them into a self-hug? She felt ashamed that she hadn't returned the favor when he was having issues.

Katie let out a sound like a mouse.

Sarah said, "It's okay. I know about you and hugging. We can expand the people who know so you won't be trapped into having to hug me." Katie's body relaxed. "But I expect full contact kisses."

Doc Timsen laughed.

Alex emoted unhappiness. Sarah knew he was right. How could they effectively fend off attacks if they were in mid-silliness?

57

TRAPPED

QUENTIN: DAY 18

I f only he'd left well enough alone. Instead, he'd been trapped for over a week.

He had managed the klaxon-like banging inside his skull. Whenever male-Alex and the Sarah-thing separated, he'd grab something to keep his knees from collapsing. The migraines were manageable, but not with any known medication. Maintenance was achieved using a distracting activity.

When studying or drinking didn't help, Quentin resurrected the skills from his short house-cleaning gig. Both bedrooms were small, but each bathroom had exquisite tile, giving him hours of grout scrubbing to calm his nerves. He started to plan and prepare gourmet meals. It turned out he had a talent and the necessary attention to detail. Cooking provided the greatest distraction. He had a routine, and if he'd kept to it, he wouldn't have been trapped in a cage of his own making.

Last week, he decided a deep cleaning of the Sarah-Alex bathroom was in order. It amused him when Sarah Beth went ballistic about his cleaning, though she never mentioned the bathroom tile and porcelain.

Then it happened.

He added cleaning their carpet to his invasion of their space. Moving the highboy to clean behind it, he nudged open the second from the bottom drawer, and a pink sock partially hung over the edge. He picked it up only to find it was attached to the entire drawer of clothes. Clothes that said, *"What the hell do you think you're doing."* It was Sarah in her camouflage mode. He'd never seen it, but over a couple of beers, Alex waxed on about how he lost Sarah, only to step on a patch of carpet that she was perfectly emulating, touch, sight, and smell.

She moved up his arm and his knees crumpled from the pain, toppling him onto the highboy.

For several minutes, he lay there afraid to move. *Alex is going to kill me. I violated his trust.*

Sarah became visible on his arm as a flesh-toned wrap. *"That hurt. How are you?"*

"Me? Me! You almost killed me like the volunteers in the old program."

"Quit being a drama queen. The pain went, like, both ways. The other experiments were with dead outers. I'm human and not controlled by instinct. Anyway, we accidentally completed the experiment Alex, and I have rejected. The lab rats will be thrilled."

Quentin's skin went clammy, and Sarah slipped. He held her surface. *"What's next?"*

"First, I'm bored. Can I hang around your neck? I can see through your eyes, but I don't hear anything." When he agreed, she conformed around his shoulders, dropping into the camouflage mode Alex mentioned but refused to show. She moved to cover more of his chest but slipped. *"I can't conform tight enough. I'll have to stay on your shoulders."*

His eyes cleared, and he saw colors more saturated since bitch-Mom had experimented on him. An enhanced state of clarity became his norm.

From that moment, he was hooked on the enhanced state. Every time Sarah Beth unblended in the apartment, he became the willing, needful, host. Katie glared but let it go. He didn't believe she or Alex knew about his dependency.

The Last Man

Alex

I fake a library trip to convince Sarah to separate. I'm still not comfortable with my tests and don't want to discuss them with Sarah, or anyone.

Quentin drapes Sarah over his shoulders as he putters all day in the apartment. He's taken to skipping classes "to keep Sarah occupied." Utterly lame excuse, but I don't have the energy to fight him on this. The Khans, his parents, are going to kill me. I was supposed to keep him serious about academics.

Katie hustles me to the WSU field house. Baseline testing is baseline testing; you never discover anything interesting. Small, but measurable improvements across the board, as expected. I'm paying more attention to eating and getting a little exercise running the stairs between floors with security. I'll be glad when they finish calibrating the equipment. My five-foot-eleven height records as five feet ten inches, and I've lost ten pounds. As I leave, Dr. Timsen huddles with her team, passionately arguing, while two technicians stare at me.

Katie walks me an unusual way to her car. I'm puzzled, but I enjoy the walk after the treadmill. We stop in a small weight room occupied by a woman who looks like she could take Katie in a fight and two similarly muscular men. Mr. Johnson and Steve from physics meet us. Katie says, "Sarah's with Quentin. The apartment guard's doubled."

I hold my peace until I'm led past the bodybuilders, and Katie stays behind. I turn to her, but she shakes her head. Something's wrong. Katie's always at my elbow outside of the apartment, except when Leala sits in for lectures. Before I allow myself to be led into a small office, I grab the doorjamb and recon the area. Twice the usual security here, including the three bodybuilders. Nothing scary, just strange.

This is one time I wish I had more ability. I'm almost blind without Sarah's power to draw on.

The scent of old sweat and dust confirms what I see. This room is rarely used, probably because it's stacked with equipment needing repairs or trashing. Johnson offers me the most comfortable chair, a small desk, a pen, and a stack of papers. I read. This can't be right. He explains. "They are what they appear to be. Once you sign and swear, you'll have compartmentalized Top-Secret clearance at the highest level in this project." I hadn't known they had compartmentalized even the Top-Secret.

"Isn't that a bit silly? I live—am—this project. What would I not know?"

"You don't know everything. Steve approached me and indicated you should be aware of what his team is uncovering."

Steve's lips turn a shade of blue, and he pops a couple of pills. "The bottom line is you were on the right path when you engaged the grad students at their weekly bull session. Your intuitive leap is staggering. With one exception, we've deflected the group by offering other interesting questions, lab assistant positions, et cetera. Please don't contact them again."

Now he has my attention. "Why deflect them from the search?"

"Because it's dangerous. Hear me out. We examined the shell of the apple you recovered from Sarah's attack. It's the same as Sarah in-shell; no inside, just the outside. Totally impossible unless you accept one hypothesis. It manifests as physical only if it's pure energy in other dimensions. We're working on which of the eleven mathematical dimensions effected the energy transfers."

"Effected?"

Steve isn't as cold as I assumed he was. He holds my shoulder but keeps the gap between us. "Yes. Effected. The affect is in our physical dimensions, not the other way around."

They've written off the theories of the admittedly obnoxious Clarice. I'm intimidated they've included me, but there's no way I'm passing up the inside scoop of the latest theories of what we are. "What about Sarah? She should be here."

Johnson wipes his bald pate. "We three are the only ones who will have access to all the accumulated data. No one else on the team can know there's another security level. You can't tell Ms. Parker. And absolutely, you cannot tell Sarah. When you access the information, you can't be in the same room with her." Katie, with her MP background, would understand, and in fact, demand that she not be included in levels of security that didn't need her. Sarah, on the other hand…

"I can't promise to withhold anything from Sarah."

Johnson interrupts. "Steve, explain what the problem is."

The corners of Steve's eyes crinkle, but not in mirth. "The best we can estimate from existing theory, for Sarah to manifest herself as a shell, she's the largest accumulation of energy on earth. Roughly double the energy of the largest mega-H-bomb built by the old Soviet Union. When blended with you, we have no method for estimating how much energy she maintains."

Something from a middle school science lab tickles my memory. A round basin filled with water and a rod repeatedly touched the surface. If the rate of the touching was right, standing waves formed in the pool, storing the energy. "She's a standing wave of energy somewhere in the non-physical."

"Katie reports that when you aren't participating in the blended entity, she can be unstable as if she's a different person."

"So, you don't want Sarah to know about her fundamental nature, in case she accidentally uses that knowledge." Alex knows that she's too sweet to understand how dangerous she is. The guard protects those whom she cares about. As long as her friends remain safe, everyone's safe from a rampage.

"Yes. From your debrief earlier this week, we know your influence has kept Sarah sane. You've been the damper on her puerilism. You need to remember that with her access to this massive energy, you're the only thing between everyone and a disaster.

"Potentially, she could release all of her energy, scouring Pullman off the maps. You're the last man."

58

OCTAGON

SARAH: DAY 18, TUESDAY

He forced Sarah to her knees, making her spill her groceries. Ancient oil stained her legs and palms. "Stay there."
No one treated her like that. Defiant, she reached for the apple rolling away. He kicked her supporting arm. "I said, stay there." Now she had grease on the front of her fave sleeveless tunic. He backed away five steps, the rod of Asclepius earring swaying, and lifted a yard-long octagonal tube with spinning lights. Green

---

S arah knew she had to fight back these nightmares. Each day, she remembered more of them, and they darkened her days.

Alex was sympathetic. He'd lived with his darkness for years. He was committed to her, but he didn't know what to make of the octagonal tube. Sometimes, she got the sense he was evading the question.

He woke as she finished her almost nightly report on Katie's project tablet. He and Katie exchanged pleasantries before they went back to bed.

Quentin pretended to not be awake.

Sarah: Physics lab extension, 2:17 PM

Katie and Sarah rushed to get to the newly re-instrumented physics experiment. Sarah had a good feeling about it. The last two days, the project had taken on new energy which she prayed meant that she would see results.

They took a shortcut and passed by Steve's office. Johnson was in an intense discussion with him. As the door closed, they overheard him say to Steve, "He still has the prototype?"

Today's physics lab included double locks and a double shift of security. Sarah and Alex knew all their energy signatures. As always, Katie sat inside with them and the cleared female tech who ran the racks of equipment with instrumentation and data acquisition devices. Everything showed scratches and dents from frequent removal and reinstallation. Several were connected with spider webs of wires, smaller boxes, and lights.

There was no fade out today from Alex. He—what was that term? — geeked out. Alex was dying to ask questions but couldn't. Sarah Beth didn't know enough for technical questions.

To mollify him, she asked, *"Does this look unfinished to you?"*

"Yes, and again, without disclosing there are two of us, I can't ask questions about what this equipment does or what they're testing for."

Waves of unhappiness flowed from Alex. Not only did he live sixteen or more hours a day as Sarah Beth, but he couldn't express himself intellectually on technical matters. If it wasn't such a silly idea, she'd check if their new insurance included couple's counseling.

The previous week's tests of blending cycles had been recorded with the video for study. Dr. Timsen and others came to no conclusions other than they blended and deblended, and that it was disturbing to watch. Sarah and Alex had talked about it and decided they'd rather not know what they looked like while blending.

This week a rack of new electronics played sentinel in the hope of capturing anything caused by the blending/unblending cycle. Sensors attached to Sarah Beth fell off before they started, so direct readings were a lost cause. For this test, they moved through their blend/de-blend process ad nauseam. Her jump time from Alex-body to full Sarah Beth body expanded from two seconds to fifteen to thirty. The separation out of blend onto the sensor plate took twenty seconds. She maintained focus with difficulty.

During each cycle, she caught part of what Alex was saying. "Can I hold a chair, to stand up?"

Separated, then reblended. "I have a headache."

Separated, then reblended. "I'm weak."

Separated, then reblended. "I'm going to puke."

Separated.

Rats. She was nauseous, too. Without a core, she couldn't do anything about it. Pressure settled on her. What the...? It was Alex. He fell on her and was quiet to all her senses. This was wrong.

She jumped him, blended, and staggered to a stand. "*Alex.*" She wobbled and fell into Katie's arms. "Alex. Forget me, save him."

Doctor Johnson shouted orders into the phone and Katie picked them up and ran to the door. A guard burst through the door pushing a gurney. In a physics building? He inserted a drip line and pushed a small hypo into their arm.

59

COLLAPSE

ALEX: DAY 19

I wake in a well-lit room reeking of disinfectant and the noises I associate with TV hospital dramas. Flexing my muscles proves I'm Sarah Beth, and securely strapped down.

I use a trick learned in the VA hospital, to not be bothered. I fake sleep and listen to what is being said. Being Sarah Beth has its advantages. We control muscle groups on a finer level, allowing me to twitch and trace lines and tubes. Excellent. We're doing well. Only a drip line, and judging from my spaciness, they recently pushed a light load of joy- juice.

"Sarah."

Nothing. Wait, then again.

"Sarah."

Nothing.

I'm riding solo. I don't sense her absence, so she's fine. I hope. Plenty of people here. I sense Katie, and Johnson, presumably in the room. A doctor or nurse leaves. Farther out, Leala and extra security people whom I recognize from around the apartment form clusters. That's heavy, they're worried. Others, again nurses and doctors, going about their business. We're secure, but I can't relax.

I don't want to open our eyes, to find only me. "*Sarah!*"

"*You don't need to shout.*"

"*How are you?*"

"*Fine, just ... dizzy.*" She sighs with relief, and someone moves next to us.

"*Any idea what happened?*"

She opens our eyes and looks around. "*Just I was exhausted, and I sensed you were also. You passed out and fell on me. I flash-blended with you, but I also passed out.*"

Johnson and Katie come into our vision. He pulls out a tablet with medical charts. "Good to see you Alex. How's Sarah?"

"She's okay but nauseous, and dizzy. Can you check us out of here." I lower our voice. "Neither of us thinks it was an attack. I know we'll need to provide a full debrief. Our apartment is more secure than an ER."

60

A FISH IN WATER

SARAH: DAY 20, WEDNESDAY EARLY MORNING

His back to was to Sarah, talking to two people who are blurs. She couldn't tell if they are male or female. His rod of Asclepius earring dangled, crystal clear. Comfortable lounge area, waiters bringing drinks. An image flashed in the picture window. It's an airplane's reflection passing by. The three of them were in an executive airport lounge.

In his hand was a large tablet. He wrote "You can't escape. I know where you are." The tablet converted the handwriting to large blinking text. "You can't escape. I know where you are." He stood, turned, stared at her and laughed.

Green.

Alex

It's a rare morning where I don't wake to Sarah bustling around. She's quiet, asleep from last night's drama. I stretch and remember this is us, not me. After all this time, it's odd I sometimes wake thinking I'm Alex-body. I hope that this is not a sign that I'm getting used to being female.

Oh, crap. It's nine AM. We're late for everything. I nudge Sarah. "You didn't wake us up. Anything wrong?"

"Not really. After you dozed off, they woke me for more tests. The last blood draw was at five AM. I fell asleep and had another nightmare and took an hour to document it on Katie's tablet. So, I shut off your backup alarm. It's not a work day. Now, if you don't mind, between the tests and my nightmares, I'm exhausted. I'm taking some me-time. Don't bother me. Watch the energy levels of our body."

I whiff something Quentin-inspired. Walking out, I find he's put on a full spread, as though expecting a crowd. The scrape of a fork on the dish signals Leala finishing her breakfast, and she carries her plate to the kitchen. "You're looking good. I heard about your accident. How's the bump on the noggin?"

I like the cover story. Simple. "Barely feel it."

"If I'd known you were joining us, I would have changed shifts. Sorry, I have to leave."

Next time I'll check the neighborhood. My first Alex-solo opportunity to be with Leala and I missed it.

Quentin slides a crêpe that smells like oranges in front of me and joins us at the dining table. "Before anyone else shows up, I have a question."

I'm stunned. Quentin doesn't question; he melds into the situation. "Sure, anything."

"I've picked up enough to know you absorbed or deflected an immense amount of energy during the quantum attack."

How'd he learn that? Only Sarah and I've speculated about where the energy went. He continues, "No one told me anything, but I'm the sci-fi geek here. The rationalists running this project can't see their fingernails even when their hand is in front of them. You or Sarah deflected that energy." He wipes sweat from his forehead. "Any chance it became an alternative past?"

My jaw drops. "What makes you think that? Is something different?" Not that there is any way we could possibly know the past was changed. Like a fish in water, you can't tell if your past is what you started with.

"Just thinking. It wouldn't take much to make someone either exist or not exist." With Katie's arrival, his stiff back retreats into the kitchen, and he doesn't look my way.

Between mouthfuls of Quentin's latest crêpe invention, Katie fills me in on the post-ER activities. "Lots of aggravation, and nothing useful discovered." She slides her tablet over to me. "Sarah insisted on not waking you about the nightmare. Here's what she recorded."

Sarah's attacker is on the move. If the analysis group can identify that executive lounge, this might be the lead they need. Regardless, I need to do something extra nice for Sarah for taking all the grief as well as the needles.

I reread the threat. No nuances there. I ask Katie, "What can we do about the threat?"

"Nothing."

61

COINCIDENCES

ALEX

I was almost six when Babushka said, "You die before twenty-five." Maybe my great-great-grandmother Babushka was on to something. Hopefully not the death thing.

For all her obsessions, she'd tried to train him in basic survival twenty years ago. When the assassin tossed the dodecahedron grenade at us, I reacted instinctively, and shifted all its energy into—where? My adhesion to the energy flow pulled me with it, and I got stuck.

Is it a coincidence I'm taking the course in Spinoza's philosophy? The day Sarah appeared, I was half-asleep when the lecturer quoted:

"I would warn you that I do not attribute to nature either beauty or deformity, order or confusion. Only with our imagination can things be called beautiful or ugly, well-ordered or confused."

Looking back on my life, I've had too many coincidences. I don't know what's intentionally pushing me around, including the friends I make, where I live, and school courses I take, but I've been brought to this point. I don't think, other than the forced training, Babushka had control, either.

My obsession with being a girl ends now. I have a role in my own story.

I make my own destiny.

I've died three times since Sarah showed up. Sarah pulled me out once, and twice something pushed me back. I won't give up on her. But realistically, I'll die unless our mysterious agency has a massive breakthrough.

This is the cusp point. I'm claiming control of my destiny, starting with Babushka's soul-piercing "shift." Two decades ago, I fought and screamed to avoid her training. But without that training, we don't have the jenergija tools. Tools I suspect will save us. For the first time in over twenty years, I'll invade Babushka's terror-vault.

My stomach knots or would if I had one here. If I remember correctly, all I need to do is …

THAT SHOULD DO IT. Let's see … nothing. Damn.

LOST TRACK, but this is attempt seven, or eight, or nine. And I see … nothing.

Double damn.

> What did Babushka scream at me? "No, no, no. You forget
> everything? Don't think. Don't see. Be. Be vermilion and shift."
> Babushka pounded her four-legged walker.
> "But Babushka, it gives me headaches."
> "Because you do wrong. Once you do right and keep doing
> right, you headache go away."

Has it been twenty years since I last thought about that psychotic's lessons? What is "be vermilion?" Deep breath, don't think, close my no-eyes … be vermilion … shift.

Oh.

Wow.

There they are. All fourteen of the Matryoschka nesting dolls. The outermost one, the set of four, and the set of nine. Exactly as I left them eighteen years ago. Impossible. Aunt Millie locked them away. Which means the real nesting dolls I played with were merely a training prop. Something else about the last session with Babushka.

> "Nudge the large one open and look inside."
> "It's empty; you had me remove the four inner dolls earlier."
> "Open it and remove next nine."
> "I can't. It's closed. Besides, I already know it's empty."
> She rattled her usual long string of Russian and German curses.
> Once I mimicked some of it in front of Mom, and she slapped
> my face.
> Babushka glared at me through her pain. "You must. I no time
> for your silliness. Now open it."
> I opened it and pulled out the nesting doll from what I knew
> had been an empty shell. When I finished de-nesting the new
> set, I'd added nine dolls to my five. This is what I now see. They
> never changed.
> Babushka grimaced with pain. "Remember you do that. Each
> time harder. The next set sixteen. That is as far as I got. I was
> told you find sets of twenty-five, then thirty-six, then forty-nine,
> up to one hundred. Please call your mother. I need to rest."

She died two days later.

It is time for me to be a full partner, the trained partner in the "Sarah and Alex" freak show.

Someone or something has been screwing with me, Sarah, and my friends. Whoever or whatever you are, it's your turn to watch out. I'm fixing Sarah; then we'll keep you from visiting this terror on anyone else, ever.

62

WOLF

SARAH: DAY 21, THURSDAY, 3:11 AM

The starched-stiff, pressed white dress shirt sticks to his damp
back as he takes one swallow of water after another.
The people in the room listen. Their faces blur.
He argues, and his actions sharpen.
He stops. Eyes glaring, fists clenched, he leans forward. The rod
of Asclepius earring swings with his motion.
He waits. Waits.
Some blurs lean to each other.
First, one side of his mouth lifts then the other until it matches.
His fists unclench, and he rocks back on his feet.
On the opposite wall a monitor flashes. "It's a matter of time."
He turns to me and smirks, emphasizing his long nose.
Green.

Katie: 3:22 AM

"Mmf." Quennie rolled over as she tugged at him, freeing her
left arm. He'd sleep through the Second Coming, Armaged-
don, and likely through Ragnarök. He'd give that big wolf indigestion.

The second knock slowed her flipping off BMFG's safety. That light touch in the knock was classic Sarah.

Even though Sarah represented Katie's lost best friend Alex Jane, she also represented Katie's salvation. This Alex and Sarah were lost souls, utterly at sea, needing help. Katie was a realist. Even living with Quennie, her future was iffy. The triangle, Alex Jane, Alex James, and Sarah gave her purpose. For the first time since she lost her child, Cissy, she had a reason for living beyond basic survival.

She opened her bedroom door.

"That had better be your secured tablet and not BMFG." Sarah's eyes welled up. Her nightmare had been a bad one.

Notifying HQ, she secured BMFG in her safe and removed the security tablet. Sarah was too agitated to type on the surface, so she used the voice recognition to dictate her nightmare. As she related it, her eyes dried up and hardened. Each report was more specific than the previous, down to the furniture, texture of the carpet, the anodization of the copper window casings, everything. While the jewelry, suits, shoes, and even carry-on cases got the detailed treatment, faces other than Tod Engle were obscured. Either something blocked Sarah or she unconsciously blocking herself. Katie's instincts bet on an outside force. After almost an hour, she finished. Her posture changed and became more erect.

Recognizing the signs, Katie said, "Hi Alex. Sarah finished recording her latest love-tap from your attacker. I'm heading to HQ. Tell Quentin to go to classes without me. Leala will be in charge until I get back."

Along with Harry, the only member of the security team she didn't think she could take in a fight, Katie, BMFG and the tablet made for HQ. She didn't want any "accidents" preventing analysis of this new intel, and she still didn't trust the internet security protocols. She allowed herself a grin.

The analyst group's debate raged. Was Engle/Y'Arty intentionally reaching out to Sarah, or was he caught in an unintentional backwash from the attack that created her? Either explanation worked for Katie, as the nightmares were a wealth of intel the agency and its covert ops partners had no other way to get. He had to be meeting in airport executive lounges. It would take digging, but there were only a couple dozen in airports, though more overseas. Pattern matching would track it down. Correlated to the location and time, images from security cameras would narrow the field of candidates. Her instincts screamed that he wasn't a singleton rogue, but an international net.

After dumping the data into the analysis network, she would requisition appropriate body armor and armament. This is something she could understand, a physical threat. It would feel good to have an M4 automatic rifle again. Her smile widened showing her canines. Once there was a clear target, she would lead the ops.

No more guard dog—she was now a wolf on the hunt with her quarry's scent in her nose.

63

TREADMILL

SARAH

T he sweat splattered on the floor-to-ceiling mirrors and left filmy spots. One of the few disadvantages of this time of day at the gym was that full cleaning happened after the morning rush. She wiped down each piece of equipment before using it, partially for sanitation, but mostly to remove the left-over pheromones and waste chemicals in the previous user's sweat. The mirror in front of the treadmill confirmed this new outfit reduced the jiggle. One piece at a time, she was ditching her wardrobe for one that fit the new body. *Remember, life is good. Remember.*

The monotony of running on a treadmill put her in a focused mental state similar to her in-shell state. It was logical and opened her to new thoughts. More importantly, it provided refuge from her residual post-attack emotional-regressions. She'd never been emotional. She'd been the vision of stoicism since Daddy, Brother, and little Sis were killed by that drunk. She needed clarity to deal with the recurring nightmares. If she missed something and Alex was harmed, she'd never forgive herself.

Alex woke. *"Why are we running?"*

"You're getting fat. Doc Timsen prescribed five miles a day. I hooked you up with a gym."

He wrinkled their forehead. They ran in silence for a few minutes before he responded. *"I don't think exercising as Sarah Beth will work. Though, given how strange blended-us is, there's no telling. Anyway, Timsen's tests prove I'm more fit than us."*

"I'm still pissed you didn't tell me about your parallel testing. Why not tell me?"

His emotions shifted, he was hiding something. *"We were afraid you'd worry. False assumption and I'm sorry. Anyway, I've kept my promise to never hint I'm skilled at sensing people. What time is it? Shouldn't we get ready for classes?"*

Bogus. She wished he were a girl. Men were hard to read. This one, in particular, had gotten too good at suppressing his emotions.

"No, it's just past six AM." Focusing on the mirror, she confirmed that no one in the gym noticed their internal exchange.

"Are you crazy?"

"No, this is the before-work session. Recognize anyone?"

"I see Leala, some people I sense loitering around your work and our classes. This is everyone with night and morning shifts."

"Judging from their energy levels, they're thrilled about combining fitness and paid work."

Alex was already sliding into his I'm-not-here state. How could she hold his attention? *"See the long gym bag over our right shoulder? I'm positive I saw a shotgun barrel when the short blond retrieved a towel."*

He continued his slide into I'm-not-here. A sexy blond with a bare-everything exercise outfit carrying a shorty shotgun didn't hold his interest. Didn't men his age have raging hormones? Did he have hormones anymore? What if he was slowly losing his maleness, his uniqueness that sustained both of them? She'd lose him until classes start or she buzzed him for help.

She got lonely. She admitted it. It was lonely in a body that didn't look like her; one that looked less like her every day.

Finally, she was finished on the torture machine. She resolved not to check the monitor. Her heartbeat was up, which is all she needed. She joined Lea at the free weights.

"Lea, I'm glad you mentioned this. I wish Alex would get out of bed and join us. Trust me, he's not a morning person." Their cover story again. No wonder Mom and Aunt Gertie lectured her about lying, even white lies. Lying was tiresome. She wanted one person outside of cleared people, and Katie and Quennie to let her hair down with and talk, and talk, and talk.

Lea smiled and tilted her head. "Well, he broke his shyness with me. He's sending the most beautiful texts. Sometimes I think he's quoting poetry."

She was wrong on both counts. Alex had been evading discussing his lack of private life. Sarah insisted that him being a monk was insane. Both of them needed non-project normality to keep sane. Besides, he was good looking and easily liked. So, when he was "out," Sarah borrowed his cell and sent Lea texts. Yes, those were poems, lightly modified Emily Dickinson. The last one she remembered: "Come slowly—Eden Lips unused to Thee—Bashful—sip thy Jessamine. As the fainting Bee." Sarah had Lea melting.

"Remember he's shy. Be discreet but assertive." She flexed her hamstring against the treadmill's handles. "Bogus. I'm as stiff as a boy. I can't extend my leg more than 100 degrees. In gymnastics this year I extended almost 170 degrees."

Lea shrugged. "Something to work on."

Thank you very much, Ms. Obvious. What she'd never tell anyone is she flexed more than 180 degrees two weeks ago, the first time she almost lost Alex. She shuddered; another crow walking over a grave. Alex's grave. She couldn't face the prospect that her survival might mean his demise. She had to keep him involved with life while they worked on their problem. Even if it meant blatant meddling with his love life.

She dropped into their sensing state. Contentment rippled among the team, and several were toweling down. Good, she'd had enough.

Back at the apartment, she rushed to get ready for work when her phone rang. It was from Shy Guy, the one who handled all the spook-ware electronics. "If it's okay, I'll be over in five, with some new interior decorations." Another change in their routine. He normally called Katie for all things Sarah Beth.

She loved Katie's "interior decorating" gag. She'd coined the term at the tea party, and security still used it when discussing monitoring of her gilded cage.

Her cage.

Alex yawned. "What's wrong?" In their bathroom, it was safe to act like a normal couple.

She emoted good morning. "Nothing, go back to sleep." She was too sad to say more.

"No, something's wrong. A tidal wave of unhappiness hit me. Now spill."

She shook her head to clear it. "Sorry, I got to thinking about my lack of freedom. Same-old. The canary in the gilded cage."

"Heads-up. Your Shy Guy just stopped at our door. Is he scheduled? Should I hang around in case a technical issue needs our okay?"

"Thanks, I'd appreciate it." She opened the main apartment door before he could knock.

Startled, he jumped back a half step, then recovered. "I was never properly introduced. I'm Jimmy Addams, with two ds." She loved his smile, his energy, his name, Jimmy. Jimmy. "Only my mother calls me

James. Sorry about all the secrecy. Now that I'm cleared, I insisted you know my real name."

Alex moved their gaze away from Jimmy's eyes to what he held. A wilting Gerbera daisy with serene pink petals fluttered in a pot wrapped in mangled foil and ribbon. It was so sweet, she squealed with delight and kissed him, for a quick second, no, five seconds. Her Jimmy's arms flew out to protect the plant and to avoid touching her. She squeezed him harder.

"Stop it, we have a bad habit of swooning, and besides, he may get fired for fraternization." Alex could be right about the firing, so she quit. Although she could think of worse things to do than swoon into Jimmy's arms.

"When have you brought me flowers?" It was petty, but Alex frequently forgot she was also a girl. With needs.

He said, *"Good point, I'll be more attentive. But did I catch a complete change in mood?"*

She emoted happiness, again and again. Jimmy had appeared right when she needed a boost. This isn't an emotion-regression; she hoped she'd gained better control. She'd go with it and let things fall where they would.

Poor Jimmy stuttered until Quennie walked over, took the plant and directed him to the couch. "Sit. I'll brew tea while you two catch up on the morning show." Quennie returned to the kitchen, straightened the foil, clipped the dead foliage, and watered it. She got his attention and mouthed "Thank you." He blushed.

She touched Jimmy lightly on his wrist and twirled her short hair. Internally, she sighed. She knew cutting her hair was going to be a problem.

64

MATRYOSCHKA DOLLS

ALEX

Sarah's life just got a needed boost. She's been lonely with only the three of us, and occasionally Leala, to talk to. I'm ecstatic she's finding new friends, and maybe a love interest. I give her a quick caution. *"Back off; give him some space. He came to you; let him initiate."*

Jimmy's timing couldn't be better. I need her distracted. I don't want her to catch on to what I'm doing until I have something solid. She's had too many crushing disappointments.

WEAPONIZATION OF SARAH. That's my deepest concern. As much as I hate not being honest with Johnson who's more than kept his end of the agreement, but Sarah's right. Even my limited capabilities can be weaponized. However, bringing Sarah back to her full body is my highest priority. My concerns and priorities conflict, to the point where I'm losing sleep. I have to keep my focus. Which is why I've returned to the scene of my greatest childhood terror.

I shift to ... I'm not certain what or where this is. This is my *else-somewhere*.

I suspect this is an *energy-space bubble* created to contain what I seek. I'm not certain if the words *what* or *where* or even *when* apply. It's open but enclosed; dark but lighted; warm but unheated.

Enough. What this is, is unimportant. What *is* important is Babushka's matryoschka dolls with the massive libraries they hide. As I left them, disassembled all those years ago, here in "else-somewhere."

I have to slow down and take a deep breath. This is getting complicated. When I was four, it took me a year to successfully "nudge" the outermost doll and take out the set of four inner nesting dolls. Babushka taught me how to read the writing on the inner and outer surfaces of each doll. Then she taught me how to separate the layers of writing under the most visible layer. I got headaches and cried until she introduced me to her poppy-seed knuffelen pastry.

Much of the text in the nine-doll set involves "nonfiction" phenomena that would have given the Brothers Grimm night sweats. How the phenomena could happen wasn't explained. It's like picking up a tourist pamphlet of someplace you've never heard of.

The most useful text occupies the set of sixteen dolls I retrieved yesterday. I plow through the Edo-Dynasty classical Japanese and … wait… when did I learn classical Japanese? How do I know these glyphs are over three hundred years old and from the Japanese Edo period? Puzzled, I back out of the layers of writing. Babushka never mentioned the change in language. Then again, she died before I opened this level. Viewing the most superficial layer, I realize something I missed in my rush to start. Instead of the classical Russian peasant paintings, these dolls decorations include Oriental religious, military, and peasant folk.

This is different. It's more of a wandering tale than a lexicon of knowledge or compendium of nightmares. It's someone's journal or family history.

65

THE JOURNAL

JOURNAL: FIRST ENTRY, 1932

I don't know what to do. I've done so much wrong, hurt so many people. At least five of my family and lovers have died. I have condemned generations of my descendants to probes of evil they are unprepared to resist.

This is my only redemption; may God take this into consideration. I was a child in Messer on the Russian Volga River when Pastor Stärkel from Norka made his monthly circuit preaching about our salvation and how we should comply with the latest Russian obscenity. They had taken over our schools, and only Russian topics could be taught. Claiming that they knew more than us, they forced the German language out of the schools.

For one hundred years we stabilized their eastern frontier, tilled the previously untillable earth, traded on the Volga, built schools and churches, and didn't bother anyone. Now that we've kept the Kazars and the other wild people from raping and stealing, Moscow showed up to claim they were in charge. Pastor Stärkel said to pray, be a good Christian, and comply.

I didn't. I went with my eldest brother on his trip to sell our woven goods. I saw how Russian women lived. I decided then I would never be Russified. I was a good German Fräulein. Tod Engel, the bastard and ambitious beyond his station, was to be my way out. I seduced him into violating me, in Papa's grain bin. We would leave together before he was drafted into the crazy war on the Pacific with the Japanese and I was forced to attend the new Russian school. Instead, my betrothed, Heinrich Merk, the son of the riverboat captain, found us and beat Tod. Tod left to save his life. I was rushed into marriage to Heinrich Merk, Jr. by Papa and Mr. Merk.

Please, God. Take pity. I'm a good person. With all my nagging, my unambitious husband, Heinrich Merk, decided peace would be found in America. Joining us was my unwed sister, Elizabet. While packing, two sealed porcelain jars arrived from Tod, all the way across Russia from the siege of Port Arthur in China. I hid them among my personal undergarments in my trunk.

I killed Heinrich through my curiosity. In 1897, in our rented house in Lincoln, Nebraska, he caught me reading the writing in the dolls from the first jar. He flew into a rage because it was a gift from Tod and because he couldn't see what I was reading. He grabbed the unopened jar to crush it and fell dead.

Please, God. Why would my husband be punished? He beat me, but only when I deserved it. He never talked to our only child. He knew he was the son of "that bastard," but he never beat him, just me.

I gathered what money I had, the dolls, clothes, and my son and ran. A geyser of black flames, a fire I didn't set, burnt the house down. I talked a friendly teamster into letting us ride his freight wagon west to Ogallala, Nebraska. The teamster and I knew each other, and we stayed with him when he traveled to live in Seattle, Washington.

The nightmares never ended.

would see my husband, not dead, burning in the fire that was cold.

I would see Tod with broken legs, returning from the Russian war with the Japanese to Messer, to a welcome of no one.

I would see a girl who was a boy who was a girl.

66

MATRYOSCHKA WEAPONIZED

ALEX

The account stops and fades from my perception. I don't think this is the end, but something interferes and blocks my reading past this point. The last part parallels, partly, Sarah's and my problem. Casting around finds no more of the diary, so I return to my search for the practical in this massive documentation of the impossible.

I need some old-fashioned Yankee know-how text to work our problem. Layers down, I find my first promising sets of instructions.

"With the eight-sided crystal rubbed on—*untranslatable word*—skin, we started our—*untranslatable word*. After—*untranslatable words*—our four servants—some *untranslatable names*—were separated from their bodies. We successfully created mixed-up people combining our four with another—*untranslatable word*—our master presented to us. Three mixed-up died right away. The fourth—*untranslatable name*—lives alone, not understanding why she doesn't look like she did before."

The writers had found a naturally occurring octagonal crystal provided the conversion and the reverse modus. Finally, my literal headaches may bear fruit. I read further, excitement building. No, another dead end. I remember something from middle school science class. Natural crystals form as hexagons. A student asked about a natural octagonal crystal used in a TV program. The teacher laughed at him. There is no such thing as a natural octagonal crystal. I need to look up natural crystals, but this is likely another dead end ... Except. Something jangles in the back of my mind.

Sarah's account dictated into Katie's secured tablet. "He pushed me back down into the oil and grease of the alley. He held up an octagonal tube..."

This is bad. Sarah's sallow-faced assailant invented an electronic equivalent to the crystals. He's using modern electronics to translate energy between dimensions. He's weaponized the phenomena. Sarah's been trying to get that point across for weeks. I've been too dense. It's already happening, and I've lost precious time. This means that anyone can recreate this horror.

Where is the rest? The claim and description stop, in mid-sentence. Skimming this layer and the next gives me no further info. Where is the rest? I would cry if I had tear ducts here.

Gathering myself together. I try a new tack. Dropping the study of the sixteen dolls, I decide to out-do Babushka. Babushka, if you can hear me, pay attention. I'm about to do you proud.

Be vermillion—shift—Nudge the master doll and open it.

I THINK I've blacked out if that is what you do here. My no-head fissured like it did when Babushka forced her training on me. The new doll, decorated with something I don't recognize, sat in the outer doll. I lift the doll out and disassemble it. Score one for my crazed Babushka: twenty-five new nested dolls added to my growing collection. Now I have fifty-five, each with massive volumes of knowledge encoded in the inner surfaces

I need some downtime to think, hard, about my unlamented great-

great-grandma. I stopped calling her grandma, using only Babushka since her death. I need some time to cry over my loss. But not now.

The decorations and layers of glyphs or symbols on these dolls cover all of their surfaces and edges. Same as before. No, different. My "instant language" talent fails here. The glyphs follow a more ordered pattern than a natural spoken language. More like … math?

The twenty-five dolls will go nowhere unless I reassemble them. They are safe until I return. With my new appreciation of grandma, I launch my

study into the sixteen dolls. How do I bring these notes back with me? Something about focus…from before she died.

> I'd been crying then shifted to petulant. "Babushka, I want to play with my cousins. Not push dolls around."
> "Alex-an-der, if you want Babushka's special poppy seed knuffelen, you must do."
> "I'm only five; you're old. I can't write without paper." Babushka's English used "writing" for anything manually put on paper. I remember that I only drew, poorly, imitations of her handwriting.
> "Age no matter, strength no matter, power no matter. Focus matter. Do again, focus on the color I tell you and write without paper or pencil."

Now I remember how I wrote those notes strewn around the first doll. I wonder if Mom has her grandmother's recipe for poppy seed rolled pastry, knuffelen. I owe her and Dad a call anyway. I've never seen the poppy paste sold, but Quentin can duplicate anything. Grandma had trays of poppy seed knuffelen for me before, during, and after I "played" with her dolls. She insisted I eat my fill before any "focus" lessons. Even Dad commented how well behaved I was after my times with Grandma.

Oh, dumb, dumb, dumb.

Focus wasn't about writing. The writing was an exercise a five-year-old could understand. Focus is everything. Finally, I comprehend. Sarah is power, but she's focused like a category five hurricane. Her power is her weakness. She wields it without understanding. With Babushka's training and more practice, I can wield power in tight beams with great precision. I'll be the quarter-mile sniper.

Oh my god, I'll be a weapon.

A shiver consumes my non-body until I can force it into a mere frisson. This research is too volatile, too ripe for misuse.

An inspiration strikes. I can transfer my notes from my paper "Cat Journal" to here in "else-somewhere." This journal is now my "Matryoschka Doll," organized the way I think and can integrate potential solutions from all the hints. Without training, the journal can't be seen, much less read. Aunt Millie would be pissed if she knew she'd stolen worthless wooden dolls the day of her Grandma's funeral. She was, and still is, so jealous of Grandma's attention to me; she'd probably burn the dolls if I asked to see them.

All well and good, but I need to save Sarah. I have tools, but not the skills and knowledge to use them.

67

BREAKDOWN

ALEX: DAY 24, 12:21 PM.

Sarah shoots a slight smile at Leala and walks through our door. She asks, *"Can you handle this? I need a nap before the afternoon labs."* She drops off into sleep before she closes the door.

I trip, losing one of her heeled sandals. I let myself fall facedown into the love seat, screaming and wailing. I'm ashamed, but I can't help myself. Pounding the loveseat arm and kicking my feet, I lose the other sandal. I haven't had a temper tantrum since I was five years old, but I'm stuck in this one and can't stop.

A sense of calm precedes a touch on my shoulder. "Had another fight with Alex?" Quentin lifts me by my arms, placing me upright and sits next to me. He pulls me to his chest but keeps his hands off.

I blubber into his chest. Opening my eyes, I see where I left touches of tear-soaked make-up on his normally pristine T-shirt. This position is comforting, and my hands note how much firmer he's gotten since he's taken up weightlifting to keep up with Katie. I didn't know he'd started to shave his chest.

Yes.

No.

I push away and look up at his eyes.

His half-lidded eyes jolt wide in shock. "Alex?" He finishes pushing away and retreats to the far loveseat arm. He looks around for another seat.

"Sorry, yes."

"I—uh—never—would have if I knew…" He flushes a deep red.

"It's okay. You're helping a friend. You just didn't know which one. You weren't taking advantage."

"Katie'd skin me alive."

"Give yourself credit, you've matured. You've even stopped the innuendos about how Sarah dresses us."

He grabs a pillow and puts it over his lap. "I … I … I'm sorry. I didn't act on it."

"I know. Sarah is pleased about how you've changed." I reach to give him an encouraging touch. No! Instead, I push into the other corner of the couch, drawing my knees into my arms. I've never been this self-conscious of my Sarah Beth breasts, they form deep cleavage. I freeze. I don't know what I can do or say without making it worse. We stare at each other in silence.

His eyes stay on mine, flicking to my breasts. He breaks the silence. "That still doesn't help with my issue of comforting a weeping girl, and she's you."

I force a fake smile and wipe my eyes. "Get over it. I will. Somehow. You couldn't see my eyes, so you didn't know it was me." I start weeping again. Since when did I become a drama queen? What is wrong with me?

"What's the matter?"

"I—I don't know how much more of this I can take. I thought I could tough it out being a young woman sixteen or more hours a day. But, this is too much. Look at me. Always in skirts, dresses, or shorts."

"She wore long sleeves and slacks the day of the physical exams. Doesn't she ever wear them?"

"Never. You said it. She's trying to emphasize her femininity to overcome her issues with our body."

"Is she not forward?"

"It was a bad day at work, so she's sleeping. I'd have to wake her."

He purses his lips. "So, you can't separate. Take a hot shower and get into something you'll feel better about. I'm calling Katie. She won't like it, but afternoon labs are off for today."

"You can't do that. Sarah and I committed."

Quentin regains his grin. "You're now down with the flu. We'll call it the pink flu. I'll decide when you're ready for the project's pressures. Now git. Shoo! Dinner is in five hours. You two can decide if you come to dinner as you with her wrapped around your shoulders. We'll listen to how you two have worked out your problems. If you come out as Sarah Beth and I don't see slacks and low sensible shoes, you stay on sick leave."

Before I decide on how to confront Sarah and her cavalier attitude about me, I yawn. A nap sounds good. Sarah was right about the new bed.

WHY AM I reading in the strange library instead of sleeping?

An overlay intrudes on my study. It's that Russian woman with the dead husband. The writing fades in, obscuring what I'm reading. Is something trying to get my attention? For the first time, I realize this is cursive handwriting, not block letters, similar to the handwriting Sarah takes joy in using.

Before it solidifies enough to comprehend, the overlay fades, and my dream about grade school mischief with Quentin resumes.

68

HOT DATE

ALEX

The virtual library, visualized as layers of writing on the inner and outer surfaces of matryoschka dolls, defies conventional explanation. Who created all this knowledge? Who or what could create the energy-bubble space to preserve the knowledge? I decide to not work on that as it's not likely to solve my immediate problem: saving Sarah.

Right in the middle of a convoluted translation, I found deep in the matryoschka library, Sarah insists on calling me. My I'll-get-back-with-you message doesn't work. Exasperated, I drop placeholder thoughts in the journal and come out.

I pull our arms back. "What are you doing with my suit? And the shirt? And tie? Where'd the tie come from? Why are you buffing my dress shoes?"

"Microphones. Remember? Say, these shoes are shiny."

"They're military Oxfords. They stay shiny without polishing. Now, why are you doing this?"

She snorts. *"You think you'll embarrass me by wearing your warthog ugly polyester tie? I found this silk Jerry Garcia tie in the new shipment and bought it for your date with Lea tonight."*

That stopped me mid-yawn. *"It's a nice tie. What? A date? With Leala, tonight? Kidding, right?"* What's she up to this time? I suppress my growing excitement and push the emotion further back to keep Sarah from picking up on it.

"No joking, you two steamed up your cells with texts the last ten days. Naughty boy, you played hard to catch. Yesterday, you caved to her hints. According to your last text message, and I quote, 'Katie and Quentin won't let this go. Would you do me the honor of dinner? See you at your apartment at 7?' She responded, 'As long as we take my car.'"

"I didn't text anything." Oh, no—I glance at the bedroom mirror—yes, we're grinning. This can't be good for me. But it is Leala …

"Lea is a caring, understanding woman. She understood your bashfulness and melted over your texted poems."

"Poems? What poems? Besides, I never text."

"You do now. Read the texting history on your cell. I distinctly remember all the key presses for each message too. Nearly burnt my thumbs it got so hot. Oops, maybe it was me, not you who texted. Please do me a favor and go on this date. I will hate being embarrassed if my blendy partner is a wuss."

We so have to talk about boundaries. Now she's involved Leala in her little-sister meddling with my life. I have to go through with it to not hurt or offend Leala. Then again, there's an upside. I have a date with Leala.

After a shower and drying off, I check in the mirror. No surprise, no need to shave. Yet another fracture in my male identity. At least I never liked shaving. I fold Sarah in-shell into her cozy-drawer. This might be a good time to stick her in a sealed jar. No, that wouldn't be funny. Besides, all this meddling has made me the happiest I've been in months.

On the way out, Quentin stops me. "Here are the tickets for the outdoor concert. You have reservations at Chez-Chez in forty-five minutes. I pre-ordered the wine; no Ripple or Mad Dog tonight."

More Sarah meddling. It doesn't ruin my good mood.

Giggle. I didn't hear that. She can emote twenty feet away, and I can sense it? She's growing stronger, but she's right about this, I needed this date.

At my knock, Leala opens her door. "Pick your jaw back up. I'm not always a tomboy." Her hair down in an asymmetric wave, dangling gold earrings, a flowing knee-length skirt, flouncy blouse, strap sandals, and matching purse. She's always perfect. She's more than perfect. I'm frozen.

Hands on hips, she waits, then blows out a huff. "Figures. If you won't, then I will." She pulls me in and kisses me. "I understand you picked someplace fancy for tonight."

I avoid looking in mirrors. I'm afraid I'll look like a grinning loon.

Sarah

As always, in-shell Sarah had no sense of time.

They were coming back! Alex's and Lea's blaze of intermingled colors almost knocked Sarah out of the highboy drawer that they used as her non-Alex place. She sensed them three blocks away as they passed the Bodega and she mentally followed them into the bedroom.

With all that movement, she worried about her poor bed springs. She could feel so much more than with KateQuen's assignations. Impossible to ignore their emotions when they ramp up.

Being the little sister pressing her ear to the door was irresistible. She couldn't help being obsessed with the happiness of her soldier, her knight in shining armor.

No! She couldn't block them. She was losing herself. This was a bad mistake. She couldn't block them.

She started a mantra to maintain control.

I'm Sarah. I'm Sarah. I ... I ... help me ...

I'm SarLeala. I ... I'm SarLea.

I'm SarLea?

SarLea!

 ... help me ...

LOST ... FOUND

SARAH

Her thoughts circled each other like cats unhappily occupying a small room:

What's this place?

I'm happy.

What's "happy?"

How do I get back?

What's "back?"

Something concerned her deeply, but she couldn't remember what. She should be panicked, but this place was too peaceful.

For some reason, she was obsessed with Russian matryoschka nesting dolls. She shook it off. Silly topic.

Boredom doesn't exist when you have no sense of time. Strange, Alex often would say something like that.

Alex.

Oh, she had to find Alex. She had to focus on Alex.

Why?

Hey. A new sensation imploded her ennui. A talking star popped up. Awesome. She would check it out, then continue her Alex search.

"SARAH. SARAH, IS THAT YOU?" It knew Sarah's name? Her focus on the voice pulled her out and into the physical.

Who was pressing on her surface? She was relieved to be back, but who dared?

"Sarah is that you?"

"Yes, and who the hell are you? Oops." How long had she been out? No one should be able to slip in this close. How did this person catch her?

"I thought so. It adds up now."

"Who are you?"

Whoever it was didn't pull away. Even with the continuous contact, its voice was staticky.

"Lea."

Great, it got better and better. Alex was going to kill her. She'd never hear the end of the Katie lectures. Katie's roiling hot-pink color overlay was fun to watch, but only when you weren't the focus.

"What do you want?"

Lea had nerves like piano wire, to continue touching Sarah's surface while talking through the temporary neural pathways. "Right this moment, some briefs. Mine got ripped, and my skirt's a mess. I'd hoped to borrow a pair, and a skirt or shorts. I want to leave before the security shift change and not wake Alex. I'll return them without Alex knowing."

"TMI! Borrow them, and don't tell Alex."

"No, we need to work this out, persona a persona."

"Fine. Pull me out. Hey. Gently! I'm not a scarf on the discount rack. Drape me around your neck like a shawl. We can talk better that way. What time is it?"

"A little after oh-five-hundred." Her sparks of fear interfered with Sarah's ability to follow what she was saying. The neural connection reverberated like a cracked piano soundboard at a concert.

"I can make this easier. Take me to Alex."

Sarah jumped Alex and blended with him. They were partnered again as Sarah Beth. Lea's energy reacted violently with multi-hued flashes. As soon as Sarah could see, she reached for Lea to keep her from crying out.

She wasn't there.

Below and to Sarah's right, a tight monotone said, "Get off him bitch." Crouched in the same attack stance Alex used two weeks ago, Lea pointed her gun at Sarah, without wavering. "I won't ask again."

"Please, don't…"

"Why?"

"Because you may wake Alex and he'll be pissed. Please don't wake him. I need to lie down, and then he'll appear."

Lea stood and backed two steps, keeping the gun pointed at Sarah's chest. "I'm his security, and you're running out of time."

"Easy, easy. This will be over in a second. Then, wake Alex and ask him." This would be quick. Afterwards, she'd get the biggest ass-chewing of her life since she bagged that hornet's nest and tossed it into the middle of the three-legged race competition during the Hergenreder picnic.

Bogus. She couldn't. What was wrong?

Her eyes opened to the barrel pressed between her eyes. Lea said, "I don't see him. Twitch and I'll shoot. I'm taking the risk that once your green eyes fade, I'll see him."

"Something's wrong. I'm energy depleted but shouldn't be. Give me a moment, I have to think." Sarah wasn't worried about the bullet. Some instinct told her neither of them was at risk. But the sound and pain would wake Alex, and he'd kill her.

"I said, time's up." Lea retreated several steps, fumbled in her purse and pulled out her phone. "I'm doing what I should have done when I found you. I'm calling in a full team."

Sarah would never live this down. She'd always be the fuzz-wit who couldn't maintain simple OpSec. "Stop. Don't do that. We're the project. I made a mistake in responding to you. Tell you what. I'll wake Alex, and he'll fix this." She fixed their eyes on Lea. "Please don't move until Alex sees you."

Jangle. Jangle.

Alex woke slowly, as usual. "Wazzup?"

Sarah was afraid to speak, to breathe.

Alex

Leala's standing next to me. What a wonderful sight the first thing in the morning. A hole in my existence fills. "Oh, mornin' Leala. Do you have to leave so soon? Quentin will be devastated if you don't sample whatever he cooked this morning."

My neck muscles loosen dropping my head to see Leala's gun. She's a mole? Her plan was to bed then kill me? "What the hell, Leala?"

"What happened to the wine last night?"

"What's with the gun?" My voice. Oh damn, I'm Sarah Beth.

"One chance. What happened to the wine?"

"Nothing." The click of the safety disengaging clears the remnants of my fuzziness. "It was corked. Ruined. We both got ill from the moldy taste. We went to the bar across the street to clear our mouths."

She points the muzzle away from us but only to one side. "How can you talk while being Sarah?"

"That's what the project is all about. I form the living core for Sarah. Without me, she might die. No one knows how any of this works." That discloses too much, but she's looking at the proof.

However, something's wrong. "Why am I still Sarah Beth?"

"I'm not certain. "Sarah's voice warbles. "We've had another energy depletion. I sense I can't separate, I just don't have the energy for it."

"How'd I get blended?"

In the light from the casement window, Leala's olive toned cheeks blossom red. "I was sneaking out before the security shift change and needed to supplement my ripped clothes. I found her while rummaging in her drawers."

Sarah says, "He meant why did I break his precious OpSec. Fine, but don't yell; I wasn't paying attention. When she touched me, I responded. She couldn't handle it, so I, well, jumped and blended with you to explain."

We're in trouble, and I don't see an easy way out. I grimace. "Leala pulled her gun on you. It's okay. You don't have the experience to understand why blending was a bad idea with a security chief watching." Sarah still doesn't comprehend the high stakes security we live under; Leala may be in trouble for not shooting the creature she saw and ask questions later.

Leala slips her gun into her purse. "I've got to go before this gets out of hand."

I grab control of Sarah Beth and pull Leala onto the love seat. "No. I have enough experience to know this won't work. We'll go out and ask Quentin to get Katie ready for a walk. The three—four—of us, will talk this out away from microphones. We'll walk the neighborhood like girlfriends getting early morning exercise. Sarah, call the magic number and tell them we're on the move. We'll stop at the bagel shop about a mile away."

We gaze directly into Leala's eyes. Lovely expressive eyes. Warm medium brown like the finest latte ready for my surrender. Her breath on my lips, inviting...I'm confused. I want, but don't want to. Emotions contradict, churning my stomach. The conflict dizzies me. I loosen control of Sarah Beth to concentrate on the strangeness.

Sarah stiff-arms us away from Leala. "You heard the man. Find what you need from my clothes and talk to Quennie. I'll contact security for our walk."

Leala looks good in our clothes, better than us since we've grown taller and lost our curves. No!

Sarah emotes anguish. *"I'm sorry, I'm not ready for girl on girl. You have your regular body for Lea."*

This is the first time we've been conflicted on an emotional level. I'm still heavily disoriented. We remain seated to center ourselves, as Sarah has the same problem. Time to apologize. *"No, I'm sorry. I let the moment get away from me. Forgive me."*

Sarah emotes acceptance. I ask, *"What do we do when you make a connection? If not Jimmy, then someone else?"*

"I don't know."

What will we do with our freak show?

70

QUIS CUSTODIET IPSOS CUSTODES?

ALEX

Puzzled, Katie comes out of KateQuenCave, dressed for a morning walk. Seeing Leala and Sarah Beth together this early, causes storm clouds to form behind her eyes. Leala and I grab her arms and walk her outside where our four discreet shadows wait. Double coverage.

I catch Sarah's confusion. I wish we could tell the control desk what was happening. *"They only needed one team. Check Katie; she's pleased they responded properly. Probably the last thing she'll be pleased about for a while."*

One team heads to the bagel shop. We follow, talking quietly, with the other two trailing at a discreet distance.

A half block later, Katie screams, "Are the three of you crazy?" The guards stop and fade into the shadows, observing before acting.

Katie's pissed, but she needs a reality check. I step forward and crane our neck up to return her glare. "Listen, and chill for once in your life. It was an accident. Leala is exactly the smart, intuitive operative you need. All I know is our cooperation is contingent on Leala staying in the same close relationship." I avoid stating the obvious. She's my most trusted security, and my girlfriend—I hope. After this, she may do the intelligent thing and distance herself.

A glare from Katie that could cut battleship hull steel. She doesn't like threats. We walk, silently, to the bagel shop and place our orders.

The shadows sit between us and the door and window. I watch Katie.

Sarah's handling recon. She comes back. *"Will this slip Katie into one of her breaks?"* I emote a *"we'll see."* More relaxed, she provides her report. "Nothing interesting in the neighborhood, except for the heavy-set guard. I assume he's from where bagels are considered food."

Savoring her cinnamon raisin bagel, toasted, no shmear, pulling a finger's worth at a time, Katie's expression clears and the corners of her lips lift. "This may help. Sometimes the project needs Alex, solo, not as Sarah Beth."

She stops and signals the four who accompanied us. They move to occupy all the tables immediately around us.

Katie continues, "It's obvious that Sarah's has been blowing off security briefings. Sarah, come forward so I can tell you're paying attention."

She does and nervously plays with her hair.

Katie drops into her not-a-friend mode. "This is a terrible place for a security briefing, but here we are. Leala knows that this is not about her or her reliability." Leala confirms with a shrug. "It's about how the difficulty of maintaining control of information and thus the situation expands with each additional person who knows about a secret. Each new person exponentially increases the number of potential leaks." She stopped to eat another finger-pull of bagel.

Leala says, "I can explain further. Quis custodiet ispsos custodes? Rough translation: Who watches the watchers? Adding me..." She checks who may be listening. "... let's say now I have to be watched, too."

I say, "Let me." I switch to internal. *"By exposing our secret to Leala, you add her to those who know. Anyone could unintentionally say something that may seem harmless but could be collected and combined to form dangerous knowledge. Your Greasy may still have connections inside the project.*" I feel the blood drain out of our face.

Katie stops taping her fingernails on the table. She said, "From the look on your face, can I assume that you finally get it?" Sarah gives a barely perceptible nod.

Katie says, "Let's walk."

Once we clear the crowds near the bagel shop, she adds, "As I said, this may work for us. If someone's shift bridged this transition, they might break our deepest secret. Mr. Johnson and I have been going crazy planning security coverage to prevent this." Relief. Katie is in solution mode. "Leala, you can bridge those awkward transitions, which means overtime. I'm assuming this is okay with you."

"Are you kidding? These two are my best friends within a thousand miles." Leala grabs our hand and squeezes.

Katie takes a deep breath. Another breath. She looks like she could stand a whiskey.

"I'll use Jimmy's encrypted phone line to talk with Mr. Johnson. You're lucky I'm both the XO and your friend." She stops, turns us, and gaze directly into our eyes. "I know somehow, Alex, you created this mess. Even if you didn't, you have the training and should be keeping Sarah from causing these problems."

71

DUST

KATIE: PROJECT HQ

The windowless office suited Katie. The eight-by-twelve-foot room decorated in corporate-beige calmed her. She reset the thermostat down five degrees below the automatic level and relaxed.

An almost-sneeze, caused by dust from the plowing of the Palouse hills didn't happen, but the pressure made her eyes water.

She'd remind someone to check the filters. When Mr. Johnson insisted she have an office in the off-the-books HQ, she had moved out all the furniture. All she would allow was a six-foot table, a cushionless, hard-backed chair, a monitor large enough to be easily read, and the Ethernet link on the secured internal net.

In her peripheral vision, the blinking red LEDs in the upper corners reminded her, she was watched. She allowed herself a small smile every time she sat down in this private retreat. Control with no surprises was what she got here. At least until a report reminded her of the effectively out of control male-Alex and thing-Sarah.

The latest was that morning when Alex's psych eval took longer than normal. At the same time, Quentin and Sarah got into a fight, and she retreated to her cozy-drawer. Precisely on schedule, Graviton was on the move. Before Alex could be rushed back to their apartment, the project had an unexpected bonus test. Graviton slid through a fully instrumented para-psychology test on a group of psychics. She wasn't detected by the equipment or the psychics.

Katie started her search again for Rashaad, her cousin who dragged her back to sanity after she knifed Alex Jane. Except, she'd forgotten that the HQ net was internal only. She approved of the security but was pissed that she couldn't do her most private search where she was in the most control.

During a particularly boring lecture, and to distract her from the on-and-off flakiness of the Sarah Beth creature, she had messaged her cousin Rashaad thanking him for his assistance. She carefully worded the message to avoid anyone digging down and discovering that Rashaad was a low-level weed booster. It didn't work. Rashaad had disappeared off her phone and her cloud contact lists. She had searched online to copy the info when a dead end—no, a brick wall— interfered. He was nowhere. She expanded to BMD—birth, marriage, death—records, then using a for-pay snoop service, a complete history. He never existed. Neither did his family, including his parents.

The unusual XO gig kept her busy. She was promulgating policy and practices as she saw the need. Mr. Johnson always approved. She'd only had brief snippets of time to find Rashaad. She might discretely request the InfoSec people, who weren't in her control, to give her an assist. They could break into anything.

She was wasting time. She didn't like to waste time. Her finger swipe popped the project summary view to the top. Her frown, along with the triple creases in her forehead, grew as she read the lab reports and requisitions. The physicists and the psychologists were fighting again. Both groups wanted more time with the Sarah Beth phenomena. The physics geeks, because her abilities were unmeasurable, and the equipment lost calibration during tests. The psychology nerds remonstrated that her readings of people pointed to new vistas on understanding the inner turmoil of subjects.

The only thing the two teams agreed on was that under no circumstances should Sarah Beth be sequestered in a secured facility with controlled access. The physicists believed she had access to enough energy to destroy any known facility. The psychologists believed she was only stable with people, lots of people, to relate to. The diversions of interpersonal relationships preoccupied her and away from self-exploration.

Katie blew through pursed lips and hand-combed her Afro. *I need another haircut.* It didn't take a Ph.D. and dozens of published post-grad papers to know how unstable the Sarah Beth entity was. She saw it every day, in their reactions, their fights, and Sarah's random fits of childishness. She also saw how they stabilized when they were in groups.

The reports scrolled past as she speed-read them. Never comfortable with touch screens, she set the reports to append to each other in a continuous stream.

She stopped and rolled back with her old-fashioned mouse control as something caught her attention. She cursed under her breath. They had identified one of Y'Arty's conference sites, this one at the Idaho Falls airport. A couple of security cams had shots of him. Why Idaho Falls? What was there? Why three times? It was on no routes, but was an end-point. She put this in her 'to check' pop-up list. The lounge where they met matched Sarah's descriptions and hand-drawn diagrams. The time was the same as the nightmare, but lounge footage only showed him. The others who he might have been meeting with were only blurs that refused to clean up with the most sophisticated imaging software. They couldn't even confirm that the female Sarah reported was a female.

The monitor flipped off the table from the force of her punch. She picked it up and waited for the inevitable polite knock. Opening the door to the OOD, Officer of the Day, she said, "I'm okay. Just frustrated."

"Sir, we're out of monitors. Should I requisition extras?" Fair question. She'd lost it the first day over all the unknowns and cracked a monitor.

Too much the professional to blush, she said, "No, I can contain myself. Before I forget, could you get someone to check the air filters? I get dust through my vent." She suppressed another sneeze.

"No one has reported dust. We installed HEPA filters."

Katie brushed the dust off her sleeve and sneezed. "Get HazMat in here. I'll be in the unoccupied room."

72

SECOND DATE

ALEX

Leala turns to speak to me. "Does Alex have plans tonight?" We're in Leala's car coming back from the lab. It's secure, but she's careful. Clever woman. As we're Sarah Beth, I say nothing.

Sarah emotes exasperation. *"Well, talk to the woman. With the engine and wind noise, even Jimmy's equipment can't tell it's you. Besides, you need to practice my cadences anyway. Stop ending sentences with an upward inflection. I'm not an airhead."*

"I, uh, he"—guffaw from Leala— "would like to catch the movie about the sniper abandoned behind enemy lines. But it probably wouldn't do for a date."

"I'd be happy to catch it. My trade mag had an article on the authenticity of the ops and equipment. Which showing do you think Alex would like, and should we go early for dinner."

"I believe he said there's a showing around seven PM. Leaving at five-thirty would give you plenty of time."

"Sounds good to me. Have him call me when you get back."

Whew. I'm glad we rarely fake which of us is speaking. It gets weird. I do my best emulation of a Sarah-beam.

Sarah

She voiced her grandmother's greatest exclamation: Holy Horned Tomato Worms! She had picked up Alex and Lea—AlLea—as they passed her reference point, the bodega over a quarter mile from her room. She could tell they're drunk, well over Washington's stringent limits.

She decided it must be late. In preparation for their arrival, she shut down her perception of others. It had been a boring night. A burst of energy suffused her in green.

Sarah: else-somewhere

Bogus. How did she get here, in what she assumed the same 'place' that Alex called else-somewhere? She'd protected herself against dropping out of the physical. That failed, but she did manage to protect her sentience. At least that was progress.

The last thing she remembered was waiting for Alex and Lea to return from their date. Hanging out in my unmentionables drawer, and … and …

Her memory fades in like a reverse Cheshire Cat smirk. *A little more. A little more. Got it.* Alex and Lea returned and jumped into bed. Like the last time, she heard their thoughts. As much as she wanted to ensure that Alex was happy, she had increased her mental 'wall,' and—something. She'd work it out. She was on a roll. Unfortunately, she still didn't know how to return.

Even with her protection up, she 'heard' their thoughts. It was if she was pushed from the outside. Something still was missing from this picture.

No matter where she went, she didn't find any Russian nesting dolls. It seemed like she'd searched forever. Wait a ding-dong minute. Why was she wasting time on dolls? Where did this obsession come from? Those dolls were from Alex's past and certainly wouldn't be here in sensing space. Alex told her the last he heard, his aunt whozzit got pissed off and locked them away.

Which reminded her, she couldn't find Alex.

When she concentrated, applied focus, memories of what went wrong came back to her. There was a strange burst of energy. Despite her blocking, she had lost her ability to disconnect from their thoughts.

73

SARLEA

SARAH

Hold on. Movement changes what I sense. Am I moving or is the material around me moving? The non-glow glow of else-some-where ebbs and other glows momentarily replaced the non-glow.

The claret glow. It was talking. It was mind-blowing. Sarah had to investigate.

"Sarah … Sarah … Sarah." The glow was saying her name. She focused on the talking thing, and it pulled her back. She needed to take this knowledge with her …

The non-glow dissipated, and she only sensed people. Wasn't there a thought she wanted to keep?

Lea? How'd she slip in so close?

Did Sarah fade out? How? In-shell Sarah doesn't fade out. Was she in what Alex called else-somewhere? She answered, *"I hear you."*

Lea said, staticky, "Alex and I were partying after—you know. You've been so sweet you deserve a treat. Alex will take good care of you." She jerked on Sarah's surface.

"Hey. Not so rough. Why can't you be gentle like Alex or Quennie?"

Alex moved closer. No, she saw through Lea's eyes, poorly. She was doing the moving, more staggering than walking. Alex was sprawled on the bed, in a stupor. Drunk.

Intense tingling flooded her shell-form. When did she ... No! Last time she felt the same tingling was the first time she merged with Alex. *"Hey. Don't do it. Take your foot away from there. It's dangerous. Not the arm —"*

The improbable happened. She had successfully combined with a new person, Lea. "Lea, what the hell? Are you crazy? You can be damaged. And Alex--yes, you--is there any other Alex in here with a stupid look on his face? How can you let this happen?" What's wrong with her voice? It oozed like a wine-soaked baguette.

Alex stood and pulled her into him. "We wanted you to feel like a woman. Leala wanted you to feel as good as she has. I couldn't think of a good argument."

"That's because you're both drunk. Lea ... Lea. Where are you? Hell, Alex, I've lost Lea."

He stood and fell backward, head snapped back. Her punch wiping the silly grin off his face. After losing all but Mom in the accident, her Hergenreder cousins took her on as a special project. That included how to handle herself, like how to punch like a guy.

"Get back up here. You bastard. How could you do this? To Lea? To me."

Alex staggered to a stand. She threw a punch, this time from her weak right side. He stopped it and grabbed both wrists. As he gathered her to him, she felt his stiffness rub against her. Oh, to wrap her legs around ... No! Stay focused. She was Sarah, not this, this, horny thing.

He crumpled like a cheap hunting lean-to during a storm. Her cousins had also taught her to knee, hard if her hands were caught.

She wanted to cripple Alex for this stupid stunt, but she had to cut this short before she lost herself in whatever this strange person was.

"People are waking all over the building. Half this building is awake. Your stunt tripped alarms. Go wake Katie, she'll wake Jimmy. He has a crash cart in his apartment. Shut up and run! Don't let anyone in here. I'll come out. I've got to check something first."

The bedroom door slamming on his exit barely registered. Everything felt wrong. She grabbed her pink plush robe and wobbled into the bathroom. Oh, no.

She'd changed. Her hair flowed in rich, auburn waves to the small of her back. Her freckles were only hints in her otherwise flawless light olive skin. She loved these high cheekbones. Her eyes, lashes, and thick brows smolder back at her. Oh, check out these pouty lips, ready to be kissed. She kissed herself in the mirror. No!

That's it. She was deblending.

Ow!

It was worse than her first disastrous separation attempt with Alex. She nearly fainted, and only her death grip on the sink kept her from falling. She waited for the spasms to stop. She couldn't deblend with Lea unconscious.

She was stuck. Stuck in this glorious body. Where was Alex? He could carry her to bed. No!

This was trouble. Lea's shadow mocked her in the mirror. But sexier. Much sexier. She was heading out to an after-hours club with a brass pole to wrap herself around. She didn't own a G-string, but she could fold her bikini thong like a G-string.

No! She was losing herself. If she didn't save Lea quickly, she'd lose her and herself.

The colors in the room kept inverting, then returning to normal.

She now understood Alex. Poor Alex. How had he survived all these weeks stuck as Sarah Beth? Once she deblended with Lea, she'd have a frank discussion with the lab cats and rats about how to up the pace of Alex's release.

Say, she could almost put her hands around her thin, sexy waist. This body shouldn't be covered with a robe. Or any clothes. No! she was losing herself. Lea had had enough time to wake up. Time to take off the "friend" gloves and bare-knuckle her.

"Leala, mueve ese trasero y sal en este mismo instante."

Spanish? She spoke Spanish? It was her imagination. She didn't know Spanish.

She would try again, but out loud. Out loud should shock her into sensibility. "Leala, muevete! Sal aqui ahora mismo."

She couldn't speak English, and she changed Spanish dialect. She was losing Sarah and Leala.

Check out those tits. They must be at least D cups. She was taller. These legs, long enough to wrap around Alex. Where was Alex when she needed him? She had something for him to fill.

No. She was losing herself. She'd never tease Alex again with her sexuality. As she left the bathroom, she pulled the robe tighter and tripped on it

Uhng.

From her vantage point, sprawled here on the floor, vacuum cleaner tracks crisscross the carpet.

She'll kill Quennie. She told him not to clean their room.

Her hair was pulled, and her head jerked back. She stared into Katie's dangerous eyes. She'd never, ever seen the whites of her eyes before. Those deep mahogany irises, you could swim in them.

No! Snap out of it. She must separate before she and Leala become ... what?

Katie focused Sarah's attention by showing her the inside of the barrel of her BMFG. "Who the fuck are you and how'd you get in here?"

For some reason, Sarah stalled, wondering when Katie got the extreme haircut. "I'm Sarah, help me." Not again, it was in Spanish. Katie's face erupted in ripples like when she had her breakdown, and her overlay was beyond iridescent. "Please help me." Still in Spanish.

"Bullshit. Who are you? Slow down. My Spanish is pobre … poor."

"I'm Sarah, blended with Leala instead of Alex." Leala? First, she was stuck in Spanish, and now she couldn't say, Lea. How much time before she became … whom?

Katie's face flickered to concern. "We'll see. When did we first meet?"

"That's easy, in Alex's Lit class, then in the ReUnion."

BMFG was still pointed at Sarah, but at least not in her face. "Everyone knows that. What did we talk about?"

"Please, I need help, not a questionnaire." Still in Spanish. Katie fixed Sarah in her glare. She didn't take back talk, never did. "Fine, mostly your threats and my giggles. I was still dealing with puerilism. You threatened to skin me off Alex."

Katie ejected the magazine and cycled the bullet out of BMFG's chamber. "Close enough, little sister, but someone will keep a shotgun on you, so don't get ideas. Now, what do you need?"

She struggled for more Sarah-speak. "Best if I sit at a table in a straight-backed chair. I study best that way, and I hope it's best for Leala." Still in Spanish, and her voice was smoother and smokier.

She remembered flashes of her family's festival at the start of May. Cinco de Mayo, that's what it was. All her cousins, dozens of them, all ages romping and playing. Her in the middle, carrying little Juanita on her shoulders while the kid made faces at the boys.

No! She'd never been to Houston. These were Leala's memories of her family. Memory leaks never happened with Alex.

Katie pulled her up, wrapped the robe around her and tightened the sash. She held her away from the door to the common room as she opened it. Satisfied with whom she saw, she sharply ordered. "You two, clear out everyone who is not Alpha cleared. Leave the street sweepers." She held Sarah from moving, so she didn't know who it was. "Tell Jimmy and Clarice to stay at their instruments; Clarice in the van. Then you two come back. You've been upgraded to Alpha clearance. Don't smile. This isn't something you'll like."

The room cleared, we go in. Only Alex and Quennie remained in the room.

Quennie glanced at Sarah and took a swing at Alex. "Of all the stupid, idiotic stunts. Don't you have any respect for Sarah? And what about Lea, what happens if..." He took another swing; they never argue. "You don't understand how much Sarah..."

Katie's grip on her shoulder tightened. She glared at Quennie and Alex. "Stop. It can wait. Both of you, be part of the solution. Sit down on the couch. Now."

The two security guards returned. Oh no, they're Harry and David, her 'adopted' cousins, and Leala's apartment mates. Why did it have to be them? Leala may be dead.

Katie said to Harry and David, "Congratulations, you're both Alpha cleared. Both of you grab a street sweeper shotgun. You"—she indicated Harry—" cover the door. No one gets in or out until this is resolved or Mr. Johnson authorizes it. That leaves you"— indicating David—"to cover little Miss here. Shell in the chamber, safety off. If it gets strange and I don't signal it's okay, pull the trigger. Yes, I know she looks something like Leala. If this goes wrong, you probably will be doing her a kindness."

Sarah sat at the dining table. Think. This was not Alex. Her limbic safety valve, with its immediate rejection of non-suitable hosts, failed. The one time Quennie pushed their friendship too far, she had fallen into a panic state. When Alex returned, he had to drag her quivering shell out of a corner.

Think. Leala's thrivability as a core? Who knew? Alex's ability to survive their blend remained a mystery. Leala was Sarah's only friend. She had never had a friend before. Alex was her core, her reason to rise each morning ready to die in the tests. She lived to make Alex free. He was her love. But he wasn't a friend.

Why did the universe hate her? First, she died, then she destroyed Alex's life. Now she'd killed Leala.

The colors in the room inverted and returned to normal. There was no outcry from the others, so only she sensed it.

Her head smashed itself on the dining table. She saw stars.

No, those were people, clearly, no fuzziness. Not in the sensing state; why did she see people? Shuffling, and the entry of a shell in the shotgun chamber caught her attention.

Impossibly jumbled senses replaced vision. Lea! She was fine, for now. She could call her Lea, a good sign. She sensed people clustering around her. Her friends. She waved them off as her body smashed her head on the table. This could be a survival reaction of Sarah-shell. Her vision clears. Blood pooled where her head landed.

She understood what to do. She climbed on the dining table, laid flat and wrapped her robe around her. Not as good as an ER bed, but it'd suffice. She shifted into the sensing state. Immediately her limbic system kicked her out. She was sprawled indecently on the table. When she tried to retrieve Alex, she fell out of the chair and nearly beaned herself on an end table. For decency, she rewrapped her robe.

"Alex. I can't deblend with her this way. She's slipped beyond my immediate reach. I'm going in. Lea's not as compatible as you. She'll need the crash cart. This may get violent. Please toss a blanket over us, just in case." She wished her last words were in English, instead of Spanish. David translated to Alex and Quennie as she …

Fluorescent green permeated… everything.

She never wanted to see or sense it again. There was Lea, in this terror-filling non-glow glow. Sarah pushed into the only place or thing that truly terrified her. It stung like a million jellyfish taking a bath in fire ants.

My God, it was full of stars. No, not stars, people. She already felt at home. If she stayed too long; she'd never want to leave. Where was Lea? Where? There. Sarah pushed towards her. No, harder. Harder. She could touch ... fluorescent green fire throughout seared her being.

Lea was back. She was quiet, but it was medical. Sarah deblend. Success.

Lea was safe from Sarah.

Where was Alex? She was drained. She needed to blend. Alex came within reach, and she jumped him. Her vision cleared in their reblended body, she said, "Okay, connect her up to the crash cart. She's back, but something's wrong."

She was speaking in English again, but Alex was knocked out. She blended too fast in her panic. She wrapped Lea in her robe and pulled the sheet around her Sarah Beth body. David caught her as she collapsed. He positioned her for maximum comfort on the couch. Quennie held her head.

Katie hovered and opened Lea's eyelid to check pupil size. "Should we run her to a hospital."

"I don't know. I'm not a doctor." She saw double, and Alex wouldn't respond.

"I am. Get the hell out of my way!" Doctor Timsen! She had never been so happy to see anyone. Behind her was Johnson. Neither was doing happy. Doc Timsen pulled back Leala's eyelids, flashed her penlight in them, checked vitals and had the tech set up the EKG. Reading it, she said, "I think she's only unconscious, but we'll transfer her to the hospital. With this type of strangeness, we don't know what's normal."

A dozen others were scattered in small clusters around and in the apartment building, apparently to avoid notice. The alarm had worked.

Timsen opened the door, barked. "Get your van warmed up. We're using it." After closing the door and checking who was in the room,

Doc Timsen said to the tech, "Could you ensure the van is getting ready?" He left. Now everyone was cleared.

She turned on us. "Now, what happened?" Angry was never a good look on Doc Timsen.

"My fault," Sarah said. "I wasn't fast enough to realize Leala was pulling me in the way that would activate my blending. Alex is okay. He's recovering from my flash-blend." She was losing her ability to concentrate. "*Help here. I'm fading.*"

Timsen grabbed their shoulders and shook. "Stay with me. Why was she trying to blend?"

Alex woke up emoting confusion. He recognized Dr. Timsen and answered for Sarah, "She felt bad for Sarah. She felt it was unfair to Sarah to not be with me as a woman." His Sarah Beth voice trembled. The flash-blending had sobered him, and reality was crashing in on him.

"Of all the stupid drunken stunts. Get into something decent. You're coming, too. You two bruisers put Leala in a chair and carry her out to the van." She opened the door. "Jimmy, clear your junk off the table in the van."

The color spectrum inverted. ENOUGH! Sarah stopped whatever it was, and the color spectrum returned to normal. She had Alex and Lea to help; stupid light effects would not distract her.

Harry and David gathered Lea into the chair and lifted. Outside of Katie, they were the best protection Lea could have. Timsen and Katie scowled at Sarah. Orders were orders. She rushed to put on modest clothes, comfortable, she didn't know how long it would be. She tossed her brush into her purse.

She staggered. Alex took over. They still staggered. Alex's and Lea's stupid stunt had depleted their energy. Quennie half carried them while they followed the crowd to the porcupine van. Katie gripped their forearm and joined Johnson in his car. Katie drove. Three cars followed the porcupine van. They were in the middle car.

Alex was still befuddled, so Sarah swept the neighborhood. Four guard types left behind. One in their apartment with Quennie. Jimmy with another in his apartment, probably monitoring. They weren't taking chances.

Sarah still wanted to throttle Alex, and she was fighting off the sensations lingering from her Leala blending. She wanted to return to normal, and not that – that sensual SarLea blend. As much as she wanted to peel his hide off for the violation of her, they had a more immediate problem.

She asked, "Dish the truth. What possessed Lea into this stupid stunt?"

She couldn't tell if it was intentional, but Alex projected an image of a boy in trouble, drawing circles in the dust with his toe. They had stopped image projecting weeks ago when the emoji-style novelty wore off. He mumbled in a wispy, soft voice, "*She busted us on the texting. She figured it out before the first date and tricked me into admitting to it when we were drinking.*" He was burning off the bravado. "*I guess I got caught up in the moment.*"

"You mean you were drunk."

Their boss, Mr. Johnson, interrupted the apparent silence. "We'll reevaluate Leala's situation on the team."

Sarah leaned forward. "Look into my eyes, and you'll see Sarah. Alex and I have undergone, without complaint, massive inconvenience, physical pain, suffering, and near-death. There is, however, an unwritten clause in our contract: no nice people get hurt. Simple as that."

Alex said, "We can't start getting rid of people who…"

"Shut up Alex. I'll deal with you later." Katie hit the brakes, checked Sarah Beth's eyes in the rear-view mirror and merged with traffic. Sarah continued. "That goes for Lea. If anything happens, she becomes distant, or unavailable, I quit; I shut down. Alex walks away. I dissipate after about a week."

She avoided mentioning she'd be uncontrollable within 24 hours; they already knew that.

"Face it. Lea was trying to do something good. Alex didn't tell her ninety percent of the cores died. With those deaths, I never thought to guard against someone initiating blending. That won't happen again." She suppressed the shudder that threatened to push her into hysteria. Only with Alex did Sarah retain her identity.

"You mean Alex got drunk." Katie tapped an agitated tattoo on the steering wheel.

Mr. Johnson turned in his seat and stared into their eyes, checking to ensure it was her and not Alex talking. "We may revisit this, but as long as Leala recovers, we don't need to make any changes."

Sarah thought, Thank you, bossman. I owe you.

Katie swerved to avoid the car that appeared to attempt to intentionally T-bone them. She said, "Sorry sir, that isn't good enough. Sarah, Alex, listen up." Mr. Johnson watched her with interest but didn't interrupt. "I'm sorry to say this with Sarah here, but I don't think she can deblend right now. Here it is. This was a rape."

Sarah gasped and started to object. "I…"

"It was a rape. The merging was non-consensual. The planned next step would have been physical rape pure and simple."

"I don't think." Sarah backed into her seat.

"That's your problem. Leala and Alex are much of your life, and your blinders keep you from admitting the truth. Their being drunk was no excuse."

Sarah didn't know if the tears were from exhaustion or emotions. "They are good people."

"Of course, which is the reason I don't pull over and gut Alex after you two deblend and follow with Leala."

Mr. Johnson touched Katie's trembling shoulder. "Do you have a suggestion?"

Katie took three deep breaths and said, "This doesn't preclude your final disposition, but both of them should be taking sexual assault counseling to get their minds where they need to be. The university has a hotline, so it shouldn't be hard to get them in."

He asked Sarah, "Does that work for you?"

She said, "*Sorry, Alex, but I think it's for the best. I think they'll escalate your restrictions if you don't.*" Out loud, she said, "I have a lot to process here. I'm having difficulty thinking that I had a part in this."

Katie slammed on the brakes and pulled into an empty lot. Mr. Johnson touched her shoulder and said, "I'll handle this. You are in denial, so you're also going into counseling. Trust is about all we have on this project. Nothing else is working. You can't think you're at fault, and you can't excuse others."

Katie said, "In a normal project, they would be summarily fired. I never thought I would use exigency as a rationalization for rape but you, Sarah, create unusual circumstances where we can't apply normal responses."

74

OLIVE

SARAH: DAY 32, 6 AM

Their friends surrounded them in an examining room at the University Hospital. The attending physician from before came in, recognized us and left. The dumpy doc with a real personality did the annoying thing with the flashlight in their eyes, took blood pressure and pulse, and left muttering something to Doc Timsen. A lab tech drew blood samples; only seven tubes this time instead of the usual ten or more. Sarah was too washed out to complain or signal Alex forward to take the pain.

What Katie had said had been sinking in as she was still beyond livid with what he had done.

Lea, still unconscious from the deblending, was moved. She was too muddled to follow Lea's movement.

Alex returned from wherever he'd been, emoting agitation. *"Why'd you speak only in Spanish?"*

"You're an ass. After what you did, that's what's important?" She was so tired, and still ashamed of her part. Their friends shuffled around but didn't say anything. They were used to their internal discussions. She didn't have the energy for a fight. *"It was all I had. I formed the*

words in English but, everything came out in Spanish. Towards the end, I was thinking in Spanish." The horror of those moments still drained her.

"Did you learn Spanish in school?"

"Never. Nor from my few friends. My people are mostly German. Some still speak old-German."

Alex withdrew for a few seconds, then came back. *"Are you okay with English now?"*

"Yes."

Alex withdrew again.

Her rage remained incandescent, but the flame guttered from exhaustion. She would hold her full ire with him until she could put in the energy to give him the serious reaming he deserved.

Their body had needs Alex was too geeked out to notice. *"Ah'm not doin' good. I need carbs."* David brought her six juice boxes and a stale burrito.

A rolling wave of questions signaled Alex's return. *"Why did you change bodies after you kicked me out? What happened before Katie dragged you out of our bedroom? She was scared. She's never scared."*

She waved a hand signaling she was okay to the shuffling crowd. *"I'm not certain. I decided we could best deal with Lea's problems deblended. It failed, and the spasms nearly knocked me out. They were worse than when I bungled the first deblend with you. When my sight cleared, I checked in the mirror. I oozed sex. I lost my ability to speak English, and something blocked me from calling Leala 'Lea.'"*

They were dripping tears. *"I remembered Lea's family, their parties, and at least four dozen family member's names."*

"Memory leak from Leala to the blended you? You and I don't share memories or even thoughts, just emotions. You slid close to the threshold of completed blending. We almost lost you as Sarah."

This was too much. How much more did she have to endure? *"What threshold? What aren't you telling me?"*

Retreating, Alex said, *"I need to check something before I lose the thought. Signal me if something Alex-specific is needed."* He disappeared, again. She checked, but he was not in trouble.

They waited for about an hour before Doc Timsen burst through the double door from the ER. *"Initial tests show you're within what is normal for you, with more tests in process."* She turned and made the right side door rattle in her haste.

Lea's apartment mates, Harry and David, paced. She remained exhausted. Whatever they used as energy remained low, so she skipped her favorite hobby, people surfing.

A breeze hit them as Doc Timsen again opened the double doors, tired but all smiles. *"She regained consciousness as we transferred her to the bed. She's demanding to see Sarah Beth, but first, we ran blood tests and a CAT scan. She's in Intensive Care, room 422. Go to her before she has a kitten."*

Sarah ran with Harry and David hard behind her. She figured they had forgotten they were security and were more worried about their apartment mate. Good for them. She stumbled, and David held her arm. Each took an arm and half-carried her. Her weak attempts to walk failed. They wrapped her arms around their shoulders and carried her.

She shouted to get Alex's attention, *"Get out here. Lea's awake."*

As the three walked in, Lea propped herself up. "I said coffee, hot and black. There's nothing wrong with me." Her nurse passed us with an exasperated roll of the eyes. Lea half-grinned.

"Alex, now. Lea's awake."

Their eyes itched; Alex was back and forced a wide grin.

Lea said, "Sorry about the scare. I had no idea putting" — Sarah frantically waved to stop her before she said anything in front of the civilian medical staff — "That much liquor in me would cause me to black out for more than an hour."

She pulled Sarah in close and whispered. "I'm beyond mortified I violated you. I'm sorry and hope to get your trust back."

Sarah leaned in, "We'll work this out. Yes, I'm steamed. Once I work out my issues, we'll have a discussion, away from microphones." A month ago, she'd have bitch-slapped Lea and stomped off, forever. Now, she was more concerned for Lea's health than about what she had done. What was different now?

She realized she needed to speak to someone neutral. Sarah turned to Doc Timsen and Katie. "Set me up with the appropriate counseling."

Lea's face flushed, and she turned her head. "I should be discharged by eight. Just some final blood tests. I feel energized. I think I can do backflips."

Alex emoted happiness. *"Our preternatural healing effect included her when blended. She'll be full of energy."* He was withholding information again. He had discovered something when he disappeared.

"Spill it. What do you know?"

She glared and stomped out of Lea's room, taking the time to slam the door. She stopped her back to the door unable to catch her breath. What had she just seen? Did Lea have freckles? Like hers?

Alex took their body, walked them to a corner, and sat them in the cold plastic chair. *"You need help. I'm your help."* He arranged their gown, so they weren't sitting on cold plastic.

Still pissed, she had to ask, "Help? What the hell are you talking about?"

"It's time I stopped sugarcoating your blind spot. Yes, Leala and I were falling down drunk, but you can stop blending before it starts. You're dangerous to yourself and everyone around you. Your obsession with your staggering power blinds you and makes you vulnerable. The combination of blending as Leala and your failed deblending almost destroyed your identity as Sarah."

"Go away. We need to talk, but not now." Forcing Alex to give up all his free time and go to counseling sounded better and better.

She got the attention of security and pointed to the lavatory. With a grunt, David pushed himself up, but a female security guard Sarah didn't know pushed him back down. "You two look like hell. Besides, didn't you notice the Ladies sign? She stepped inside, and checked under, over, and inside everything before she waved Sarah in. Retreating to a corner that couldn't be seen from the door, she loosened her pistol in the holster. One more reminder of the professionalism they had surrounding their every moment.

Then another problem announced itself. In the mirror, the impossible stared back; a freckled girl with a light olive-skinned oval face. Gone was the round face with ruddy skin.

She washed her face to hide her tears. Her face had changed when she and Alex partnered. Now she'd changed again. Reaching for the paper towel dispenser, her finger stubbed on the metal.

What the …?

Her fingers—they were longer, thinner. She wanted to cry. But her retreating to her apartment and her bed to mourn what was happening would have to wait. Once she told Katie, whom she sensed hovering outside the door, she'd be rushed to the anthropometry lab for yet another intrusive exam and measurement session.

A chagrined half-smile tweaked her mouth; she must be maturing. She was about to give up the comfort of a hissy fit over being violated, to fulfill the needs of the project.

A project that had yet to yield results.

75

NO HERO'S JOURNEY

QUENTIN: AIR FORCE BASE, MOUNTAIN HOME, IDAHO

T he first morning of his trip home, Quentin woke to a rumble and his bed wobbled. It sounded like Air Force jets taking off.

Puzzled why a jet would be passing over his Ballard home, he tumbled out of bed, hit his shin on the TV console that never was there before, walked into the closet in the wrong wall, and finally found the outside door. Outside, he didn't face his kindergarten class photo on the opposite wall. Instead, an open field was in the process of being stripped down to rock. From the sign, it was to be a new hotel. In the distance, sun-dappled snow-capped mountains scrapped the skyline. The heat of the day had already raised the scent of fresh asphalt sprayed on the road bedding.

He shook away sleep fuzziness. Where was he?

Back in his room, he queried the location app on his phone. He was at a hotel in Mountain Home, closer to the Air Force base than he'd thought when he checked in. Flipping on his phone's GPS history, he discovered where he'd made two wrong turns, one outside Coeur d'Alene in North Idaho, and once in Idaho Falls, taking him two-thirds of a full circle heading back towards Pullman. He still had over twenty hours of hard driving to get to his home next to Alex's in Omaha. At least he was refreshed, and with a quick oversized Styrofoam cup of coffee, he headed out to his Omaha home.

Omaha. Home?

The disconnection in his destination stopped him as he pulled out of the parking lot.

Omaha. Home? Was it home?

Seattle's Ballard district, lying the other way, was home and always had been. He remembered his and Alex Jane's modern late 70s single level homes abutting each other at the base of the cul-de-sac. They'd broke the sliding patio screen door several times as they raced in and out to Alex's room the first door to the right. Once or twice a year, they would save money on redecorating by exchanging sports and grunge rock band posters. Behind the posters, they hid the real treasure: semi-nude underwear models for the two boys. Boys?

Alex James and Quentin.

He remembered the Omaha street, laid out in the perfect mid-West grid, with an alley providing access to backyards and detached, unpainted garages that opened to the alley. Hidden between the garages, he and Alex Jane would lean a rotted board against their turn of the twentieth-century houses and scramble to the second floor and into each other's rooms.

Alex Jane and Quentin.

Even when Alex Jane had started to fill out, they exchanged visits but kept their noise down. Both his parents and her mother spouted nonsense about boys and girls mixing. It was only by piecing together their different sex ed courses did they understand. It made no differ-ence. He was the one who finally convinced Alex Jane wearing a bra wasn't a violation of their bro-ship.

Him and Alex Jane. Except that wasn't her original name. Why couldn't he remember her name from before she changed it?

His head bursting, he left his car in the lot and walked down

Gunfighter Avenue. No destination, at least until he decided where home was. On Interstate I-84, two cars and a semi with an Idaho Potatoes banner swerved to avoid hitting him, still dazed, as he crossed.

He returned to cognizant thought when the AJ's Restaurant menu was placed in his right hand and coffee poured into the cup at his left. His eyes unfocused and he slumped until the menu was pulled from his hands.

"They've done a right proper fuck-over on you." Deep blue eyes filled with mirth, surrounded by wrinkles, and topped by silver-caterpillar eyebrows greeted Quentin. The eyebrows had more hair than the rest of the head, except for the ratty ponytail held by an Indian-beaded elastic band. A dusty scent, like an abandoned cave, marked the stranger's presence. The stranger's open toothed smile closed and inverted into a frown. "Sorry. Sometimes I forget how to talk to you people." He flipped the laminated menu pages back and forth. "Let's get some food into you first. Some Omaha soul food is in order."

For the first time since leaving Pullman, Quentin came to full attention.

Omaha?

His uninvited guest mumbled while playing with his greasy ponytail. "Has to be something suitable for an Omaha boy. No Frenchies on the menu. Hmm, also no deep-fried Mac and Cheese. Wedges won't fit the bill. No pork tenderloin sandwiches, or raisin pie. Too much to expect a runza this far away from civilization.

"Ah, here it is. A Reuben. Invented at the Omaha Blackstone Hotel by Reuben Kulakofsky for his poker friends."

"Who are you?"

"You gave me a scare at Coeur d'Alene, and I lost you in Idaho Falls. Something odd is happening in Idaho Falls.

"You're the most stubborn of the group, and that is saying a lot given whom you shack up with. I've got you heading in the right direction now. You can't go to Omaha. Your Omaha doesn't exist right now. You don't want to know what has happened to Omaha. Once your friend's reality shift relocated all the technology companies to Seattle, reactionaries took over the political power structure. Gangs of illegal aliens filled in the rest of the power niches. The governor pulled the National Guard out to cut down on causalities. They've totally hosed it in this reality bubble."

Meadowlarks sat outside on the windowsill.

"*What* are you?" Quentin's full geek kicked in. Mental lists formed: gods, demi-gods, demi-urges, titans, angels, djinn, demons, time tunnels, tame black holes with coincident mouths.

"None of that. Besides, it's not important. Either you return to college and vegetate into a mindless mush or go to Ballard and prove to yourself you're right."

The man curled his pinky inward while keeping the rest extended. "Procure a couple crystal memory drives." A code for five-finger-discount, aka steal. "Then return to college. Wait."

The entire conversation had taken place without either of them speaking.

Quentin's coffee cup spun across the table into the void left by the imploding stranger. A stranger who could read his mind.

His Reuben sat in front of him, half covered by a pile of limp fries slathered with brown gravy. The stranger's disembodied voice said, "Brown gravy on fries? Are these morons refugees from Baltimore? Oh, I forgot. Don't do anything. You anchor several pasts. Anchors don't have Hero's Journeys. Seriously, just be there. If you act, you can cease to exist. Your job is to remember what should be."

The meadowlarks disappeared without flying off.

Twenty-four hours later, Quentin collapsed into his bed in Ballard after using a retinal scan to get into his home overlooking the Ship Canal. In his rush to find his sister Aliyah, he'd left his home keys on his dresser in Pullman. For once, his father's paranoia had benefited Quentin. Otherwise, he'd have been waiting hours for his father to come off shift.

He'd found what he expected. There were no signs Aliyah had ever existed.

76

DAUGHTERS OF THE AMERICAN REVOLUTION

KATIE: LATE AFTERNOON, THEIR APARTMENT

*I*t's amazing how you can force normality into the weird.

While opening neglected mail at the dining room table, Katie scratched her freshly shorn Afro, peeling another dried flake of chemical-agent neutralizer from her scalp. She'd deflected both Sarah's and Leala's questions about her new shorn head. Anger flashed behind her eyes as she added it to the tissue paper she had secreted in her lap. The project had had a complete chemical warfare sensor and test kit, for what reason she didn't want to guess.

Several items puzzled her when she wasn't ready to throttle someone. The attack at HQ had been targeted. Only her office had the dispersal device. But why her? Granted she combined personal and official relationships with Sarah Beth, but she was replaceable.

The attack itself was amateurish. While the chemical was CR-like, a solid aerosol sometimes referred to as military-grade tear gas, it hadn't worked properly. The particles didn't remain almost invisible but clumped into noticeable dust which reduced its effectiveness.

At least they'd been able to identify the powder before she washed it down in a sink. The water would have activated it, causing the real damage. She'd helped clean up a Russian-chemical attack; she knew the wrong decon protocol could kill.

The hazmat response team had mixed up a solution that mimicked Army decon chemicals and sprayed her. Her clothes sacrificed, she borrowed a gym warm-up suit from the tallest male at HQ. Two triple-sealed containers with her hair and the clothes went to Aberdeen for analysis.

The attack at HQ was not a one-off but coordinated. Mr. Addams sensors recorded that at the same time, there was an upsurge in energy at the apartment. Not the almost unreadable environment affects caused by Sarah, but hard radiation, focused, and in the energy bands of the dodecahedron grenade. The attack on Sarah had failed. Fortunately, they hadn't breached InfoSec and didn't know that Sarah spent time as a pure energy thing. If anything, she absorbed the energy of the attack, without noticing it.

The favorite theory was that attack had had one affect. The energy absorption slowed down Sarah's reaction and sensing responses. Which was the reason she didn't stop the blending with Leala and couldn't reverse it?

At the next debriefing, she would ensure that Sarah was paying attention when the current theories about the attack were discussed. What did she do with all the energy? They may have to find another safe house. For now, having Sarah out and about would discourage and confuse those behind the attacks.

This didn't mean Alex and Leala were off the hook. The first counseling sessions had already happened.

The question of who was involved churned the entire project. The most obvious, and disturbing, answer was this—they had one or more moles. FBI agents were now embedded and lent their expertise. Moving Sarah/Alex wouldn't help if they didn't catch the mole.

She had her preferred suspect across the table from her: Leala. The Houston FBI field office was in charge of investigating her extended clan of over two hundred. Leala retained her position of close-in security, which required she stay where Katie could watch her. When Sarah made her threat to quit if Leala was removed from the project, Katie nudged Mr. Johnson. He got the message and pretended to acquiesce. However, her weapons were secured at HQ, and she was no longer the only close operative. She was watched 24/7.

Leala asked, "How is Alex?" She kept her eyes down on her homework from the math class she shared with Alex.

Sarah likewise kept her eyes down, suddenly interested in a passage of Spinoza. "Depleted, like me. He's fine but doesn't want to deal with any drama."

Leala raised her eyebrows, she got the message. He didn't want to get between the women in his life. Or, he was still dealing with his part in the violation.

To Katie, Alex's response was another sign of a returning Alex Jane. This was exactly her reaction when Katie and her brother got into a fight after her brother had dated Alex Jane. She withdrew until the fireworks were over.

Her other suspect was Quennie. He'd been brooding for days about something to do with his mother and had announced at the hospital he was leaving right away. He was being shadowed in Seattle, and an illegal set of microphones had been secreted in his parent's home. The preliminary reports were suspicious as the installation team had had problems getting access without being detected. That level of security in a private home was always a red flag.

To her left, her strong side, and within quick reach, Leala sat fidgeting and muttering to herself. "Where are they?"

Katie didn't want to play the suspicious MP, but that was her role. "Now what?"

Leala avoided looking up. Katie used her height to lean over enough to see the screen. She tried to cover it up, then turned the laptop to where Katie could also see. Leala said, "I was sending a message to my niece, Juanita. The response said that there was no such account. Now I can't find my brother or his family. My contacts list doesn't have them." She frowned and tried to find different ways to recover the lost info.

From her favorite seat, back to the kitchen, facing the door, Katie watched while pretending nothing was amiss. Her foot nudged her briefcase with BMFG's lump, comforting and centering her. Her hard-won poker face was being tested.

Katie wanted more than anything to jump on Leala's problem and run with it. She knew from project snooping that Sarah had been searching for people with her mother's maiden name without any luck. This also had to connect with Rashaad's family's disappearance and now Leala's belief that she had lost relatives. Something was either screwing with the memories of project personnel or even more dangerously, changing history and the databases that recorded history.

Her role was to stay in the moment, watch for more problems. She would report that maybe her and Leala's families were disappearing during the nightly HQ debriefing.

Opening and responding to mail was not only an excuse to stay watching these two women as they pretended everything had healed between them, but also was a way to distract her from her darkest thoughts. Thoughts that surfaced with the latest piece of mail in her hands. The request, to join the local Daughters of the American Revolution was innocuous, but …

Right then, Sarah looked up. "What's with the colorful letter you've been glowering at? What's a dar?"

A rare pensive expression appeared on Katie's face. "D-A-R. Daughters of the American Revolution. You are eligible if one of your ancestors fought in the War of Independence. I have two who did."

"Is that where you get the Parker name?"

"No, that's a slave owner's name from after the Revolution. My two patriots were black freedmen with full manumission. It was common, but little reported in history books or movies. The DAR has been on my back to join for years; my membership was authenticated by an aunt who's been paying the dues. She died, and now they've caught up with me. There's a push to recognize all patriot descendants, especially those of color. The Alice Whitman Chapter across the Snake River has been all over me to become active. Their next meeting is one o'clock, this Saturday. I-I-can't. They may want to talk about my military service." Katie's head dropped the table. Maybe this was the opportunity to exorcize her demons.

Sarah reached her first. "Should I get Alex?"

"No. He has enough issues. Besides, he already knows."

Katie's phone rung and Lea intercepted it. "She's indisposed. Do the shift change on schedule … No, you don't need to talk to her. Then come to the apartment."

Security implemented the standing no-knock rule and barged into the apartment, hands over their hidden guns. Katie shrugged her shoulders, got up and walked over to them. "We're off the clock. Make certain the monitoring is functional, so you don't need someone inside, just outside."

Lea opened her purse for them. Sarah stood so they could tell she didn't have a purse or bag to hide weapons in. They checked both bedrooms and bathrooms and left.

Lea said, "Sorry about that. My answering your phone put them on edge."

Tap. Katie thumped her pen on the dining table. She stared into the distance. "That'll go into the daily security reports. If not, I'll cut them another orifice. Are you certain Alex isn't listening in?"

Tap.

"Positive. Why?"

Tap.

"Because, outside of the classified reports, he's the only one who knows. I've never told Quennie, and probably never will."

Tap.

She waved Sarah to her seat. "Knowing Alex, he never told you."

Tap.

Katie slumped forward and peered into her mug. "I can't keep this in and trust myself on the project. You two should know. It's the reason I pack heat and always carry at least two combat knives. It may be up to you two, or Alex if something goes wrong."

Tap.

"My last deployment, to Afghanistan, I was handling the night security at the airport. My second finally got vid-time with her fiancé, so I did the external rounds myself. I was hooded, thrown in the back of a truck, and held for four days. They did everything to physically violate me, day and night. Even the local boys were brought in to give them the experience. They only stopped during the hottest part of the day.

One of them could speak English. "Women don't order men. Women don't wear pants."

"That's when I realized I was about to die at the hands of religious zealots. If my people didn't find me quickly, I was dead. Instead, on the fourth night, all my bindings snapped at the same time, and I escaped."

Tap.

Her face rippled, not with tears, but from poorly controlled rage. "When I mustered out, I couldn't handle home in urban Newark. Newark is like any American inner city controlled by one political party for decades. Decaying with the occasional token project declared to create real jobs and better schools but in reality, funneled money into further patronage and more regulation. I was about to blow.

"The VA has had me, and Alex scheduled for help for our stress disorders for the past fifteen months. They have promised help in no more than another nine months."

Tap.

"I found this campus, non-urban. Despite the atmosphere, I was about to … I don't know what, but it would have been violent … when the whitest gr-guy I've ever met, Alex walked up and talked me into coffee. Alex has kept me non-violent, with the one exception, up to the day the project showed up and threatened Sarah."

Tap.

Sarah held Katie's shoulders attempting to mimic an Alex-hug. At first, Katie shrugged to try to loosen Sarah but melted into the embrace. Sarah's face alternated between concern and pensiveness. She asked, "It's good the Army kept this confidential, but why classified?"

"Ssshhh." Lea shot Sarah a glare that could cut tank armor.

Katie stiffened. "It wasn't the rapes. It was the souvenirs the patrol confiscated when it found me."

"Souvenirs?"

"Seven of the rapists will never rape again, assuming they didn't bleed out first." Sarah stared at Katie's huge hands, as Katie unwound her arms. Hands that had dismembered her attackers.

For a moment, Katie had forgotten herself. These were not Alex Jane, but two people she had to continue to be suspicious of. One was a possible traitor. The other was the reason Alex Jane wasn't there for her.

Her only hope, the hope that kept her going, was something she would never tell anyone. A voice like crackling leaves, during three separate times of extreme stress, said in a strange Germanic-Slavic accent, "*She need you.*"

The first time was those days in that filthy hut. They never removed her gag. She'd never told Alex Jane how she kept her sanity. That voice kept saying, "*She need you.*"

The next time was twelve months ago after a rage-inducing run-in with the rule-bound university bureaucracy. Alex Jane had stood on the lower level with papers in her hands and a dazed look in her eyes. The voice came again. *"She need you."*

The last time was as she started to squeeze the trigger on BMFG held to Mr. Johnson's head. *"She need you."*

77

HOPE

ALEX: DAY 36

The first two counseling sessions didn't go well. The mandatory videos and lectures were fine, and I came out of them convicted but angry.

The first counseling session had me gripping the chair arms so tight that my knuckles turned white then red. They switched counselors but even though the second was a man, it didn't go any better. Until they coughed up the promised psychiatrist cleared into the project, the sessions were a waste. My anger came from my failure, just like almost two years ago. I'm failing Sarah.

My anger at failing Sarah bread the juvenile thought that I could help her more as a man. To prove that, I had to prove that I was a man. It went downhill from there. The thought of how I let my anger over failure had overcome minimum decency …

I'm going to fix this, and it will not be by baring my soul while laying on a couch.

The first step is tonight, as soon as Leala returns. I pace and chew on the side of our manicured little finger. Hopefully, Sarah won't catch it before I find her nail file.

A light hand knocks on our bedroom door. Excellent timing. I open it, and she slides in. A quick check outside, no one in the common room. As part of our security, she has a key to the apartment. Katie never dreamed that giving all of the security team copies of our apartment key would simplify my love life.

As I close the bedroom door, Leala searches my eyes. "So, how are you after the crisis."

"You don't need to dissemble. She's out. I can knock Sarah out like she can me. She's never caught me. In her case, some overstimulation while I'm mentally detached from the body usually works. She thinks I'm merely frisky."

She flushes. "I should leave. I can't be part of this.

Grabbing her arm, too tight, it may leave a bruise, I say, "Sorry, but I need – Sarah needs – your help. Separating without her assist hurts. The first time I tried, we were in the bath, and I almost drowned. I need a partner to revive me. Some topics panic her, so when I work them, she can't know." I don't tell her this should also save me. Saving both of us is my, somewhat unrealistic, goal. I may have to settle on saving Sarah.

Every day I worry. Greasy's been gone too long. Too convenient. His supporting organization, or at least our suspicions, grow with each nightmare Sarah suffers. I struggle to keep Sarah from having a meltdown from the pressure. Debriefings are tough because they have to be.

Leala waits for the shiver to signal my attention returning. "Are you with me again? Were you always this moody, or is this a blended Sarah Beth thing?"

"'Fraid so. Sarah is never moody. As Sarah Beth, I find more opportunities to be moody." Anyway, I need to recover faster. That's why I asked you to come. This won't be pretty. I've carb loaded and put extra sports drinks on the desk. This time, you're here. We'll sit on the love seat, and you'll watch and decide what may help."

"I'm betraying Sarah. Again." Leala stops pacing. Her heavy eyebrows knit into a deep, worried frown.

"You aren't. I need non-Sarah time to work on some theories with Clarice. Any discussion of what she is terrifies her into hysteria."

I'm positive Babushka doped her "famous" poppy seed knuffelen rolls with her cancer pain opiates. When I ate them, the lassitude carried me through the terrors of her mental training. No wonder she was always in pain. Every muscle synapse suddenly fires and fires and fires. My left foot competes with my right to exit my body through my mouth. Hearing and vision are lost, my world is defined by pain.

Lips touch my forehead, paradoxically cooling my head. Leala systematically massages each major muscle group. My Alex-body calms to where I can talk. "That…was…awful. How long?" I wrap Sarah into her preferred tight bundle.

Leala retreats from the love seat. "I didn't think to take an exact time but about ten minutes. The first two minutes had me scared Jimmy's sensors would blow a fuse, or you two would die. It looked like you changed your mind and started to reblend, then restarted the deblend. It happened twice. Both your Sarah Beth and your Alex faces alternated between sheet white and eggplant purple."

"I didn't know it was that bad to watch. Thanks. I'll save forced-deblending for my most urgent needs. You saved me about fifty minutes, and I need that time."

I already know what's next. Leala is as easy to read as any. "Doesn't this hurt Sarah?"

Good woman, always worrying about consequences to others. I fold Sarah into her favorite gown. "I can sense that she's happy and thinking she's still blended and dreaming."

"I'll take your word for it. I'm not touching her in that state. We still don't know how I went under when we blended."

I need to clear the air. Otherwise, my guilt about tricking Leala will interfere with what I need to do. "Were you briefed about my ability to deblend without Sarah's assistance?"

"No. Nothing about unassisted separation in my briefings. As it's new to me, your forced-deblend trick will go in my daily report. You're lucky Sarah blows off security briefings. Do you think Katie will have a seizure over the leak?"

We're sitting on the love seat. She plays with my hair where it almost touches my shoulders. I turn, gaze into her eyes, and lightly kiss her. Dirty pool, trying to influence her this way, but the stakes are Sarah's life. I whisper against her lips, "How deep do you want to get into this mess Sarah and I are in? No one but you and I know about my self-deblending ability." Good thing the monitoring is only for abrupt noises, like a gunshot.

Leala pulls away and breaks eye contact. I was afraid of that. I'll take my licks for breaking project test protocol and the hit to my squeaky-clean security profile. "What else are you withholding from the project?"

I shrug, hoping to lessen the tension. I've never felt safer than with Leala. "Only the self-deblending and what I want to talk to Clarice about. Four weeks ago, before any of this started, she hypothesized a controversial ten-dimension theory at the weekly Physics Grad Students' bull session.

"I believe the formal experiments based on conventional thinking about matter and energy, ignore quantum biology, weak force manipulation, and time dilation. They're watching for the sunrise on the western horizon. That's why the data appears random. I can't tell them because the physics department head doesn't want me to mix with his grad students.

"Sorry, I'm rambling. Sarah's on the verge of a melt-down even without more on her plate. As long as Sarah hates Clarice, I can't work with Clarice if Sarah knows. The project scuttlebutt is that Clarice is a sucker for chess games."

Leala snorts. "Figures. She and Clarice are sisters-in-spirit. They're near twins in outlook and demeanor. Clashing is almost inevitable."

We don't speak for several minutes as Leala continues to hug me. "So, what do you want from me? I'm female, so I can't be your Father Confessor."

"Funny. I deserve the jab. Two choices. The first is to fulfill your obligations; report my deblending talent. We continue as great friends, with benefits."

She kisses my forehead again. "The second choice."

"You don't report and join me in the unauthorized research. As you can tell, I need help to get around Sarah. This may go nowhere other than my deblending ability, or it could blow the project apart. You may lose your career if they discover your involvement."

I stand. "Do I call security as you're off the clock? I'm almost late for my chess game."

Leala laughs so hard it's interspersed with snorts. "No wonder I love you. No matter what, if it's a matter of principle, you march ahead. I'm in, but with conditions. I'm not oblivious to the national security implications. The security briefings stay vague, but Sarah is scary dangerous. You're shooting in the dark hoping to hit something. Don't deny it. You can cause serious problems. If something goes weird and you can't—or won't—come clean, I'll report it immediately. Okay?

"I'll call security about your game with Clarice and put myself back on the clock. You be a good boy and don't or say anything that breaks security rules. Once on duty, I'll report your skinny ass." She pinches said ass. "One question, when did you start cross-dressing?"

"What? Oh." Sarah's bra binds my chest, and her panties rub the wrong things. Otherwise, her new clothes hang loosely. "Thank you. That deserves a kiss. I'm so used to being Sarah Beth none of this stuff feels strange anymore. A bit binding in the crotch, but I keep Sarah out of whale-tails." Leala waves me to my chest of drawers while she indulges in rolls of belly laughs.

Quentin lays his book down as we walk through. A textbook? I guess he's taking college seriously. He won't talk about his trip home and what happened. "How's Sarah after the heroics?"

"She's still heavily carb-loaded; we cleaned you out of casserole and potato salad when we noshed at two AM. She's resting. No feral signs, so she's folded into her drawer."

———

LEALA'S WHISPERED hints in my ear distract my fourth game with Clarice. To be honest, if I'd listened to her, I wouldn't be this humiliated. I'm down three games and sixty dollars. I didn't know Clarice played chess for money, to keep it interesting, but that's all right. I didn't expect to win or even compete competently. I only need Clarice happy. She's been moody and unapproachable since the physics discussion group.

While Clarice contemplates her next humiliation of my limited chess talent, I do a careful scan of the neighborhood out to fifteen kilometers. Sarah doesn't know I've exceeded her range. Nothing notable other than shift changes. Most importantly, Jimmy is still tied up across the campus in a meeting with Mr. Johnson and the Physics Department Head.

Clarice gloats and thus is vulnerable. I lay my trap. "While you're having difficulty beating me this time, I'll give you a break. Whatever happened to your insistence that a three-dimensional skin that retained life could only exist if it also occupied other dimensions?"

Taking the bait, she glances over her glasses to the left, then grins. "You were paying attention. Yes, I remember you. Your question about an epidermis being a viable living entity was the best moot question in months.

"I'm afraid I got overexcited. They put me on time-out for four weeks because I got too snotty. Well, they're wrong and too arrogant to admit it. Why'd you bring it up?"

This is it. I've been banned from talking to any off-project grad students. Leala's eyes flicker between us. She knows I'm violating orders. Either Clarice has the key to the start of Sarah's rescue, and is in the right mood, or …

I take a deep breath. "I'm thinking of switching from electrical engineering to physics when I declare this fall."

Clarice does her nervous glance to the left and returns to her half-smirk. "I barely see you as an electrical. As a physics major, you'd be a novelty. A hunk in the physics department. As much as that would be a pleasant change, what does your major have to do with my apparently discredited seven-dimension manifold theory?"

"Seven? You talked about nine dimensions out of the theoretical ten."

"I did more work and the equations more or less resolve themselves using seven dimensions. Leala, you'd better look the other way, I'm about to kiss Alex for remembering to say ten instead of eleven dimensions."

She leans across the table. I shrug my shoulders and turn my head for my cheek kiss, hoping Leala will understand. Anything to finesse me into her equations. Clarice grabs my chin, turns my head and lays on a full double lip slobbery kiss, pauses, and inserts tongue.

I'm too startled to resist. Leala laughs. I'm offended. She should be jealous.

Clarice's eyes dance as she lingers on the release. "Oo, soft lips! Leala, you've got a good one. He even knows how to kiss to make a woman want more. If you toss him away, I'll catch."

I blush. I don't generate the crackling heat of a Sarah Beth blush, but this is intolerable. Remember the equations and your and Sarah's escape clause. No embarrassment is too much to save Sarah.

"Uh, thanks, I guess, for the kiss." Now both women laugh. The heat ratchets up approaching Sarah Beth levels. "Any chance you have the equations where I can see them?"

"That's what you humiliated yourself in chess for? You're sweet. But it's the oddest foreplay I've ever heard about. I've changed my mind. Leala, find yourself another one, I'm keeping him. On second thought, Sarah Beth is already jealous of Jimmy, and he's my brother."

Leala clears her throat, and we both turn her way. "I'll let the kiss go, but are you really not telling him?"

Clarice crosses her arms. "What? I don't know what you mean."

Leala places her right hand to her forehead and spreads the thumb and index finger into an L.

"Oh that. You're a serious kill-joy."

"Comes with the girlfriend territory."

Keeping her arms folded, she exhales theatrically. "Fine. I'm a lesbian."

"Outside of Sarah, I think she's propositioned every woman on the project," Leala adds.

My pop-eyed, open-mouth look of incredulity puts them into rolling laughter. "Then, why, how?"

"One, you're sweet. Two, I wish people would quit thinking lesbians don't have a sense of humor."

"Back to business." She lays down her chess king. "I forfeit, which makes you only two games behind, and I expect full payment of the forty dollars." She leaves and returns skipping from her bedroom with a laptop. "Small screen. Pull your chairs close to me on this side. This is the first set of equations. Notice how complicated it got on the twelfth page? Since no one believed me anyway, I put it away. Four nights ago, I woke in a flop-sweat and visualized a new approach. I worked through the night and finally fell asleep mid-afternoon. That night I woke again and pushed through to this. It doesn't snarl into a Gordian knot like the previous attempt."

I ask, "Mind if I do the scrolling?"

Clarice assents, and I slow down the equations scrolling off the screen.

The new set of equations resonates with something deep within me. They resemble the sixth over-written layer on Babushka's matryoschka dolls.

I shake, hard. Leala holds me. She says, "Sorry, low blood sugar again. I keep warning him. Do you have something sweet."

Eyes wide, Clarice topples her chair backward, runs, and returns with a handful of cookies. I eat them to maintain the lie, but it's Leala's comforting hug that stabilizes me.

Once calm enough to not stutter, I say, "This is tough to follow, but I'd love a copy."

Clarice's eyes sparkle again. "Of course. I trust you not to steal my Nobel Prize. I'll compress and send it with a provocative tag. That will push it the top of the to-be-examined, and you'll get it faster."

Both Leala and I jerk up, and Clarice's eyes dance again. "Must be some firewall if you didn't catch on. They tie all our server pointers to their firewall. Most of us techies spotted the lag on the first day. Mr. Johnson and Katie called us together and admonished us to quit 'debugging' the network."

WE'RE IN OUR ROOM. I don't remember leaving Clarice's apartment or even arriving here.

Leala asks, "What's your password?" I give it to her. "Our InfoSec people are efficient. I'm downloading it before they change their mind. Do you have a thumb drive for secure and hideable backup?"

I slowly work past my mini-breakdown. I need to marry this woman. She's everything a burned-out vet with granny issues could ever want.

Pulling up my shirt, I wipe my face with it. "I have to ask something."

"Yes."

"Why didn't you stop the kiss? You knew I didn't want to."

"I didn't think she would. Remember I said she and Sarah are like siblings? Both overcompensate for what they perceive to be a flaw. Sarah overdresses girly because she has body image issues. In Clarice's case, it's her appearing six years younger."

"I don't understand what..."

"Her kissing you confirmed to me how special you are."

Give me honest women like Leala and Katie; you always know where you stand with them. Sarah and now Clarice are too much for me.

As I thought, her equations line-up with the most difficult of the writing I've found in the matryoschka dolls. I have my translation Rosetta stone.

I can't hold it any longer. I break into deep sobs. Leala wraps her arms around me. I've been too long without hope. Almost two decades. The week she died, my Babushka showed me the proof I'd die before my twenty-fifth birthday. What demented fool tells a five-year-old when he will die? Grandma, you never opened the fourth and fifth set of dolls. You didn't think there would be an escape clause.

For the first time in seventeen years, I have hope.

78

EXISTENCE

ALEX

F or convenience, I've created an area in the energy-space bubble occupied by the matryoschka dolls to use as a study zone. I'm puzzled about where all the free energy comes from. The normal state of non-glow glow disrupts all my senses, including some I can't name. After experimenting with my bedroom and study desk at home in Seattle, I decided a less distracting space was needed. There were too many mementos of my youth, combined with the Army gear I left behind.

After trying several "optimal" study spaces taken from online articles, I stumbled on the obvious: a study carrel from the Owens Engineering Library, surrounded by shelves filled with books. The books, leather bound with the appropriate amount of mustiness, contain all the layers of writing I transferred from the matryoschka dolls. With this level of familiarity, and not needing to look at the dolls anymore I'm not distracted by memories of the lessons forced on me by Babushka.

The non-sound sound of the study space itself distracted me, so I added the bustle of students whispering in collaboration and the squeak of the reshelving cart's left front wheel. To keep my notes straight, I've added a lab notebook, and the Cat journal that duplicates my notebook in real space.

An overlay intrudes on my study the Russian woman with the dead husband. The writing fades in, obscuring what I'm reading. Is something trying to get my attention?

Before it solidifies enough to comprehend, the overlay fades away, and what I'm studying reappears. Large chunks of information remain concealed. So far, Clarice's work and what I have from the matryoschka dolls point to only one conclusion.

I don't exist.

79

CARLA

SARAH: DAY 38

S he hated her new body. Her fave robe was too short now for outside the bedroom, so she wrapped Alex's around her shorty pajamas. When did she stop calling them jammies? No matter, this robe reached to her midcalf. Even though the fabric was stiff and the drabbest brown possible, it was serviceable and not too hot.

She ran her fingers through her hair and glided out for Quennie's latest breakfast invention before hopping the transit bus for shopping. Having learned her lesson about security, she wouldn't chat up her guards.

Oops. Jimmy was sitting at their table, eating breakfast. She'd forgotten to check the neighborhood. Jimmy couldn't see her "normal." Jimmy would only see her at her best.

She spun on her heel and slipped into their room. Turning in the door, she caught Quennie's eye and flashed five fingers three times for fifteen minutes.

First, a quick shower to wash off night sweat, and a minimalist application of makeup. Putting makeup on while grinning is more difficult than she would have thought. Tossing clothes frantically over the bed, she decided on the perfect "oh this, I just tossed it on" outfit.

Twenty minutes later, she was ready for Jimmy. Quennie just happened to deliver her plate as she sat. He was a wonder.

Jimmy's patented shy-guy smile replaced the fork he pulled out of his mouth. "The word is you need a shadow for shopping, and I found just the guy."

She dropped her fork. Alex came forward. "Are you okay? I caught an emotional surge. I lost my place studying."

She turned to Jimmy and pointed with their chin. Alex remained confused. "Half of the project team drops by for Quennie's meals. Jimmy does a couple times a week. What's the big deal?"

"He's taking me shopping!"

"Oh. Good solution, he's not security so he can drive you. Release the body. I need to do something."

Puzzled, she released. Alex sidled over to Jimmy, bridging the gap between their chairs. His rising heat warmed their hip and shoulder, matching his reddening neck. Alex nuzzled Jimmy's ear and whispered in a husky voice, "She's all yours. Please keep her occupied all day, so she won't keep waking me."

She was going to kill him. But how?

He bailed, leaving Jimmy and her flushing deep pink and eye to eye. Oo, she'd forgotten his tan-flecked eyes. She pulled back. *Behave—take deep breaths and control yourself. Don't let this blended body get the better of you. I'm an adult.*

Jimmy pulled a fabric measuring tape from his pocket. "We have some ideas on how to better sense your shifts. Hold out your hand. We have an idea for a self-monitor you can wear."

Huh? Her hand? Her hand! Jimmy wanted to hold her hand. Easy. It's like she'd never had a boyfriend before. Except, she hadn't. And to be honest, he was just a nice guy who went out of his way to smooth over her rocky existence. No one else volunteered to take her shopping.

She regained control and extended her dominant, left, hand. He took it and wrapped the tape around her ring finger. After entering the measurement on his phone, he did it again, wrapping the tape in the opposite direction. She loved his patience, his care, his eyes, his … *down, girl.*

He finished but didn't let go. "I'll be back in fifteen. Is that enough time for you?" His warmth pushed from her hand into her cheeks.

Jimmy drove her all over town. He was such a dear, and never let on it wasn't something a man should be doing. He watched countless changes of clothes tossed back and forth over a dressing room door, and dozens of boots being tried on. She shopped herself crazy. She knew she was playing a stereotype, but with the project, classes, and work, she hadn't had any time out. Acting like a real person intoxicated her.

She missed her curvy body. In the fitting room mirror, Sarah Beth grew taller and lankier each day. Her lower lip protruded. She upbraided herself. *Suck it up.* Jimmy deserved a happy Sarah for all his effort. No moping while she was out with Jimmy.

In the second store, she spotted two women who had been at the first store. She nudged Jimmy, and he whispered. "I've been calling in the next stop. Sorry." She flashed him a smile and headed to the shorts rack.

In the end, her new body didn't do better with the new styles. She passed on a beautiful pair of lavender over-the-calf buttery-soft leather boots. Her heart ached for those boots, but she didn't know if her Sarah Beth feet had stopped growing. She bought only a thank-you gift of overpriced Claret wine for Quennie. Claret, the color of her Jimmy's energy.

As they left one store and the full sun in their eyes blinded her, Alex returned. She stumbled. Jimmy caught her.

She asked, *"How much did you see?"* There were a couple of moments involving a dressing room door that wouldn't stay closed.

He emoted amusement at my situation. *"I finished something and forgot you're out with Jimmy. Judging from your mood, he's been good to you, when he's likely dying to immerse himself in some obscure techno riddle."*

She blushed. Jimmy's lips opened, and his eyes softened. He cradled her like she was a thin-shelled porcelain doll. They both flushed. "If you keep me in this position, I will assume you want to kiss in public." Alex faded while back emoting caution.

Jimmy blushed more and almost dropped her. His perspiration ran into his eyes, making him sexier if that was possible. Just like the bare shirted men during wheat harvest. Romance novels begone; this is real life.

Standing on her own two feet, she decided a change to safe topics should deflate their heavy breathing. "Any news on the project? Anything usable from all the tests on me?"

Jimmy squirmed and gazed into the sun. "We're zeroing in on some theories. But, please don't ask. One theory is the more you and Alex know about the equipment and tests, the less valid they become—you can alter the outcome."

The last part confused her. "Okay, but isn't that impossible? I mean how can people change reality?"

"I don't know. I've purposefully left the room whenever the subject has come up. Due to my sensor duties, I'm frequently in close physical proximity close to the two of you. I don't want to accidentally mess up your chances."

Her lack of reaction left his face scrunched as if he smelled her sludge from last week. Before she recovered, he said, "I should be clearer. We believe you put everything into making the tests work. The more theoretical people think you may create successes through the strength of your desire. No one believes you would mess up a test intentionally. You have too much riding on success."

It was too much of a downer; her mood was spoiled, but she kept her smile riveted to her face. She was happy Alex had faded and hadn't heard that. Alex didn't admit it, but the test failures depressed him.

They drove to the next test in silence. She needed to talk to Alex about this whole causality thing. Hopefully, he would have a better grasp on it. Also, their body still slipped into silly mode. She knew he was affected but did the stoic thing. Together, they would get some quality time with Doc Timsen. She might be able to help.

Her interlude with Jimmy ended with him dropping her in the care of chief-cop Katie at the physics department. No Lea. She had some family crisis back in Houston.

Back to work. Normal life faded into a fond memory.

AFTER HOURS of the stupid test behind various barriers, they left the lab. The techs kept straight faces, but disappointment shadowed their eyes. She aced these tests. She even spotted the ones they had rigged to force a false response from her. They needed a breakthrough.

She needed some encouragement. She needed Alex, but he was in his study zone. Katie didn't hug unless it was Quennie and no one was looking.

Ah, Jimmy stood at the far end of the corridor. She turned and walked to him. Maybe he'd let her hug him in public. He was talking with someone she didn't know. She turned. She?

Sarah wanted to scratch her eyeballs out. Then she'd stick paper clips through them and use them as earrings, dangling ones. Ms. Willowy Model closed in on her Jimmy. She didn't care if she wore a lab coat and thick glasses, it was nothing but camouflage. Who did she think she was kidding behind those black rims? She was after Sarah's Jimmy.

Sarah clenched her fists, stepped forward, then spun on her heel to head to the next lab test. Her first victory over her immaturity left her cold. She'd never been like this, not even in middle school. She bit her lower lip to maintain control.

Katie stepped faster to catch up. "I'm proud for you. That had to be difficult." Sarah looked up, puzzled. "Her name is Carla. If she wasn't so important to the analysis, she'd been fired by now. Jimmy is one of a few men immune to her charms, like Alex. Not that she hasn't been trying."

CATATONIA

SARAH

S he. Hated. Needles.

The day he died, Daddy had let people put lots of needles in her, needles with ugly stuff in them. The needles stung when the stuff went into her. Later, Daddy, brother, and sister died in a car accident. She couldn't think about needles without remembering how she and Mom were left alone in the world.

Mr. Sharp Dresser had set up shop with a staff of seven apparent mutes. All she knew was that he was an extremely expensive consulting endocrinologist. He had even brought his own techs. Even for a med room, this one reeked of stainless steel and high-end antiseptics. Even the chairs' sci-fi film modernity offered no comfort. The eight whispered to each other. He was polite, proper, and without even a flicker of emotion in his face or eyes. One mute strode over with a stainless-steel tray with eleven sample tubes and three needles, the longest six inches.

The chair tipped backward with her jump. *"Alex. Alex. ALEX!"* Where was he? She needed him.

Alex

I can't move.

I can't see.

"I think something's happening." That sounds like Dr. Timsens. What's she talking about and why can't I move? "The brain waves changed. This is not baseline Sarah. We might have Alex back."

"Anything we can do?" The feminine rumble calms me. It's Katie. She'll know what to do.

"Once we get the drip line working, talk softly in their ear. Nothing exciting, old reminiscences, funny stories, that type of thing."

"We've been close this past year, but we haven't had much in the way of funny times."

"Then make it up. Tell lies he'll appreciate."

Air movement caresses my right cheek. "Do you remember that time in the CUB, when we picked up sandwiches?" Katie's low voice, whispers into my ear. "We didn't want to take it outside, so we sat at a table with a couple of nerds? I was on the side with the girl, you with the guy?" I think I remember, but it wasn't a funny moment. "They shuffled and tried to make eye contact with us. Especially the boy, who accidentally touched you more than once. After eating most of our sandwiches, you winked at me, and full-on kissed the guy. I followed with the girl."

I remembered it differently. Katie, concerned about her sexuality, decided to experiment. We sat with the two, and when it didn't seem like they were a couple, Katie came on to her. Surprised, the girl glanced at the guy, then followed through with a kiss. I bought the guy dessert to distract him while Katie and her new friend made plans. After one failed date, they stayed friends, but Katie decided she was definitely heterosexual.

All of us remained friends, and over beers, we would joke about Katie's experiment and joke about when I would find someone to date.

I drop back to force control of our body. I'm too far back to know who says, "The brain waves are collapsing. He may be crashing." I can't tell them I'm fine, or as fine as I can be.

I push for control. The voice says, "Erratic jumps in all the brainwaves."

Another voice, male, asks, "Do we know what it means?"

"He-maybe both are dying."

This still isn't working. Whatever holds me is solid. I retreat deeper. I have to find Sarah.

Deeper. No Sarah. I may not exist, but I can't fail Sarah.

Deeper. I'm at the end of my Babushka's training. I'm in unknown danger, without a guide, even a psychotic one. Nothing I can do but push on.

"Needles. Why all the needles?" Sarah's muttering to herself.

"Sarah."

"Needles, my Daddy, brother, sister dead. Needles."

She's not responding, so I try for a comforting emanation, simulating, I hope, a hug.

"Needles … Alex? What are you doing here?"

"How are you?"

"Needles…"

She's slipped back. This is all my fault. My attempts to not confront her issues with her attack and her strange existence led to this. Her overre-actions; clothing, several showers a day, flash hysteria—were all signs of some form of stress disorder, maybe even PTSD, but other than the ineffectual VA treatments, I don't have anything to offer. I repeat my comforting emanation.

"Alex. Is that you?"

Joy expands within me. *"We're catatonic, or at least our body is. That's what I'm assuming. They have us on a drip line. They may start a chemical treatment, or even shock therapy. I couldn't break out, so..."*

"... you came for the fragile lily that caused it."

My anger, built up from months of poor treatment by the VA, finally bursts. *"Stop that crap. This is my fault. I've seen it. Katie's seen it. You're suffering from stress disorder from your attack. Sharing a body with me, a male hasn't helped either. I should have pushed to get you, us, into therapy."*

"No."

"It's the only choice."

"No, it isn't. I'm not ready to talk about this, except with you. Promise me you won't, even when you're in Alex-body, bring this up with anyone."

"I can't. Katie and I understand and want to help."

"You can talk to Katie. I trust her, but no one else," agrees Sarah. *"I remember how this happened. We have to talk about a childhood trauma I had, later. For now, we'll work on how to come out of catatonia. But, if any needles are waiting I'm retreating, and you'll have to handle it."*

A span of time passes, then she says, *"I sense, no, I see. We're coming out of it."*

I'm overdue in my hi-how-are-you for Sarah. We're no closer to solutions or even workarounds. The ancient scripts I study will need years and a team to organize, much less create a solution for Sarah. My inability to effectively help Sarah other than being her core builds my anger. My anger that opened me to my irrational violation of her.

I knew the second day we were together, I'm the worst person for her.

Sarah, on the other hand, other than brief stress symptoms such as showering, bounced out of our catatonia, cleaned up, and demanded to go to her sales job at LDOs. People interactions give her stability.

Sarah catches the eye-itch when I look out our eyes. She emotes "love you, busy here." Curious, I hang back and observe. As I expected, she's at LDO, but in an ultra-happy mood. No wonder, it's the End-of-Summer sale, and she has three shoppers waiting to talk to her.

She's talking a fleshy thirtyish woman out of an outfit that conceals too little skin. She's been promoted again, this time to women's clothing sales. "You have a lovely neck. This dress will emphasize it and draw compliments at work." Her interpersonal skills make me jealous.

I emote "love you too; see you later," and bounce back to my study space. The Edo Japanese shells contain a set of translation pointers to shells in the strange glyph-based language. Fear ripples through the Edo writings. The Edo-Japanese translator warns for pages against the originators of the math-logic shells. He or she—no pronouns in this translation—calls them "Rational, without souls or concern for any moral consideration." Another long passage warns that exclusive mental life degrades the Being, "allowing the expiration of any infants, children, or adults who don't demonstrate full ability to participate in society." Today I skip it. Libel is for washed up politicos and wannabe journalists on news networks.

So far, there's no relief from my prophesied expiration in ten or so months per the German set of matryoschka scripts. I search for the "escape clause" hinted in the Japanese and glyph-based matryoschka palimpsests, which report that someone attempted before but failed. I think; it's vague.

The old records support the same conclusion. Sarah must stop being power. No sensors should go off. She's destructive. She breaks things every time she does something. The breaking ripples move wave-like and disrupt the physical environment. It's the disruptions that trip

Jimmy's sensors. My inadvertent moderating influence keeps her from destroying herself or others.

My influence is the only counter to my growing suspicion I'm not real. How can I moderate Sarah if I'm not real? Could I be both?

81

THE JOURNAL

TWENTYONE YEARS AGO

I've done something terrible. May God forgive me. I broke my promise to my second husband. He's been dead for forty years, from that terrible fiery consumption I wrote about.

Alex

H old it. What second husband? Rolling back in her story, I hit a figurative brick wall. Something doesn't want me to know decades of this Russian woman's life. Blank pages smeared beyond reading, hundreds of them. Then the dated entry from over twenty years ago pops into painful clarity.

Journal

I found him worrying over my old nesting dolls that came from China. Words formed on his lips as his finger traced the inside and outside of each one. He could see the words, which were in Russian, not English. But they aren't visible to anyone but me.

My children, and their children, never saw anything but faded and chipped decorations.

He always was the strange child. When he was born, he didn't cry, but looked right through you, his eyes following something you couldn't see. My four-year-old great-great-grandson saw the Russian words. I taught him how to read what isn't there. The words aren't on the shells but are in else-somewhere. I grind my cancer-pain pills into the poppy seed paste and fed it to him. Otherwise, he would get such pain in his head and fall over quivering.

Please God, forgive me. I taught my poor great-great-grand-child, Alex, how to read what can't be seen.

Alex

Oh, shit. This is about me.

82

VICTIM NINE

SARAH: DAY 41

While driving, always the back-seat passenger, next to the armed guard, always the fragile cargo, to the Psych labs, she expressed what had been bothering her. "I miss Mr. Johnson. He doesn't even run the briefings anymore."

Emoting understanding, Alex took their voice. "He's preoccupied. No one, except maybe Dr. Timsen, knows anything."

Lea, driving the car, touched her earbud and said, "Lea here." She pulled over to the curb to talk on her earbud-only phone. "Got it, we're almost there." She pulled out and made a U-turn. "Psych department lost their slot."

Even here in her car, scanned at least once a day for listening devices, she was careful. She swung by the Merrill Lynch building. Katie, holding a tray of coffee for all of us except our guard, sat next to Sarah in the back seat. Sarah always felt sorry for the guards, but protocol was that they never accepted food or drink in case someone tried to drug or poison them.

They pulled up next to the University hospital's loading dock dumpster. Alex raised their eyebrows to the person waiting for them.

She said,m "Orders" and shrugged her shoulders. As Alex was in charge of their body, Sarah took the sensing duties. She said *"Everyone nearby is in the dark. Also, no one near us other than our people."*

Alex nudged Katie and Lea. "Sarah says nothing's out of place." They relaxed.

A double security detail escorted them through the complex into the sub-basement. They passed the second perimeter of security.

Alex emoted deep concern. "We haven't had this much security since the first week. This can't be good."

A sign on a double stainless-steel door said Morgue. The crow walked over her grave again.

Their escort left them at the next door, and Katie opened it, inspected inside and waved them in. The guards and Lea stationed themselves outside. Sarah would have liked Lea in here with them, but after Alex's lectures, she understood.

An emaciated woman with long, blonde hair laid on a gurney. A drip tube fed fluid into her veins, so she wasn't dead. Mr. Johnson held the woman's hand. Sarah cringed at the long and curly nails. What was going on?

He inhaled deeply and exhaled with a small shudder. "Cindy Worth, age nineteen, died from a brain hemorrhage in a car accident. She was the last shell created in the old program." Stone-faced and clipped in his delivery, he stood rigidly in one place.

Sarah's stomach clenched. "Ah'm leaving, I don't like dead people." She grabbed control of their body, and she had no intention of letting go. Three more steps and she'd be outside.

The strongest wave of anguish she'd ever felt halted her in mid-step. It was Mr. Johnson. "The volunteer core isn't dead. She put on the shell created from Ms. Worth, and collapsed, but didn't die. She's blended and alive. My authority at the time didn't cover stopping the experiment." His breath shuddered, tears glistened.

Doc Timsen guided him to a chair, and said, "Your episode with Leala taught us something we didn't anticipate. Cores can collapse but can still be recovered. You saved your incompatible core, Leala, because you're a living, sapient shell."

Sarah: ten years ago, mortuary, Omaha, Nebraska

Mom, Auntie. Don't make me. I don't want to touch Daddy. He sleeps in a box, his eyes closed, hands folded over his chest. No, not Brother and Little Munchie. Please, let me leave. I promise to be good for weeks. Just don't make me touch them.

TEN YEARS AGO, Sarah had touched dead bodies. Never again. "Ah'm still leav'n." Garroted by Doctor Johnson's emotions, she had to get out. "No!" The small room echoes. Too many people stood between her and the door. She retreated to the nearest corner, slid down the wall and hid their head under their arms.

Alex gently took over, limb by limb, and pulled them into a hug. "You've no idea what you're asking of Sarah. The threshold your volunteer is behind if she even exists is sheer terror. After each time, I took on the Sarah Beth duties for two days."

"Each time?"

"Don't tell them. This is not the time to go Boy Scout."

Alex emoted an apology and said, "Before the Project started, before you found Sarah Beth, even before Katie and Quentin discovered us, I got lost. You fall into bliss and don't want to come back. Sarah went in and saved me. She's kept me secured ever since."

"Can you talk to Sarah?" Dr. Timsen asked.

"She's still conscious, and responsive."

More stable, Mr. Johnson rose from his chair. "I think she knows what we want. Can she first verify if the host has fallen into whatever state that is? Then pull her out?"

"Wait." He asked me, *"Can you? Will you?"*

It was the gentlest Alex had ever been. They rocked in the corner, head down.

After several minutes of rocking, she peeped at Katie, Doc Timsen, and after hesitating, Mr. Johnson. "I may not return. Each time I go into deep sensing space, it's more difficult. The desire to stay is unbelievably strong. I never sensed this—this—thing other than while blended with the affected host. Whatever it is, it sucks on your soul, drains your will, demands you stay.

"I'll try, but I won't risk Alex. I'm stronger blended, but I won't risk him. My other condition is I won't blend with the cadaver. I just can't. I'll try skin to skin contact instead."

She separated into his hands. *"Are you okay wearing my clothes?"*

Alex emoted amusement. *"Now you ask?"* However, his unhappiness leaked to her.

He carried Sarah to the woman, arranged her for maximum skin-to-skin contact, but left his palm on her. She couldn't believe his stupidity. Exasperated, she said, *"Soldier, take your hand away. This could be dangerous."*

"No. Don't ask again."

She writhed to toss off his hand and failed. *"Your funeral. At least the morgue is next door."*

"Good, keep your sense of humor, but stay focused."

She thought. *Oh my God. The threshold was humongous.* It filled the view almost filling the entire sensing space.

She rushed back to physical reality. *"Let them know I sense someone cognizant behind the barrier. Weak, but there. Whoever it is, they aren't in distress. Also, the barrier is many times larger than either yours or Lea's."*

After a few moments, he responded. *"I told them."*

"If you feel anything, pull your hand away. I mean it; you can't help me if this goes bad. I'm going in."

WHAT AM I? What is this place? I am ecstasy. The freest I've ever been. The only place I've ever been. No. That is wrong. Why is it wrong? I am ecstasy.

A tiny, annoying buzzing. Buzzing? No. A voice.

"Sarah."

"Sarah."

What is a sarah? I am ecstasy.

Another annoying buzzing.

"Focus."

"Focus."

"Focus."

What's a focus? I'm ecstasy.

I like drifting along. No problems. I keep bumping into these cute glowing things. Some squeak as if they feel me. I'm ecstasy.

That last one was odd. It murmured. Too bad I drifted by so quickly. I would have liked to have checked it out. Say, I reversed directions. Think about my direction, and I change direction to match. Automagically.

Okay, little murmurer, here I come. Who invited the scorpions, angry wasps and fire ants?

THE FIRST THING she noticed was that the green was gone. A deep wrongness enveloped her when she returned to physical normality. Two, no five people intruded on her space. She finally understood. Her existence was a mistake. She didn't belong in the physical reality. Depleted of energy, she prepared to slip away for the last time.

But, a tie held her back. It was Alex, he was dying but did not know it. She was all that kept him alive. Gathering what she had, she anchored herself in physical reality and waited for Alex to grab her essence and try to force a blend.

A THOUGHT, important, critical even, wouldn't let her rest. She couldn't remember what it was, but her mind buzzed with its importance.

Awake again, she was cold, empty-cold, like when her attacker left her. Hands wrapped heated blankets around her. Someone wept. Her? No. Alex? No, someone, she'd never sensed before.

"More blankets. Hot liquid. Juices." Was that me? No. Who?

BEEPS, boops, slushes invaded her, confirming her presence in her most hated place, the hospital. "Alex are you there?" That was odd. She had intended to talk internally.

He opened their eyes. Knowing she would want to examine her surroundings, he moved their head. This room had lamps with a pinkish color. The green indicators looked brownish in the pink glow. He said, "*Barely. When you crash, girl, you crash hard. We thought we lost you.*"

She was too muzzy, so she only emoted confusion.

"*After you conformed over the woman, the visible spectrum in the room blue-*

shifted, red became yellow, yellow became green, blue disappeared, and you disappeared. Not just invisible or chameleon-like but gone. The spectrum reverted to normal. You were gone except if I pushed my sensing."

"Everything's fuzzy. How? How am I here? I couldn't reblend." She needed to warn Alex, but about what?

"When you reappeared, I tore you off her and wrapped you around me. After the legs, the arms, and head, you closed over me. I passed out. I woke up a little while ago. I told them we're fine and asked them to leave so we can have some peace."

"Of all the stupid stunts. You and your Boy Scout tendencies. You might have been trapped inside a cadaver. You remember what happened to everyone else? They died in extreme pain."

She had a deep disquiet as if she'd left behind an object of great value. It had to be part of her experience in the else-somewhere. Like before, the knowledge didn't pass through the barrier with her. She could only hope that it wasn't important. Then why did she fear for Alex?

Alex chuckled. *"Honey, like I had a choice?"*

"Not fair, that's my line."

"You passed the test. You're arguing, so you're fine. They're doing their best pretending not to overhear. Let's get out of here."

Being alive was great. She decided to ignore her sense of loss and enjoy life. "Hey, where is everybody." A swarm of faces, disembodied, formed around her. She still must have been out of it. Her sensing abilities failed to differentiate people.

"Good to see you back Sarah." It was Lea. Jimmy held her hand, but she was too weak for a real smile to her Jimmy. Towering over them was Katie. What a wonderful sight.

Tears pooled on their cheeks. She said, "Can someone do something about this allergy?"

She fell asleep. She sensed fewer people. Doc Timsen at a distance,

Katie and Mr. Johnson nearby, or in the room. Someone strange, red, orange, and green, nearby, flickering. She opened her eyes.

Alex said, "*I possumed waiting for you. Until you were ready, I had nothing to tell them.*"

Laying here was a waste of time. She said, "Hi, when do I get out of here?" Katie jumped out of her chair and held their hands. The door slammed, and Doc Timsen stepped into view. A presence cried on the other side of the bed. "I'm not dead," she said, Why the tears?"

Doc Timsen said, "We thought we lost you. You saved the volunteer. After you returned, the shell, turned to dust, leaving the volunteer in good condition and aware. She's awake and wants to see you."

Sarah jerked out the drip lines, sat up, and fell back. "Get me up." One good thing about freakish healing, they never stayed long in hospital beds. One glance confirmed this wasn't a hospital, but some storage room with exposed plumbing. Heat from one end made her suspect this was part of the building's environmental controls. Her eyes adjusted since the last time, and the lights weren't pinkish, but the standard fluorescent with the violet cast.

Alex emoted satisfaction. "*I've been listening to the staff and Dr. Timsen. You're ready for release once you say so. You're stable, so I'm turning Sarah Beth duties to you. I have some things to check out.*" Gone, he pulled his dump-and-leave again.

At least she was an expert in avoiding observation, and they'd be home soon. They set warm blankets in the wheelchair, then lifted her into it and covered her with more.

She was wheeled into the next room, where a plain looking girl, with high cheekbones, long white hair, seventeen or eighteen, laid propped up in her bed sipping juice.

Sarah said, "Hi, I'm…"

"Sarah Beth, with your flaming red hair. You're all I've heard about from Father." She was holding Mr. Johnson's hand. He dabbed the corners of his eyes. *Father?*

"What's your name?"

"Karen—Hunt. I can't tell you how much I owe you. I was at peace but not alive. It was terrible." She choked up and stopped talking.

Sarah leaned in to hold her hand. "I know. It's a terrible place." The exchanged weak hand squeezes. Unable to lean in more and hug her, she stayed with the hand squeeze.

Mr. Johnson also choked but continued. "Karen was the last volunteer. In her research, she identified another approach. Unlike the others, the shell didn't disintegrate, killing the host. She collapsed and stayed blended in a vegetative state for over a year. I killed the research project and put her on life support. The theft of the portable prototype and your discovery reactivated the project. You know the rest."

"The white hair? Did you have white hair before?" She was jealous. Auburn was fine, but Karen's platinum blond was to die for.

Karen's smile dimpled her near-perfectly symmetric face. "No, and I hope my mousy brunette comes back quickly." Her father wasn't ugly, but in the right, or wrong, light his face appeared to be two different people stitched together. Sarah wondered who this beauty's mother was. No one should look that good after what she went through.

Sarah twisted in the wheelchair and repositioned it to better see her. She was right. Ms. Hunt appeared to be high school age. "I know this is rude, but sorry Doc, but how can you be her father? For that matter, why didn't you tell me?"

"My daughter is forty-four. I didn't want to let emotion force your decision. It needed to be truly voluntary. I'm sorry about the breakdown." He swept his thinned hair back with this hand. "I wasn't the stone statue I'd planned on being. We suspected age regression from the autopsies of the eight volunteers. The telomeres at the end of the chromosomes lengthen, and blended hosts become younger. We don't know the limits. That test will never happen, as long as I am the director." His eyes were hard, and flinty, with lightning behind the irises like Katie at her angriest. His stare, verging on a glare, held her still.

She was the only one who could initiate his forbidden test. To the bottom of her soul, she agreed. She would never volunteer again. Each time she ventured into those spaces, she almost lost her conscious life. Time to change topics. Fast.

"Karen, when you feel more energetic, drop by our apartment. You won't believe what Quennie concocts for dinner, or lunch or even breakfast. Now, let me hug you. These people will wheel me out of here. I can recover in my own bed."

Sarah needed to think. Something had happened to Alex. If she and Alex put their heads together, they could sort it out.

Sarah: In bed, their apartment

"No side discussions until you practice focus. You almost lost it rescuing Karen." Alex had the focus bug up his fanny again. He started with focus lessons; then he turned to wave theory. Back and forth. He didn't let up. Even riding in the car returning from the hospital, he wouldn't let her rest.

She. Couldn't. Handle. This.

Each focus success exploded her mind, filling her with imagery of surreal objects. She couldn't take any more. *"Pffft. There is nothing you can teach me I can't already do."*

Alex remained patient. *"You do it by breaking things, which sets off Jimmy's wall gear. If you focus on the minimum power needed, you won't create problems. Now try the nudge again, but as gently as you can imagine."*

"No!" She found another place in sensing space to hide. She didn't understand why, but every success with focus terrified her. Humans shouldn't be able to think this way. Her mind flashed kaleidoscopic colors each time she succeeded.

Alex arrived. Her peace from running away got shorter and shorter each time. Alex shouldn't even be able to move between these spaces, much less rapidly find her.

He metaphorically hugged her in his wonderfully strong arms. *"Sh, sh. I understand. I think my Babushka drugged me by doping my favorite poppy seed pastries to help me over the initial terror."*

"Can't we stop this?" She wanted to cry, but couldn't here.

"No. Without control, you can die, and kill others."

83

FUTURE'S ANCHOR

QUENTIN

S ince his return from Pullman, Quentin participated minimally in what happened around him.

Most of the time he'd curled up on their bedroom's lumpy gray and white loveseat cocooned in his VR hood, external sounds blocked by massive, temperature-controlled audio couplers, and wearing sensitive, elbow-length tactile gloves. He'd brought these back from his bitch-Mom's lab. Actually, he had stolen them as she walked him through it. She had taken his renewed interest after the blow-up five years before as a gesture of reconciliation. His only purpose had been to acquire beyond the state-of-the-art prototypes.

Hour after hour, except for runs to the toilet or his beer cooler for drinks, he twitched his eyeballs to organize data and twitched muscles in his forearms to kick off elaborate correlations and analyses.

He'd stopped cleaning their part of the apartment. If the musk of daily living got any higher, it would overwhelm the olfactory stimulators in the hood.

He usually took care of all Katie's needs. He was the nurturer, she the protector and provider. They both reveled in the compatibility.

That compatibility had ended. He'd stopped interacting with anyone. Someone dropped in to replenish his cooler with beer. He didn't bother to check who, but from the footfalls, Leala, Sarah Beth, and Alex alternated. From the vibrations of Katie's footfall and the slamming of the door, she'd had enough.

A turquoise glyph at the periphery of his VR vision popped up again. It happened occasionally, and always after Katie left their room. As long as it remained turquoise, those who broke in only saw the lame-o VR FPS, a first-person shooter interactive game his AI was playing with the other slackers. He'd quit FPS, then all other gaming once Alex Jane, on their last night together before her deployment to Iraq, raged on and on about how utterly lame, and pathetic it was to shoot imaginary people. He should be leaving the house and interacting with them.

Quentin trusted that no one noticed this gear wasn't a high end and overpriced toy but top-secret virtual hacker gear he'd stolen from bitch-Mom's lab while pretending to bury the hatchet during his visit. He was on a mission. The mission was given to him by the greasy-haired, geriatric neo-hippie while Air Force jets rumbled the restaurant table. The gloves were a top-secret wonder. They used muscle twitches in the arms, wrist, and palm to initiate complex data mining and analysis. The fingers moved data from the active memory to the crystal memory. He'd never heard about crystal memory before the neo-hippie told him to acquire it.

Stabilizing his life history was a priority. If he could untangle the two, maybe three pasts he remembered, he could work on male-Alex, and Sarah. He remembered the original Alex Jane and her obsessions. Only he and Katie remembered her. Except he couldn't remember anything before he met Alex when they were both five. Neither could he remember her given name she had abandoned at age eleven. Why couldn't he remember? At the age of eleven, in reaction to the training bra, she demanded everyone call her Alex Jane: Alex for her dead father and brother, and Jane for her dead sister. She'd started self-injecting soon after. Years later he discovered someone had been slipping her hypos of testosterone and anti-estrogen.

When he hit a dead end in his life history, he shifted to examine what he could find about Alex and Sarah. He was drawn by their strange, interlocking family histories. For over one hundred fifty years, their families stayed in two tiny villages, less than one hundred people total, less than two kilometers from each other on the banks of the Volga river. Their ancestors emigrated to the USA, on the same ship, but different dates in the same year. Most of their ancestors shared the same family names, but nothing showed that they ever knew each other or intermarried. He was fascinated at how something like this could happen. With a shrug, he turned back to the problem of his twin memories of growing up in both Omaha and Ballard.

A non-screech invaded his skull bouncing from temple to temple like a wild thing writhing in pain. Alex and Sarah had deblended again, likely to allow Alex some me-time.

He knew from his tête-à-têtes with in-shell Sarah she felt no pain, so this was merely how his bitch-Mom-amped senses interpreted the environmental disruption of their separation. He would have to give the jangled neurons a chance to ease, then he'd invite Sarah to drape over his shoulders. Dragged into briefings he didn't want, he'd been repeatedly given stern lectures on how to interact with Sarah-thing, mostly—to never, ever leave the apartment with her attached. Also, to hit the help-button on his phone if Sarah was able to do more than drape over his shoulders. Any adhesion would bring an immediate response.

He'd try to continue his work but ask her not to watch. Anything to remove the brain-mush she created when she was Sarah-shell. She was good at not watching when asked. The eye-tingle that betrayed her watching never was there when he wanted privacy, like in the bathroom. He countered her amused kidding about that with a suggestion to ask Alex for the experience. That shut her up. This Alex, like the original, was a private person.

His VR hood was jerked from his head, and the olfactory stimulators hooked and tore at his left nostril. He blinked until he could see the missing Alex Jane standing in front of him.

She said, "How could you?" She formed a fist and pulled back, the coming blow signaled by her bent knees and the opposite foot's forward step.

"What do you mean?"

Male-Alex stepped back. For the briefest moment, Alex Jane had been back.

He asked, "Why didn't you tell me?" His flushed face caused Quentin to back-step.

Still disoriented from the Sarah-disruption of his nerves, Quentin asked, "What?"

"You've been my best, almost my only, friend for as long I can remember…"

His briefings on male-Alex had never considered this contingency: Alex James had become self-aware of his precarious existence. All briefings had centered on his likely PTSD. Quentin had been the only one who suspected the male-Alex was not complete, was, in a way, unreal.

Quentin leisurely stripped off his opera-length gloves. "Cut the crap. What are you blathering about?" Wiggling his right hand's fingers, he confirmed that the shigawire attack the AI received had severed his fingers in VR, not in real life. He never got used to the extreme pain that the VR mono-molecular weapon inflicted. Even without the sensory-gloves, the ends of the fingers stung from the virtual amputation. Turning the sensor gloves inside out to dry any perspiration, he checked his nose. It had already stopped bleeding.

"Me," said Alex. "You of all people could have told *me* that I didn't exist before a few weeks ago. You could have told me that I'm not Alex."

Without telling anyone, Quentin had prepared for this. He might be the slacker who read fantasy and science fiction in his youth, then a wastrel submerged in total-immersion VR, but he'd known a crisis was brewing. These two, the mismatched parts of his best friend Alex Jane, were the greatest danger.

Readying himself for the inevitable confrontation, he asked, "What do you need?"

"Need? I need for someone on this god-forsaken project to be honest with me." Another sign that this is not Alex Jane, but the fake-Alex. Mistress of the dysphemism, Alex Jane would never pass up an opportunity to slip in a scatological or profane swear word. Or words.

Quentin stood to face Alex, almost nose to nose. With Alex's height loss, they were even. Alex Jane had been taller since early middle school. "I'm here. Ask."

"Am I Alex?" His eyes pleaded for a lie, but he needed the truth.

"Yes and no."

The blow sent Quentin sprawling over the bed. He rolled off onto the side opposite Alex. "You shouldn't have asked. Everyone has been jumping through hoops to keep you unaware."

Alex dropped to his knees, face pulled with conflicting emotions. "I'm a Velveteen Bunny?"

Alex or not Alex, Quentin jumped into his natural response and joined Alex kneeling on the floor. He worried that any of the couple dozen experimental sensors would trip, or worse, their interaction would catch Sarah-thing's attention.

Quentin said, "No, you're not a children's story, you are real, but not…"

An unhearable non-screech banged around the inside of his head. Alarms sounded, including the extension in Katie's and his bedroom.

Too late, Sarah-thing was on the move. A disorientating implosion of his senses left him …

HIS VR HARNESS was torn from his head, and his nose bled from the olfactory stimulators that hooked and ripped his right nostril. He blinked until he could see the missing Alex Jane standing in front of him.

She asked, "How could you?" She formed a fist and pulled back, the coming blow signaled by her bent knees and the opposite foot's forward step.

"What do you mean?"

Male-Alex stepped back. For the briefest moment, Alex Jane had been back.

"Why didn't you tell me?" He asked angrily.

Still disoriented from the VR, Quentin asked, "What?"

"You've been my best, almost my only, friend for as long I remember."

Quentin unstrapped the prototype harness holding the sensor-feed-back and action-control activators on his arm. "Cut the crap, what are you blathering about?" He checked his nosebleed. It had already stopped.

"Me," Alex said, "You of all people could have told me that I didn't exist before a couple of weeks ago. You could have told me that I'm not Alex."

Ready for the confrontation that he had known was inevitable but had avoided the past weeks, he asked, "What do you need?"

"Need? I need for someone on this god-forsaken project, to be honest with me." Another sign that this was not Alex Jane, but the fake-Alex. Alex Jane would never pass up an opportunity to slip in a scatological or profane swear word. Or words.

Quentin stood and faced Alex, almost nose to nose. With Alex's height loss, they were even. Alex Jane had been taller since early middle school. "I'm here. Ask."

"Am I Alex?" His eyes pleaded for a lie, but he needed the truth.

"You shouldn't ask." Before he could complete his thought, a blow sent Quentin sprawling over the bed. He rolled off, onto the side away from Alex.

A non-screech banged around the inside of his head.

Too late, Sarah-thing was on the move. A disorientating implosion of his senses left him …

THE VR HEADSET he bought six years ago was torn from his head; he blinked until he could see the missing Alex Jane standing in front of him. With the headset in her hand, she glanced from his face to the headset several times. "You're not bleeding?"

Her face tightened in anger. She said, "How could you?" Her fist formed and pulled back, the coming blow signaled by her bent knees and the opposite foot's forward step.

"What do you mean?"

Male-Alex stepped back. For the merest moment, Alex Jane had been back.

He asked, "Why didn't you tell me?"

Swimming in déjà vu, Quentin knew he'd been experiencing some form of rewriting of the near past. After his Mountain Home meet up with the stranger, he'd been waiting for such an event. He remembered at least two other times this had happened, with him being slugged, a reset and the two of them reliving the scenario afresh. Unless he wanted to get caught in a time loop, he had to tread carefully, without knowing the cause. Quentin asked, "What?"

"You've been my best, almost my only, friend for as long I remember. Not that that has been long."

Keeping the plastic action-control gauntlet on, Quentin asked, "What do you need?"

"Need? I need for someone on this god-forsaken project, to be honest with me."

Quentin scooted to the bed, and male Alex joined him. "I'm here. Ask."

"Am I Alex?" His eyes pleaded for a lie, but he needed the truth.

"Yes." Quentin bit back the qualifiers. He put his arm around Alex's shoulders.

> *"The time has come,"*

Quentin said.

> *"To talk of many things:*
> *Of an Alex Jane whose soul died three times.*
> *Once when she watched her great-great-grandmother die,*
> *Once when her father—brother—and sister—died,*
> *Once when she watched two street children die."*

Alex tried to interrupt, but Quentin held a finger up.

> *"Of her promise to never fail others,*
> *but failing again and again."*

> *"Of how she never grew up,*
> *but remained the child of five,*
> *nursing the unknowable training—*
> *and her father's betrayal."*

> *"Of her inability to reconcile*
> *her childhood trauma, with her adult reality.*
> *Of her warring parts sundering into two,*

One, the child whose innocence had been stolen, and
One, an adult who had witnessed too many deaths."

Alex leaned back and dropped onto the bed, his face asymmetric with conflicting emotions. "I'm a walrus? Wait a minute, who is Alex Jane?"

"I needed to slow you down, get you where you could think. I wasn't about to kiss you like Katie did, so I went with something from our favorite childhood story, *Through the Looking Glass*. It fits what I need to tell you about Alex Jane."

"Has anyone told you that you're shit as a poet."

Quentin loosened his grip on Alex and sat next to him on the bed. "It's come up."

"When's Katie coming home?"

"Likely not for four hours; late meetings."

"How many beers do you have left?"

Quentin popped the lid off his cooler. "Four." He pulled out two and handed one to Alex. "Slugging me might help your tension, but otherwise would be disastrous." He took a long pull on his beer. If he didn't handle this perfectly the two of them would accidentally reset time, and they'd repeat all this. "When I'm using the VR, I haven't been gaming—I've been cataloging data anomalies. These are the ones that the media has tagged, *electro-putsch*. Nothing but data was damaged. The missing data crashed systems worldwide until the links between data could be rebuilt. This happened at the same time Sarah was created.

That was what everyone thought. Following a hunch, Quentin had collected everything available about their backgrounds.

"The damage correlates strongly with the dispersion of your ethnic group. Everywhere your ethnic group exists—the central USA and Canada, Brazil, Argentina, Germany, Kazakhstan, and Siberia—

including its homeland on the Volga River in Russia, databases collapsed in the same way. It's as if a massive change in the past occurred, but the database links were the only thing that didn't adjust. Something happened to the past that only affects your ethnic group." Quentin decided to not disclose his ability to remember the multiple pasts. Or, that new database collapses happened in the past week in Newark and Houston. Two acknowledged freaks—Alex and Sarah— were too many.

Alex's face loosened into his "I'm listening" pose he used whenever his friend went off on a weird idea. "So? Why do you or I care?"

"Remember that you asked why there was no blood on my VR headset?"

"So?"

"That was *déjà vécu*. You remembered something that happened and expected to see it. This will be weird, but you and I have fought about this at least two times. Each time Sarah came to your rescue, and the project's alarms went off. The next thing I know, I'm reliving the previous several minutes. This keeps happening. I think you two create a disruption to the present when one gets distressed, causing new pasts to be created. You must stay in the moment, and not become violent."

"Why me, if it's Sarah that's the energy thing?"

"If I'm right, you both are energy beings. You are one person, the person I remember as Alex Jane. You two are her." Quentin pulled out a memory chip, also stolen from his bitch-Mother. It was crystal based, write-once, and still experimental. He expected the Feds knocking on his door, trying to find the missing equipment. Jail loomed if the pasts didn't realign, wiping his massive felony from existence. He inserted the chip into his old-style laptop. All the files were there. He was right, the crystal memory was immune to time displacements.

"Read the summary; it's in the form of a log. It has all my data."

Alex's face and posture took on his rigid thinking mode as he read the log with Quentin's anecdotes about Alex Jane and two files about his and Sarah's ancestral villages. "Uh, ah... Take care of Sarah before she starts to move and create panic? I have something to do."

Before Quentin could respond, Alex fast-dialed central control. "I'll be next door in Clarice's apartment. Is someone available to cover?"

84

ATTACK

SARAH: DAY 42

A whisper of familiarity drew her through the walls of a building, made of metal panels, inside another building. Inside the inner building, in front of a large three-screen terminal, he grinned like a whippet eyeing a mouse, contemplating dinner. Head first or tail first this time? He pulled out a thumb drive and typed something into the terminal. Smiling, satisfied as the three screens flickered into garbage, he rolled his chair to another terminal. A buzzer sounded, and everything stopped. He examined the results on the right-hand display. His carnivore fleer reflected in the screen.

The middle screen blinked. "Now."

He turned and smiled directly at Sarah.

Alex: 0121 AM

Persistent whimpering wakes me. *"He's here … He's here … He's here."*

It's not a Leala sleep-over night, so I'm Sarah Beth. I listen. Nothing. Even the air conditioner cycled off.

Then.

"He's here ... He's here..." It's Sarah.

"You're having a nightmare, wake up."

"He's here ... here."

We're drooling, both sides. "Okay, who's here?" Our pounding headache drowns the whispering.

"Greasy, here, now."

No, impossible. Bullets and electronics ring this place. One day, a drone circled the apartment. When I confronted Mr. Johnson, he confessed it had been a trial. I encouraged the trials.

"Are you certain?"

"Greasy, here, now." Too soft, but I understand. Sarah's preternatural abilities exceed anything I've ever heard about. Our satchel sensor kicks in; the buzz alarm confirms her warnings.

The anticipated attack slipped past all our defenses, like a kitten stalking a cockroach.

Greasy, I had no idea you were that stupid. You're facing a trained, deployment-hardened veteran. With all my work with Leala, I should be one hundred percent Alex within a minute. I start my deblend, the internal organ fireworks start, and I barf Quentin's supper over Sarah's favorite coverlet. Failure. That should have worked. She's too far gone for me to force a separation.

That's fine. Sarah Beth still has Alex's training, with Sarah's speed, and flexibility. I roll us off the bed, pull my service footlocker from under the bed, and grab the gun case with my father's Colt 1911A military-issued semi-automatic. I heft the magazine. It's full of bullets, and I slam it in. Cycle the receiver, safety off. The cool blued steel reminds me that I might not be real, but steel and lead bullets are. Good to go.

The pressure between our eyes combined with a shift in the light from my cell phone from blue-white to red then back. The satchel alarm escalates into a scream, eliminating all doubt. We're under attack.

I force the pressure away. Better, a little. The alarm steps back to merely annoying. I might be the Velveteen Bunny, but I have teeth. If I'm going out, I'm taking Sarah's enemies with me.

On our knees, I poke our head up, using the mattress to support our double grip while searching the dark for a moving shadow. I only look like a naïve coed. I'll fill you and your shadow with lead. Then reload and fill you again until you're too heavy to walk.

This ends tonight.

"Olly Olly Oxen Free." I drop my Sarah Beth voice into the best growl it can sustain.

The door smashes open, and I sense security in the door. Lights blind me. I drop Dad's Colt on the mattress and slowly stand, arms as high as possible. Katie and Leala compete to be first to scramble over the mattress to protect Sarah Beth.

The two nightshift guards check all the nooks and crannies. "Clear. Clear. Clear. Clear."

Turning to the guards, Katie says, "Check the whole apartment. Check our apartments on this floor and above. Detail a double squad outside. Wake Quennie to make coffee; it's going to be a long night. Set up the command post at the dining table." Katie studies us and decides we're okay. "Several alarms went off, including a couple never tripped before. What happened here?"

"Greasy's here." Just Leala and Katie are left in the room; they're cleared. I can talk.

Katie listens to the "clears" coming from the other rooms. "Apparently not."

A breath, barely vocalized, comes from Sarah. "The skiff."

I turn to Katie. There's only one possibility. "No, he's at the SCIF." Why didn't I know about a secured InfoSec room?

Katie frowns and folds her arms. "What SCIF? There's no SCIF?"

Leala runs to close the door. From Sarah's drawers, I pull on the closest things she has to combat wear, loose jeans with cargo pockets and a cotton shirt. I tie my camo handkerchief over my hair, Babushka style.

Blood? The mirror reflects blood trails from our ears. I reach into my deepest military training to avoid going into shock. We don't drool, we bleed. Sarah Beth bleeds out of our ears and nose. I grab a washcloth, wet it and wipe.

The pressure increases between our eyes. I push again at whatever it is, and it stops.

"Katie, I accept that you must stay to coordinate and be the boss. Leala, are you coming? After you dress?" Leala leaves.

I retrieve my satchel, dump Dad's Colt and all the forty-five caliper cartridges into it. "I'm going hunting." As an afterthought, I toss in the washcloth.

Katie steps in front of me. "No."

"Yes. Think about it. He's here." Whatever Greasy's doing must be stopped, or else Sarah's toast. We can't separate. If I'm lucky, I'll remain Sarah Beth. It will solve my unreality problem but in the worst possible way.

"No."

"Yes. She's our only hope of stopping Greasy and his friends. I won't lose someone again due to my failure. You didn't know there's a SCIF, what else don't you know? Now get out of my way."

How would you mount an attack from within a SCIF? They're shielded; nothing electromagnetic gets in or out.

Regardless, this may be my only opportunity to be more than the unreal meat engine for Sarah. I draw on the training and skills of that other person that Quentin wouldn't talk about when he confessed that I had existed for only a few weeks. He returned to his VR hood and gloves and since then has only eaten when Katie has brought him food.

Katie follows Sarah Beth out. Quentin and Jimmy assemble equipment on the dining table. Harry and David have slung 12-gauge-street sweepers over their shoulders.

I have to do something for Sarah. I walk up to Jimmy, hug him and kiss him on the cheek. In my best Sarah voice, I say, "Sorry we never got together."

Quentin stops his helping Jimmy and grasps my forearm. "No matter what happens, I'm always here for you."

In the hall, Leala waits with a street-sweeper shotgun, a bag of ammo, and the keys to her car. As we walk to the car, I grab the street-sweeper from her. "That's mine." Leala moves to take it back, and I shake my head. "The street-sweeper is mine."

In the car, Leala adjusts the mirror. "Where?"

"Do you know where the SCIF is?"

"Sorry, I don't know about a SCIF."

"Let's start at the physics building at the top of campus hill; it must be close to there."

As I transfer the 12-gauge cartridges to my satchel, a small parade forms up behind us. Four, no, seven, no, nine in three cars. Leaving three to stay behind with Jimmy, Katie, and Quennie. Smart. This could be a feint. I load the shotgun and check the safety.

I check in with Sarah. She's almost unconscious. "Hold on. We're on our way to get him."

She fades more. "Why is he on a boat, a skiff?"

"Not a boat. The only thing that makes sense would be a Sensitive Compartmented Information Facility, S-C-I-F, pronounced skiff. Usually, a metal-lined building within a building used to process the most classified information. This is one spooky group we're entangled with. Which way? We'll find it ourselves."

"Past the physics building. Distance is not reliable with energy, nonlinear. Hurry. I don't know how long I can hold out."

The washcloth saturates with my oozing blood, which hasn't stopped. "On the other side of the Physics Building, anyone closer?"

Leala speed dials. "Target somewhere on the other side of the hill past the Physics Building. Do we have closer assets? And does anyone know where the hell the SCIF is?"

I sense two cars taking lateral routes starting at or near the Merrill Lynch building across from our tea party weeks ago. I always wondered where they kept HQ. Right over our noses every time we met in the square. It was obvious that Katie had an office there, but I was satisfied to not know, in case something happened to me.

We pass the physics building. "*Sarah, where?*"

"*To the Left ... Best I can do.*"

She weakens. I can sense her only when I concentrate. This is her chance for reckoning with her attacker, and she's been taken out of the fight. It's up to me, the person who doesn't exist, to take it to Greasy.

A low, drab prefab building with a loading dock appears around the corner. "That looks good. About the right size. Pull up by the dumpster." I thumb off the safety and cycle a buckshot shell into the chamber of the street-sweeper. Good to go.

The loading dock door's open, but I'm pulled back. Sarah's "cousins," Harry and David rush forward, followed by two more.

Leala and I go through. Yes, this is a SCIF. Sealed metal building inside a building. I've only seen one before when I took a shortcut at a base. The officer who caught me ordered, "You never saw it."

"Christ, please tell me this isn't ours." I think that's David, voicing the general disquiet. They spread out. Excellent team, well-trained. Nothing will come in or out.

"Sarah, can you see out? Is this it?"

"Yes, but he's moved. Which direction are you facing?"

"East."

"He's moving north. Fast."

To the crowd, "He is now moving north, fast." I open the action, remove the shell, and thumb the safety back on. The team doesn't move. "Leala, keys. I'll go myself." She keeps the keys, and we run to her car.

Someone yells, "Airport. It must be the airport."

We're the last in the line of cars. Sarah confirms our direction. I'm happier leading from the rear. Less chance of running into an ambush. Like Tikrit. I shudder at the memory. Those children's deaths. After a half-hour, the red-green-white lights of an airplane take off on the horizon.

"Moving, faster." Sarah fades more.

"Honey, you have the skill, but I have the power." How many times did Sarah say it? We'll see about that. I'm almost certain that I'm a mere shadow created when Sarah was attacked, but I'm still capable of independent action.

Mr. Greasy, your reign of terror ends tonight. I'll spit on you through prison bars.

I drop into the deep sensing state. Four, tight together. Must be a small plane, Greasy in a back seat. I fight down my gorge. Sarah's right, he's ugly. What happened to him to mangle him that badly? Single pilot station, good. That one must be the pilot. I don't give a shit if I melt every Jimmy gadget. The entire northwest electrical grid can collapse.

I mentally shuffle through the hundreds of choices that my obsessed and dying Babushka made me memorize. Oh, I like that one. Hell yes, this will work. Good to go. I'm the quarter-mile sniper.

"Yoo-hoo, Mr. Pilot. Meet my buddy, Qiulong. Qiu is a one-horned dragon and has a problem. He only eats dead emperors. You realize there have been no Chinese emperors for decades. Have you ever seen and felt a classical Chinese Dragon eat your legs? Hurt doesn't it? Dragon killers wait back at the airport. Turn around. Save yourself."

Nothing. No. I sense his discomfort, and his determination to continue east. His willpower is staggering.

I ask, *"Can you give me a boost?"*

"Trying." Sarah goes silent.

All the lights flicker: the cars, the farmhouse, the airport in the distance and the plane, then they blue-shift. The yellow-ish road lights became green, the blue-type headlights go dark, and the temporary emergency red flashing lightbar becomes yellow. Another flicker and all the lights return to normal. Overhead, a light show like a spectacular Aurora Borealis streaks across the sky.

We are dead on the road, and Leila pulls me upright. "Are you okay?" I shrug. What is "okay" for something like me?

All the cars have stalled. Then they start again. The airplane drops into a dive, corrects and barrel rolls three times. It levels off, still heading east. Damn.

I faded at the critical moment. I failed, again. The washcloth drops blood. I use Sarah's blouse and my scarf. We bleed more, including from the eyes.

Then the stench hits. We've sludged again through our skin. Leala lowers all the windows.

Giving out from the exertion, I slump back in the seat, and say, "Let's go home. Your people can do whatever you do when someone gets away."

Leala asks, "How are you doing?"

"Give me a moment." Sarah doesn't answer. I jangle her. Nothing. "I can't tell. Get us back to the apartment."

Leala slows and turns around. The other two cars speed over the hill and continue to the airport. I push my senses out, trying to get anything useful about our attackers.

In the plane, the other two people have disappeared from my senses. One gutters like a candle. The other shines like a cheap flashlight with a bad battery. *Monster.*

I've killed two people and crippled two others. *Monster.*

I can't find Sarah. That last push did something to her. Leala fireman-carries Sarah Beth over one shoulder through the apartment building doors. When did we get back?

Leala says, "I don't know about you, but I need a beer." She holds us on our feet while she fishes for her apartment's key. I wave her to my apartment, next door. Plenty of people will be there. I'm too weak to explain that we need to get to help.

The stench precedes, follows, and wraps around us. I try to sense who is in our apartment, but only give myself a blinding headache. Sense-blind, I knock on my door; it beats being shot by a nervous guard. Leala carries Sarah Beth in and puts us on the couch. Once she positions us upright, I hold up our hand as if holding a beer. Quentin comes out of our bedroom. He drops the bloody sheets and brings over my favorite Hessian brew.

I say, "Sorry, domestic." Quentin immediately understands.

Leala examines my eyes to see who's there.

"Barely. We need help."

I'm surprised that she heard us or that Dr. Timsen responds. "Then for once don't fight me." I don't let her know that it's me and not Sarah. Dr. Timsen shines a light in our eyes and applies sensing patches to our skin, cursing the way our skin slips from under them. A moment of faint buzzing passes, before she says, "As normal as you get. I see that you're Alex. What about Sarah?"

I shake my head.

I don't know if Sarah was hurt by the weapon or the energy drain from my counter-strike. Or both. I pray she has not slipped past the sensing threshold. She could be toast, taking me with her. All this research and we still know nothing about Matryoschka Sarah. I've only started to layer my notes in the Cat Journal. But nothing, ever, from the matryoschka dolls. They're evil. *Monster*!

I try the trick Sarah used all those weeks ago to bring me back from my spiral into self-oblivion. *"It's your favorite domestic. Come forward and taste it. The efflorescence. The hoppy bitterness."*

Command Ops bustles around the mini-command center at the dining table. I hear something about trying to track or physically tail the plane. A couple of fighter wing interceptors have been scrambled out of Mountain Home AFB, Idaho, but they're having no luck either. More whispers, this time about activating a missile defense grid under test at the submarine base north of Coeur d'Alene, Idaho, but a debate starts over disclosing our project.

None of that is my problem. I need to think about what happened, and what to do next. Greasy's ops included more than a raid on a secret facility. He also mounted a directed energy attack. My defense was automatic, like jumping on the dodecahedron grenade. It didn't feel like a person, more like a machine. The defense made me sense-nauseous as if I'd swallowed something living, and it's fighting to get out of my stomach.

He'll pay.

Katie leaves the argument at the table. "I don't know what you did." She stops to check who's in the apartment and changes what she was saying. "But don't sit on my couch with that stench. Into the shower with you, little sister."

She looks into my eyes, and only sees me. I shake my head. No Sarah. Not yet, if ever.

Leala sniffs her uniform, pulls us up and heads to our shower. She strips Sarah Beth. All I can handle is swilling beer and teasing Sarah to rally her. "*Sarah, first one gone.*"

Leala strips her clothes and pulls Sarah Beth into the shower. "*We're taking a shower without you. How will you ever live it down?*"

Out of the corner of my eye, Quentin stuffs our clothes and sheets into garbage bags, then double bags them. At least Dr. Timsen will be pleased. More Sarah Beth sludge than the first time. I have no idea what data she gets from scooping through that disgusting stuff.

After Leala finishes with Sarah Beth, I scrub her. She got sludge into her hair while carrying us. I hope her hair doesn't fall out.

"*Sarah, ever feel how thick Leala's hair is?*"

Dead silence including energy effects. No! Breathe slowly. You can get Sarah out of this. Karen's rescue stripped Sarah of all her extra energy, and she hasn't had time to recover. Greasy's attack hit her at her most depleted. It's up to me, and I have no power, just training. Training that couldn't have happened but exists.

Katie laid out sweats for Sarah Beth and Leala. Sarah's are too small for our Sarah Beth body but fit Leala. Clothed, we return to the couch. It stinks. Towels cover where we sat. Quennie replaces the empty beer in our hand.

My teasing Sarah remains mental. "*Feel the coolness of the bottle, the sweat from the humidity.*"

Sarah stirs, far back.

Leala happily drinks her beer oblivious to the crisis next to her. Dr. Timsen reapplies sensor patches and makes more noises about how poor the contact is.

My attention is one hundred percent on Sarah. By the deep concern, I sense from Katie and Quentin, they know. We've become that close.

I try to tease her out. "You know, the second tastes better. The alcohol in the first dampened our taste buds."

Katie pulls up a chair, ignoring the panic around the dining table, to sit and watch. Quentin returns with six more bottles, and coasters. He falls into the overstuffed chair and waits.

By the clock on the dining table, over twenty minutes pass. Jimmy comes in, sees our distress, and whispers to Katie, "Complete loss of most sensors. Here and in the van. They were over ten miles away. More than a quarter million dollars of active sensors, melted into silicon and plastic slag."

Katie points to us and puts a finger to her lips. Jimmy's eyebrows knit in confusion, but he pulls a chair from the dining room table and joins the wait. Clarice and others on his staff come in and report, distressing him further.

Later Mr. Johnson arrives with our loud, angry, and burly security chief. We hadn't seen him since the second day when he checked the apartment before letting Dr. Timsen's techs set up. Katie puts a finger to her lips and points to me again. I start my third beer.

"Sarah, only two left. I checked the fridge. That's all until shopping day on Friday."

Katie takes Mr. Johnson and Burly to KateQuenCave. Katie outshouts Burly. His security failed. He couldn't even secure the SCIF, a stationary building. However, there will be other butts to ream about outing the SCIF, followed by mind-numbing rounds of debriefs. A SCIF's existence is never, ever acknowledged.

If they find the dead bodies ... No, I don't give a damn.

Sarah tastes the beer.

85

SHADOW COMMITTEE

ALEX: DAY 45

W e're going stir crazy. When you heal this fast, and you're blended 24/7, energy builds up. I've gotten over that sense-nausea from my defeat of the energy attack.

Leala's been bringing over lecture notes. Katie doesn't take any and Quentin's are inscrutable. We need an outlet.

I prod Sarah from her study space. "Nothing left to study. What about you? Are you up to finessing ourselves out of here?"

The forced sequestration during the security lockdown enervates her. Her joy lights our face. "Same here. I've caught up with you on math, and I'm our Medieval Romance specialist. Let's get out of here; it's been days. I'd love to stretch our legs and see something other than these apartment walls."

"Some geek or geekette out there is dying to lay his or her hands on us. Let's get Katie on it."

We march over to KateQuen Cave and knock, politely. She comes out. "You look like trouble. Which one is it and what do you want?" She grins. She never grins. Our recovery sequestration reduced her aggravation level by keeping us under surveillance, and to be honest, under control.

Sarah returns Katie's grin. "Both of us. We're fine, and security is back to normal. Time to return to work."

"Any luck remembering what happened when the plane took off?"

It's a sore topic. The project deserves straight answers, but I'm stuck looking evasive. "Nothing. It's exasperating. Sarah was out of action, and I still have a complete memory block of about twenty seconds. All I know is what Leala's told me." Whatever happened during the crunch time remains hidden from me?

Quentin follows Katie to the couch. She shakes her head. "You shouldn't be here when we discuss project security." She pushes him towards the door. There she says, "I'll tell you this, then you go shopping. You know everyone better than I do. If anyone shows a change in behavior, don't wait to tell me. Tell the nearest security. If they don't respond immediately, run. Find a safe place and try to contact me. Now leave. I won't risk you any further. Wait, contact control for an escort. You'll always have someone with you."

With Quentin gone, Katie brings out a round of beers. Two for us, one apiece of our favorite brands for our differing taste buds. We alternate who drinks.

Katie says, "I love Quennie, but please remember that his love of the strange doesn't make him cleared. The attack confirms Sarah's nightmares that we haven't been dealing with one rogue agent but an organization of unknown resources and reach."

I jump in before my turn to drink. "So, they're finally taking all of Sarah's reports of a fully resourced enemy organization seriously?"

"And about time. Major fault finding has been happening above Mr. Johnson's head. A full debrief is being readied, and some people will be reassigned. The project's inner core remains in place, as we never had a say in the bad decisions."

She pulls on her beer. "This is the short version. With the reach they've exhibited, sequestering you in some isolated piss-hole bunker would only make it easier for them to stage another snatch attempt. The decision is to continue to use the college campus as our bunker. All the civilians and dozens of video monitoring networks make it difficult for anyone to skulk."

Damn. That has to be the best finesse, ever. I leave Sarah to her drop-jaw, pop-eyed use of our face.

The biggest danger has never been external. It was and remains Sarah. All known barriers are transparent to her, which means they could never hold her. The only protection the world has is her attachment to people. The more people the project gives her to relate to, the less danger there is from her disassociating and going feral. She's a people person.

Take that away, and she'd break. Taking who knows what else with her.

86

THE RING

ALEX

"Come in," Katie responds to a knock at our door. Interesting, we normally get security sweeps this time of day. They don't knock. Jimmy enters with his omnipresent metal briefcase. Katie retrieves Jimmy's favorite brew from the fridge.

He frowns, then smiles at the two different beers in front of us. "A two-beer day? This early?" Sarah shrugs. He says, "I should give you this."

This is my first glimpse of his metal-clad briefcase's interior. It holds at least four coils fabricated from thin copper wire wrapped around different diameter plastic cylinders and fixed in different orientations. He must be testing for magnetic flux. I don't tell Sarah; we may be twisting physical reality which would explain our perfect test results. Even tests set up to force failures don't fail. If Sarah doesn't know about the magnetic flux test, then they might catch Sarah's unconscious manipulations.

He unwraps aluminized mylar from around a small loop. With our attention so obvious, he does the responsible thing, flips two toggles and closes the briefcase. Damn.

Our attention is more glued to a loop, the size of a wedding ring.

Sarah's emoting off the charts over the obvious size. It glows in the fluorescent lights and changes color as he lifts, and looks through it. At least he doesn't toss it first into an open flame to check for hidden writing.

Jimmy says, "If you don't mind, I'd like to catch a video of this." He props his phone to cover our mid-body.

I hold back our hand; this thing doesn't react to light or my other senses as it should. Strange. I need Sarah's opinion; she's stronger. *"This loop has a presence we can sense. That's wrong; it's more like a non-presence. Where it physically is, there is a corresponding 'nothing' to our abilities."*

Sarah emotes interest, and she follows the issue. However, she's running off the boards in curiosity. I let her emoting go without comment as it parallels mine. She asks, "What's that thing? It's the size of a wedding ring."

Jimmy treats us with his shy-guy smile.

Now I get to be the bad guy. *"Stick to business. His demeanor is pure business. Behave."*

She humphs back, then adds. *"I'm working on it. The emotions are mine, or what I remember as mine, but overreactions dog me, even after all these weeks. Any ideas on how to work it."*

"Don't have a clue, but Jimmy's waiting for us to stop talking to each other." Sarah flashes our brightest smile. "Sorry about that, it takes a moment to sort out our responses."

He says, "You agree faster than Clarice ever does." He blushes but regains his professional demeanor. "Since Alex is available, I would like his opinion when I put it on."

Turning on his phone's video camera, he places the ring on our left ring finger. "This is the reason I measured your finger. This is made from a material called SZ. Its real name is over fifteen syllables long. It can't be machined, so we made a cast and cured it to the shape of your finger. It took over a week."

The ring fades to near transparency, feels like nothing and doesn't reflect or refract light. I've never seen anything like it. I emote for control. Sarah's too happy about a ring on her ring finger to carry on and hands the body back to me. Days without puerilism, and now she's succumbed. I avoid mentioning it to her. She'd be mortified.

I ask, "No circuits? What does it do?"

"We think it will interact with your phenomenon. I think if we'd had it earlier, it would have tingled to warn you about the attack. We would appreciate it if you would wear it and report what you sense."

I'll remind Sarah. I'm afraid that as I don't exist, I won't notice.

87

DESPAIR AND JOY

ALEX: DAY 49

L eala walks in and spots me at the bar. She pulls out the stool next to me and sits. "I'll have whatever he's having."

"Go away. Did Katie or Sarah send you?"

"Neither. You forget I'm both your girlfriend and a security lead. You have two disturbed shadows outside. They called me. Give me your keys." Without asking further, she fishes them out of my pants. I'm too drunk to stop her. She goes outside and returns.

"Your car is heading back to the apartment. They'll notify Katie, so she doesn't activate a general search. Your shadows are now our ride home. Or their shift change. As of now, I'm clocked out."

We drink in silence. "Go away." She doesn't take the hint. She rotates the SZ ring on my ring finger. Somehow it resizes itself when I'm in my own body. Jimmy and I had expected it to either disappear or drop to the ground when we separated.

She pulls a slug from her bottle. "Can't. We have the same ride home. Are you blitzed enough so your macho-ness can tell me what is wrong?" Leala drags me to a back-corner table. "Now spill. What's up?"

"I'm losing my male stability." And my belief that I'm more than a quantum shadow of the real Sarah.

"Even after sixteen hours as Sarah Beth, you're as much male as any woman can handle."

"The healing is awesome ... I'm glad you never saw my droopy cheek ... but all my blood chemistry is inverted, with massive amounts of female hormones."

I drop my head to the table and bawl like the five-year-old who lost his grandmother twenty years ago. Leala holds me and says nothing. Embarrassed, I glance around for something to blow my nose into. Leala offers me a paper napkin. Someone put a stack on the table, along with a steaming pot of coffee. Reserved signs sit on all the tables around us. As she counts a stack of greenbacks, the blond barkeep smiles up a storm. I should have known Mr. Johnson's project would cover my meltdowns. What I wouldn't do for some privacy.

After a couple cups of coffee, something occurs to me. "Did you say you're a lead on our security detail?"

The barkeep refreshes the pot. "I was hired for the role of LDO friend, but they neglected to tell me about Sarah's rep. I only saw a pleasant, lonely girl who was struggling with her first time away from home. Sarah and I clicked, and I got a promotion without understanding why. My intuiting the reality of the Sarah Beth duality caused Katie to create a new role of bridge between Sarah Beth's and your public presences. That assignment jumped me to security lead. Two promotions in less than three weeks. Like I said, being security for you two has been sweet."

"What are your plans after this project? Will you continue the security gig?"

She flushes. "No. My original goal was to earn enough money to work towards a Master's in Business. Now I'm thinking of combining the degree with my security experience and create an independent consultancy specializing in unusual security needs. Great training this summer, 'Sarah Beth' constitutes unique security needs."

In unstated agreement, we continue talking, but about everything, not Sarah Beth or Alex. I haven't had a normal conversation for over a month. We even argue about the Seattle versus Houston game this weekend.

After an hour, Leala's cell phone buzzes. Puzzled, she picks it up. "I put out a do-not-disturb. What could be this important?" She frowns, then. "… Thank you." She puts her phone away. "Uh oh, you're in trouble. That was Quentin. Did you forget about Sarah's date with Jimmy?" She rolls her eyes, a rare thing for her. "She only has four hours to prepare."

"I forgot. We need to get home. This is embarrassing. I'm all morose about my own petty problems and forget others."

Leala grabs me by my chin and her pupils expand. She kisses me. "That's for being too sweet for words. You needed the time to process your issues. How much does Sarah know?"

I ignore the question, stand, and only partially weave to the door and our waiting car.

At the apartment, we meet a jittery Quentin. "Thank God you're here. She has been threatening to blend temporarily with me to start. Yes, Sarah, I know you're kidding, but wearing a cranky woman around your shoulders is no fun. Ouch, stop it."

She jumps the distance to me and blends. *"Oh. You're sad. Can we talk while I'm getting ready?"*

I emote good to go, and she turns to Leala. "Thanks for bringing my soldier back in one piece. Did I taste lipstick when I blended?" I come forward in time for Leala's blush and stutter. Sarah grins.

With that, she cheek-kisses Leala and Quentin. "Quennie, that's for putting up with a bitchy Sarah. You know how I miss Alex. Leala, I can't taste or smell anything about Alex when I blend. But I love how you blush."

She turns us to Katie. Katie says, "That's all sweet, but I'm late to a meeting with Jimmy next door." She leaves, walking around the other side of the dining table, avoiding a kiss on the cheek. Remembering the theory that we bend reality at the sub-atomic level, I suck it up and don't ask if the sudden meeting is about what Jimmy's geek-briefcase recorded.

In our room, she lays out several outfits, all modest blouses, and slacks. I take over the body. "What's this? Your first real date with Jimmy and you want to dress like a nun on vacation?"

"Nothing fits. Lea fills out my clothes better." She wipes at a tear with the back of our left hand.

"I know, and I know you knew. How tall are we?" This is the break question for me. It's time to get it all on the table.

"Two days ago, at the med tests, we were five feet ten, four inches taller than when we met. We gained about twenty pounds, despite the reduced curves. They say it's from adding muscle which is denser. From now on, you need to stay engaged during physical baseline testing. I'll roust you so you can participate. Denial is no longer a good idea." A smile in the mirror. She's handling it.

It's time to push her out the door like she did for me. "Don't you have a hot date in three hours? I'll stay forward, and ensure you behave, clean up, lay on the makeup, and wear sexy clothes. Something will fit. Tomorrow, you and Leala go clothes shopping. No blendy partner of mine goes on a date dressed like a tomboy."

Our smile grows wider. She emotes cautious happiness.

One more thing; I run our hand over our legs. I thought so. *"And don't forget to shave. I may not need to shave, but we certainly do."*

88

IDENTITY DEATH

ALEX

S ome of Sarah's emotions leak even to the space I use for studying. She's the happiest I've ever felt her. Her date must be going well.

With Clarice's equations to use as a Rosetta stone, I've deciphered maybe five percent of the math dolls of the fourth doll set. Whoever created and wrote on these dolls had an ordered mind. There is both a table of contents and an index. The index is by concepts, not alphabetical, which would be useless anyway. I spend the time reading layers of writing on the shells searching for the concepts closest to our problem. The clarity is stunning. Not metaphor or analogy-laden like the other shells. Something about the orderliness calms and centers me.

Psychotics must have written the first set of dolls my Babushka found, the set of four. The nightmare writings of the second set of nine are not much better. The set in Edo-dynasty Japanese is not psychotic but is disturbing. Several people wrote those. All the accounts about blending end abruptly, as if the writer abruptly died. Sarah will never see these. I push everything non-psychotic but useful to my Cat Journal in my personal study space.

Now to translate the next segment of glyphs. Oh.

Identity Death.

It took me too long to interpret this section. I might have been subconsciously blocking. Identity Death. I wasn't ready for this. I was thinking of physical death. This guy or gal is deep. The contention is the least energized person doesn't die but undergoes an identity death. The more energized person remains conscious. The remaining blended person evolves into the best characteristics of the two. The less sophisticated tracts written centuries later said physical death.

I'm so dead.

The warmth of the breeze, freshened by the soybean fields, tickles my legs. If I had known we would be walking outdoors, I would had worn shorts or slacks, and lower heeled shoes. None of that matters, Jimmy's hand in mine more than compensates, threatening to flush my face into the stereotypical redhead's burn.
Jimmy says, "This overlook is the best, and the family with kids left it while we were walking." There, he spreads out a quilt, and gallantly holds my arm so I can sit while straightening my skirt.
While he pulls things out of the rolling duffle, I watch his cute ass. As if he knows what I'm doing, he turns with his shy guy grin. I feign watching some meadowlarks singing on the other side of the trail. A precisely folded set of napkins and plastic ware gathered in ribbons come out and are placed on the sides of the plates. I keep my smile, while inwardly grimace. This is Clarice's work. She packed the duffel.
No. I won't let my fuss with his sis break my mood. He pulls out individual sealed containers and pops the lids. Reaching to help, my hand brushes his. He's been so sweet, that I can't help myself and kiss him on the cheek. If he had moved ever so slightly, it would have been on the lips. Then it would have been an "accident." He's so cute, so naïve, so *mine*.

A sharp tingle stabs the palm of the hand I'm using to position myself to be in harm's way. Two meadowlarks start to fight. I pull back and pick up a shiny shard of stone. It tingles familiarly, mimicking a vibration in the ring Jimmy gave me.

Warmth at my side. Jimmy's next to me looking down. "Is it the ring? What do you feel?"

I lift my head at the same time as Jimmy bends closer to look. Our lips brush, then we gaze eye to eye, his breath adding to the heat from the top of my head to my toes. "I'm not certain." He leans closer.

Yes! A kiss.

89

BFF

ALEX

N o!

I—I'm Alex! I'm not Sarah. Again, I almost lose my identity. I retreat to my library to exercise my intellect. Fuzzy impressions of Sarah and Jimmy doing something clouds my attention. Finally, my concentration returns and I'm back in my study space.

Jangle-Jangle. Huh? Oh. Jangle-Jangle. Sarah's calling me. Sarah must be home from her first real date. Time to be the friend she's been to me.

"He had a corsage!" She screams in delight. She had undressed, removed her makeup, and completed all the female night stuff before contacting me. We're even wearing her baby doll nightie. She sits us cross-legged against the headboard the same way she does when she does BFF with Leala.

I can take a hint. "Please, we're in the same body, remember. You don't need to scream. Besides between our female hormones and your emoting … let's say I get the idea. Now, why a corsage?"

She giggles like she hasn't in weeks. I'm glad I pushed her out the door and dropped back into the study zone before she greeted Jimmy. This is 100% Sarah. She's been lonely with only my friends to talk to. Even Leala is more my girlfriend than her friend.

She slows down her giggling. "That's the sweet part. Remember the corsage for Lea on your first date? We bought it as a joke. Lea loved it. She told Jimmy about the gesture. He told me if he was dating a romantic, he would do it right." She returns to giggling. This will be a long night or morning. It's past two AM. It's too late to call Leala to pick up the BFF gig. I'll be exhausted in the morning.

I resolve to not point out to her that she's succumbed again to puerilism, given her over-reactions. She needed a boost, and I'm not taking it away from her.

"Instead of dinner at a restaurant, he surprised me with a drive north past the airport. We ended up at a county park, Kamiak Butte, walked up and around."

Now she's coy. Obviously, I'm to jump in and bite. "So, all you did was walk?"

"Grasshoppers?"

Now I'm confused. "Small children?"

She giggles, obviously, I said the right thing. "No silly, real grasshoppers, more different types than what I've seen before. The Butte is a natural native species preserve." For the first time, I note the small rock she turns in our hand. I'll let her play this out. "Almost no wildflowers." She huffs. "That is in the spring and early fall. Anyway, we walked back to the car – did I tell you he borrowed his sis's Corvette – and pulled out a wheeled duffel and took it to the overlook. We clinked champagne glasses as the sun set over the wheat fields. It was glorious."

I decide to bring her down easy before I say something stupid from my exhaustion "The rock?"

She stops playing with it. "Oh, this? I forgot about it." Right, like I forget to stretch my back out each morning. "It's quartzite, a crystal found only on the Butte. Extremely old, pre-Cambrian, it sparkles. Jimmy says that the crystal is extremely stable. I'm thinking of cutting off the shiniest part and making a necklace."

I decide to not tell Sarah that the transparent ring has taken on a silver under-glow. Keeping in mind the physics department's concern about bending physical reality, I'll inform Jimmy and Katie. If they get an okay back, I'll just happen to notice and tell Sarah.

I need time to assess how much Alex remains.

90

GOOD TO GO

ALEX: DAY 55

I need sleep, but I need to find some answers before the next crisis.

Knowledge, manipulation of perception, and effects in the sensing space affect nothing physical. That's Babushka's lesson she thought she never taught me all those years ago. Somehow, I must release Sarah from dependence on her power. She'll be whole, undetectable, and free.

Four months. My twenty-fifth birthday, the expiration date on my Alex-body, is December. The project data and the history recorded in the Matryoschka dolls offer no hope.

Evil comes from rationalizations and denial of responsibility for our actions. Evil never comes from inanimate objects. I understand now. There is only one solution to Sarah's mess.

Yep. Good to go.

We need to talk. A voice like stepping on a pile of dried autumn leaves.

Crap. Babushka, my crazed great-great-grandmother has returned. I haven't heard from her since Sarah showed up.

"Go-to-hell, Babushka, I have plans." Rage always exorcizes her voice. The last thing I need is great-great-grandmother Babushka's interference. "I won't walk out on my own story, even at the end."

We need to talk.

91

GONE

SARAH: DAY 55, 2 PM

S arah burst into the KateQuenCave without knocking. "I can't find Alex! I've tried rousting him, but I don't even sense his presence. He's gone." Startled, Katie and Quennie untangled.

Sarah erupted into crying and collapsed on their bed.

Katie rolled out of bed and grabbed her phone. "Quennie, pack three days of clothes for you, Sarah, and me. I need to make some calls."

Into the phone, she said, "Mr. Johnson, good, it's you. It's happened. We need a crash wagon, stat."

By the time they got to the airport, bypassing two hospitals including the University teaching hospital, a medevac jet sat with the engines warming up. The clipboard jockey checked our group. "The patient?"

Mr. Samuel flashed a badge she'd never seen before. "Don't ask questions. When we're airborne, I'll give the destination."

The sun came in the left window; they were heading west. A med tech installed a drip line with saline, but Doc Timsen didn't let him push anything. Emotionally exhausted, Sarah fell asleep until they were setting down at a fogged-in military base. The mist hung on her as she was half carried into a waiting EMS van.

Through the mist, she could hear an exaltation of meadowlarks singing.

A gurney waited at a low building barely visible in the mist and without any exterior signs. They lifted her onto the gurney and wheeled her past three checkpoints where everyone, including her, were retinal scanned. After each checkpoint, the door opened outwards with a rush of inward air. Sarah wished Alex was available to explain why the doors opened the wrong way. Finally, they entered a room with lots of equipment making medical room noises. Her attention waned. Katie leaned over her.

"Sarah dearest, please repeat what I'm saying, so we know that you understand. Yes? This is an experimental med lab specializing in quantum biology. The project's medical staff has been studying Alex's weakening condition for weeks but has had no solution. If anything, his deterioration accelerated when you two were unblended. The best theory is that he was a living macro-level example of quantum biology, which is why the treatments didn't help him."

Was that the reason he was the only person she could partner with? Why? Her head slumped onto the thin antiseptic-smelling pillow.

Katie said, "Stay with me. We need you to separate. Quennie will drape you over his shoulders so you can follow what's going on. If we need to talk to you, he will give the signal, and you will have to blend with Quennie and blend so we can talk. Now repeat."

Sarah repeated what she said and then separated. Quennie's physical contact soothed; his deep empathy calmed her.

Day 56, 2 AM

To sustain Alex for the trip, she had dipped into energy reserves she didn't know existed. If he didn't improve, she doubted she had another day. She was worse off than when she first found Alex.

Only Quennie's natural calming kept her from going feral. She struggled to maintain her sapience so she could warn them before … before she became deadly.

She faded in and out and had problems following what was going on. Sarah came out of a fade with a sense that something important was happening. She felt the signal and gathered her strength and jumped Quennie.

Oh, she was dizzy. He or she rejected the blend. She couldn't maintain it. Several hands grabbed her, keeping her standing. Katie leaned down to her level to talk eye to eye. "Sarah, you need to get back with Alex, so we can explain the rest."

She sighed and flash-blended with Alex. Hands helped her move. Someone wrapped and conformed her to Alex. She'd never needed help before.

Where was Alex? She wanted Alex. "Alex, I can't sense you, wake up!"

Mr. Johnson's eyes teared up. "He's brain dead. His body is fading. You need to stay together."

"No! I want to die and be with Alex."

Doc Timsen motioned to a person in a lab coat who pushed a large hypo into the drip line.

No! Alex, She couldn't hold the blending bond …

… oh no …

She did this. She started it all …

Her one purpose was to keep Alex alive, and she failed.

She thought, "If I can retrieve a stranger, then I can get Alex back. I'm coming for you Alex … goodbye, Sarah Beth."

PART III

SARAH BETH

"Though by your kindness, my fond hopes were raised,
Long, long ago, long, long ago,
You by more eloquent lips have been praised,
Long, long ago, long ago.
But, by long absence, your truth has been tried,
Still to your accents I listen with pride,
Blessed, as I was when I sat by your side,
Long, long ago, long ago."

— "Long ago" – German Folk Song

92

TAPS

SARAH BETH

I've no idea what time it is.

Leala holds my hand and damp-wipes my forehead. I finally get enough moisture in my mouth to ask. "What time is it?"

Katie says, "About 2 PM. It's Monday."

"It was touch and go." Says Leala. "Your body went comatose with minimal function. Then the entire base lost electrical power and all the colors blue-shifted."

I accept the ice chips Leala offers. The melting cool moisture helps immensely. That spectrum inversion had to be me. I must have gone totally wacko to take that type of risk.

At my nod, Leala puts the ice chip down and says, "Your heartbeat dropped to less than one beat per minute. It was as if you were in hibernation. They didn't know what to do, especially since your brain didn't show any electrical activity. Katie threatened to shoot anyone removing life support."

Katie sniffs and wipes away a rare tear. "Then you revived, and all monitors showed you sleeping. The only thing different is that your Theta waves seem on the high side."

"Where's Alex?" I push out with all my senses. "I can't find him!"

Katie looks sharp in her full-dress Army uniform. "We buried Alex today in Seattle. Mr. Johnson handled all the details. His family, friends and Army buddies attended the memorial and funeral.

"But how can I be here if he's buried."

"We buried a weighted coffin." She waves the remote, and a video of a funeral appears. There are many people. I don't know any of them except for Doctor, Katie, Leala, Harry, and David, and some of the lab rats. Katie in uniform leads an honor guard, a bugler, and pallbearers in full uniform.

No Quentin.

Katie holds my hand while I cry. I'm alive. I guess. Why me? Why not Alex?

An odd movement in the ceremony startles me out of my weeping. A girl, in a two-toned beige scarf—a hijab, open at the neck—fights to stay with the coffin. When a short woman, in a purple hijab tries to pull her away, she casts off her hijab and stomps on it. Wiggling away from the woman, she climbs on the coffin and hugs it.

"Who...?" I point.

Katie expands the view around the girl and her struggles. "That's the girl Alex saved from the ambush set for his squad in Iraq. She was already a street child, all the adults in her life were dead, and she was running feral with her two brothers. The brothers died in the crossfire." Her face, normally a deep umber, paled to ash gray.

Sarah Beth's memory, actually Alex's memory, fills in the details. Alex raised holy hell to get an exemption granted to get the girl into this country. The Kahns, his next-door neighbors, are fostering her until they can adopt her.

"Her name?"

"Aliyah. I think it means "free" or "freedom.""

"Could you roll it back and turn up the volume?"

Aliyah screams, half in Arabic, "He's alive. He died when he saved me. I saw it, but he came back. I know that he's alive." When did I learn Arabic?

I glance at Katie. She says, "I got the med and after-action reports from the incident. The medic and base triage got it wrong. They listed him as dead, but during the mortuary prep, he groaned."

Exhaustion prevents my joyful reaction. Best that I keep to myself my belief that Alex's still alive unknown. I remember Alex's surprise when he awoke and stared back at the field mortician.

Alex can come back. There was no mistake in Iraq. He did die. That crazed Babushka did something to him. I release real tears. They think it's from sadness. Wrong, these are tears of joy.

I demand. *"Enough. Stop this stupidity and say something."* I get no response, no tingle, nothing. Nothing but hollowness.

Leala says, "He's gone. We need to be strong for each other." I don't agree with her, but something's also different about Leala.

93

NOVAE SPES, A FRESH START

SARAH BETH: NOVAE SPES APARTMENTS, PULLMAN,
WASHINGTON, DAY 63

Most of the 'whatever' they've pumped into me must have cleared. I don't want to know how much meds they used to knock me out, but unlike before this summer, their affect ceases the moment I raise my head.

I'm back in Alex's and my room. My room. Sarah Beth's Room. I have to get used to that. Sarah Beth in-the-whole. How, when, did I get here?

No matter, I need Alex. *"You've had your fun. Time to stop whatever you're doing. "*

Silence.

Except for my weeping for the bone-crushing hollowness

I'M AWAKE AGAIN, and I smell something cooking. As far as I'm concerned, energy depletion plus smelling food equals time to get up.

When did I get this cotton nightgown? I must look like my mother.

I find only one tube, a drip line, which I tear out. Using a tissue to clot the blood, and I walk into the living room weaving all the way. In the room, Jimmy, Mr. Johnson, and Katie chat over lunch.

It must be early afternoon as Harry and David are on duty. They all jump up to stabilize me, Harry and David get there first, not by much before Katie. They sit me at the dining table, and soon I'm inhaling some Darjeeling. Someone slides a small plate of food in front of me. I can't taste it.

The front door opens, conversation filters through, before it closes.

Footsteps drag on the carpet. It could only be Dr. Timsen. "You're up. Good. Let me look you over." The pain! I feel pain in my knees, even though I'm sitting down. I realize that it must be Dr. Timsen's knees. She needs to get her knees replaced. But why do I now literally feel her pain? I've had limited empathic abilities since my partnership with Alex, but I've never before sensed other's physical pain. This can't be a good development.

Dr. Timsen starts her examination. While that's happening, Katie and Mr. Johnson exchange glances. Katie says, "You must have questions."

After the obligatory questions about the date (August 18), time, (after 1 PM), my health (excellent), recovery time (nearly over), and when can I start school (as soon I can walk across campus.), I break down. "I killed Alex!"

Katie says, "No, you didn't, you saved him." she looks at Mr. Johnson.

Mr. Johnson says. "Everyone out. Keep everyone out until otherwise ordered."

When they leave, Dr. Timsen turns to me. "What killed Alex was a fistula compounded with an embolism on the last day. We found it in the emergency CAT scan. The muster-out physical missed it and wrote it up as PTSD. The VA didn't question that, and so it remained misdiagnosed. His dark moods would have been treatable if anyone had checked. We depended too much on the VA records. Your blending kept re-healing the fistula and prolonged his life.

"His body changes may have been slowing down, but we'll never know. Bottom line, his fistula could have ruptured at any time, even without his body changes. We believe you prolonged his life."

I finish my snack and return to my room.

Nothing supports my belief that Alex can be restored. I don't care. He will be restored.

94

LIFE, MORE OR LESS

DAY 64, SATURDAY, 10 AM

I'm more stable. Weeping is for schlocky romance novels. Well, more than three days of weeping. I'm numb from the emotions.

I'm alive. I got what I wanted, I'm whole. But now all I feel is hollow. I hope if I move and do things; I may recover my ability to feel.

I gather my emotional will up and peek out my door. Good, no one. I dress in a modest blouse and shorts. I'm not in a flirty mood. Will I ever be again? No makeup is my new look. I comb enough tangles out of my hair to be presentable. I need another haircut to tame this mop.

It's strange Quentin isn't prepping everything, keeping me and everyone else out of the kitchen. I eat dry cereal in silence and return to my room for a quick cry.

I need to do something. Anything is better than this worthless crying. Anything to fill the hole of my hollowness. Two ideas present themselves. One is to register for the fall semester. The other is to jump in Chitty-Chitty-Bang-Bang and do a James Dean. Mom didn't raise a sensationalist, so I go online to register.

Déjà vu envelops me; I've done this before. My mind refuses to let me register for my freshman year. Sophomore engineering is what I should register for. I have to find my faculty advisor in Sloan Hall and get the ball rolling on my major. Wait. Sloan Hall is the electrical engineering building. That was what Alex was going to do, not me.

The pressure of Alex's needs, wants, and plans toss me into a fugue. I need to pull myself together and talk to Leala. But not until I can help, instead of hindering her. Alex died regretting that he was the taker in their relationship. How do I know that?

The phone rings. "Hi … I … uh … how are you? Are you okay?" It's Jimmy!

"I'm fine, thanks for calling." Horrors, I'm sniffling like a drama queen.

"Do you feel up to going to the mall in Moscow, say, about three PM? We can pick a quiet place to talk."

"I would love to, but could you give me a day or so? I'll call you. Is that okay?"

"Yes." Oh, he sounds disappointed, maybe I will rethink this later. "Remember I'm on call, and my commute is short." We both laugh. Old joke. Between friends, old jokes are the best.

That helped. I'm refreshed, not weepy, and eager to wrestle the first-semester course load into submission.

I don't have a direction.

Getting nowhere, I shuffle around our small bedroom. My small bedroom. At the bottom of the closet is the short trunk where I found his pistol all those weeks ago. Not yet, this is Alex's core. Soon, I'll have to go through it to package for his parents.

What else? Alex's laundry sits jumbled in a corner of the closet. Strange that Quentin didn't find and launder it, violating my orders and threats. I pull out Alex's shirts. They hold his smell. I grab the entire stack and lay down on the floor burying my face in it. This one smells of spilled beer. The blue polo shirt retains traces of Leala's favorite cologne.

He has to come back. For me, for Leala.

I can't curl up within my pain. I must get my act together and be there for others. I'm not alone in my pain.

Time to face my grief head-on. I'll organize his things starting with his trunk where he stored his most personal belongings. I open it. All of Alex's lecture notebooks sit in neat stacks. I take them to the bed, curl up and read what I can. This is all I have of Alex.

I touch the covers; feel the indentations from the ballpoint pen. On one, he spilled his aftershave. I run my nose over it, inhaling deeply. I trace my fingers along the edges and breaks of his printing. Everything we meant to each other, and it comes down to class notebooks?

The first year's core-curriculum course notes are here. As I read them, I begin to understand how the confusing course catalog becomes real courses with understandable subjects. These notes are familiar to me. Why?

With a start, I'm chilled. I need a break.

In the bathroom, I wash my face to clear my head. It doesn't help. I've never had a class in this. Why is it familiar? The notes are a year old. I was still in High School.

I'll think on this before I mention it to anyone. The notebooks for second-semester courses include chemistry, calculus, and freshman engineering. On a lark, I look through these. Sucking on the papercut on my finger, I feel a familiarity and the same chill.

Note to self: ditch the paper notebooks and buy a high-end tablet that really understands handwriting.

This ability to remember things I haven't experienced is a new phenomenon. I won't report it. I didn't sign on to be their indefinite lab subject, just exploration of the shell effect. I'll continue the current tests when asked, I owe at least that to them – even though they failed Alex.

There is no host. There is no shell. There is me, Sarah Beth Merk. That is enough, it has to be.

I have two ideas that don't take years of study or advanced degrees. They were in front of me for days, but I've felt too sorry for myself to think clearly.

95

APPOINTMENT WITH MS. COLT

SARAH BETH

I'm alive. I've gotten what I wanted; to be whole.

Hollowness deeper than the Marianas Trench engulfs me. It's much, much worse than when I accidentally took over Alex's life. Why?

He's gone, and I'm here, with an ache that fights my every step. Alex had a solution, and in the end, he was right. There won't be a me without an Alex. The government can go screw itself. They didn't save Alex. The Shadow Committee rumored to support Mr. Mort Y'Arty can find someone else to attack.

My solution rests inside Alex's service locker. His Grandfather's service Colt 1911A cools my hand. Two boxes of cartridges offer their polished brass sleekness to motivate my fingers to fill the magazine. With a twist and a slam, the magazine seats into the gun. Sliding the receiver draws the round into the chamber. I thumb off the safety. Good to go.

Damn sniffles. Someone in the building is suffering from allergies, and my sinuses leak in sympathy. Jimmy's SZ ring vibrates on my finger.

Do I do it now when the building is the emptiest, or early morning when most are sleeping?

I vote for right now. The satchel's alarm starts.

Pop!

96

CISSY

SARAH BETH

The crack of the failing door jamb amplifies the popping of the broken door lock.

Locked in a tableau, we freeze, me with the barrel of Alex's Colt pressed tight under my chin and Leala in mid-rub of her shoulder and gape.

Leala's expression changes to shock as she's knocked to the ground by Katie's cross-room flying tackle. She falls too short to grab the Colt or my wrists. We struggle with her beartrap-grip threatening to cut the blood flow in my biceps.

"Leave me alone. This is what Alex wanted. I'm only finishing it."

A haymaker stuns me. "You bitch!" Leala?

Makes no difference. I buck Katie partially off me and use my now freed left hand to wrestle Alex's solution to my head. Katie crawls higher and reaches for the gun.

Leala hits me again, this time on my temple. The ringing and triple vision distract me.

Leala pries the gun out of my death grip, flips it, and stops before her swing drives the pistol butt into my forehead. "Have you had enough? Or do I let Katie finish it?"

A hand reaches over her shoulder. "I can take that," says Harry. He ejects the magazine, thumbs the safety, and removes the round from the chamber.

Katie rolls off me. "All of you leave. Leala and I have a little sisterly love to give to our Sarah." As they close the door, she shouts, "Secure the area, and notify Mr. Johnson that we've had an incident, but it's been handled."

I'm pulled to my vanity chair and forced to sit down. They sit on the loveseat, which they moved in front of the door. I glare. They watch my eyes. They're looking for signs. Signs of Alex exerting control.

I glare more. How dare they demand that? Alex is gone, and the hollowness begs to be filled with a .45 slug.

They don't say anything. Why can't they go away? Katie answers her phone, listens for a long time and says, "Yes, sir."

I give up outlasting them. "Okay, what's next?"

They have a whispered conversation. So they have something to tell me. Leala leads, "A full set of labs, just in case something changed. Some psych tests, and you'll get a psychiatrist. He was already contracted and set up for you and Alex. If you're stable, we need to vacate the bedroom. You'll have video monitoring installed in your room."

That caught my attention. With all the dollars dumped into the project, I'm surprised they hadn't already done it.

"Before we head out, are you going to be okay?" Katie's eyes soften, and her forehead smooths.

Beats the hell out of me. I shrug my shoulders. "I think so. I don't have the overwhelming desire to off myself. I can promise today."

"Today is all any of us have." She grimaces over the cliché. If the situation wasn't so tense, I'd tease her about it.

Leala leaves and Katie motions for me to remain sitting. "Leala double checked, the audio is off. You know about my flash-violence. There is more to why I react as I do. After this, you should know. Did Alex ever mention my daughter?"

"Daughter." Something awakens in me. Katie's lost daughter. I had planned on helping Katie to find her. No, it couldn't have been me. Must have been Alex. Alex … no not Alex, but Alex. Something important to me struggles to awaken, then slides back, deepening my hollowness.

"Her name was Cissy." Waves of conflicting anger, anguish, and helplessness buckle my knees. Katie doesn't emote—until now.

Alex never made the connection to her natural musk scent and her imminent breakdowns. Alex had awesome friends; then again, Alex was extraordinary in the extreme. Who would have put up with being the opposite sex most of the day, especially with an intelligent but insuppressible joy-spirit like me?

At least until he … died, taking my joy-spirit with him.

"Yours and Alex's situation gave me something to latch onto, to remain sane. It's time you understood why you two are critical to me. Only Alex, and now you, will ever know."

"Six years ago, I was training in Military Police school at Fort Lewis, Washington. There was no childcare available that I could afford, so my aunt in South Seattle took care of Cissy during the week. One day, there was an electrical blackout, and Cissy disappeared from an interior room. The doors and windows were locked, and the only way out was past my aunt. The neighbors and the Seattle Police looked for her for a week. The MP Training Company added their resources. No trace. Nothing missing, other than Cissy.

"Unlike Alex, I've never lost anyone from my company or non-combatants to enemy fire. Some to stupidity or accidents, but I don't have Alex's issues. However, my daughter, sweet Cissy, is gone. No trace. First Alex, then you, filled part of that hole. I couldn't save Alex, but I won't let you die on me." She stiffens and doesn't move. Alex always sat next to her and waited. How do I know that? My movement to join her on the loveseat is interrupted by her snapping into action.

She gazes into my eyes. She's still looking for something. "I'm trying to work on my flash anger. Both Alex and I have been on the VA's schedule for treatment before the end of this year. Let's get out there before we worry them."

IDENTITY

SARAH BETH

They lift me onto an EMS gurney, place an oxygen mask, a coolant-driven compress around where Leala slugged me and secure the straps. "Hey, I don't…"

Dr. Timsen's pissed. "No backtalk. We've got to get you out of here in case you got undesirable attention. We're going to the Intensive Care wing where we can control the flow of people. Now shut up for once."

At the hospital, they finish all the samples and a trip through the MRI. They'd used the MRI out of hours to minimize the attention to us.

"I'd like to use the toilet, then lay down while we wait, alone." They place me in a small room with bare walls, a commercial toilet with a stainless steel seat double bolted into the toilet and a stainless steel sink. Pushing the single reclining guest chair to a different location, it doesn't move, as it's bolted to the floor. Nothing I can use to harm myself. The steel door double deadbolt drives home. Perfect.

They misinterpreted my perspiring palms, elevated heartbeat, trembling fingers. I can't tell them I'm not in here for biological reasons, but literal soul-searching issues. The mysterious hollowness stems from a dislocation in my soul. Afraid of what it means, but afraid of not understanding, I sit propped up with pillows and calm myself. After a minute, I ask, *"Sarah, are you here?"*

Nothing. I should have gotten confirmation of some sort from myself.

I wrestle with my memories of being Sarah, her love of life, deep infatuation with Jimmy, the joy of walking to class, and of course, commitment to Alex, but I am not Sarah.

Why do I think that? I grab towels, wet them, and hold them over my mouth like a paper bag to control my hyperventilation.

I'm Alex, or at least his memories, pain, gender dysphoria, and his utter devotion to saving Sarah. His pain over those poor children killed in the ambush almost two years ago doubles me over. How do I remember the hole in the boy's chest large enough for Alex to put four fingers in to stop the bleeding?

Anguish. Deep, bone grinding, tendon popping anguish. Alex lived with this, with only Katie to help?

What am I?

A rap on the closed door brings me out of my Alex-anguish. How'd they know I was curled up on the floor? The door opens. A female guard I don't know talks into her comm. How did they … there it is, a central all-angles camera in the ceiling corner.

Pushing off my anguish, there's something else, there's a stillness I associate with outdoors away from all civilization. It's here in this room. The door seals with copper, and a fine grid glints from behind the air exhaust. They've installed a Faraday cage to contain me. It doesn't work. I easily sense outwards. However, it does block out all the electronics frequencies I must have sensed since becoming Sarah-the-shell. I may fake some illnesses and get a bed in here. At least in here, electronics won't disrupt my sleep.

Oh no! I'm a freak. I shouldn't know anything about Faraday cages. This is Alex's knowledge. Am I really Alex?

I drop into the sensing state but keep my scan tight to follow a lead from my Alex memory. Before he died, my energy states remained invisible to me, but I caused what could be called ripples in physical reality. I wish I had paid more attention to Alex's leaps of intuition. I found them amusing and endearing but otherwise ignored them. I can't sense myself, but I should be able to sense my nano-distortions in the environment …

Nothing.

No!

I wash my face. Suck it up. You're alive. You can get through this. Whatever you are.

A blackness rushes from the back of my head closing out my sight. Dizzy …

Alex!
I can't hold the blending bond …
… oh no …
I did this. I started it all …

The stringy man with the greasy hair insisted on carrying my groceries from the bus stop to my apartment. He wouldn't listen to my protests that I wasn'tt a fainting lily. Halfway down the alley to the apartment, he placed my groceries on the hood of a dark blue Chevrolet Caprice.

He said, "Please don't be alarmed. I have something to show you." I edged down the alley when he came back with a manila portfolio. "You don't remember me, do you?" He held the port-folio out at arm's length. "I'm going back to the car. Look through this, and we'll talk when you are ready."

Bogus. Major freak alerts competed with my curiosity. He did look creepy familiar. I leaned on a detached garage facing the alley. Stapled on the flap was a decade old photo of me as a child. After removing the cord, and I saw lab records and more photos of me at different angles, in only underclothes, when I was a child.

He said, "Read the consent form first. That will explain the photos. I know that you could be disturbed by the photos. Please read the consent."

The form was Daddy's consent for me to be in an experiment. This was me at eight, in only my undies, photos taken throughout a year. Notes indicated normal age-appropriate maturation, with no visible affects of the treatment regimen. I remembered this. "You. You. You were the one who stabbed me with needles."

"No, we had a registered nurse install the drip line. I pushed the test fluids through that. Do you see the report? Read the last page."
I back-stepped at his advance, and he retreated to his car. I assumed it was his car.

The final paragraph scared me.
"Subject shows the first stage of energy sensitivity. The expectation is that even without added treatments, she will continue to progress in her development. Monitoring is needed. The second instar can take place in ten years. At that time, she will have a significant ability to handle energy transfers. Continual monitoring for potential early development is needed.
"Personal note: I know that testing on my own daughter would be frowned upon, but she showed significant potential in the screening exams. I'm convinced that she won't come to harm. The completion of this series of instars in ten years will guarantee my legacy."

"Signed: Alexander Joshua Merk."

I was a guinea pig? Daddy was the researcher? What did he mean "instar"? If I'm right, that's a stage of grasshopper development. I was a grasshopper?

My staring into nowhere was interrupted by the guy. "Sorry to interrupt. My name is Tod Engel. A long time ago, a wit changed my paperwork to Mort Y'Arty, and I've never been able to shake it. I worked with your father. I'm here at the university and would like to continue your father's legacy. He will become famous."

I wasn't certain about all this. Mr. Y'Arty who'd been run out of town by my cousins. Lifting my groceries, I ask, "If I agree, what is next?"
He lifted a tube, about a meter long, an octagonal cross-section, with components soldered on its sides and inside. "First I would like to take measurements." A fleer exposed all his teeth.

A wave, like the morphine given me when I broke my clavicle, swept me with ennui. I shouted. "Hey!"
Green.

DAMN, Damn, Damn.

You bitch. You left me with a body and nothing else. I never wanted to exist …

Now I have to live with the guilt of my Sarah-forbearer's starting this chain of events through her naïveté. Living with Alex's guilt over his great-great-grandmother, the Tikrit children, and Sarah pulls me into a near comatose fugue. I'm a monster created by the improbable meeting of two freaks of nature.

But I was the one with the naïveté. I was the helpless one when others died. How? What am I missing?

I wish Dr. Timsen would take that penlight of hers and stick it where the moon doesn't shine. I push her hand off my face, releasing my eyelid and blink. I stall to gather my wits. "How long this time?"

Leala pulls me off the floor and sets me on the reclining chair. "About ten minutes. You stopped moving, so we came in."

I don't want to talk. I'm the hollow person. Hollower than in-shell Sarah. Alex and Sarah have departed. Sarah is...somewhere... searching for Alex. What am I?

Dr. Timsen grabs my face again and continues her examination. "What happened?"

She won't leave me in my gut grinding nausea. What am I? I push her hand away again. "I remember things, but fuzzy. I need time, alone."

A lie. My first as Whatever-I-am. Those were Sarah memories. I remember being devastated by all the lies I told while gathering information for—what? No, Alex had the issues with lies. His Boy Scout sensibilities clashed with his need to—what? The memories are close to the surface; I need time and quiet.

I broadly smile. "Whatever it was, I'm feeling great!" Not a lie. I may be Hollow Sarah, but for some reason, a part of my hollowness fills. A small part, but I've moved beyond some crisis.

98

MATRYOSCHKA ALEX

ALEX

Surrounded, infused, and suffused with Sarah. But there was no Sarah. She was with him, but not. As usual, standard definitions failed in this alternate space.

His self-awareness puzzled him. Everything he believed pointed to his dropping out of their body partnership would stabilize Sarah but leave him in nothingness. He retained cohesion as if he was being fed.

"We need to talk." Even without the accent, he knew that this was Babushka, his great-great-grandma. She's the one who screwed him, and consequently, doomed Sarah. "There's something different about you. Care to explain?"

"Fuck off."

He picked up a sense of amusement, and she said, "Your grandmother would've washed out your mouth with cod liver oil. Okay, I messed with you when you were young. Something was happening back then. I would disassociate at a precise time every Wednesday and Friday. Towards the end, I could see through my hands. I was afraid that it was an attack. You were to protect me. I'm sorry."

He still had fond memories of her. She reached out to him when his cousins thought he was too strange. It was no accident he had found her matryoschka dolls. No one would play with him, and both of his parents worked. Babushka had kept him occupied in her home.

His lack of passion puzzled him, but his old sense of right, wrong, and duty remained. He still had a purpose, and he hadn't written his destiny, yet. "Not good enough. I have something to finish." As long as he remained coherent, he had to find a way back to Sarah, and ensure she was stable, maybe even happy.

"You were always the stubborn one. Even with all my avatars I sent you, you never listened."

"Avatars? The meadowlarks? The false memories?"

"No, the lilac scent. You wouldn't pay attention to my nudges, so I had to get creative with false memories. I know nothing about meadowlarks. You've been beyond stubborn. What part of don't die before you're twenty-five did you not understand?' "

"You never said that. You said, "You die before twenty-five."

"No, you may have been laid out with the opiates, but I told you *not* to die. Instead, what did you do? You joined the Army and almost died saving gutter-children. And now, now, you died. Stubborn. You may have been the smartest grandchild or great-great-grandchild, but kiddo, you always were stubborn."

"What happened to your accent? What's with the proper grammar?"

Her smile came through, the one she only had for him as a child. The lack of a body didn't diminish it. "Think. We aren't talking. We overlap, I guess, so we communicate. There is no accent or grammar, just meaning."

"I don't buy that I screwed up, but how do I finish what I started?"

A warmth touches me from my Babushka. "Maybe you can help, but neither of us has the energy to do the bridge. If you bridge back, get to Lincoln, Nebraska."

"What's there?"

"*IT*. Something evil. I buried it under my house when it killed my husband. I left that night with your six-year-old great-grandfather."

"What is it and what does it do?"

"It's the second jar. It scared me too much to open. I'm afraid that when Tod, my lover, found and removed it from where it was, it created a change. Something went wrong that will correct itself."

"A change? In our family?"

Babushka lets out a mental sigh. "I don't know. IT gave me nightmares about how it would build allies, then merge them when the time came."

"A causality branch. It must be talking about a change that is ultimately forced back to the center. Like a stone tossed into a stream. The ripples eventually disappear and don't affect the course of the stream."

"If you say so. I can't say I understand."

"How do I find it after over a hundred years?"

"Ask our family in Omaha. They all left Lincoln and settled around Omaha." A new ripple infused him, followed by a sense of her don't-sass-me. "You didn't answer my first question. What's different about you?"

"Uh…"

"Don't be coy. When I left you, you were a girl."

99

COINCIDENCES

SARAH BETH: DAY 58, NIGHT IN HER APARTMENT

A untie Mildred pulled the reluctant Sarah across the rise.
Aunt Millicent pulled the squirming Alex James up the rise.

The giant's teeth, row upon row, threatened to consume the unwary. Some gleamed as if porcelain capped. Some are stained tobacco-tan with the passing of the ages, or green verdigris leached from pennies left on them. Two, over there, exuded the scent of whiskey poured out by old buddies. Occasionally, a cross or an angel capped a tooth. More rarely, a voice that only she/he heard stood guard over the most neglected tombstones. Blessed were the deaf.

No one came here except for those who remembered from their grandparents' insistence that they do their ancient homages every Sunday. Generations ago, the one-way lanes were jammed with people rushing to visit great-uncle-whozzit after the end of the Sunday Sermon and before the Sunday pot roast could overcook. Blessed were the dead.

Yesterday's late evening chinook had melted the powder snow, but only the surface, before a blue norther refroze everything. The glare from the milky ice covering the snow combined with bands of winter fog to create a dappled world of half-light and half-terror blindness. Blessed were the blind.

Someplace back there, hidden by the low rise and the flat-bed truck that had skidded off the lane, was Aunt Mil's car. Pulled in her iron grip, Sarah, dug the toes of her Sunday-only patent-leather single-strap Mary Jane shoes into the milky ice covering the powder snow. Alex James dug in the toes of his lace-up Sunday shoes. Behind her/him was a trail alternating between her/his left, then her/his right, then her/his left toe trying to get traction. She/He couldn't easily stand on the ice, but her/his Mom and Aunt Mildred/Aunt Millicent broke through the crust. Each snap of the breaking ice reminded her/him of dogs cracking pot roast bones for the marrow.

Her/His silent beseeching eyes were met only once by her/his mother's. She exchanged glares with her sister, Aunt Mildred/Aunt Millicent, but she/he only scored a regrip, harsher than before.

The adult's silence, punctuated by only glares at each other, didn't make any difference anymore. They would have been drowned out by the sentinel voices anyway. She/He even heard the meadowlarks that kept vigil during the summer.

The guardian at the destination row of giant's teeth, a gnarled Bios d'Arc tree, reached out to stop her/him and tore her/his dress/jacket. Angry, her/his aunt expelled a huff and jerked her/him free. The motion left a vertical bleeding scratch on her/his right cheek. In twenty years, a bullet would open her/his cheek along the same line.

"Sar-ah-Beth, it's been ten weeks. You were too ill to go to your Babushka's funeral." It was her mother, Anna Marie Merk, barely holding back her tears. This was her daughter's first Sunday not huddled in her closet since the death she'd witnessed.

"Al-ex-an-der, it's been three months, you were too ill to go to your Babushka's funeral." It was his mother, Annie Mary Monroe, barely keeping her own composure. He had thrown himself off his Babushka's roof the day she died.

An ugly gray carved rock, something like concrete, shiny except the letters, is my Babushka.

Here lies beloved Wife, Mother,
Grandmother, Great and Great-great-grandmother.
Anna Maria (Hergenreder) Simpson
"Babushka"

4:37 AM

EEEEEEEEEE! EEEEEEEEEE!

I can't stop screaming. EEEEEEEEEEE! I curl into a tight ball tangled in my sheets. EEEEEEEEEE!

I-got-to-stop.

The lights flash on. Leala grabs me.

I-got-to-stop. EEEEEEEEEEE!

Finally, I come around. Double vision, but no puke or blood. I hate to admit it, but I'm proud of my regained control. My first nightmare as Sarah Beth, except it was a concurrent nightmare. Or was it a false memory, like what tortured Alex? I didn't realize it, but I remember most of Sarah's and Alex's memories. Then which memory is false? Both can't be true, can they?

Leala won't let me look away. She's searching in my eyes. I know she's searching for Alex.

I pull away. "I'm okay. Just an unusually vivid dream." Looking around, I remember noticing Clarice. "Clarice, why are you here?"

"Jimmy's out of town. He'd have my ass if there was a sensor misfire, and I wasn't here to fix it." Holding up a tablet I hadn't seen before, she says, "Two weeks of no readings, and now the sound pressure transducer fires. Did you scream?"

"I think so," I say. "I'd like to take a quick shower, change sheets, and go back to bed. I'm very sorry about getting everyone out of bed for nothing."

"I'm staying." Leala squeezes my hand.

I catch a flare from Clarice. "I'll stay. I need to calibrate the sensors anyway. May as well do it now. Now get into the shower, and I'll change the sheets."

No. Not what I need right now. A freaking slumber party when what I need is some quiet. What if both are true memories? What if this, including my dual existence, is part of a plan?

I know that they watch my calls. I can't even ask 'Mom,' the former *Anne Marie Hergenreder* before she married Alexander Merk, my dad. Well, Sarah's dad. I'm having difficulty keeping my identity straight.

100

WHAT AM I?

DAY 60

My phone's alarm kills a perfectly magnificent dream at five AM. I forgot today is a gym day. A moment of indecision. Am I a gym person? In the bathroom mirror, I grin. Why not?

In the hall, I'm greeted by the morning shift carrying gym bags. "It's nice outside. May we walk?" A call to Ops and we're off.

New students move in, filling the vacancies from the departing project staff. I wonder what they're like. Pushing to read people gives me a sharp pain behind my eyes, and I tilt to one side.

All three, the two escorts and Leala, gasp and stop. "What's wrong?"

"I'm sorry. I tried to–ah–do something. I can't anymore."

At the gym, the monotony of the treadmill clears my mind. I take inventory. Lost are tagging or any sensing talent. Lost is my sense of energy. I get hungry, like a real person. Gained is my clearest sense of being. A veil lifted, not only on what my attack caused but my entire life, everything is more vibrant. I think thoughts deeper and more placid than before.

I stare into the floor-to-ceiling mirror in front of the treadmill. None of my bras fit, but I'll replace them only when stuffing doesn't work, or they wear out. In addition to being five-foot-eleven – an additional five inches in height – my leaner body has defined muscles, especially in the abdomen and biceps. Lost is Sarah's cherub face; my cheekbones protrude high like a cosmetics model.

There's something else I'm missing.

No! Double D; I'm dense and in denial, just like Alex. I hit the emergency stop and hop off the treadmill. Arms folded over my head, I hide from my own reflection. I wave that I'm okay to whoever rushes up. We're so stupid. The reality has been staring the entire project in the face, and we ignored it. The Karen-corpse blend was mostly Karen in appearance. The Leala-Sarah blend was Leala with some Sarah. The host dominates the appearance of the bonded person. Stupid! It's obvious.

I know where Alex went. I see him in every mirror, the shade overlaying old-Sarah. We thought Alex "wore" Sarah. But we were wrong. Sarah "wore" Alex. Sarah Beth was always Alex, feminine, and female, but always Alex.

My pity party finished, and not wanting to scare anyone, I use the treadmill arms to scissor vault onto the tread. Show-off. Who set it so slow? I double the speed, still too slow. Another two miles per hour added, and I'm feeling fine. This is the way a run should be. I love how I look in the mirror. A lean, mean, red-haired running machine.

Sarah's sports bra is too large and chafes. The faster speed screams for a better fitting sports bra, something seamless so I can exercise longer. While I'm at it, compression tights to show off my trim body and those well-defined abs. Yes. Life is good.

I'm running still too slow and push twice on the up-speed and once on the incline increase. My smile in the mirror spreads wider and wider. A sheen of perspiration covers my body, soaks my outfit. I've never perspired before. Scratch that, the blended version of Sarah and Alex never sweated.

The gym goes silent. I check the mirror in front of the treadmills.

Everyone has stopped their exercise and is watching me. I shrug my shoulders and wave Hi! in the mirror.

Wait a minute. My smile disappears in the mirror. What happened? I forgot my unhappiness. No, that was residual-Sarah. Hey, I have residual Alex and Sarah in my personality. Don't have a clue how or why I know that. I'm Sarah Beth. I'm the best of Alex and Sarah. I just had an integration. I'm Sarah Beth. My smile returns. I'm integrating the old, residual personalities. I wonder who I'll be.

I check, and I'm running more than triple Sarah's speed from before my pity party. Better than Alex's, when he would run. He was a stair-well runner and hated the treadmill. Time to quit distracting everyone. I slow down, dismount with a reverse vault, and towel down.

I am Alex.

I am Sarah.

I'm Sarah Beth. Time to get used to it.

<hr>

THAT AFTERNOON FROWNS greet me at the end of each lab test. I've nothing for them. Our—my – only active ability was sensing, and I'm blind. The only trick we had was blending and deblending. I won't try that again. The brain swapping uncovered by the PET scans stopped with Alex's death. I need to huddle with Dr. Timsen to find out why the PET scans were exciting. All medical tests confirm a healthy, actually unusually healthy, young woman of eighteen.

Doctor Johnson observes each session. I don't need sensing abilities to see his worry. This turquoise-eyed red-head has torpedoed his project.

We head to the next appointment, a tightly controlled psych eval where I disclose my emotional condition. Each day I hurry to this appointment not for the intrusive eval, but for the room. It's the metal-lined room that shields me from sensing electronics.

Before I got into the heavier, and classified stuff about me, I got Katie's and Mr. Johnson's okay. I go full disclosure, hoping this phase will wrap up and leave me with only one, integrated personality. It may be intrusive to the extreme, but I need to stabilize. I suspect Leala ratted out my personality flip-flops, in her daily reports. I should do something nice for her. After all, she's also lost Alex.

A knock on my special room announces the end of today's session. This may be helping me, but I'm clueless how the project benefits. That's for Katie and Mr. Johnson, whom I hope wait outside the door, to answer.

Psych-guy gathers his encrypted tablet and finds the glasses, which he mislays each session. Per protocol, he knocks, and the door opens into the room from the outside. There is no interior knob. Doctor Johnson and Katie stand there, with Jimmy off to one side. I say, "Glad you could come. I'm taking advantage of my B-and-B here. I understand checkout time is in a couple of hours. Could you come in? Oh, Jimmy. This may be a while, but could you hang around? I want to check out that new bistro. I'm paying."

I have some unloading to do. Things neither Alex nor Sarah wanted to talk about.

101

SURSURRATIONS

The air hisses through the copper-mesh seals as the door closes. All electronic noise disappears, not completely, but I have to concentrate to notice it. I love this room. It's too much to expect this level of shielding at the apartment, and they only use this room when they absolutely want to avoid all possibility of eaves dropping, except their own, of course. After they take the two chairs at my insistence, I stand to face them, balancing on my right foot. With a start, I remember that this is how Alex always initiated his "happy dance."

"Rather than set up a secured meeting, I'd rather unload what I know right now." Katie pulls out her secured tablet and swipes on the audio transcription mode. "First, but likely trivial, I can sense active electronics. I only get relief here inside your Faraday shield. Don't act surprised. I told you that I've inherited Alex's knowledge and most of his memories." Katie's posture changes, more erect and what I can only call a hopeful look crosses her face. "The copper strips on the door give it away. For that reason, if you want to do nighttime monitoring, I can sleep here to help."

"That won't be necessary." Doctor Johnson said. Damn. He's right. Having me doing sleepovers in the physics annex would be noticed.

"Okay, but keep in mind that I don't mind meetings here. If you thought that this would dampen my ability to sense people, no joy there. I wouldn't have minded if I could be dampened, but I'm stuck with knowing people are around. "

I want something, so I'll break Alex's and Sarah's pact over his abilities. "I'm limited compared to either Alex or Sarah." Stoic Katie's face rippled in surprise; I've caught them off guard. "Sarah's sensing was good out to about twenty kilometers. Alex was about five, more if he wasn't ill. They never thought of trying to combine and extend their reach."

Doctor Johnson asks, "Did they have a theory on what limited them?"

"Just what Alex stated. He believed the uncertainty principal clipped accuracy. As you know, distance accuracy went first. They never disclosed their true range because they were already exhausted by the formal tests. Those were limited to no more than ten meters as they didn't see the point of extending the test range. Before you ask why Alex didn't tell you, he wanted your attention on fixing Sarah. Besides, it was likely her influence that he was merely reflecting." That last is an absolute lie, but I'm not outing his family.

"Do you mind some tests?"

"Only if it's in this room. That way I can get some peace. Distance? Give me a moment." I push outward to where people "flicker." "I don't catch anyone moving at traffic speed, so I'm constrained to this building, no more than about ten meters. I still can't tell who I'm sensing or anything about them, just that they're there."

"We'll set it up. Is that all?"

"No. I'm trading. You got something. I get something. Do I make *that sound*?"

"I, ah, how did you know about it?"

"Alex's memories and knowledge, remember? Now quit stalling. Do I ever make the susurration sound Sarah did when she moved in her shell state?"

"I'm not certain that…"

"Jimmy's right outside. I didn't ask him to come today just to have lunch. He'll know. Do I open the door and ask?"

"Don't. We'll keep this to the chain of command." Mr. Johnson opens his hands and flips them palm up. "We have sensors everywhere you go. Sorry, but it was prudent to extend the coverage after Alex died."

"Let me make this easier. You depended on Alex to rein in Sarah. He's gone, so what's my control? That's why I'm asking. Do I show any signs of quantum level movement?"

"No. Other than your rapid healing, probably a quantum biology phenomenon, you're completely human."

"So I'm only part monster. I can live with that. Keep the sensors running, just in case."

I'm still not ready to expose Alex's deepest fear. He disclosed everything but this about Sarah. She was a Golem, created out of quantum froth, the clay of the universe. The project screwed up when it accepted Sarah's belief that she slipped through alleys until she found Alex. The distance from Sarah's attack to his/my apartment is over ten kilometers, and there are no dark alleys. She slipped in and out of physical reality, transporting herself to her target, Alex.

I will recover Alex. I swear it. Then recovering Sarah-the-monster becomes *his* moral dilemma.

102

REVENGE PREPARATIONS

DAY 62

As we return to the apartment, Harry catches up and asks Leala. "Can you make requals?"

Leala says, "Certainly. The next shift started, so all I have to do is drop Sarah at her apartment."

"Hey. One, I'm right here, and two, what are re-quals?" Shouldn't be that touchy, but she insists on calling me Sarah. Besides, my life is shit.

Leala grins. "Testy, today, aren't we? We need to go to the gun range and re-qualify. We're overdue, due to the excitement lately."

"Can I come? Wait for me. I'll be right back." Before they can answer, I've run to the bedroom and load Alex's satchel with all the cartridges I can find in his footlocker.

"Okay, I'm back." I trip and dump cartridges over the hall. "Uh, any chance Katie will let me use Alex's gun?"

Leala snorts, "About as much chance that the moon will go backward in the sky. This is the slow time at the range, so we can try to get clearance to allow you to join us."

Harry fingers the cartridges as he helps me pick them up. "These are old. No telling how many will fire. I can help. I had my old .45 cleaned last month but haven't test fired for a year. If ops approves, you can use it. I'll carry it. You don't have a license."

It takes over an hour to decide on the new SOP for my unusual choice of recreational activities. The four of us wait in their apartment, drinking either water or pop. They don't want to mess up their scores, or even worse, have alcohol on their breaths. Finally, psych-guy and Katie confirm that the outing is likely to be beneficial, as I've had no violent ideations since the first one. However, Alex's gun remains under her control.

At the range, I sit quietly until Harry comes over and checks that I still have my firearm-safety earmuffs and glasses on. He touches the bottom of my chin, smiles, and shouts close to my head so I can hear through the muffs, "It's okay. Since Alex died, Leala frets about you constantly."

He puts up a paper bullseye target on the range line and programs it for ten feet. I shake my head. "It's seven meters." He frowns and runs the target out to seven meters. I load five rounds in the magazine.

"How'd you know five rounds?"

"Alex told me." No, just another damn memory leak. I did it automatically just like the seven meters. Five is the number you use for quals. Feet spread, lean slightly forward, breath in, out slowly, hold it and miss the bull's eye target with all five rounds. "I don't like this target. It's distracting. Could I have one like you are using?"

Harry shrugs his shoulders, buys the standard human outline target and is waylaid by both David and Leala, who look at me, then the target. Worry creases their faces, but they say nothing. "That's better. Put it at ten meters." Harry complies. It's the same distance they qualify at.

This is more like it. I'm more comfortable now. Breathe slowly, deeply. Visualize your target. *"Call me Uncle Mort."* Hold your breath, and the first round hits on target but high to my right. *"I'm Mr. Y'Arty."* Second round hits closer but to the left. Third round about an inch high. *"I work with your father*." The last two rounds punch touching holes in the crotch. Reload. All five rounds again punch touching holes. Hell yes!

All shooting stops. Leala, Harry and David cluster behind me in my booth. David whistles, and says, "One in the heart. The rest are low and to the left. With practice, you'll get them all in the heart."

"No, I got it right. Could you get me five more targets? Hold it. I changed my mind." I reach into Alex's satchel and remove his wallet. Pulling out two hundred dollars, I say, "Make that nine targets, some cardboard, so the target doesn't move between shots and all the rounds this covers."

The nine new targets sport pink body outlines. Pink? Very funny. Which one is the wit? I'll kill their fun by not responding. Let's see. One target each for Alex's and Sarah's death. One each the deaths of my daddy, big brother, and little sis. One for what Mom went through as a single mother. One for Alex's parents. One for Katie. If she gets too close to Mort Y'Arty, her sensitivity to the types of energy he commands may kill her. And one because this is calming. Fifteen rounds in Alex's target and it falls apart at the hips. I put up Sarah's target next

Life is good. I revel in my Alex-Sarah Integration moment. I'm something neither Alex nor Sarah could be. I am Sarah Beth.

Maybe not all violent ideations have disappeared. Suicide has fallen off the table and has been replaced with revenge. "Call-me-Uncle-Mort," Ah'm com'n for you.

103

WHO AM I?

DAY 64, APARTMENT HALLWAY

B ack from another day at the test mill, and I'm about ready to drop. My bed will get a couple of hours of use before dinner. I've got to remember to ask Katie where Quentin's been.

Jimmy heads out to do whatever he does in the late afternoon. Alex believed he reported each afternoon on the readings captured by the electronic monitoring in my walls. Which reminded me, that stuff is extremely irritating to one or more of my preternatural senses, and the wall looks like hell from all the patchwork trying to make it appear that nothing is there.

This is my opportunity to help myself and to take care of a loose end. "Jimmy. Do you have a moment?" Leala backs off from her position at my elbow. She's expecting a reprise of Sarah's infatuation with the geek. But, I lost that with Sarah's exit. All that's left is a deep respect for Jimmy's abilities, inherited from Alex.

"Certainly. I'm sorry it's been almost two weeks, but we've both been busy."

"I can help on part of that. You put in three new sensors yesterday."

"How'd you..."

I turn to Leala. "Come closer. It looks like I've slipped, and you'll need to put it in your report." She steps forward but only within easy listening distance. "I've always been able to tell. Probably would make an interesting test. Since my incident, my mind's been clearer, and I can pinpoint the location of each sensor. You've filled almost the entire wall. It would be easier on me if you moved in a standard electronics rack and put it all there as you replace or come up with new stuff."

"Our agreement was…"

"We're past that. I won't be offended if you have to put a security cage around it. I'm only trying to minimize the points of distraction."

I wave off Leala. This is as good a time as any to let this nice guy down as easy as I can. She steps back, maintaining the illusion of privacy. "I wanted to thank you for putting up with my ridiculous silly-attacks. I'm also past that. You don't need to feel any obligation."

I step past him on my way to a needed nap. He holds his hand out. "I understand. Any chance you could join me for coffee at the CUB? I'm fascinated by your sensing the monitoring. We can correlate what you sense with my location matrix."

Why am I playing with my hair?

Day 65, 07:11 AM

My phone rings. Cozy and whole, I curl around my warmth. It rings again. "Go away." Another ring. I uncurl, roll over, stretch and answer on the next ring. Morning eyes keep me from checking who it is.

"If you are finished abusing Brother, could you remind him he has an early morning meeting with Mr. Johnson?" Busted by Clarice. Now Sarah Beth's overnight stay with Jimmy would be everyone's knowledge. Clarice. It had to be Clarice.

"Why don't you come in here and tell him yourself, or better yet call him?"

"I'm outside the door. I was coming in, but I worried that what you two may be doing would warp my fragile mind." To prove it, she pounds and shouts through the door. "Jimmy, wake up call."

As I turn over, Jimmy's patented shy-guy smile greets me. "You're lucky she likes you. She usually barely knocks before she walks in. When we were younger, she'd sit between me and anyone she didn't approve of. You can see how that killed my social life."

My skin tingles. I push down the gut reaction that I don't deserve this happiness; that it should have been Sarah's, not mine. Emotions don't lie, I hope.

After the CUB, we walked in the park until dusk. We parted to ready ourselves for dinner out, and I put on my first makeup and skirt. He's the first to fill me with hope, and to be honest, happiness.

Jimmy starts his shower, and I curl around his pillow. With his scent and warmth, I still feel the sensation of him next to me. Waves of happiness overwhelm me, making me giggle. Huh? Sarah Beth doesn't giggle. Who is it this time? Bound to be my residual Sarah, the part not yet integrated. Several deep breaths and I regain control. No, I'm wrong. It's my unintegrated Alex? He's giddy happy for Jimmy and me and my lost virginity. This is a side of Alex I never saw while he lived. More for me to think about.

Back to more important things; I curl up and enjoy Jimmy's warmth and scent on his pillow.

Another knock, soft and polite this time. Puzzled, I wrap the sheet around me toga-style and open the door to a rarely diffident Clarice, clothes in her arms. "I checked, and you don't have anything on the schedule until the weekly debriefing in the late afternoon. I hoped you would stay a while and look at my dissertation's equations."

I almost blurt out a retort, but she's biting her lip, and toeing a circle on the carpet. In a way, it's sweet. Curious about what's up, I say, "Sure, once Jimmy finishes I'll shower and come out." At this, she breaks out in a grin. She skips to the kitchen with the tea box.

Jimmy comes out, a towel wrapped around him, thank goodness; I'm not ready for full nudity in daylight. He spots the clothes in my arms and asks, "Something early on the schedule for you?"

"No, Clarice asked me to stay for breakfast."

We hug, exchange a quick peck, and I'm into the shower. He'll be gone before I get out. That's good. Last night's strip was in the semi-dark. The only man who's seen me nude was Alex. Who has the biggest issue with stripping before a man, Alex or Sarah? I don't know. Time to grow up. I need to get over this. I'm eighteen – or is it Alex's age, twenty-six, for goodness sake? And finally, after last night, not a virgin. I start giggling again. Stop it Alex. I'm Sarah Beth, and I don't giggle.

Mental adjustment over, the bathroom's gestalt stuns me and the sheet slips from my hand. Standing nude, for the first time truly seeing myself in a mirror, my normality and that of my surroundings flush me, I'm flushed, not with embarrassment but with strength and purpose.

Jimmy's musk cologne strangles the other scents. A curl of toothpaste proudly presents itself on the faucet handle. The shower tiles slip under my fingers with the accumulation of soap and Jimmy. Normality; that's what I've missed. If Quentin doesn't stop cleaning my room and sanitizing my bathroom, I'm moving in with Clarice and Jimmy, even if I sleep on their couch.

Before I jump into the shower, I text my plans Leala and Katie.

<<Staying w LS in apt>>

They know Sarah dubbed Clarice LS for—little snot. Now that I know that I'm not Sarah, I've taken over her identity. That or I'm without an identity.

Katie knows me well. She's sent boxer shorts, plain cotton bra, a T-shirt, and jeans. Much better than the lacy outfit I wore last night for Jimmy. I can move in this. Slipping on the gray leather sandals, I weep. What's wrong this time? Who's weeping? I need better integration. A couple of deep breaths and I have my answer. Sarah's weeping for her lost Alex. Drawn to the mirror, I understand why. Except for the bra and belt, these are all Alex's clothes. I grab my skinny belt and cinch the extra six inches out of his jeans.

Stop right there. I've had worried messages asking why I wasn't on LuRRk during my incident and crisis of identity. My overnighter reeks of the opportunity to keep up the campaign to solidify back home that I'm the Sarah Beth Merk sent to college. I return to the bathroom and snap a LuRRk in the mirror catching me in silly-pose but more importantly catching Jimmy's mess in the background. This will keep Omaha's tongues demanding more.

I root through my – Sarah's – floppy pink zebra-print purse for transparent lip balm. I have no luck, so lipstick it is. A clink in the bottom catches my attention. It's the quartzite from Sarah's first and only date with Jimmy. Warmth, not of embarrassment, but of strength, infuses me. Monday I'll drop by the jewelers next to LDO and have it secured to a strong necklace chain.

Sarah's memory combines with Alex's facility with Clarice's equations. His thoughts, notions, and suggestions threaten to overwhelm me. My bright smile precedes my entry to their common room. I can help someone. I can help someone!

———

"… what do you think, Alex—Sarah Beth?" Lips slightly open, eyes wide, almost beseeching, Clarice tilts her head back and stares up into my eyes. Sitting, our height difference is more pronounced.

A whiff of perfume, not the question, jolts me out of my reverie. Pursed lips with perfectly applied lipstick match her freshly manicured nails. Foundation flawlessly applied with an expertly blended blush. Her eyes lined and shadowed. Who puts on full makeup in the morning?

She sidles up and sits hip to hip without me realizing at first. Heat radiates from her exposed leg below the short skirt. She waits for me to make the first move. She wants—no, needs—Alex. The Alex who took care of her deep hurts and abuses at the hands of her peers. The Alex with the insights into the potential of her work she never saw.

I can handle the latter. Alex left all his memories of her work and his ideas. I can make an installment on her other need, but as Sarah Beth, not as an Alex surrogate. "Hold that question. I need to stretch." I retrieve the afghan from the couch and place it on her shoulders. Dressed in a skirt and thin blouse, she'd been shivering in the air-conditioned room.

"Now, I recall a thought about your fifth line…"

————

WHEN OUR HEADS come up from an intense argument about her dissertation, Clarice says, "Four hours. Where does the time go?" Saving her markups, she stretches. "You're a wonder. We only made it through two pages of equations, but they were the ones Alex couldn't help me detangle. With your intensity, now I know I'm right, but it needs more work."

104

CAUSALITY BOMB

An icon on the last page catches my attention "What's that?"

Clarice's face falls. "It's a pointer to something not on the page. A lemma."

Lemma. Sounds familiar, a vague memory from middle school math—trigonometry? —refused to expose itself. I'm forced to admit. "I can't remember. What's a lemma?"

"A secondary or supporting theory. Whenever I find something of interest that is outside of my research, I document it as a subsidiary theory for the next generations of grad students. The last thing Alex did was to collect all the fragments for me."

I'm still missing something. "Why the face?"

She holds her hand over the icon. "My Lemma of Embarrassment."

"Why Lemma of Embarrassment?"

"Just this one." She touches the icon, and a new flow of equations appears. "See how future potentialities pile up? If this is right, then a trivial change in energy of the extra-dimensions can create a cascade of coexisting futures."

"So? At least the sci-fi fans would be happy."

"My rep is already fragile enough. It can't take the burden of a theory that all futures co-exist and can interact."

"You're no fun."

"I want my physics Ph.D. and a fellowship at a leading physics lab before I expose my nutso side."

"What's this?" I don't know how I'm even following, but a clutch of Curl equations seems odd.

"Up to now, it's been bad. This is the 'worse.' I stopped before my mind hemorrhaged. Under the right set of extra-dimension conditions, the futures create a reverse-time effect ripple and affect the past. There would be multiple co-existing pasts."

"Do you have a beer? I've had too much caffeine. I'd like to look this over."

"Yeah!" Clarice fist pumps and dances with hip swings to the kitchenette.

I stretch out on the couch, feet over one arm. This will take a while. Hmm. I'd better activate the notes overlay feature so I can write suggestions as I go. "I can't see why this bothers me and I know that I don't have the background or the math, but..."

After almost an hour of stiff-arming Clarice from looking over my shoulder, I have something, but what? "I'm certain that you've made a bad assumption." Without looking up, I raise my right arm and block the blow from Clarice. "That's a bad habit Jimmy shouldn't enable. Take constructive criticism like a woman."

Flipping the laptop to show Clarice, I say, "It isn't time, but one or more of the x-dimensions interacting with our reality. Poking around to find a favorable future would energy-ripple physical reality until the past supported the new future."

Lost in thought, I sip my beer with Clarice in silence. This means something personal to me, but what?

Clarice starts, "I…" then goes silent.

I rise, and in Jimmy's bathroom, comb out my hair, re-arrange his stuff, and examine my pupils again. Still turquoise. On his bath vanity, I exchange his amber and emerald bottles three times before recognizing what I'm doing—I'm stalling.

Back at the couch, Clarice puts down two new brews, called *ZeitGeist*.

I open the window to mitigate the humidity in the room. After sitting down, part of what disturbs me bubbles to the surface. I ask Clarice, "Do you smell flowers?"

"No, what type?"

"Lilacs."

"It's been more than three months since they bloomed."

"I don't hear meadowlarks singing."

"They don't hang around during mid-summer. They come back in the fall, then migrate south."

That's what's been itching in my mind since Alex's and Sarah's death. I've lost my personal totems. Alex was close to the answer. The lilacs were a signal that his Babushka was interfering somehow. The meadowlarks, especially those that hung around windows, marked a different interferer. Who could do that?

Clarice interrupts my thoughts. "Do you know about the Butterfly Effect?"

From my Alex side, certainly. He inherited a massive pulp magazine collection from his grandfather. There was also the best-forgotten movie series. "An ancient sci-fi story. While hunting dinosaurs from a suspended path, a tourist accidentally squashes a bug. Killing the bug totally changes their present."

"This is worse."

"Agree."

"This can be controlled by someone."

I watch a drop of condensation slide down the side of the beer, breaking into two paths. Two futures. Tipping the bottle for a slug, the perspective changes. The two drops compete to create a compatible past.

I say, "The future, once messed with, creates a targeted past…"

" … with enough finesse, it can be limited to selective pasts," finishes Clarice.

"Or extended."

"Many alternative pasts and futures could coexist."

A causality bomb.

This is it. My answer. And to think that it was pain-in-the-tush Clarice who stumbled on it. Mr. Johnson wasn't subtle about keeping her away from the core aspects of the project, only tolerating her presence on the grunt work because of his need for her brother. But now she's busted the project-wide open. I may have to kill her.

Something shattered the present and future, creating two simultaneous pasts, one that had Sarah in it and one that held Alex. "Each past-present-future combination would be fully consistent. Each combination would be aware of each other."

Clarice finishes her beer. Her eyes glisten. "The phenomena would spawn more."

"Until something catastrophic and energy-intensive stopped it."

Clarice lets the bottle slip from her hand; it rolls and clinks against the leg of the coffee table. "I disconnect from the net when I work to avoid interruptions. No back-ups have been made. I'm wiping the whole drive."

"Better yet, copy all your work except the lemma into the backup.

Copy the lemma to your personal encrypted chip and hide it. Then wipe and restore your drive."

I've added to my lengthening list of things to take care of. First and obviously, Mr. Y'Arty. He can't be allowed to bounce around destroying lives. Likely he doesn't know the future-past phenomena, but once dead, he can't find it.

Then there's that shadowy group that supports him.

Most scary are the interferers that Alex discovered, tying into physical reality via meadowlarks and lilac scent. I no longer think the manifestations are real. They were Alex's and Sarah's preternatural perception of interferences by others.

I now know who I am.

105

I KNOW WHO I AM

Clarice is in the same mind-space that Jimmy disappears into. She even has the same cute face as Jimmy when she's thinking. Similar to the male-Alex. Alex's intense concentration could only happen if Sarah was ready to take over. Of course, Sarah was always ready. I'd never considered how useful not worrying about your body could be.

I don't exactly have an abundance of friends, but this sideshow wagon is leaving the fairgrounds.

"Clarice, something came up. After I handle that, I want to go clothes shopping with you." I pull on the five-inches-too-large waistband of Alex's jeans.

Clarice comes out of her reverie to giggle at my dilemma. "Only if I can get you into a beauty shop. You've let yourself go since Alex..." her hand goes up to her mouth. "I'm sorry."

"No problem. Having people walk on eggshells only makes it worse. Please pass that word around. I'll text you to see when you're available."

Showtime. I touch the "magic button" on my phone. For some reason,

Alex's phone has disappeared, as did the one Sarah's mother sent from Omaha. "I'm heading over to HQ. I'll just use whoever's on call." The call center stalls and I hear them readying a denial. "Let me put it this way, either you bring me there, or I'll find it myself."

Clarice doesn't follow me into the hall for the handoff. Another sign of her distraction. Clarice's breakthrough, if accidentally made real by Sarah Beth's channeling male-Alex's intuitive abilities, is too deadly to let out.

I hope that I won't have to kill her.

I know who I am.

Free will is a bitch. Especially when you don't have free will. Why'd I ever work on those equations?

106

FREE WILL

PROJECT HQ, 3RD FLOOR SUBLEASED SPACE ABOVE THE TEA
SHOP ON THE SQUARE

E ven with the full-height windows, there's something spooky about this conference room. The window coating obscures direct sunlight and reflections, but not any other light. It's a technology I'd never seen before, but I decide to ignore it for now. The ceiling lights focus on the table space in front of each seat making the conference table look like an Appaloosa pony drawn by a child. The chairs are metal with mesh seats and make a strange *thnnng* sound every time Mr. Johnson changes position.

I ask, "Sir, is this all the available data on Alex and Sarah? It seems thin."

I like this interface. Data for Sarah and Alex occupy the center two of four floor-to-ceiling computer displays. I hand-swipe chronologically tagged data on both Alex and Sarah to the right. It automatically arranges the data by date. Factoids that don't seem to correlate get sent to the far-left.

Mr. Johnson says, "Wait until I make an adjustment." The exterior windows opaque, leaving only the cone lights and the self-illuminated displays. The rest of the room drops into a gloominess that would make a haunted house enthusiast ecstatic. "This is all of it."

I stand back to examine the results. The factoids on the right form a chronology. The far-left fills with factoids that don't fit the chronology but tells a story that may be a real-world validation of Clarice's lemma.

Some data is missing, but this is it. My life. I haven't remembered snippets of Alex's or Sarah's life. I've remembered my own. How did I get so screwed up?

A screech and clunk outside announce Katie's arrival. She should get that lower ball joint replaced. How'd I know that that sound is a ball joint? Of course, I would know. I'm not Sarah.

Katie enters with her normal window-jostling door slam. I turn to the two, Katie and Mr. Johnson. "Now that both of you are here, when were you planning on telling me the truth?"

Mr. Johnson swipes perspiration off his pate while Katie edges her briefcase onto the conference table. He asks, "What are you asking?"

"When were you going to tell me that I'm Alex?"

"The psychologist warned about telling you more than you asked. He doesn't know the classified exclusions, but his observations indicated that you're unstable."

"No shit. I'm a damaged veteran who's had two sex changes in less than three months, all while maintaining a third persona as a coed who never grew up."

Katie pales, and her hand reaches under the flap of her briefcase. I say, "Take it out, make certain it's loaded and the safety is off." Katie's face calms as she readies BMFG. "We have some stuff to talk about, and it will go better if you're confident you can handle me if I go feral.

"I'll lay it on the line. I'm Alex. I renamed myself Alex – Dad's name – when I was eleven. I legally changed my name from Sarah Beth Merk to Alex Jane Merk before I went into the military to show that I could follow in my father's footsteps, survive, come home and have a family. Which reminds me..."

Tsssk. A mild pressure starts in the back where my neck merges with my skull. *Not now.*

Mr. Johnson pulls out a tablet. "Read this, sign, and place your thumbprint on it. Then you'll be cleared at the highest classification for the project."

"I already did this."

Katie's hand hasn't left BMFG. "No, male-Alex signed into the project. We think you are the same person, but your DNA and fingerprints changed."

"Anything different than what male-Alex signed?"

Mr. Johnson flips his hand. "No."

"Then I'll sign and thumb-verify so we can get the important stuff. Is that okay, General?"

His face flushes and the perspiration returns. "General?"

"Of course. It all fits. No civvy would be in charge of a joint command project, and generals … well, generals exude a sense of authority whenever they're in the vicinity."

"Did Sarah or the other Alex know?"

"I'm going back to Sarah Beth. "SB" for friends," she grinned to ensure they were included. "It'll be easier, and I no longer need to emulate my dad. As for my two predecessors, Sarah, of course not. Alex was too distracted by all the strangeness, but he knew you had to be someone important. Sir, if you're finished trying to distract me, I'd like to see the vid of Alex's funeral."

The general finishes wiping his forehead. "Can't."

"Why the fuck not? What game are you playing?"

"It's gone. All records of the funeral and his extended family are gone. In fact, everything we didn't record on the experimental crystal matrix we were testing is gone. The crystal appears to be immune to whatever wiped conventional servers and our memories.

Our only link is memories of those closest to Alex or Sarah, mostly Katie and a little of Leala. We've been racing to record their memories and those few who remember anything. So far, we've only identified Dr. Timsen, Mr. and Ms. Addams, Leala, and myself as having memories of Sarah and male-Alex. Everyone else only remembers you as you now are and believes that only you have been on the project. We've recorded our memories and play them back when we forget. Replayed, personal memories become more resistant to fading."

I've got to stop this. That bastard Mort Y'Arty created future branches, and they're erasing the past. Clarice's lemma is deadly.

"When did this start?"

"We don't know for certain, but definitely after Alex's funeral. We noticed small discrepancies, like who was in the funeral vid. Then everything disappeared."

"Alex's family is gone?"

"His entire Ballard neighborhood is now a naturally occurring sinkhole."

A handy way to create an entire back history without tearing the entire fabric of a community to shreds. I may be able to use that in the future.

I had found Quentin's second crystal chip under the dining table. It was the only physical evidence that he'd ever existed. Should I give Quentin's two crystal chips to the project to help their restoration of lost history records? No. That I'll hold onto.

I examine my reflection in the office window. "Why do I look like this?" My side view reveals not the flat chested, small hips that I remembered growing up, but small breasts, no larger than B sized, and a modest swelling of feminine buttocks. "Get Quentin here. He always ate this weird shit up. He's likely to have some theory from some pulp book." I'm not disclosing his research until he and I can decide how dangerous it is.

Katie's reflection pales into ash. "You remember Quentin?"

The general perks up and thumbs on the audio recorder on this laptop. "Is this one of those outages?" Katie motions a yes in the combat sign language the two of us, and now the general use.

Katie's eyes glisten. "You and I are the only ones who remember Quentin." Katie's deep anguish jarred her from her own issues of dislocation in time. She wasn't the only victim. How broad did the ripples go?

The future created by integrating her errant selves, Alex and Sarah, required that Quentin not exist. Quentin, her best friend, had gotten caught in the rewritten future. Therefore, he no longer existed. Bullshit and stinky pig shit.

She remembered the past where Quentin spiraled into slacker hell when she enlisted. He had set that aside to come out to Pullman to help her.

Her new future required that Quentin be dead. In addition to her memories of the slacker Quentin, she also remembered his death. Eight years ago, during the summer before their Senior year, they hiked the entire Cascade Trail. Quentin dived into the glacial fed pool. He hit his head and died from the injuries because she didn't know how to save him. She screamed for hours for help.

Only Katie and she remembered him. But how long could we resist his erasure? I grabbed the window ledge to stabilize myself. Impossibly, the double thick ballistic-resistant window transmitted the songs of the meadowlarks covering the parked cars.

There was a solution, one that needed massive amounts of free energy. I push the problem to my subconscious, confident that the intuitive part of my mind, my male-Alex mind, resided there.

A new visualization of Clarice's lemma forces itself into my conscious mind. Manipulating the future to create alternative pasts is like preserving a soap bubble by putting it in your pocket. There was a way, it only required the intuitive push that my Alex mind excelled at.

Turning from the window, I channel Alex Jane, for the last time. "I'll need a secure laptop. I'm now on the study end of the project. Load it with all the surviving public and military records about me. I'll report on how it differs from my memory." The stoic, kick-ass Alex Jane needed retirement to let my real persona, Sarah Beth to…

Tsssk

I wake to Katie's eyes showing whites and BMFG pointed at my chest. "Damn, Katie. That's a hell of a thing to wake up to." Dr. Timsen collects blood, perspiration and mouth spit samples.

"You crumbled like a sand castle hit by a wave. I ordered her to cover you." The general's eyes betray more concern than fear.

"Good move, for Alex or me. However, Sarah never had military training, and she might have overreacted. No telling what would have happened to this building. Any signs of Sarah?"

Jimmy arrives. Swell, this has become a party. "Nothing on the sensors."

Clarice is jumping to see over the taller people.

"Have you finished blood sucking?" I'm annoyed but refrain from interfering with Dr. Timsen.

"Yeah, and I doubt that I'll find anything, again. Your brain waves peaked again in the theta. But now they're near normal." Dr. Timsen removes the blood draw needle and the EKG patches.

"Jimmy, anything interesting?"

Clarice has to nudge him.

"Um, no. The log shows a rise in what we're tracking, then it disappeared."

I wave around the room. "You all have to leave. The general and Katie and I have something to discuss. You'll be brought in as they decide who will be involved. Oh, Jimmy stay. I want to discuss your readings some more." I pull on Clarice's arm. "You too."

Once everyone else vacates the conference room, I motion for those left to sit, and I bring up an aerial map of Pullman.

"I'm going hunting."

107

HUNTER AND HUNTED

XTREME GIRLS SHOPPE, PULLMAN, WA.

"You know Katie will never forgive you. She hasn't been out of earshot since your accident." Clarice brings yet another outrageous tank top and short shorts combination into the dressing cubicle.

"I swear, you're trying to make me look ridiculous. Katie is too conspicuous the way she glowers all the time." I drop to a whisper. "We're going for girl-friends innocently shopping for party clothes. Remember, if anything happens, drop and cover. Wait for someone on the project to retrieve you."

Clarice holds the ensemble in front of her, checking the mirror. "I think this color also works with my darker skin and hazel eyes. If it comes in my size, then we can hit the bars as sisters. Hmm, turquoise sandals. Definitely needs turquoise sandals." She drops back into her whisper and hands me a data chip. "I've wiped everything and reloaded my dissertation work without any hints about the lemma. This is the only copy of the lemma. You're the only one I can trust with this. My life is an open book, and I need Jimmy's help to keep my computer working. He's bound to stumble onto it if I leave it there."

She cracked the door and checks for anyone nearby. "I don't like this. I don't remember you as ex-military, but everyone tells me it's true."

I stop shedding the previous outfit to look into Clarice's eyes. She isn't pretending. So, the quantum entanglement that protects some people from forgetting includes her. "Do you remember Alex's funeral?"

"Of course. I made a fool of myself. I didn't stop crying for a day."

Clarice's connection is on an emotional level. I wonder which type of memory is the most robust. I have the opposite problem. My own memory increases in size and strength and, like the previous night, the conflicts threaten my hold on reality.

Who am I? Sarah Beth of course, but those fifty-five days I was Alex and Sarah jumbled me as each persona's experiences demanded dominance. Again, I'm grateful for the psychiatrist's attention.

"Mention this to Katie when you have a quiet time. She'll want to know. Don't worry about me. When we're out drinking, I'll fill you in on my service; it included some covert ops training."

Clarice initiates a fist bump. When I don't respond, she pulls my hand to hers. Then she splays her fingers, and I follow, puzzled. We interlock fingers. "That's what girlfriends do. I know that you've had a tough time, but you're overdue being a real person." Clarice glances out the slotted door again. "I don't see anyone from the project out there."

I release her hand. For some reason, the girl-friend grip causes an unprecedented warmth in me. "That's good," I say, "We gave them time to preposition, and no one we know should be out there. We need an apparent security protocol violation to lure our quarry out."

"And you're the bait. I still think the plan stinks."

Clarice leaves to find more outrageous outfits. I try on more of the almost-slutty outfits. "Clarice definitely prefers skin showing. Maybe we should hit up the bars after all. She needs a woman to take that edge off. I should be able to guide a couple to her." I realize I've slipped into an old habit, muttering to herself, that I'd thought died with my father. I will take that as another sign of healing.

Tssskt. The energy is building.

The solution pops to the top of my mind like a methane bubble rising in a swamp, but it's incomplete.

More. I wait for the Alex part of me to deliver something to grasp. What I need is a future that makes Quentin critical.

I have it.

Not knowing how I do it, I hug into submission a future where he stops me from accidentally killing someone. Alternative pasts immediately presented themselves, too many to count. To avoid screwing with others, I ignore any that anyone but me to change their past.

Bright, like a rising full moon, the adjustment to my past lights my consciousness. All I needed was to force a past where I quit Girl Scouts over Mom's objections, because I didn't relate to the girls' stuff. Instead, I joined Quentin in Boy Scouts. Merit badges, training, and internships gave me training in lifesaving, CPR, field triage of trauma, including concussions. I'd save Quentin, and to hell with other damage I create.

All it needs is a massive burst of free energy. Someone is stupidly delivering it on a silver platter.

Tsssk. Not internal. But external.

This one will be larger than the one in the cafeteria, and double any of the remote attacks. A half smile forms on my face as I pull on the least revealing ensemble, capri slacks, loose, too large but I don't have time for a replacement, and a loose vee-neck tummy-exposing T-shirt with half sleeves. I leave my shoes off. Good to go. *It won't be long now.*

I check Jimmy's sensor through the open flap of my satchel. The alarm hasn't activated, which confirms my suspicions that I'm more attuned to quantum level events. A single three-finger tap on the case sends the signal that the attack is imminent.

Sometime in the past hour, my pink zebra-print floppy purse disappeared, and the Alex-satchel replaced it. Good riddance. I hated that purse.

The tooled pink leather clutch is replaced by my old Alex-wallet, made from bison leather, with a zipper enclosure. Some pieces of my former life are aligning with my memories. The only thing I know with certainty was that I have no need to be Alex Jane. Besides, it would please Mommy.

Mommy. How long had it been since I've called her mother that?

More importantly, I remember how I had forced my macho-bitch form. From the age of eleven, I talked Quentin's mother into supplying me with testosterone and estrogen blocking injections. I was obsessed with replacing my father Alex, in all things that my preteen mind understood. That meant being rough and stoic. In the mirror was the Sarah Beth who would have developed if I hadn't been in extreme grief over the deaths of Babushka, Daddy, brother, and little Munchy.

Something has healed in me. I owe that to Alex and Sarah. Separately, they came to grips with their part of my craziness that I couldn't handle as a single person.

Everything pink disappearing from my life confirms my deepest fears. Before the attack that sundered me, a few of my items were pink, mostly for variety. Now I'm living an almost pink-less existence. Something was still spinning alternative futures. What future required that I be macho? It's my base persona, but what was happening?

Clarice's lemma points to a future-adjusted reality recreating the requisite past. Is someone already doing that or is it an unexpected outcome of that cursed experiment started ten years ago by Y'Arty? Regardless, this is probably the only thing more dangerous than Sarah had been. If necessary, I will kill anyone who might be able to change the future.

Tsssk. The Jimmy sensor remains quiescent.

Tsssk. A familiar hand, the same one that dropped the quantum grenade in the cafeteria appears over the wall of the dressing cubical. The same dodecahedron, but smaller, spinning and casting colors as it drops.

Green.

Yellow.

Red.

A color without a name.

Indigo. Jimmy's alarm sounds.

Caught it! Now to keep the blast from hurting anyone. Like male-Alex, I instinctively wrapped myself around the grenade. It refuses to stop spinning, even as I clutch it against my gut.

108

HOLDING QUENTIN LIKE SOAP BUBBLE

T he no-space with the non-glow does exist. It isn't a false memory from Alex and Sarah. No sign of the threshold, so I'm probably safe. Unlike the Sarah-thing, I'm not pure energy and feel the infusion of the grenade's energy. Which also means I can consciously contain, absorb it and focus the energy later.

I ponder how to get back to physical space. The no-space exhibits an organic ebb and flow. A pull toward no-direction catches my attention. Two entities, one quiescent and one iridescent to my senses appears. "What the hell are you doing here?"

I EXAMINE MYSELF. No damage. Strange. The last attack broke the sternum of the Alex/Sarah blend and pulverized concrete. Only the walls of the flimsy privacy booth bulge out. I grin. No sign of the grenade anywhere and my clothes and skin remained spotless. Another grin forms on my face.

Confirmation! I've absorbed its energy, and just maybe, I can use it.

The door crashes in on broken hinges, and I'm confronted by the willowy model-like researcher that my Sarah persona had been so jealous of. So, Carla is the mole. Another woman, heavy set, in black fake-tactical gear, is a shadow behind her. "You can't be conscious." The last syllable comes out as a screech. The mole slams the door shut, knocking it off the last hinge.

I'm rattled but determined. I kick the door out and sail after the two, over their heads, right into a circular display rack. *I leaped fifteen feet?* I scramble to my feet as four women pull out pistols and converge on the couple. I shout, "Stay close, but they're mine."

Exploiting my Army training and experiences, I dodge around two other racks and jump the pair at the entrance door, carrying all three of them onto the blistering hot sidewalk. My Sarah memories about how the mole flirted with Jimmy takes over, and I pummel her, aiming more for maximum disfigurement.

Pop. Pop. Pop.

A rosette of blood appears on the mole's forehead, and fire burns in my left chest and neck. The pain makes me slump. I'm cradled in what could only be Katie's arms.

"I thought you were staying at HQ?" My eyes narrow.

Katie snorts. "Since when did I ever take orders from any of you?"

"Glad you're here. There's a shooter."

"I know…"

I wake to my most hated place in the entire world: a hospital ER room. The klink of metal hitting a metal pan catches my attention. Dr. Timsen and Mr. Johnson, the General, watch me over surgery masks.

Dr. Timsen says, "I know that I'm not a surgeon, but damn you're tough to operate on. Your wound kept closing faster than I could cut. I finally grabbed the bullet with the forceps and ripped it out along with some flesh. You're already healing. Didn't you feel it?"

"Maybe some pressure. What happened?"

Mr. Johnson asks, "You don't remember?"

"The shooter. Did the mole survive?"

"The shooter's job was to kill you and the mole if the ops went bad. She got away. A true pro. She drilled you in the heart and tore open the carotid artery. You had no life signs for almost twenty minutes."

Sarah Beth closed her eyes, trying to remember anything, no matter how trivial that would help. "She attacked Alex when they were searching for evidence about what happened to Sarah. She was with Y'Arty at that time. Do you need me to help ID her?"

"No need. We had time to position several hi-res cameras. A few seconds of facial recognition, and we know who she is."

"What's her name, and where is she from?"

"No."

"What?"

"Katie and I believe that you'll try to find and kill her." The shrug of my shoulder rockets too much pain from my wounds. "It wouldn't get what you want. She's a mercenary for hire and wouldn't know anything useful. She'll be lucky to survive her employers."

Mr. Johnson continues, "What happened to the quantum grenade?"

"I grabbed it, just like last time. It should be in the dressing room." I don't want to disclose what I believe. Not yet.

"Not there, and no damage, except to the walls from the pressure wave. I have reports that you leaped over their heads."

"What about Jimmy's sensors?"

"Readings climbed until the sensors overloaded, then dropped to standard background noise."

"I think I have an answer, but a debrief will have to wait until we are secure, like in a SCIF."

Crap, crap, crap. I've absorbed who knows how many terajoules of raw quantum energy. Great-great-grandmother's mythical Jenergija courses through my being. Wellness ripples through me. I'd been concentrating on stopping the damage and didn't stop to think about what might happen to me.

The building pain in my muscles, like a bad flu, is scary. When the medical staff is distracted, I palpate my puffy legs. Not puffy, but tight, solid muscle. Defined calf and thigh muscles, at least double in diameter. Panicked, I drop into one of my great-great-grandmother, Babushka's mental exercises.

Has it really been over twenty years since I've thought of that crazy old lady?

The mental exercise pushes the energy out, and the muscles recede to what is my new body's baseline. Good to go. Always present, the Jenergija prods parts of my body. I'm not going to be a freakish cartoon character, I'm already a monster. For safety, I shove the energy into Alex's else-somewhere, for study and possible later use.

I'm a monster. What future is sucking me into its reality? I have to stop this before more than whole families cease to exist. I'm in a university hospital surrounded by best medical and freak-science gear that exists. I sense Jimmy in a nearby closet working on his geekware to monitor my monster side.

I'm using the Jenergija before it slips away. This is the best opportunity that I'll have to implement my adjustment of the future, make Quentin indispensable, and then force him back into existence.

After again forcing the energy out of my extremities, I'm ready. If I'm wrong, I may kiss reality goodbye. The absurdity made her grin. If I'm wrong, I may as well bend over and kiss my ass goodbye.

I need a baseline to give me a before and after my adjustment to reality. A quick sweep of everyone I know and their positions out to my new limit of one hundred meters should provide adequate information. If someone significantly moves, disappears, or appears, I'll know.

This is it. I send the right type of quantum energy down what I interpret to be the best application of Clarice's lemma.

All to create the future that requires have a living, active Quentin.

109

QUENTIN

"She's awake," Dr. Timsen flashes her penlight across my eyes. "and no obvious damage. Do you care to explain yourself? You were out for over ninety seconds with all the med and other sensors going berserk."

Mr. Johnson says, "Clear the room except for Ms. Parker, and Dr. Timsen." He checks the door and asks, "What did you do? The spectrum of colors blue-shifted for a second then righted itself."

Then, I succeeded in moving the free energy. My rescan of the area confirms that nothing obvious had happened to the people near me. I have failed. There will be no Quentin in my and Katie's life. "Nothing that I know." If my hubris has resulted in my hopes becoming dust, there was no reason to discuss it.

Dr. Timsen returned with a tablet scrolling dozens of medical images and tests. "As usual, nothing shows up. We'll take another sequence in the morning. For now, go home and relax." Leala comes in to take me home.

I sit up in the bed. "I meant it about the SCIF. You may want to revise your protocols, but I'm mentally wiped right now." A wave of ennui drops me back into my pillow.

All the colors in the recovery room blue-shifts. Then everything was normal. Anyone who blinked wouldn't have seen it.

Quentin says, "I'll help you." Quentin? He hadn't been there, hadn't existed a second before. This wasn't my doing unless there was a time-delay buried in Clarice's lemma.

Quentin pulls me, arm in arm, to my feet. I say, "I guess we're back, old buddy." Quentin's grin lights the room. I lean into him and whisper. "Call me Sarah Beth. I don't need to be Alex Jane anymore."

His grin disappears, as we breach the final barrier in our relationship. I think about how we never ended in bed together, and never will, but also how many times I had been his wingman. He never had problems scoring, but me, the eternal macho-bitch with bulging muscles, could rarely finish the first date.

His *little extra* is a topic we have to resolve, but today, I'm thrilled that my risk with the quantum grenade closed down more alternative pasts. I wonder what else has changed back to before the attack two months ago.

My body remains that of the blended Sarah Beth, not the testosterone-molded Alex Jane. An internal sigh was all I will allow myself.

Life is to be lived, not fought.

Katie stands statue-rigid. "When did you get here? How did you get in.?" She breaks her fixed stare to grab Quentin, lifts the smaller man, and twirls him, kicking the medical equipment table.

Quentin grins. "I don't remember. Why?" His grin fades slowly into a frown. "I was at the other medical facility thinking about Aliyah." He pulls out his phone. "This is important. I have to call my family."

I roll over to check the medical monitors to hide my relief and the start of a tear. Both Quentin and Aliyah exist again. I'd saved Aliyah again.

In opposite corners of the recovery room, Leala and Katie are both on their phones. Katie returned, all smiles. "I'm sorry, but something pushed me to call my cousin Rashaad."

"Everything okay?"

Leala and Katie respond in unison, "Never better." They stare at each other. "Everything is okay." This creeps me out.

Quentin also returns with a smile. I motion for him to come closer and say, "My ears are still ringing. Talk into my ear, but quietly." I prepare for the worse, but if it is good news, I don't want complications with the project until she was ready.

He says into my ear, "Aliyah is fine, and aced the wall art contest for the elementary school."

This is the crunch question. "In Omaha?"

His eyes knits in a frown. He started to say something, then changed his mind. Finally, he said, "In Omaha. For some reason, I was going to say Ballard."

An eye hurting turquoise peasant blouse and short skirt lands on my stomach. "Change. It's already 10 PM, and we have to celebrate to do. Kick loose, the bad guys are on the run, and you're doing fine." Clarice spins to show off her matching outfit. "You're my wingman. Big Bro Jimmy sucks as a wingman. Everyone I like wants to mother him instead." She holds up turquoise strappy shoes with three-inch heels. "I have a pair for you, too."

Katie clears her throat. "I was expecting a quiet night in the apartment. Okay. The debrief can wait until tomorrow, but no way am I wearing anything but slacks."

Clarice scrunches her face. "Could you at least ditch BMFG and smile some? You'll scare away anyone who approaches."

I intervene, "No to both ideas. Katie, you, and Quentin need some private time. I'm crashing at Clarice's." Katie started to object. "Don't give me any grief. Assign a couple from the security team that likes clubbing and you and Quentin go home." I'm glowing from my success.

I'll need confidence and more for the clean-up and the hunt that tickles the back of my mind.

110

MATRYOSCHKA DAUGHTER

DAY 70

A happy Sarah Beth pounds on gophers popping up in a mechanical game counsel. Alexi, Alex's and Leala's ten-year-old child, screams in delight as she struggles to catch up. She misses or doesn't hit hard enough. Flashing a shrug over her head to Leala, Sarah Beth starts to miss more gophers. The kid catches up and laughs in delight, causing other children to come over to watch her beat the grown-up.

Then it's not Sarah Beth, but Alex standing there, pounding the gophers. Then it's Sarah Beth, then Alex.

"What the hell?" Leala grabs my arm and forces my wrist under the kitchen faucet, washing the blood off it. In my other hand is Quentin's sharpest paring knife with a thin line of blood on its edge.

"What happened?" I ask.

"Your face went blank, then you went into the kitchen and cut yourself."

Another monster thing of mine. I flashed on a possible future – no two, because the second was Alex's future… one that didn't include my survival.

I disassociated and attempted suicide? How screwed up can I get?

Wait, flesh fragments along the edges of the cut jump, then dissipate, then jump again. I remember this. Sarah discovered the self-healing by accident. Alex believed it was a form of quantum healing.

I say, "Watch." The blood on my arm disappears, and the wound closes. The blood on Leala and the sink remain. I don't have a clue why I disassociated and cut myself during my future vision, but I can cast this in a positive light. "I don't know why I did this, but now you know I self-heal. Dr. Timsen has experiments set up to test it."

"Are you going to keep trying to harm yourself? Do I have to move in to replace Alex?"

"Dr. Timsen's setting up a wearable monitor and tests to quantify it. I doubt my strangeness will last. Once I get the monitor, you can sleep without worrying."

More important to me is that there's a future where Alex returns to his wife and daughter. A preternatural reach with my senses confirms it. Leala is pregnant with a child that they'll call Alexi.

Alexi, the Matryoschka Daughter.

Saving Alex moves up to the top of my list. His daughter deserves him. Even if his recovery forces me into non-existence.

111

QUENTIN'S BETRAYAL

NIGHT 72

A wild-eyed Sarah Beth gathers her electronic counter-measure modules. Hair in a careless bun, stray hair blowing in the car's A/C, she pulls a long vermillion gym bag from the back seat next to the ten-year-old Alexi, the dead Alex's daughter. She removes a double bandolier of shotgun cartridges and an assault shotgun. These she hands to the short woman in the driver seat. "These are for you."

She turns and leans over the front seat to unbuckle her back-up, the ten-year-old Alexi. "We're going to have some fun. We..." Sarah Beth shakes her head and sits back in the front passenger seat. "We, uh..."

She opens her door. "Keep the kid safe. That's your only job."

Sarah Beth slips from shadow to shadow towards her target, an anonymous warehouse on the Baltimore harbor. Inside, five people guard her goal. Five people who are dying from what they guard.

Quentin slips into the sedan. "Don't follow her. You'll die from it. Guard the child like she said." He turns to Alexi, still strapped in. "Can you sense her? Can you push when she needs it."

Alexi asks, "Why couldn't I go with her? I could do better."

"Because you'd die. Your Aunt Sarah Beth may need your help but do it from here."

———

QUENTIN WILL BETRAY ME. In ten years, I'll need the push of a ten-year-old Alexi, and he interferes with my chain of thought. Alexi stays in the car, and I die that night. This isn't the future I thought I had created.

112

QUESTIONS AND RIDDLES

NIGHT 77

A blazing headache wakes me. The oversized time in the corner of the mirror/clock, 12:37 AM blurs. Even with the lights on, everything is fuzz. Where is my phone? I reach to activate Jimmy's help me function.

Wait. Wait. Something's familiar. I wonder if …

Braving a worse attack, I drop into the sensing mode. Beautiful. A psychedelic display of colors I can't describe interact and create waves of more colors. It's everywhere. The complexity, the movements, the interactions are indescribable. Too much to handle, I back out.

Over two and a half hours in real time gone. Screw this. I have a life. Along with my deep angst over failing people, I've lost my desire to escape my issues. Sarah and male-Alex in their fifty-five days cured me.

In the morning, I'll report recovery of my abilities, though unless I want to spend hours comatose, I can't see what good my sensing abilities are.

S<small>KIPPING THE BREAKFAST SPREAD</small>, I grab a banana and a bowl of dry cereal from Quentin. "I'm in bed today. I'll be out to finish my talk with Katie later." Since I'm not Sarah and eating for Alex and their energy needs, I've been packing on the pounds. Back to eating like a girl.

What to do first. Several opportunities clamor for my attention. I'll try the easiest and open the textbooks I've bought. My credits and student ID from before the attack exist again, so I'm a non-declared sophomore. I've schooled myself to periodically look at the lens of my 24/7 friend, the camera that blinks in the upper right corner of my room to assure the duty officer I'm not comatose.

Screw that. I might not have meaning, but I'm not self-cloistering. I pull on my Army PT uniform, my new running socks and shoes, and sprint up the hill to campus. The green sedan follow-car is joined by two runners, and it backs off. The urgency drained, I pace myself to a slow run. The woman runner hands me a scrunchie, and I pull my hair out of my face into a ponytail. "Thanks."

We circle campus hill, except for where the SCIF is. A quick left keeps it out of sight to avoid triggering an alarm. We run clockwise around the college of agriculture and into the eastern end of Pullman. A glance at Alex's favorite watering hole evokes a sigh. I could stand a quick mug, but it's too early.

Up the hill, over the basalt ridge toward the Sloan electrical engineering building, but as I run my hollowness increases. Damn. Alex was an electrical engineer or would have been if he had survived. His engineering career and Sarah's humanities plans compete for dominance. This is my sophomore year; I should pick a major.

Rounding Sloan on the north side and sliding to the south of the Morrow Journalism building, we continue up the hill, to the top. My legs burn, and I'm gasping for air. Love it! Before, like Sarah or male-Alex, it seemed that physical exhaustion was non-existent. Exhaustion defines me as a real person.

On a south-facing grassy knoll, an older guy, who looks like even sitting makes him sweat, waves us over. Fat rolls threaten to cover his sandals like his beer belly has consumed his belt. Pasty white complexion combines with a musty scent that make me think of a blind cave fish. At least five meadowlarks surround him. For some reason, I scan the area before joining him. It dawns on me that neither male-Alex nor I have ever sensed the meadowlarks except visually.

He shields his eyes and looks up at us. "Nice day for a run. Take a couple of squirts to make it more enjoyable."

He holds out a triangular shaped bottle, or skin. I look askance at it. He says, "It's a Bota, you squeeze it and squirt wine out the narrow end." To demonstrate, he shoots a steady stream of dark purple liquid into his mouth. He's about the same age as my great-uncle Helmut, he exudes a natural bonhomie. I ignore his late-60s, crudely hacked-off jeans, too-small madras short sleeve shirt, and tire-tread sandals.

A diversion from my personal weirdness is in order.

He says, "I'm Terry Niemand." More meadowlarks land between me and my escort seated higher on the slope to maintain station.

I say, "I'm Sarah Beth." I extend my hand, and he grips it mid-forearm. More birds land on the slope.

For the first time, he looks down to my chest. "I could have sworn you were a guy. *Mach Nichts*, never mind." e slur-sings something like, "Boxes and Foxes, all made from ticky-tacky," while squirting wine into my mouth. I fight back a gag reaction. Grape juice? He says, "Mad Dog 20–20, Kosher Concorde grape wine, twenty percent alcohol, useful lubricant to get bras to fall off."

Another questioning glance from me and he hastens to add. "In the late 60s. It would never work today."

I laugh at his raw audacity and take another squirt. He motions over his shoulder where my two companions sit higher on the grassy knoll. "Will they join us?"

"Not their thing." More birds land and I check around for the nearest building. Birds gather en masse, making me nervous. The anthropology department in College Hall, about two hundred meters away, is closest.

He places his right index finger to the side of his nose. "Reminds me of fun days toward the end of the Vietnam War. We had party poopers like that around, also." He waves across the street to an old parking lot. "The basement got plenty of their traffic. Fun times." He squirts himself another dark purple stream and slurs, "It was paradise. On one end—the geeks, not that we called them that back then—watched and argued over *Doctor Who* and *Dark Shadows*. They never knew that the other end held true paradise and terror beyond their wildest imaginations."

I accept another squirt and wave an okay to the two watchers fidgeting behind us. They don't seem to notice the swarm of meadowlarks surrounding them. "Basement?" For the first time since becoming Sarah Beth, I'm mellow.

"Oh, I forget. That was Ferry Hall, a dorm with an unusual basement. Fun times down there. It abruptly became obsolete in the mid-70s and was torn down. I was homeless, stuck in a dirty cave. For fifty years, all attempts to build something in that lot have been blocked."

The conversation has taken a non-mellow turn. I ask, "So what happened there?"

"If you can blame your emotional problems on your parents, and your genetics on your grandparents, what can you blame your great-great-grandparents for?"

A riddle? I motion for more of the fortified grape juice. "Beats me." My weird partner squirts it into my mouth. It's late summer, but the meadowlarks break out in mating calls.

"Time. What you think you seek is in the *ticky-tacky*. What you are looking for is in slow or fast Time. Also, don't trust deserted parking lots. You never know what's below the macadam. Fun times." I shoo a meadowlark off my lap and my pendant made with Jimmy's quartzite swings with the motion. His eyes follow it. So he wasn't ogling my chest, but the tiny stone.

His eyes meet mine. "I've exposed myself. That rock confused me. You're not ready. You're only at third instar. I need you at five instars."

Pop!

Pushing myself up from where I face planted in the grass where he'd been sitting, I look around. He's disappeared, and the implosion pulled me toward where he sat. There's no evidence of anyone but myself and my two companions. All the meadowlarks have vanished.

The woman shadow places her hand on my shoulder. "Are you okay? Do we need to call a car?"

"Did you hear the old guy?"

"You were the only one here."

We pick up the pace as we're near the top of Campus Hill and the rest of the run is downhill. The steady plodding gives me time to think. Who calls himself *Terry Niemand*? Now that I think of it, his aspect never wavered from open friendliness. Like a computer simulation, but he'd been solid. I still can taste grapey wine. Did I have another hallucination, a flash-forward, or something else? I wasn't by myself, and wrist cutting wasn't involved. My bet is that this was something else. I think I've met my personal Tom Bombadil, who calls himself Terry Niemand.

113

UNFINISHED BUSINESS

W inded, but feeling alive, we skirt the bus stop, and I'm greeted by some unfinished business. Today is as good as any to start the clean-up of what Sarah and Alex left behind.

I say to my shadows, "Katie's in the entry. She'll take it from here. I'll cool down by walking around the parking lot. Thanks for putting up with my unplanned run. I'll schedule in the future."

They peel off, and I slow to a walk. When they're more than a block away, I turn from the front door. Unfinished business beckons from the gravel end of the parking lot.

I walk up with the sun behind me. "Hey-ya! Studmuffins! Look'n for some fun?"

The String Bean, like the previous two times, once with Sarah and once with Katie, takes the lead. "Always." His heavy-set friend slides to get behind me. Excellent. "What do you have in mind?"

3—2—1

I'm grabbed from behind. Exactly like my Sarah-memories recall. Excellent. To distract this block of muscle, I bite him between his thumb and index finger as hard as I can, then grab his wrist, and twist out of his arm. I've practiced this in my Sarah and Alex memories, and now I move into a Sarah gymnastics flip while maintaining a death grip on his wrist. A satisfactory snap and scream reward me. I never took gymnastics, but I revel with in my Sarah skill.

Not as tall or heavy as Katie, and without any weapons, I have to keep moving while the three Einsteins puzzle out why they don't already have me in the bed of their truck. Arms raised, just like their attack on Katie, the remaining two move forward. My vision narrows into a red blur. Each time they grab at me, I'm not there. Every time I elbow, grab or twist, their appropriate body part obliges. No punches, I work with the strength of my lower body. If any of them thought through what they were doing, I'd be toast. I'm rolling from pure adrenaline, not thinking, just following memories.

In seconds, all three are on the ground, and two are bleeding. I kick String Bean in the ribs, and my shoe meets resistance before moving deeper. Another rib was broken. I lift him by the chin and stare into his eyes. "Remember this. I didn't have a weapon. From now on, I will. Don't ever come anywhere on this side of campus again."

Leala races up, reaching under her shirt for her gun. I intercept her arm. "No need. Let's keep this simple." One of the three groans behind me.

Three down, with no telling how many more in Alex's, Sarah's, and my back-history that need my personal attention. Next in the queue is the man who "accidentally" killed my father, brother, and sister. I'm kicking off a search for any money transfers or other connection to my father's company. Part of my new personality slides into place. I'm comfortable with who I'm becoming.

Leala spits on String Bean and asks me, "What the hell are you doing?"

"Going to lunch, joining me?"

Katie joins us as we walk in. "Is there any point in chewing you out?"

"Nah."

"You're damn lucky their IQ is so low. First, returning to the same hunting grounds, and second, in not taking basic self-defense classes. Sooner or later, they were bound to meet the wrong girl. Alex isn't around to save their pathetic asses."

The most ambulatory of the attackers loads the other two into the truck and leaves, the back wheels throwing gravel. Leala grabs my arm. "Not only was that stupid, but you made several mistakes. We," -- she looks over at Katie -- "need to get you to our self-defense classes. You don't seem to be into avoidance, so at least you can be prepared. The first lesson, do not, I repeat, *do not* engage someone bigger than you. All the talk about size not mattering is bullshit."

The front double doors crash open as Clarice and Jimmy race out. Jimmy has his stubby screwdriver in his hand. I kiss his cheek for being so sweet.

Clarice says, "We saw them attacking you in the monitor. Sorry for not getting out in time. Why'd you get near them? Everyone knows they're trouble."

Katie uses her superior reach to grip one of the project's surreptitious cameras and snaps it off the ceiling. She hands it to an ashen-faced Jimmy. "Immediate all-project coms. No one comes to the apartment unless they live here. Everyone living here stays away except to retire for the day. Grab all the hall and exterior cameras. Let's make it for 24 hours until we see if there will be a police response."

I say, "I'm hungry, and Quentin said he's cooking meatloaf. Joining us?"

I'm not my past; neither Alex nor Sarah. I'm my future. I am my own story, and unlike Alex and Sarah, I'm not walking out of it.

114

HELENA RETURNS

DAY 79

Walks around campus hill, downhill to work in Pullman keeps me centered. In late summer, the verdant rolling hills of eastern Washington hold the promise of fresh life, of restarts. The dust from late summer planting has subsided, and the breeze remains brisk and keeps the heat bearable.

I am real.

I'd only walked to work once before the logistics of covering me was declared insurmountable. After that, I acquiesce to the realities of my situation and have been shuttled in Leala's car. Unlike Sarah, I have no difficulties with the continual inconveniences imposed by the project, but I demand an explanation.

If security or other leads go to the hassle of creating a non-laughable explanation, then my part is to comply. Once the hard-case security chief whispered to Katie, "What happened? She was always a bitch about OpSec." That brought a smile to my face.

The reality of who I really am, the re-integration of Alex and Sarah into one body and one psyche, was kept even from the head of security.

Returning home from work, Leala asks, "Do you want to keep the retail job? It was Sarah's thing, and the term is starting soon."

I hadn't thought that far. Leala is right and deserves a considered response. "Give me a few days, I need to work this out with the other stuff I'm wrestling with."

I don't bother any project personnel with my search for Alex's manias. Sarah never sensed the interferers in their lives. Lilac scents and meadowlarks have stopped dropping in and out of my perception. My childhood and later memories align perfectly with my Alex memories. The lilac was the favorite flower and now is the avatar of my deceased great-great-grandmother. The meadowlarks remain a mystery. I wish that Alex had huddled with Jimmy on developing a portable sensor. That opportunity gone, I decide the avatars' absence was a well-deserved break from the weird.

I'm tapping my overflowing bank account and get off the paper notebooks. I'll switch my laptop to a strange ultra-thin tablet device called a 'Flat.' Its eight by ten size is easy to keep stable on my lap and folds into a four-by-five-inch package. Once folded, it was still less than a quarter inch thick. I'm not going to be the 'old-fogie' who used old tech. I'm going to fit in.

Between the Alex/Sarah fiasco, and my initial difficulty in regaining my equanimity, I'm late in completing all the necessary registration forms. Linda and the Physics Department head used their pull to get me a waiver for late enrollment.

When I completed my online forms, I discovered a set of medical study tests offered free by the Health Department. Curious, I printed out the notice, then trashed it anyway.

Where is it?

At the bottom of the second and final garbage bag of Quentin's outgoing trash, under damp coffee ground, of course, I retrieve the pages and reread them. Conducted by the obstetrics and gynecology departments, it provides the perfect cover. I will be the subject, arguing that a set of independent and free baselines will be useful to the floundering project. The catch is that I agree to allow quarterly updates and let the result be accumulated under an anomalous ID.

In reality, the unwitting subject will be Leala.

After clearing it with Dr. Timsen and the always argumentative security chief, I join the study. I hint Leala was the least obvious of her shadows. Katie took the hint, "More time for me to catch up with the paperwork."

During the running test for oxygen uptake, my phone rumbles the opening bars of Bach's Toccata and Fugue in D-minor. As always, Leala cringes at the choice of alert but pulls out the phone, thumbs open the text message and frowns. Her frown grows into her protective-fleer.

Leala reaches for her gun then she changes her mind and reaches for her encrypted laptop. I pound on the guard rails of the treadmill for attention. Leala first shakes her head, then brings the phone over to the treadmill.

The text >>STAY AWAY BITCH OR...<< was punctuated by a shooting-gun emoticon.

Leala returns to her laptop and runs a full-out security screen of the message and sender. I pound again on the treadmill and motioned and shake my head. I don't want this followed up until I check something. Leala stops but moves to where she could watch the door.

Finished and toweling off, I ask, "Who?"

Leala said, "A Helena Hergenreder, do you know her?" I knew something like this could happen. "I'm calling in full lockdown and a team to investigate her."

"Please don't. At least until Katie, you and I talk. What's available?"

"The Box." The Faraday shielded exam room. I love it, but it wasn't suitable for my needs this time.

"We may need to call out. What about the apartment?"

"I'll call Jimmy to scan early today."

I call Katie, "We have a situation, I'd like to brief you and Leala at the same time." I wait for Katie's affirmative rumble. "And no Quentin. Not until we decide what to do." He'll be pissed about being cut out, but it's for his protection. He doesn't need to become one of the subjects of the project.

At the apartment, I make coffee and find the fresh baked cookies Quentin laid out. Quentin leans forehead to forehead with me and whispers "CUB coffee shop." He leaves, slamming the apartment door.

Katie sits, propped her legs on the unoccupied chair and leans back. "What's the mystery?"

"This."

Katie reads and rereads the text message. Her face ripples with unpleasant features. She checks the details of Leala's search. "Helena Hergenreder, Ogallala, Nebraska. Elementary School Principal. 42 years old. Why the fuck hasn't there been an alert?"

I reach and hold both their hands. "Because this is not what it seems, it's bigger and affects the two of you."

Pulling out the crystal memory data drive, I hand it to Katie. "Sarah discovered that my extended family bifurcated to lend historical verisimilitude to her and Alex's existence. Of course, she thought that this was her family. This went all the way back over three hundred years, with two new villages being created on the eastern Russian frontier where only one had been before. On this is Alex's documentation of her research, on crystal memory, so it survived all the causality disruptions."

"Where'd he get the crystal memory? It's top secret and rare."

I shrug my shoulders. "Not certain, my Alex memory is blank on that." A complete lie. Quentin gave it to him.

Katie purses her lips, tapping them. Leala takes advantage of the quiet moment to ask, "Why not investigate?"

"You two have the same issue." This brings Katie out of her reflective mode into bunched eyebrows and flashing irises. "In addition to where Quentin went and how he returned, both of you have family members who disappeared during the Sarah/Alex period. You never said it out loud, but it was obvious."

After waiting for both to indicate, slowly, that I'm on the right path, I ask, "Are they all back?" Katie nodded, and Leala smiled. "You see the problem? I can see the need to explore the phenomena," I slide the crystal memory chip to Katie, "but who knows how much our innocent families would go through. It's all documented here for my families. Do you want to record your families? If not, right now, and forever, we must agree that this conversation never happened. My condition is that all contacts with my extended family are pre-vetted by me, including the methodology."

Silence drops over the apartment. The fake pendulum clock clicks the seconds, and the air conditioner cycles twice. Leala and I watch for Katie's response.

Katie drums her fingers on the dining table. She clearly understands the implications for both innocent people and the project. Katie says, "You're giving up your family to protect our families. Why?"

"My disruption affected hundreds. Your disruptions only involved a few people. Helena may not be the only person who remembers both back histories. In that regard, she's like Quentin. One or more may be pissed off enough to do more than a lame-assed threat. This way the project will be ready."

"Leala. I think we should go with this, but if anyone in our families demonstrates Quentin's abilities, we'll have to reassess."

I head to my room to switch shirts to the one where I secreted Quentin's memory chip. I should have returned it before now. This would be an unpleasant couple of mugs of coffee. Quentin has several life-changing decisions to make. I will be there for him, despite his legitimate anger at my cutting him out.

115

A FISH NOT OUT OF THE WATER

DAY 80

A fish doesn't know it's living in water.

Alex, at the most basic level, knew. We all are energy entities. He knew the secret of existence, but never developed the ability to study or even explain it. We, everyone, float in the else-somewhere, never sensing it.

Sarah's apparent physical existence was an illusion. Even her flesh-tone of her amorphous state was her forcing meaning into her existance.

All the time, asleep, running, shooting, all the time. I sense Alex's else-somewhere. It suffuses all matter and energy. Sometimes it reminds me of a living thing, with a purpose, but that has to be my overactive imagination. The geek tests confirm I sense electromagnetic fields, but this is different.

Yet. I will know. Like the melting of a lighted multi-layered candle, it's only a matter of time before the integration releases all his memories to me. An Alex thought dominates. *"The greatest pride, or the greatest despondency, is the greatest ignorance of one's self."* Spinoza, of course.

That damn meadowlark sings outside our—my—bedroom window. So, the interfering agent, the one that I perceive as a meadowlark, is back.

CORDITE PERMEATES THE AIR, and even with the safety ear protection, the pop, pop, pop from my four companions reminds me I'm not alone in this pistol target range. They replaced the lamps idiots shot out, and it no longer looks like a cave. Instead, it's a room, like any industrial concrete building, except with the isolation booths at one end, we shoot from and the heavy bullet no-bounce barrier at the other.

I squeeze off five more rounds and all fall in a satisfying row in the groin. Three more rounds and the lower part of the target, from the hips down will drop. Every other day, a couple hundred rounds of target practice at the gun range center me. I've shot up their stock of pink outline targets, and I've switched to the standard olive on black. After cleaning and lubing it, I'll return old-Alex's Colt to his father tomorrow with the presentation gun case, and all his service ribbons, Purple Heart, and Bronze Star. Family heirlooms belong with family.

Hold, I'm Alex. I have four military commendations more than male-Alex did. I'm not certain how the fractional past he occupied resulted in him having fewer commendations. One of the many mysteries that can't be answered now that his and Sarah's pasts have collapsed, rebooting mine.

I'll still return the heirloom Colt 1911A and service medals, but to Mom for safekeeping. I had brought them to college as a totem to help me stabilize.

I tried Katie's hand howitzer, a ten-millimeter Smith and Wesson, dubbed BMFG, *big mudda fk'n gun*. It fits my hand, but the weight bothers me. I remember having the same reaction last year when ... no that was Alex. The security gang and I will gun shop in Spokane this weekend. I like Leala's Walther PK360. Security will keep the gun until I get my license and can legally carry it.

I cut the target in half at the groin. I retrieve it and toss it in the trash.

Home, and I strip for a much-needed shower. Even Katie complains I can stink like a guy. I'm going to enjoy my next meeting with Mr. Y'Arty. I'm nearly a match for Katie in the weekly martial arts class she takes for relaxation. Alex couldn't keep up with Katie and dropped out.

Something hangs on the edge of my consciousness. Alex hid something about my—our—last encounter with Mr. Y'Arty. *Monster*! Another seal blocking my memory. What happened to male-Alex? What frightened him?

What did I hide from myself?

I love this needle-spray shower-head. Just what you need after a grueling day of imagining beating the crap out of your personal villain.

Alex and Sarah, I owe them. As they healed, they healed me.

Sarah was the part of me that never dealt with the trauma from the experiments her father let happen to her. My father who died the same day in a mysterious accident. I avoided the discussion, hid it from my family, and became the macho bitch that protected herself and others. The past that got Sarah created a Sarah who was an irrepressible joy-spirit. Her swings in emotion drove Katie to distraction, endeared her to Quentin, and were a trial for Alex. At the end, she regained control, took responsibility, and gave her life to find Alex.

Alex was the part of me that didn't deal with Babushka and the street children dying, and my unwanted skills creeping into my abilities. Alex learned to deal with the deaths and the joys. He also embraced his abilities.

They didn't know it, but it was time for me, the original Sarah Beth, aka Alex Jane, to deal with life.

It isn't fair they died. I will devote my life to finding a solution for them, and to kill Mr. Y'Arty or Engle, whatever he calls himself, and the shadowy organization that backs him. Their experiments sunder the present and future, creating co-existing pasts. I can't let that happen.

I know this doesn't make me sane, just functional. I'll settle for functional.

116

DUST

I'm tired of dramatic moments and gestures. I'll clear some of the dust in my life. The small stuff also needs attention. I speed-dial Leala. "Hi. Are you up for a walk and fresh air? Can you be on duty so we can have privacy?"

To get a rise out of HQ, I wave at the not-discreet-enough camera from the desultory lobby couch. Finally, a double-tingle from her tricked out fitness band confirmed they'd had enough. A single tingle confirmed monitoring, double tingle for pay attention, and three for out of monitoring range or to look out for a potential problem. A triple tingle, I will immediately stop what I am doing and find monitoring coverage. If there was a danger, my phone goes into intercom mode. With the project winding down, this saved on staffing.

Something impinged on my consciousness. Something familiar I thought I'd shed forever. *"Sarah Beth, we need to talk."* A voice crackling like a footfall on dried leaves. My Babushka was back. Not Alex's as he never truly existed except as a fission of her. My Babushka and I was ready.

"Piss off." I reach into the male-Alex's else-somewhere, retrieved a soupçon of the remaining free energy from the quantum grenade. With

that, I sever the channel my great-great-grandmother has exploited all these decades to harass me. *Bitch. She was the first to experiment on me with all those doll-exercises. If she hadn't; everything else wouldn't have been possible.*

Dead silence evolved into an undercurrent of bliss. So, this was the silence of those who were deaf to the manipulations of the dead. I decide to stop waving at the camera, and I let my first wide smile in over a decade stretched from ear to ear.

For a moment, I feel sadness for her male side, Alex James. He used rage to shut Babushka down. My ability to choke her off didn't transfer to male-Alex. The extra energy I also pack helped. The irony of using Babushka's Jenergija to banish her improves my mood.

Five minutes later, Leala joins me. "Had to get confirmation I could combine being on duty with a private discussion. Did you have something to do with lifting that restriction?"

"I've renegotiated my contract. I'm on the project, not just the subject. You were part of the deal. Things have changed. I'm not what you originally protected. I'm what I seem, a twenty-six-year-old veteran starting her sophomore year. Let's walk."

Around the apartment complex, across the graveled extension of the parking lot, I find the pocket park I'm looking for. Three new trees, sodded grass, and a pine plank park table form the core and a lovely place for girl talk.

I keep pace with Leala to practice my newly formed ability. My time in the medical tests gives me opportunities to be close to pregnant girls, training my preternatural senses to recognize every nuance of pregnancy. I use my trained senses on Leala's and Alex's child. It was only a cluster of cells, but with no indication of distress or abnormalities.

Dust everywhere, of course. I wipe both benches, the table with the towel I brought. Leala joined her. A tingle on my wrist com confirms we're being monitored, probably by the fake toy drone that hummed overhead. From my satchel, I take out two mugs and a thermos of tea.

"Quentin?" Leala asks.

"Yep. If we don't finish it, I'll dump it to keep him happy."

We sip in quiet. Leala's posture loosens. No meadowlarks bother us.

Leala asks, "Can you tell me about your plans or is it classified?"

"I'm on-project, but I have to wear this for monitoring and comm." I tap the band of the fitness monitor. "Beats an ankle bracelet." Leala snorts. "I'm switching to physics. The physics lead, Steve, has wrangled a work-study internship in the department, likely to keep me near him." I can monitor all research for anything that might threaten to disrupt time. "And you?"

"I'm planning on staying to finish my business degree, and then hopefully an MBA."

"Then let's room together. Quentin is showing all the signs of not getting enough of Katie's attention, so they'll be moving to a single apartment."

"I hadn't thought of that. Harry and David are leaving, too. Okay, but only on the condition you'll be honest with me if it gets uncomfortable." We fist-bump, followed a splay of fingers and interlocking of our hands. More bonding rituals, the macho Alex Jane never put up with. Me, I'm now healed and can smile the wide smile I really want to display. We sipped tea and discussed our plans for classes in the upcoming semester.

Alex and Sarah had healed me by taking on fragments of my irrational psyche, suffered the consequences and fought their way to emotional health and belief in themselves. They each deserved a life, independent of needing to share a body. Someplace in the old Matryoschka Doll transcripts and Clarice's research was the answer. There had to be an answer.

Alex's and Leala's daughter, Alexi, the Matryoschka Daughter, grew, while forcing back the quantum rules that should have made her nonexistent. Just as Quentin had been her reality-anchor, Alexi would be Alex's reality-anchor. With Alexi, I have a chance to effect their return.

Rooming with Leala, I will monitor and assist the pregnancy and birth. Leala was orthodox Catholic, so abortion was out of the question, but to ensure it... "I would love to go with you to Mass." I practice the occasional upward lilt at the end of my sentences.

Leala's eyebrows rise, then she says, "That would be nice. I've had no one to go with me."

The dust from the morning breeze cleared.

117

ARCHIVES: SOUTH PACIFIC CRISIS, FOLIO B.17.119, INTERVIEW WITH SARAH BETH MERK-ADDAMS, AGE 147

The record halts here.

The next question, about her children, upset Ms. Merk-Addams and she walked out.

She strolled through five locked and sealed security doors. Despite the alarm that caused a general site lockout, no guard was able to touch her as she calmly walked to a waiting hover-van. The hover-van passed through two closed security gates without damage to it or the gates.

The next opportunity to interview Ms. Merk-Addams was three years later after sustained interventions by third parties. Despite this, she refused to discuss the next ten years, instead started her narrative ten years after the end of this record. See *Folio B.113.017, "Matryoschka's Daughters"*

———

COULD YOU DO THIS AUTHOR A FAVOR?

Please consider writing a review. In the modern age, the number of mentions, especially in a review, counts more than individual book sales. The book sellers' algorithms push books/authors with more reviews. Even an indifferent review helps.

It is easy, on your reader, click on the review link. If you have a paperback book, click here >> https://t2m.io/sqfi0J6F <<.

Many thanks!
terry gene

SARAH BETH AND FRIENDS HAVE JUST STARTED.

This is a four novel and twelve short-story character, theme, and story arc that started on the Washington State University campus in Washington, and ends forty years later in the defeat of the nine nation South Pacific Task Force sent to turn back the alien invaders. Generations risk their existence to create a solution.

Sign up for occasional mailings of releases, free giveaways, and free fiction at http://eepurl.com/dCo78z

EXCERPT OF MATRYOSCHKA'S DAUGHTERS

R elease November 2019 to all distributors.

Archives: Witness' statements:the South Pacific Invasion Crisis, Folio B.113.017, interview with Sarah Beth Merk-Addams part 2, age 150

Quitcher bitch'n.

I see that dropping into my childhood dialect stopped your whining. This is my story, and I'll tell it as I see fit.

Never heard that dialect before? It is mid-American, eastern Nebraska, Lincoln to be specific. Look it up. I'm not your info-daemon. Here is a hint: Lincoln has been a deep hole for forty years.

Oh, you're pointing to your mic, and you want me to identify myself, again? Fine. I'm Sarah Beth Addams, maiden name Merk, the coward of the South Pacific Invasion. Happy? For such a nice guy, you are a serious pain.

My origin story was a bit long, but now you know that I'm not one person but two cohabiting people in the same body.

Okay, that's a bit confusing.

This is what happened. I called myself Alex Jane to overcompensate the death of my father, Alex, brother, also Alex, and younger sister, Jane. After two tours serving with the Allies in the Muslim 100-year war, I returned broken over my inability to save people. My second year on campus, I prepared to commit suicide. Before I could, that insane Tod Engle sundered me into two people playing out my waring obsessions and failures, like matryoschka nesting dolls. Alex the suicidal veteran, and Sarah, the woman-child who never grew up, managed to work together, and I was whole again.

I haven't answered why I didn't join the resistance during the alien invasion. The power to manipulate gravity and time dilation should have thrust me into saving the nine-nation Pacific Task Force. Outmatched, it was placed in a bubble by the invaders, as if it was a curiosity for the mantle.

Life is never that simplistic.

Life is not a video game. So start using your brains instead of your thumbs.

Impatience is not a virtue. Each of us is the total of our pasts and how we coped. A simple answer would be misleading and wouldn't be satisfying.

Nothing much to report about the next ten years. Each day I struggled to regain the sense of oneness stolen from me. I got married, to Jimmy Addams of course. I'm too strange for anyone but the sweetest, most distracted geek to want to marry. I became a hermit with three obsessions: restore Alex and Sarah, protect the world from the millennium old transnational Shadow Committee, and to find and protect those like me. They remain in danger from monsters like me.

Oh, before you interrupt me again, yes, the male-Alex conceived a child with their chief guard Leala. Alexi grew like a weed. Sorry for the cliché but it fits. At ten, she's age-appropriate chunky, with the personality of her missing father, Alex, and the drive of her mother, Leala. She was the only person who could get me off the hunt for the Shadow Committee or out of my high energy lab.

I'd downplayed my matryoschka nature. I may have been one again but being able to sense changes in energy states at the quantum level continues to distract me at critical moments.

Sometimes I created great errors and greater monsters. My next cluster of disasters was nearly eleven years after I re-incorporated.

READER GROUP QUESTIONS

1. *The novel starts with the overarching question: "If you're hollow; what will make you whole?" What are the various forms of hollowness each of the main characters faces?*

2. *Alex failed both his great-great-grandmother, Babushka, and three street children. Was either his fault? What did he have to do to fill his hollowness?*

3. *Sarah has been betrayed by those she loves and trusts. Is this hollowness worse than the physical one she suffers from, and how?*

4. *Katie finds purpose in her protector role. Will this form a solid means of becoming whole, or will she need more?*

5. *Quentin plays the perpetual good guy. What issues does he have?*

6. *"Good to go" is frequently used by Alex in preparation to act. Contrast this with "Life is good" which Sarah uses to settle her ennui.*

7. *"Most compatible couple ever made by science." We get a glimpse of what made Sarah and Alex "right" for each other. Why couldn't this evolve into romantic love?*

8. *Sarah interferes with Alex's personal life. What need is Sarah filling in herself?*

9. *Love is not telling the full truth. Both Alex and Sarah don't admit to*

it, but they practice withholding information for each other's good. What could have worked better if they had never withheld?

10. *What do you see as Leala's and her daughter, Alexi's, future?*
11. *What is signaled by the actions of Aliyah at the funeral? Does this tie into Quentin's unexplored something-extra?*
12. *Is the re-integrated Sarah Beth deranged? What are the signs of sociopathic behavior and what are the signs of adjusting to normality?*

ACKNOWLEDGMENTS

First, I want to thank my wife, Betsy. Despite all the late hours, two AM jumps out of bed to write, she has always been supportive. Who knew that she was also an ace proofreader?

Second, I thank Lexi Robins. She wrote a short story "Sarah" which set up one of the concepts I use in this book. She graciously released full rights to me to develop into a different novel. Five years and 375 thousand words later (250 thousand deleted), you can see the result.

Third, All the beta readers and critique partners created an ecology that kept me on my toes and challenged my creativity. Thanks!

A shout-out to Public Libraries!

In my case, when I couldn't write one more word at home, the Bonham Public Library http://www.bonhamlibrary.net/ *offered their swing space, with excellent lighting and closing! door. Much of the Matryoschka Heritage novel arc was written there.*

ABOUT THE AUTHOR

About the Author

Dear Abby,

I'm engaged to a wonderful man, who is kind, giving, and well established in his profession. My problem is his family and if I should tell my parents about them before the wedding day.

His father is serving 10 years for embezzlement, and his mother makes ends meet via having many male friends. His sister has been arrested for horse theft. His younger brother has a master's degree in engineering. You can see my problem. Do I tell my parents about the engineer?

–Dreading in Tx

———

I'm an engineer, now retired, and know all the engineer jokes. I'm blessed that I'm not a lawyer. They have more jokes, but…

After thirty-plus years of working in nuclear power plants, anti-aircraft missiles, and third, fourth and fifth generation wireless communications systems, and various esoteric sensor networks. Obviously, after all that, one should retire to Texas to farm and ranch. It was the biggest fail of my life. I still have the fifty acres, but now I'm a certified Texas Master Naturalist busy restoring the native Tall-Grass prairie.

Before and since my retirement, I've helped build houses for *Habitat for Humanity*, worked directly with veterans at the VA, served as a *Big Brother*, mentored elementary students, ensuring that every day was a success, mentored adults in literacy/GED, filled shopping carts for the clients of the local food bank, and ran meals to clients for *Meals on Wheels*.

The richness of interacting with diverse people, especially the most important diversity, that of *thought*, lead me to put ideas down on paper and ultimately to my four-novel *Matryoschka Heritage* novel arc: *Matryoschka*, *Matryoschka's Daughters*, *Matryoschka's Effect*, *and Matryoschka's Time*. I hope you enjoy Sarah, Alex, Sarah Beth, Katie, and Quentin as much as I have.

facebook.com/terrygene.author
twitter.com/TerryGeneAuthor
instagram.com/terrygeneauthor

ALSO BY TERRY GENE

News on novels, short stories and weekly free fiction can be found at: http://matryoschka.com with free sign-up at http://eepurl.com/dCo78z

Matryoschka Heritage is a four novel and twelve short story arc.

- Matryoschka, https://t2m.io/l3Rkk5fj will take you to all stores that sell it.
- Matryoschka's Daughters, release 2019
- Matryoschka's Effect, release 2020
- Matryoschka's Time, release 2020

www.ingramcontent.com/pod-product-compliance
Lightning Source LLC
Chambersburg PA
CBHW070924100726
47908CB00001B/94